THE GUARDIAN
A YEAR AT KILCHURN CASTLE

DIANA KNIGHTLEY

ONE - KAITLYN

JUNE, 1706

I awoke with a start to the sound of Magnus crying out. He whimpered and thrashed. I held onto his shoulder. "Wake up, love, wake up, you're having a nightmare."

He whimpered again and then startled. "What?"

The room was very dark. The fire had died down to a few hot embers. I kissed his shoulder, holding on. "You had another bad dream."

He said simply, "Och."

He reached over to our bedside table and switched on our solar lamp, turning it to the lowest setting.

My arms around him — he was tight and bound. He had gone to high alert. It would take a moment to bring him back with kisses on his skin and caresses, until slowly he relaxed. I rubbed my fingertips down his arm and around his hand and felt it slowly lose its grip, its tenseness. Finally I rubbed my hand down his taut stomach to his hips and around to his front, in his ear, I whispered, "You want me?"

"Aye, mo reul-iuil," and he kissed me with his lips full of urgency. His hand traveled up to my hair and I crawled onto him with his hand pulling me there. I straddled him, pulling my linen shift up in gathers around my hips and settling on him. I had caught him in a nightmare because I had been lying awake, staring at the ceiling — it had been a long day and I had thought about waking him to make love to him, but had decided to let him sleep. His day had been longer, yet here he was, wanting me, as if my dreams had come true.

And it had been my dreams that had me ready as soon as he had said, "Aye," with breathless desire, his voice rumbling through my mid-region like a train of desire — I smiled to myself, *next stop, sex station.*

That settling was such a wondrous feeling, full of opposites, equal measures of anticipation and completion, want want want, *oh god* — breathlessness and deep — *exhale.*

I bowed down over him, my lips near his cheek, and wrapped my hands in his and rode him through his fear, past his climax, and sat up on him and followed him over the edge, to release, and then, I grew weighty and he was calmed, as my body draped across him.

Gone from needy to satiated. I hugged my arms around his head and kissed his sweaty forehead.

"Better?"

He nodded quietly.

I rolled off him, and pulled his face to my breast, an arm under his head, my leg across his waist. I wrapped around him holding him close.

And waited, for what I knew would come...

Because he had something he needed to talk about, but it always took Magnus a moment to think it through before he could speak.

Then in the darkness, his voice low, he said, "I ken I hae made a mistake."

I rubbed my hand down his back, breathing, listening...

"I am nae sure when, but I ken with certainty there has been one. I canna understand how I came tae be here, but tis nae right."

"I don't understand..."

"Ye ken there is a feeling ye get when ye feel as if ye ken something a'ready? As if we hae lived it before?"

"Yes."

"I think we hae lived this before. It daena sit right with me, this..."

I drew my fingertips in circles on his shoulder.

He said, "I am hidin' in the past, with all these people around me, living in Kilchurn castle, and my kingdom is lost. Hammond must be dead. I daena ken how tae..."

I pressed my lips to his forehead.

"We are protectin' Isla, I ken it, but I am beginning tae believe I am cornered. I am without options."

I decided to speak. "Or... Maybe you have the upper hand. You have almost all the vessels, hidden. You have the Trailblazer. You've secured them. It means that you might have changed the outcome in your kingdom. We don't know yet, we're just waiting for you to get strong."

He stayed quiet for a moment, then said, "I ken and I daena want tae worry ye. This is where we are living: tis easily defensible, and we will do it for a time. Until we can verify what is happenin' in the kingdom. Until I am strong enough tae make the world safe for Isla."

"Yes, but I believe you already have."

He chuckled, a sure sign that he was feeling more relaxed. He joked, "If I had truly made the world safe I would be eatin' ice cream right now."

"True, I would be taking warm showers and pissing in a flushing toilet."

"The composting toilets are a fine addition though."

"What else do you miss? I should add to my list for the next time James and Quentin go back."

His voice was muffled between my breasts, "I miss towels."

I thought about it for a moment, "What... *towels*? Like bath towels?"

"Aye, ye ken, when they are warm from the dryer and they

are soft and yet they have the fibers tae wipe ye clean, but they are nae scratchy, this is the important part — they are soft and ye can wrap them. Tis always verra nice when I see ye come from the bathroom with yer towel wrapped around ye and then when ye drop it tae the ground, tis a pleasure."

"So what you're saying is that you miss bath towels because they feel good and you like to see me drop them to the ground so I'm naked?"

"Tis all the same thing — a bath towel has all of it. Hae ye considered them? Think of when wee Isla is in the bath and we wrap her in the towel after — she is damp and funny and smiling. Och, I miss towels."

"Well, now I miss towels, too. We might have to send James and Quentin back for them pronto. Or better yet, we'll send Hayley, she can go to the store and get good towels. She'll know how to find the best ones."

He nodded against my chest.

"I'll add it to my list tomorrow," I said as I began to fall asleep.

TWO - KAITLYN

I woke up and first it was that damned rooster, Master Buttnugget was his name, crowing as if his life depended on it, too stupid to know that if his life ended it would be because of his racket at dawn.

Then Beaty started in with the bagpipes.

Fine, she had gotten rather good.

I was resting with my eyes closed, when I heard James and Quentin arguing down in the courtyard.

"Ugh, they're going at it again." I kissed Magnus's chest.

"Aye, they are regularly furious with each other. Twas m'day tae sleep in — first the bagpipes sounded and now there is a battle below."

"And don't forget that goddamn rooster."

I listened to the fight down in the courtyard.

James: "Some fucking respect, that's all I ask!"

Quentin: "Yeah? Because you can swing a hammer suddenly you're lord and master?"

I asked, "Why do you think they're fighting so much?"

Magnus said, "Because Master Cook needs a woman."

"All he does is complain that all the women are married."

"I fear that until he finds one we will hae tae suffer more family meetings."

My head shot up and I looked down on him wide-eyed. "No! The last one took hours! Ugh." I dropped my head back on the pillow and groaned. "Emma wants everyone to be heard. You know what? I kinda think we need more of 'everyone shut it. Shut your mouth. Shut up.' Unless it's me of course, my list of grievances is freaking long."

Magnus's chest shook under my head as he chuckled.

I sighed. "Most of my grievances involve Hayley this week—"

Through the open window came Hayley's voice from a window farther down. "Will you two shut up! James, we get it, you brought the composting toilets, you set them up, we get it—"

"All I want is someone else to dump it out, smells like hell in there and—"

Quentin said, "Why the hell you looking at me? I dumped it last time, it's not my turn."

Fraoch's voice, "What are ye yellin' about? I can hear ye down at the docks!"

Emma's voice, "Well, I did not want to say this, but you've driven me to it, we need a family meeting."

I groaned. "Here we go."

Magnus kissed my forehead. "Looks like we will need tae go down tae pass the Feelin' Stone."

I scrambled up. "Well, as long as we have to have the meeting, I might as well get my notebook."

I got dressed, grabbed my list, and headed down the cold steps to the Great Hall.

TWO - KAITLYN

The room was full. We had guardsmen and servants living with us, plus their families. Most of the stable boys and field hands lived in the village, but came to the castle for breakfast.

James, Hayley, and Quentin had traveled back and forth for supplies, being very very cautious, so we had outfitted the castle pretty well. We aimed for comfort and convenience, while trying to keep waste to a minimum. We had solar powered lights in our private rooms, because that just made sense. We had comfortable shoes for everyone. We had enough food stores to keep us living if there were issues with crops. But we tried to be sparing and kept all the magical things hidden behind the scenes.

By the time Magnus and I made it to the Great Hall everyone else was already there, sprawled in chairs, dressed, complaining that it was too early. We had run out of coffee three days before, so their irritation was building.

As soon as Magnus walked in, Quentin said, "Boss, tell James we need to stop bitching about this toilet situation and work on the pump house we need the—"

James folded his arms across his chest. "Forgive *me* for thinking *waste management* was *also* something that needed to happen."

Magnus sat down in a chair. "Do we hae coffee?"

Zach said, "Nope, gone."

Magnus said to everyone, "Do ye see we are without coffee yet we are in a family meeting? I worry about our priorities."

James said, "Mags, ya gotta weigh in."

"I think we need both of them tae happen."

Emma was standing and rocking little Zoe in the sling, passing her a toy to suck on and then when Zoe dropped it, passing her another one from a bag in a chair. All Zoe wanted these days was to shove things into her drooling mouth with dripping, sticky, reaching fingers. "And *that's* why we need this meeting to discuss—"

Everyone groaned.

Emma said, "I know, I know." Zoe dropped a wooden ring,

Emma passed her a silver rattle. "You're irritated, but just bear with me. Let's go around the circle. Each person can name one issue, then we'll address it."

I opened my spiral notebook and tapped a page with my pen. "First, I need to remind—"

James put his palms out incredulously. "Why does she get to go first?"

I tapped the page again. "Because I have the list, did you make a list?"

"No, but reminder, I installed composting toilets."

Quentin groaned. "And I cleaned them last, what, you think you do everything?" He crossed his arms. "I've been keeping you all protected for months, jumping back and forth, running security, and getting bossed around by you — is that the thanks I get for keeping your ass safe?"

Quentin waved his hand at me. "Put this on your list, Katie, I think we say, 'Fuck this,' and go to the future-future and fight Paddy-whack."

I said, "Noted, but I'm trying to cut out the f-bombs, because of being more classy. So, maybe, fudge this." I screwed my face up. "I do not like that as much, it's stupid."

Quentin said, "You didn't write what I said down."

"Fine." I read as I wrote: "Quentin says, 'fuck this.'" I underlined it twice. "Happy?"

"Not exactly. And who got you the notebook? Me — regretting it."

"You, last time you went home. I don't get to go home because of Sir Padraig." I wrote, "Quentin wants to go to the future-future to fight."

Then I turned to Hayley, "Okay, your turn—"

She said, "Come at me, I'm blameless, all I do is help and no—"

We all groaned.

I said, "I'm not going to discuss all your varied issues, but I do need to ask, have you *seen* the scissors?"

"The... like the black handled ones?"

"Yeah, the ones you didn't put away. The ones that are supposed to be in the upper storeroom."

Sean walked up with a big smile and a bounce to his step, then he froze. "Och nae, I wondered where everyone was... Are ye havin' another meetin'?"

Lizbeth heard him as she entered from the kitchen, wiping her hands on her apron. "Another meeting! For what purpose?"

I said, "James and Quentin were having an argument in the courtyard, so—"

"So ye decided ye must talk about whose turn tis tae kick the rooster?"

Beaty was sitting on the floor beside a low wooden box filled with straw. Mookie was rooting through the straw looking for his favorite stuffed animal she had hidden there, a blue moose that Isla named Moosy. Beaty covered Mookie's ears. "Kick the rooster! Ye canna kick Master Buttnugget! He is the father of all the wee chicks! Daena hurt him, Madame Lizbeth."

"Och, Madame Beaty, tis just a thing tae say. I am nae going tae kick him — though Madame Beaty, if *ever* there was a rooster tae deserve it, tis that one. He is nae fit tae live in a civilized castle. He was chasin' Isla just—"

"Och, he daena mean anything by it."

Just then there was a loud chant of children's voices from outside, then the kids swarmed in. Ben and Archie were leading, then Sean's son, Gavin, and Lizbeth's son, Jamie, and then a trailing of cousins including Lizbeth's other son, Ainsley, who was still a bit wee, and other kids, and then at the end Lizbeth's daughter, Mary, with wee Isla riding on her hip.

Maggie, Sean's wife, followed behind. "My apologies, Queen Kaitlyn, I see ye are havin' another meeting. We dinna intend tae interrupt, the kids were wanting a parade."

The kids marched around, taking food from the trays, scratching Mookie behind his ears, scattering crumbs as they circled us and then departing through the great door.

Maggie said, "I will follow, but wanted tae ask ye, Master James, ye said there would be plentiful water? Tis needed for the laundry."

He said, "Aye, Madame Maggie, it's coming. Quentin and I were just discussing it."

"Good, I am verra much looking forward tae it. Cleanliness in the eyes of the Lord, is the surest way tae eternal reward." She kissed Sean sweetly on the cheek and headed out of the room

Lizbeth said, "Madame Emma, please allow me tae hold the Feeling Stone."

Emma passed her the rock, a stone from the shore that was about the size of our palms, and had two googly eyes stuck to it, and no one would fess up to who brought them. First Lizbeth chuckled, as she always did, at the funny eyes on the stone, then she said, "Master James, Master Quentin, ye promised me there would be water by the end of the month, and tis almost upon us."

Quentin said, "Yeah, I know, we brought all the parts."

"Aye," said James, prone to having a Scottish brogue these days. "Quentin and I will start building it later today."

She said, "Good. Now Master Fraoch, ye ken ye need tae help them. I ken ye want tae fish, but we need the water, now we are luggin' it from the docks, and I winna say it in front of Maggie, but I heard it might be warm? Twould be a lovely thing tae hae warm water and if ye lend a hand it will go faster. Twould be excellent. Madame Hayley, I need ye in the storeroom taeday, we need tae go through the cloth. Kaitlyn will ye speak tae auld Eamag in the kitchen? She has been arguing with Zach even more than usual."

He said, "Is that what she's doing? I can't understand half of what she says. I thought she was agreeing with me."

Emma asked, "Zachary, with her hands going like this?" She gestured angrily.

He joked, "Oh, you mean, when I said, 'What this soup

TWO - KAITLYN

needs is more spices,' and she was shrieking, 'Nae! Nae!' She was arguing? Now that I think about it, you might be right."

Emma said, "You think?"

Then Lizbeth turned to Magnus, "And finally, Magnus, I need ye tae—"

Magnus laughed, "Ye dinna advise Madame Emma!"

Lizbeth put her hands on her hips. "Because Madame Emma daena need my advice. Ye on the other hand..."

"Och nae! I am perfection, I will help wherever I am needed and..."

Sean laughed. "Ye ken what we need is much less talkin'. We need tae put down the Feeling Stone, and there needs be more doin'."

Lizbeth laughed. "Here Sean, so ye can speak." Lizbeth passed him the rock.

He said, "I hae the Feeling Stone so ye must listen tae all I say. We ought tae hae some games of strength and battle this out like friends and brothers."

Fraoch said, "Or we could send them out tae the Eilean a' Chombraidh tae settle it. Ye can come back from the Island when ye hae finished the argument."

Quentin said, "Shit, I can't even remember what we were fighting about."

James said, "Me neither, great plan, Emma, we talked for so long we ran out of steam."

Emma laughed, "My work here is done." She passed Zoe a stuffed turtle.

Sean said, "We hae one more issue tae agree upon. Master Cook, ye need a woman tae settle ye down."

He passed the stone to Fraoch who said, "Aye, Master Cook needs a woman."

We all laughed.

The stone was passed to Hayley. "James needs a woman."

It was Magnus's turn, he patted the stone, "I concur," and then tossed it to Quentin who said, "Yep, gotta get laid."

James sighed. "Seriously, y'all gotta come at me with this? I will say it again, there are no unmarried women in this entire castle. I've looked, I would find them."

Quentin said, "Okay, fine, no need to be tense. This is what we need to do, one big hug, come on!" He stood up, put out his arms, and gestured us near. "Come on, bring it in, hug it out."

Beaty joined him first.

Then Zach who said, "Hell yeah, we have not had enough big group hugs in the eighteenth century."

Emma joined in next, and then Hayley, Fraoch, and Magnus and me and finally James, Lizbeth, and Sean. We all hugged and held on laughing and then we broke apart.

James said, "Good talk. Glad we got that all settled."

Sean crossed the room for the door, but said over his shoulder. "I still say ye need tae use yer bait and tackle, Master James."

James laughed. "Everyone is married!"

THREE - MAGNUS

We sent James and Quentin tae the year 2387 tae see what had changed, begging them tae please bring coffee when they returned.

I sent them tae the location of the safe house. Though it had been embattled at one time, I hadna been there since, and keeping it hidden had been General Hammond's top priority. I doubted Sir Padraig kent of it and I guessed Mrs Johnstone would hae remained there as caretaker if she could.

We loaded Quentin and James up with gear, weapons and ammunition, and outfitted them in bullet-proof armor — things we kept in our armory in case they were necessary. Quentin carried a letter from me, allowing him safe-passage and giving permission tae m'subjects tae share their knowledge of the current state of the kingdom.

My hope was that the war had ended, and the dispute had passed, and the worst case was that the king was in exile without reason. This would be a good problem tae hae.

So we sent them away, and expected them back the following day. We needed them back, we couldna do without two of our guards for verra long.

Our day was watchful.

I dinna like having a vessel out from the cave and being used. It caused me tae feel exposed. Tae protect us, they had traveled a distance away before leaving, so the storm would nae be associated with our castle. I sat on the walls, with the binoculars pressed tae m'eyes, scannin' the horizon for the storm, and also focused on the caves.

The walls of Kilchurn were different from the walls of Balloch, older. This castle had a five-story tower house with a long view of the loch and the mountain passes. There was a large courtyard defended by a high outer wall.

By the time I was here, guarding the castle, the stones along the parapet were already aged and ancient. Watchmen through the years had marked and grooved the stones with their blade points, out of boredom, or tae keep track of scores.

From where I liked tae stand in the center of the parapet, there was a good leanin' wall, and a row of letters: F, Z, Q, J, M with notches beneath them. The objective was 'How long can ye go without complainin' about the food'? Fraoch was beating us handily. The letter M had so many notches below it, I would never come close tae winning.

My stomach growled.

Twas difficult tae be hungry, when I kent twas m'own fault for having brought us here.

There was plenty of fish though. Kilchurn sat upon a peninsula scarcely larger than the castle itself, almost completely surrounded by water. Access tae it was along the causeway, barely more than a road.

We had another score, farther down, that James had started, a notch for every time ye won an argument. All had tae agree that the argument had been won, so far there was one notch, below his name.

There was a stone, farther down the parapet that had the

year, MCDLVI. One of our arguments, tae pass time, had been: was 1456 the year this castle had been built? Or were they the initials of the six men who had stood guard long before us, a way tae keep score on their arguments?

I believed this castle tae be at least that auld so I argued that MCDLVI was the year. I kent Sir Colin, the man I met at Balloch in the year 1551, had improved this castle by adding chambers to the north of the tower house, and remodeling the parapet. I figured that he couldna improve it if it hadna been built long before.

Plus, the circular corner turrets had many carvings from this time.

But I hadna won the argument yet.

I raised the binoculars tae m'eyes once more and looked out over the loch and Ben Cruachan tae the stone-covered entrance tae the cave. Then I swept the binoculars along the shoreline and then the southern horizon.

Nothing.

I thought about Sir Colin's son, Sir Duncan, the bairn that Kaitlyn had once nursed. He had built the Great Hall along the inside of the south wall, and the chapel in the southeast corner.

It caused me an immense sense of pride tae stand upon the parapet of my forebears and guard m'family inside. There was a long history here, of Campbells under the shadow of Ben Cruachan, and tae hae Archie growin' strong on the hills around Kilchurn felt comfortable. Much of this felt as if I had come home.

There was a connection here — the wind sweeping m'hair as I stood under a blue sky, on hills covered in their deep green. The colors of the Campbells. Twas a land that was etched inside of me. I could remember racing up the stairs tae see m'Uncle Baldy standing right here, on this spot, guarding his family.

Liam and Sean, young men and long friends, had once carved their names and scores intae the stones.

I had wanted tae be just like them.

I remembered calling them tae come tae the hills and they would say, "Nae, Magnus! We are tae be on watch!"

And I would be angry and resentful, but would get halfway down the causeway tae hear them yell down, "We are comin', Young Magnus! Wait for us!" And they would race down tae the causeway. "Baldie told us we could go!" And we would rush tae the hills, racing up and near tumbling down, and exploring the woods and streams. I loved those days.

Archie and Ben, along with Sean and Lizbeth's sons were now the ones tae race off and explore. Because they were younger, they were told always tae stay within sight of the castle, but with this high wall they were easy enough tae find.

These were my thoughts as I stood watching, massagin' my left hand — somethin' recently developed and now persistent. Twas disconcerting that I had been resting and yet my left hand had a numbness that needed tae be rubbed. The numbness bothered me, and I had seen the concern in m'fellow guardsmen's eyes, so I tried tae hide it, tae give m'self somethin' else tae do. I raised the binoculars tae my eyes once more, watching the sky, the mountain, and along the shore.

Fraoch and Hayley were already in the clearing, waiting for them tae arrive, and then finally, mid-afternoon they returned.

They rode up the causeway tae the walls, and looked freshly washed and smiling. I met them at the gates, "What say ye? Ye look fresh and well!"

Quentin swung down from his horse. "About that, Boss, you want the good news or the bad news?"

"I expect the bad news first, but there are ears around, let's go intae the office."

THREE - MAGNUS

We climbed the steps tae the second floor, but then I found myself gripping the rail and haltin' mid-climb.

"You cool, Boss?"

I gasped but tried tae swallow it in so they wouldna see. "Aye, I am fine, the lunch dinna agree with me." I pulled against the railing tae hoist m'self up the steps.

Twas the way with my stair climbs these days. I was often winded from them, and dinna think they were getting better, but rather worse as the days went by.

I dinna want tae mention it tae the men.

Once in m'office, pokin' the logs tae get the fire going, Quentin reported, "The bad news: Your kingdom is being ruled by Sir Padraig.

"Och, all this effort and nothing has changed?"

"Nope."

Everyone looked dejected.

"So what is the good news?"

"Well, if you think about it, we've been here for almost two months and no one has messed with us. I believe it means we are hidden well enough."

I nodded. "I dinna want m'best skill tae be 'hiding well enough.' I want tae fight him."

Quentin shook his head. "That's not possible. He's amassing power and strength, and you're still not in condition—"

"Are ye callin' me weak?"

James and Fraoch both shifted in their seats.

He said, "No, but I am calling it as I see it. You aren't ready to fight. You aren't strong enough yet and he is—"

"Ye are calling me weak. Tis nae a question anymore, Quentin, ye think me weak."

He exhaled. "Look, Magnus, I went and saw it with my own

eyes. I interrogated Mrs Johnstone. She told me about how the kingdom has changed since you were driven into exile—"

"Och, this is nae the way the history should go."

"As soon as you are strong enough we will fight him—"

Fraoch said, "I will fight him. Ye could make the challenge, Og Maggy, I will fight in yer stead."

"All m'enemies would ken I am weakened, they would all challenge m'throne, ye would be fighting all the time, Fraoch. I canna ask ye tae trade yer life for mine."

"The offer is always there."

"I ken, all I ask is that ye fight alongside me if I am in need."

Quentin said, "James and I were talking about assassination — It wouldn't be that hard. We just have to plan it well and sneak up on him. Until then, we hide. We hide well and then sneaking up will be easier, that's all I'm saying. You're not weak, you're just playing the long game."

Fraoch said, "I agree with Quentin. We are nae weak, we are playin' a verra long game, like World of Warcraft, a game James introduced me tae one rainy afternoon in Florida. We are just strategizin'."

James chuckled. "I love it when you ancient guys talk about video games."

Fraoch said, "Speaking of video games, ye look verra clean?"

James said, "Hell yeah, we stopped in Florida on the way back, got hotel rooms. I took a luxurious shower, bought a couple of coolers full of food just for Fourth of July, and even some fireworks. We're going to have a good old fashioned or in this case, since the country wasn't even founded yet, a good old modern Independence Day barbecue."

Fraoch said, "I am jealous about the hotel room, I get tae go next."

I nodded. I had lost interest in the conversation because m'mind was ruminatin' on m'kingdom. "Can ye leave me? I need tae do some thinking on it all."

Quentin said, "Aye Boss, but don't let it bother you too much. This is exactly what you thought was going to happen: nothing changed."

"Aye, I thought it, but I hoped I was wrong."

FOUR - MAGNUS

The following morn, Quentin, James, Fraoch, and I pulled carts of lumber, pipes, and equipment tae the river mouth, where we planned tae build a water mill, though James said its official name was a micro-hydropower system.

He had all the parts. We were going tae build it encased within a wooden house with a water wheel tae hide the machine within. Twould be verra efficient, James thought, the pump would be enough tae carry water tae the castle.

I dropped a spool of wire where we were buildin'. "Will it be good enough tae get water up tae the third floor?"

James answered with a long explanation about the varying river current and the strength of the pump and added, "We will have water up to the first floor at least."

I joked, "Tis nae a full answer on whether I will hae water up tae m'apartments."

He said, "Well, Mags, there is a possibility we'll have water up to the second floor sometimes, and that's definitely better than nothing."

James clapped me on the shoulder. "And the good news is it will be warm sometimes too, once we install the heater."

I groaned. "Warm only sometimes? Och, I believed the magic tae be more magical than this."

James leaned against a crate. "The pump will be good enough to get water up to the castle, hopefully to the upper floors, but worst case scenario, we're bathing in the kitchen. Eamag will love it. With the electricity we generate, we'll be able to power the water heater. We'll install it in the corner storeroom. Again, worst case scenario, we have to double up in the bathtub in the kitchen."

Quentin, Zach, and I groaned.

It all seemed magic tae me, and tae the other eighteenth century inhabitants of the castle, but we told them, if we build this, ye will hae water without needin' tae carry it. Warm water would be an extra benefit.

We placed tools out, James laid out the plans, and we made verra orderly rows of lumber, pipes, and coils of electrical wire. Twas one of the things about him, when he was building he was verra particular about how tae do it, and bossed us around a great deal, but we respected him because he was good at it.

Twas a fine day, the sky high and blue, the grass waving around us.

Sean and Liam stayed away while we got the pump set in place. Twas wet work and we were often in the water wading and hollering at each other over how tae do what needed tae be done.

Quentin waist deep in the water, shivering, his arms huggin' himself, said, "While we have the men all gathered we should take another vote."

I waded out of the water tae the shore with him following. "Och nae, Colonel Quentin, I daena want tae hear of it again."

He shook all over like a dog. "Do we need a vote to decide to vote? Because I had to stand out there in that ice cold water and I think you should let me have a vote."

"Fine, a vote."

Zach said, "None of the women are here — we don't give a shit what they think?"

"Daena matter, tis nae goin' tae change my mind."

Quentin's teeth chattered. "Those of us who *want* to stay here, in the past, and live like this indefinitely, wet and cold and depressed, will vote 'nae'. Those of us who want to fight, come up with a plan, make something happen, will say 'aye'. We do this every few weeks, and so far no one has changed their mind, but in light of the new information, that the future is still like it was planning to be, that the raid on the vessels didn't affect it, maybe we need to try something new."

By now all the men were standing in the circle. James asked, leaning on a shovel, "Is this a secret vote? Because I do not want to go against Magnus."

Quentin said, "Hell no, it's not a secret vote, you need the power of your conviction. Plus, last vote, I was the single solitary vote aye, and he didn't hold a grudge about it. He knows I'm just ready to make a move. Boss isn't going to hold a grudge, he's going to take our opinion under advisement is all, right Boss?"

"Aye, I will take it under advisement, tis good tae ken how ye feel."

Quentin said, "Okay, all those that vote to make a plan, to go to the future, and seize back Magnus's kingdom, at the very least make it safe enough that we can return to Florida, say 'aye'."

Quentin and James said, "Aye."

Everyone else, when asked, said, "Nae."

Quentin said, "Great, I hoped I'd be doing something besides building a pump house today."

Sean and Liam came mid-afternoon tae help with the building. I took a break, picked up the binoculars, and directed them tae Ben Cruachan.

FOUR - MAGNUS

Fraoch came tae stand beside me. "Ye checkin' the vessels?"

"Aye, because of this project I haena been able tae go there taeday. I ken they are hidden well enough, but I still hae tae check, I canna ease up."

Fraoch said, "I ken, my eyes travel up the ben all the time. Tis a lot of pressure tae hae that many vessels."

"Aye."

He clapped me on the back, picked up a beam, and carried it tae James tae build the structure.

FIVE - KAITLYN

 𝓘 had finished the bulk of my chores, so I took Isla and a wide wool blanket down to the grass north of the castle and spread it out with a view of the water's edge and the work that the men were doing.

The sun was high. It had been cold so it was nice to be warmed on my face. The scent of flowers and grass and breezes mingled with the smell of loch and castle. I wondered what that would be called in a candle fragrance — Fresh and Old? Medieval Glen?

Isla and I picked flowers. I called Hayley on the two-way radio: "Hey babe, you should come out and see this, summer is here, for sure, hot hot summer."

"I am doing crucial work today. As Lizbeth put it, the line between life and death is *me* in this boring storeroom. I think she's just kidding, because this does not seem important — why, got a better offer?"

I was making a daisy chain for Isla's hair but my gaze was across the grass on the men, who one by one were stripping off their shirts: Magnus, Quentin, James, Zach, Fraoch, building something — *shirtless.*

Sean and Liam even, helping to build.

FIVE - KAITLYN

I said, "It's like an epic 'hot guys in kilts' calendar down here. Bring Emma and Beaty if you see them."

A few moments later Hayley and Emma appeared. Hayley joked as she raced down the grassy incline to where I was sitting, all her bosom and skirts bouncing. "I heard it was an emergency — hot damn, those are some..."

Fraoch hefted a piece of lumber to his shoulders and carried it to the small wheelhouse. She said, "Woo wee."

Emma stood with a hand on a hip, the other hand shielding her eyes. "Hot damn."

I said, "Ain't that the truth."

Beaty rushed over, her camera around her neck, Mookie trailing behind. "Madame Hayley did ye want me tae take a photo of the scene for ye?"

Hayley laughed. "Not for me, no, silly girl, not for me. I want you, heck, you *need* to take photos for all of womankind. Look at what is happening! We have men, half a dozen, all out there in states of *disrobed*, all kinds of masculine, testosterone, boiling..."

Fraoch looked up and waved. She waved back. "Was I talking about something?"

The women sat beside me on the blanket, in the warm sun, little Isla toddling around, with Mookie following her dotingly, while we watched the men work. Lizbeth wandered up.

I whispered, "Uh oh," to Hayley.

"What are ye doin' out here in the...?" Lizbeth stopped and watched for a moment. "Och, I am finding it quite warm out here taeday."

We moved over to make room for her on the blanket. "Is this what we are tae do?"

I said, "Not all day, but we ought to take a moment to appreciate what God has given us in the bodies of these fine men."

She laughed. "I will try nae tae look at m'brothers, tae nae think on the other men of the group, but my husband, Liam. He does look verra fine, I believe."

I said, "Then that's a good enough reason to rest from our work and spend some time here in the sun."

∾

The men worked on their project all day.

We had many things to do as well, but...

The one thing I felt very irritated about was that the men's work, as brutally, physically hard as it was, took them outside a lot.

They got to spend time out in the sun and weather.

My days were spent walking from one end of the dusty, dark castle to the other.

We had two-way radios, but they didn't cut down on my walking. It seemed I always needed something at the far end of the castle, I would need something from the storeroom on the second floor, or someone would ask, "Did you tell Eamag...?" And because she didn't have a radio I would head down to the kitchen. Or, "Did you check the pantry?" Or, "Look in the nursery..." Or, "He's out in the courtyard, I think..."

Magnus's work was backbreaking, mine was foot pounding. Every step on the cold hard stone of the castle — dark interiors, dusty rooms, mildewing walls. He was kind in that he let me complain and even gave me some nice foot rubs sometimes, too.

Because the thing about foot rubs? They often headed straight into pound town.

I chuckled to myself as I dressed for dinner.

∾

It was very hard to dress in these uncomfortable clothes everyday. We complained a lot.

The one thing we did compromise on was modern shoes. We

FIVE - KAITLYN

wore them hidden under our eighteenth century clothes. The men wore boots that were warm and well fitting. Most of us had shearling boots with proper rubber walking soles for inside the castle. We did our best to keep the styles plain but that meant no athletic shoes which were sorely, begrudgingly, irritatingly missed.

Us women had to force ourselves into the bodices, and we griped the whole time. They were tight, uncomfortable, and took forever to put on.

As Hayley said, "Would it kill them to invent a zipper?"

I was dressing in my favorite mantua, a floral silk, for dinner, when I overheard Magnus and Beaty in the hall. Magnus said, "Madame Beaty, I had another complaint on ye, for nae wearin' a bodice and hitchin' yer skirts up as if they were pants. Ye were shewin' yer knees."

She said, "I ken King Magnus, but tis more comfortable and I canna bear tae ken I *could* be comfortable but I am simply nae allowed tae be. I ought tae do as I like, daena ye think?"

Magnus sighed. "What can I do tae make ye comply with the rules?"

"I daena ken. Tis much better tae walk without the skirts around m'ankles."

"But tis complicated for me tae answer for it. What can I do? I will do somethin' for ye, if ye will keep yer skirts coverin' yer legs."

There was a pause where she considered, then her voice, "Fine, I get tae play the pipes after dinner, I hae some new songs and I want ye tae say I am verra good, and ye must look like ye enjoy it."

∽

He returned tae our room chuckling. "Och, I believe tis Madame Beaty who runs the castle."

I said, "Yup, she wakes us up in the morn, and serenades us tae sleep at night. Was Mookie with her?"

Magnus said, "Aye, he was lookin' up at me with his sad eyes the entire time I was speakin' about her skirts. He is verra good at arguin'. I daena mind him so much though, tis her chickens — they are always underfoot." He shook his head. "But I canna complain on them either, they lay verra good eggs."

I laughed. "I agree." I pulled at my stays trying to get the laces to loosen. "So she'll be playing tonight?"

"Aye, twill be better than long recitations of her ballads, remember the last one, twas all about the pig?"

"It was very good though it went long." I put my finger and thumb together. "She's this close to persuading Ben to be a vegetarian and I wonder if Zach might get arrested for murder. I marvel at how patient you are."

I shoved my feet in my boots.

"I hae asked for a great deal of sacrifice from everyone, the least I can do is listen tae them recite their odes tae farm beasts and applaud their songs."

"I guess that is true."

Done getting dressed, I took stock of Magnus. "Och," I said, "You are red as a lobster."

He said, "Every inch of me is on fire."

SIX - KAITLYN

$\mathcal{W}$e held hands and went downstairs to the meal.

All the men were bright red except Quentin, but he assured us he was feeling it whether he looked beet red or not. But, he cracked up whenever he laid eyes on James, Zach, or Magnus who looked hot to the touch. Fraoch, Sean, and Liam were inflamed, as if they might spontaneously combust. I had to remember to ask for sunscreen on the next supply run.

Eamag cooked a large meal. The kids came down for food and then returned to the nursery. In the Great Hall we had celebratory grownup drinking and conversation, but perhaps the most exciting thing of all was the addition of a widow.

She was a young widow at that.

As soon as she walked through the wide carved wooden doors, we all turned, saw her, then met eyes, nodded, and all at once we turned toward James.

Who had a full-body, hot under his sunburn, totally flustered blush. He had gone poinsettia red.

He shifted, and then it was as if he gravitated to where she stood.

She was dressed well. Her mantua was made of orange silk with ornate gold details, accentuating her curly red hair, the kind that stuck out in wild wisps. Her skin was very pale, and she had a peppering of freckles across her nose.

I said, "A widow? Who invited her?"

Magnus said, "She sent a letter ahead. She was travelin' and has asked for a place tae rest. Sean has vetted her, she was raised by cousins in Edinburgh—"

"Cousins? Uh oh."

"Aye, but cousins on Sean's side of the family. Nae mine, so tis fine. Sean thought James might like tae meet her"

"Ah, I see. He was right." James glowing like a supernova, was standing right beside her, speaking directly to her. "And you said she has been vetted? How well? What do we know about her?"

"She was married verra young and is now widowed. She daena hae an army or even any servants tae speak of."

Sophie's eyes looked up at the ornate ceiling of the Great Hall, at the paintings of Campbell ancestors along the walls, and then a furtive glance at James, she batted her eyes.

"Sean trusts her, but I am remainin' watchful. "

"So heightened security?"

"Aye."

It was odd watching James put his attention on a young woman from the eighteenth century, she had sparkling pretty green eyes, and blushed at most of what he said. The rest of what he said she found amusing — showing off a broad easy smile.

She was pretty and beside her he looked handsome, even if ridiculously sunburnt.

What the heck was this former quarterback, a good ol' boy from the twenty-first century and the American South, saying to her anyway?

Just then Hayley walked by, "What are they talking about do you think?"

"I have no idea. I guess I'm just excited he has a young lady to talk to."

James said something close to her ear, she laughed flirtatiously, then blushed pink.

Magnus said, "Och, I am going tae hae tae pay for another marriage tae a woman with nae fortune. The men of m'clan are costing me a fortune."

Quentin laughed. "I think he's been warned about the price of paying attention to young women in the eighteenth century."

Beaty leaned in and kissed him on the cheek. "Was I too high a price tae pay, Quenny?"

"Never, I would have paid twice for you, three times."

"That's sweet, I wish I could take a photo of ye and put it up on Instagram and tell m'followers how much ye admire me."

I asked, "How many followers do you have Beaty?"

"Thirty thousand, but they are missin' m'posts, Queen Kaitlyn. Tis a terrible loss tae nae be able tae speak tae them. I daena mean tae be negative on it, I ken tis important tae keep the bairns safe, and I ken we must hide here for a time, but I do feel it verra much in my heart."

I said, "I remember what it was like. When I lost my YouTube channel, it was devastating. I didn't know what to do with myself."

Beaty sighed. "It might be the most 'daena ken what tae do with myself' thing in the world."

Magnus jokingly groaned. "All right, Madame Beaty, would ye like tae perform for us — bagpipes or poetry tonight?"

Her face brightened up. "Bagpipes, King Magnus, let me run tae get them."

She rushed away from the table.

I leaned in to Magnus and kissed his shoulder.

The widow, Sophie Milne, was brought to meet us. She curtsied and made small talk and then James pulled out a chair for her and we returned to our seats.

James said, "Madame Sophie was just telling me something super interesting, I thought y'all might want to hear."

She cast her eyes down.

He said, "It's okay, you can tell them what you just told me."

"About the weather, Master James?"

"Yes, about the weather."

She seemed nervous, "During our travels we heard tell of terrible storms in Glencoe."

Fraoch leaned forward. "What kind of storms?"

She said, "It was told tae me that it was a verra different sort, as if God himself had come tae force the people from the land with lightning and thunder."

Fraoch, Quentin, and Magnus all glanced at each other with a look of recognition.

Fraoch asked, "Was it described as building upon the land, or as if the wind was pushing it?"

"The men who spoke of it said twas as if the storms built from a spot, and rumbled toward the heavens. They said the lightning was terrible tae see, they were verra afeared. M'hair stood on end as they spoke on it."

James and Magnus nodded.

Quentin said, "All right then, that sounds familiar, right?"

Fraoch said, "Did the men say how long it had been happenin'?"

She said, "Tis why I took note of it. The men said it had been goin' on for a fortnight, with nae signs of pause. Tis why they felt it best tae head south. Twas how I came across their band, as I left Edinburgh tae come tae Kilchurn."

Lizbeth sat down just then.

I asked, "Have you met Sophie Milne?"

Lizbeth said, "I hae met her and heard all about her travels, but now I hae had an extra drink and was thinking she ought tae tell me more." She grinned. "Madame Milne, my new cousin, what is interesting about ye?"

Sophie considered for a moment then said, "Master Milne taught me astronomy."

Lizbeth's eyes went wide. "Did he now? That is a verra interesting thing. Tis a wonder he allowed it."

"Aye, I was the one tae write down his findings and he would allow me tae look through the telescope tae see what he found. I helped him replicate the face of the moon and the patterns of the stars. After Master Milne passed, I continued tae do his work, but after a time I was warned that the minister was speakin' on me from the pulpit — he called me a heretic and a witch and wanted me tried for it."

Lizbeth clucked her tongue. "Och nae, a young widow — ye had tae flee Edinburgh or else be tried as a witch? Tis a monstrous behavior of otherwise-educated men."

Sophie's chin trembled as she nodded.

Lizbeth patted her hand. "Tis a good thing ye found us. We are a safe harbor, Madame Sophie."

I squinted my eyes. "But I do wonder, *how* did you find us?"

She said, "I was raised amidst Campbells, cousins of Sean and Lizbeth, from their father's side, the Campbells of Lowdon. I had heard that m'cousins resided here. Twas the only thing I could think of tae do."

"So you are here long term?"

She said, "If m'cousins will allow me tae stay."

Lizbeth nodded. "Of course we can take in a cousin in such a dire situation."

"And I hae brought my telescope, I might shew ye the moon and stars."

Lizbeth said, "Wonderful! There has nae been enough witchcraft afoot in this castle, as m'mother has nae visited in ever long."

Everyone laughed.

SEVEN - KAITLYN

Beaty arrived with her bagpipes and began to play Blondie's Heart of Glass.

We had another round of whisky brought to the tables.

And as the night wore on we sang and danced to the music as she played.

Fraoch sang us a song. One of the stable men, Smelly John, played the lute. And James borrowed it to play Hotel California. We danced and sang for hours and the kids came down and played and danced with us. Then the youngest were taken up to the nursery, but Zoe stayed with her mama fast asleep on Emma's lap and Isla fell asleep on my lap. I shifted her onto a bench beside my table while I danced.

Finally everyone left to go upstairs, first Emma and Zach with Zoe. It was Fraoch's turn on the walls, so Hayley returned to her apartment, and James escorted the young widow up to her guest room. Then Magnus picked up Isla and heaved her little body up to his shoulder. Her sleepy brow resting against his chin, her little pudgy arms around his neck. Her eyes opened to find me, she smiled, and then fell back to sleep on his shoulder.

We stopped at the nursery, weaving through to the little room in the back, with wee beds for the kids, where once, long ago, my husband had slept beside Sean, near the window that looked out over Ben Cruachan. It was a window he showed me, years ago, as his whole other self — Old Magnus.

I kissed Archie on his brow, "Sleep little guy, see you in the morning." Then I turned to see Magnus placing Isla down in her own little bed, tucking her in, and my heart skipped a beat for a moment. I stopped still.

He whispered, "What did ye just see?" We turned and walked from the nursery into the hall.

"You — I turned, and half expected you to be the young man from that moment on the deck, when you asked me to marry you... remember?"

"Aye, I remember. I told ye I wasna worth ye, but that I planned tae marry ye anyway."

"So romantic," I teased.

Just then James came strolling down the hall and we met under a wall lantern that created a small pool of golden light. "I'm headed to bed after seeing Madame Sophie to her room."

I joked, "Very kind. You like her?"

"Yeah, she's great, and beautiful, don't you think?"

"Yes, I agree." The hallway echoed, so we talked in hushed tones.

"And she's an astronomer, she's going to put up her telescope tomorrow night. Can you believe she assisted her husband, and actually noticed things he didn't, but he took all the credit, even for her findings?"

"It's not surprising, I think that happened all the time."

"You're always the feminist, huh?"

"That is literally one of the reasons feminism came to be."

James continued excitedly, "And she came this close to being tried as a witch."

"Another reason why feminism came to be. She might be an original feminist. This is very enlightened of you to be interested in her — a lady of science."

He smirked, "Plus she's got no children, she thinks I'm amazing, and she's gorgeous, right?"

I chuckled. "Well, there goes your enlightenment. But yeah, she sounds perfect. Don't forget to keep your eyes open though, she's a wildcard, we can't be too casual."

"Sure, of course, but she doesn't have a vessel, and her story checks out. Hey, I'm going to go back down to see if anyone is still up for a drink."

Magnus said, "Quentin is still up, he will join ye."

James wandered off. Magnus and I walked and I was thinking about what it was like to fall in love, how it was such a chemical bath, a stew of hormones that overrode our best senses — we meet, we enjoy them, then somehow it's turned into desire and passion and love. To take that person and become their lover, and then their mate — it was a miracle that it happened at all.

I wondered if James would be able to do it with a woman from the eighteenth century? They had nothing in common at all, but then again Quentin had fallen in love with Beaty... theirs wasn't a 'traditional' marriage. She didn't defer to him in everything. They were partners, because he honored her — quirks, foibles, and all.

We came to the door of our rooms and Magnus got us inside and stoked the fire in the fireplace. I was taking down my hair in front of my mirror when Magnus came up behind me. His arms around, a longing kiss on my neck. "What else?"

"What do you mean?"

"Ye said ye were thinking about the day we decided tae marry..."

"Oh, yes," I met his eyes in the mirror. "I know we have been traveling through time, and we've lost people we care about and gained people we love, and so much has happened, but I just saw you tonight with Isla in your arms and I had a feeling come over me, love. That fresh love, that nervous love from the first days, when you promised you would marry me. But it was also *that* feeling *plus* seeing you now. You're older — did you know?"

He kissed. "Aye, I am. I am much older than I was. What, like thirty?"

"By the year, you are now the ripe old age of twenty-five."

"Och, add a few years."

"In Florida time I am twenty-eight, so let's assume you are twenty-nine in time travel years."

I turned in his arms and wrapped my arms around his neck.

He smiled. "I finally overtook ye in the years."

"I think it is so lovely that I can look at you and see the years, the comfort and steadfastness, the loyalty and commitment, and still feel that flutter in my stomach, have the breath leave my lungs, my heart race, because of my feelings for you."

He kissed my jaw. "Tis a fine thing tae be loved by ye."

"That's a very nice thing to say."

"Come tae bed and I will say more nice things, I hae tae go tae the walls soon; I want a stroll in yer gardens first."

"Definitely."

EIGHT - KAITLYN

I loved dawn here. My room had a nice window and light fell upon my bed just when I needed to get up so it wasn't obtrusive, it was a gentle wake up. I had proper sheets and a mattress, everyone in the castle did. It was one of the perks of living with a king from a distant land.

Magnus was already up on the walls. He loved the morning watch, as the sun peeked over the land. Fraoch loved the night watch. James and Quentin liked the day. Zach made sure all the troops were fed, and guarded when he was needed. So they had organized an efficient rotation that suited most everyone, and there were extra men from the castle and the surrounding environs to fill in when necessary. We had men in the stables, women in the kitchen, young boys and women doing the work of the castle. A great many mouths to feed. A great many people who we had to hide our modern lives from, but sheets, and comfortable mattresses were something we decided to share along with the proper shoes.

We kept any lights or other 'magical' things well hidden.

But also, Magnus and Fraoch and Sean and Lizbeth were well liked and admired by the parish minister. He was a kindly man, respected by all. He was happy and healthy and greatly

EIGHT - KAITLYN

liked his new mattress as well, and the occasional largesse from Magnus — fine food and drink. And of course we were all regularly at church. Magnus managed to keep the villagers comfortable enough that no one complained about him.

He was easily the wealthiest person in the entire world in that year.

If he needed more, one of us could go and get it, but we weren't doing that right now. We were not traveling. We were staying close to home, over three months already.

The pool of sunlight on my face was warming. Then, like every morning since arriving, my lady's maid knocked. "Queen Kaitlyn, Mistress Isla is comin' through the—"

Isla burst into my room. She rushed to the bed and climbed up.

"Mama, come food?"

I was surrounded by sheets with her fresh face grinning down on me. I said, "Mama must first wash her face and get lovely for the day. Do you want to go eat or wait...?"

Like most mornings she said, "Wait."

Then she watched as I washed up and my maid helped me dress. Then she lost interest, climbed off the bed, and said, "Go eat!"

And I said, "I'll be down in a moment."

I knew she would be followed by the maid out to the hall and somehow her father would sense she was about. Most mornings he would find her in the hallway, and by the time I was presentable enough, my children and husband would be down at breakfast.

The only thing that would make any of this better would be to have a coffee maker in the room. The prospect of putting on layers of skirts and tightly laced dresses every single day really required caffeine.

. . .

When I got down to breakfast Magnus was helping Isla get butter on her oatmeal. I said, teasingly, "How'd you two meet up?"

Magnus said, "I thought, I am hungry, I should go tae breakfast and I found her in the hallway thinkin' the same thing. We hae the same stomach, daena we, wee'un?"

Isla nodded, pointing at the butter. "More."

We all carried our oatmeal to a table where Archie and Ben were already eating. Hayley and Fraoch walked in, fully dressed, as if ready to ride.

"Where are you going?" My eyes were wide because there had been no plans.

Hayley said, "Glencoe, of course. There's a storm!"

Magnus, Fraoch, and Quentin stood at the edge of the room, holding bowls of oatmeal, spooning it into their mouths, discussing Fraoch's trip.

Hayley was buzzing around packing, organizing, and discussing with Emma what needed to be done in her absence.

As Hayley hurried by carrying a bedroll, I asked, "So how long will you be gone?"

"At most a week, Fraoch and Magnus are deciding on a date we need to return by."

I looked around to make sure I wasn't overheard. "And you can't take a vessel?"

Hayley stopped, hands on hips, "As you know, and this is your rule — vessels are off limits without damn good reason."

"Sure, but I'm kind of used to everyone going to bed under the same roof, not sure I'm ready for you to go gallivanting around."

"Well, I am ready, man, am I ready. I can't wait to gallivant upon hill and dale. It's going to be grand. You're just going to miss me. That's what's got you all weird this morning. I will miss you too."

EIGHT - KAITLYN

"You're an adventure junkie."

"That's what sober does to a gal, I suppose. Any-who, we can't use the vessel anyway, because whoever is activating a vessel in Glencoe is doing one of two things, probably doing it remotely, like Donnan did, right? So it's someone looking for the vessel. We need to get there first, but if we jump in with our own vessel they will see us arrive, through their monitoring. *Or* some layperson has found the vessel and is messing with it, turning it on and off trying to figure it out. Either way, a vessel being played with — Fraoch and I are going to go find it."

"You're not taking anyone else with you?"

"Nope, everyone else needs to be here, and don't worry about us, we are heavily armed. We will have a monitor, and we will have the two-way radios. At that distance, we won't be able to reach you here, but coming and going we'll be able to connect. We're ready for all emergencies."

I teased, "You're just excited you get to use lights at night."

"Hell yeah, for the chance to listen to my downloaded Spotify playlist and use a flashlight in a tent and pretend to be a twenty-first century girl on a camping trip for a few days? Heck yeah, I'll go on an overnight to Glencoe."

"It sounds like you've thought of everything."

"Yeah, probably not, but that's okay. I've grown used to chaos management by now."

"Time travel sucks."

"I was talking about being an owner of a temp agency."

I laughed. "That was so long ago. You gave up that job for a cushy life as a wife of a Highlander."

"I wouldn't change a thing."

I hugged her, and kissed her cheek goodbye.

NINE - HAYLEY

Fraoch and I rode for about six hours, with a short rest for lunch, but then my ass would go no farther. We came to an idyllic stream, dismounted, and built camp. When we were done we had a modern tent nestled in the grass near a lovely glen, a perfect little spot.

We took off our shoes and splashed in the water, washing our faces and feet, and Fraoch jokingly saying, "Because I love m'bhean ghlan, I will also wash m'balls tae make them 'bearable'."

I laughed and said, "Thank you, and for you my husband..." I lifted my skirts and splashed ice cold water between my legs with a shriek. "Cold!"

We built a fire to make dinner as the sun was going down. "It's like a second honeymoon," I said. "We could stay here all day tomorrow and just mess around."

"Och aye, tis verra romantic, with the fish in the stream calling tae me," he joked.

"Fine, you can dream of fishing all you want, but guess what I would do if you actually did go fishing?"

NINE - HAYLEY

"What would ye do?"

"I would go into this little tent here beside the stream, in this little glen of romance, and I would play with myself without you."

His eyes went wide. "Och, I would hate tae miss it, I daena think twould be fair."

I shrugged playfully. "Fair or not, I would appreciate some attention, and I am much better than a fish."

"Tis true, yet — what if we are tae starve, m'bhean ghlan? Could I be the kind of man who can fish for yer dinner, feed ye nicely, and then give ye the attention ye require?" He stretched his legs out beside the fire. "Ye would be the kind of wife who would rather be hungry in the tent by herself?"

"Ha! I didn't think about it that way, good point. Yes, I would like a full stomach too, but see, that is why I am a modern woman: I love when you fish for me, obviously, you're adorable, manly, and you provide for me very nicely, but also, sometimes, like now, with the tent right beside us, beckoning, I think it might be nice to go by McDonald's and grab a meal for the quickness and ease of it. So that you have time to spend on my attentions. What I mean is that sometimes my attentions are priority over my stomach."

"Och I ken it, Hayley, I live with the same thing every day."

"That's why we are so perfect together, you get me, and I get you."

"Tis true. Ye are a funny wife, full of spirit — did ye ken when I was growing up the elders told me 'Daena marry a woman with a wise mouth, she will make yer life miserable,' and yet they were mistaken. Ye are a fine wife, with all yer opinions, even when ye are complaining about my fishing."

I grinned and then lay down so my head was on his lap, looking up at his unruly beard. "You know I'm not really complaining about your fishing. I just like to spar. The fun of teasing you sometimes means I'm saying something I don't one hundred percent mean. And though I do want to go play around in the tent with you, I am also very much enjoying this — the banter, and sitting by the fire as the sun has gone down. I like the quiet and the dark and the scratchy wool of your kilt under my head."

He joked, "Dost ye want me tae take it off for ye? For yer comfort?" He shook his hips so my head jiggled.

I giggled. "You've been riding a horse all day, and those splashes in the water earlier weren't enough. I probably don't want to have my head that close to your arse, not that you're not handsome, and hot, but we are very horsey-smelling, both of us."

"Och, but I put the water upon m'whirlies, and twas verra cold. I might need some appreciation for the effort."

I laughed. "Appreciation for a dip-in-the-stream ballbath — the very lowest form of bath for your balls? Have you met me sir?"

"Ah yes, m'bhean ghlan, I hae met ye. I hae fallen in love with ye, and though ye think me a foul beast, I ken ye love me as well."

"God I love you so much." I rose up and kissed him and then enjoyed it so much, deep kissing and making out near the fire that before I knew it I was climbing on him and then astride his lap, kissing more.

The fire crackled beside us. The stream glistened as it flowed in the moonlight. His lips pressed to mine, his beard against my face, he was soft and warm like a bear. My arms around the girth of him. His big man-hands on me — I felt small compared to his bigness, my mountain man.

I mounted him.

And then I laughed because that was funny.

"What is amusin'?"

"You got me on you without going into the tent. We're outside by the fire and the stream."

His hands rose up under my skirts and I pulled his kilt up his front.

He said, "Aye, ye wanted the tent, I wanted ye by the fire. We hae had too much of it indoors..."

— his breaths so close to my ear, my skin. I said, "Shhhh, forget I said anything, this is good," as he pulled me closer.

∽

The next morning we were up very early. I groaned. "I can't understand why we're up so early. What's the point of it? This is like Katie: she gets up so early and wants everyone up."

Fraoch rolled to his front and did a push up to all fours, growled, and shook his head like a wet dog. I laughed.

"I am wakin' up, do it, ye hae tae give it a try."

I groaned and slowly pushed myself up to all fours in our bedding and then growled and shook myself. I laughed. "Okay, you're right. I am much more awake now. But coffee... coffee needs to happen."

"I will make it before we ride."

We actually spent some time splashing around in the stream, watching fish swim, jumping from rock to rock, and getting pretty muddy, and then we finally loaded up onto the horses.

We took our time as we rode. Fraoch described the view, named the mountains, explained the route, and talked endlessly of the flora and fauna. I loved listening to him. He was excited to return to his childhood home. He had come back every now and then, but he wanted to show *me*...

Then we came over the final rise to Glencoe where a giant thunderhead had climbed to the highest point of the sky, settled on the gorgeous green valley, and was pelting the landscape with rain, as lightning arced to the sky.

"I've never seen one of the storms from a distance before."

"Aye, tis terrifying, but at least we can see where we hae tae go."

I gulped. "Yes, and maybe no." Lightning sparked up and

down from the ground to the billowing storm clouds. "I mean, we could just turn around and go home."

"And what would be the fun in that?" He urged his horse down the trail in the direction of the storm.

TEN - HAYLEY

As we descended into the valley, we couldn't make out what was happening above. It simply looked like we were coming up on a storm. There wasn't much special about it, at least from here. Ahead of us rain poured down and wind gusted. Lightning lit up the sky, the hallmark of our intense storms.

Our approach brought us to a small croft where Fraoch engaged the farmer in a long conversation that was difficult for me to understand, though I wasn't expected to participate anyway because of sexist bullshit.

I took the moment to unpack our raincoats and so when he was finished with the discussion we pulled them on, just as it began to sprinkle on us. Fraoch mounted his horse again and we turned our horses back to the path. "Och, Hayley, the man said these storms hae been rainin' down upon the valley since last month."

"That's awful." Thunder rolled through the sky.

He snapped his raincoat up to his chin. "Aye, he is feeling verra religious about it all. He is sure there has been a judgment from God. We need tae find the vessel and deactivate it else they will become superstitious about it all."

I grinned. "Very modern of you to be so skeptical."

"What does skeptical mean?"

"To not believe in God, or magic, to not believe in superstition."

He chuckled. "Aye, thank ye, m'bhean ghlan, but though I would like tae be more modern, I hae tae believe in God." I followed him as he steered his horse around a wide, deep looking puddle, watching behind to make sure my horse stepped well. "I do verra much like tae think on the science of how the world works, but ye must still ken that God is drivin' it — Did I catch fish? Aye, then God is smiling fairly upon me. If nae, then God is givin' me a lesson. Tis important tae hae belief because life can be verra dispiriting without it."

I said, "This is true."

He added, "Tae be modern is tae pray tae God tae help me find the fish, but also tae ken the tide, the current, the weather, tae use m'GPS, and understand where the fish like tae be — do they want the heat of the sun or the shade? And then if I catch fish, I hae had science and God tae thank."

I nodded. "Well, that definitely sounds like a modern, independent man."

He grinned. "Daena get me wrong though, I must still leave gifts for the fae for a good yield. Science can take the credit, God might watch over me, but I must be careful nae tae anger the fae."

I laughed as we came upon the edge of the storm and spent a moment looking at the monitor we had brought. It showed a vessel with a marking that wasn't on Kaitlyn's list — though who was I kidding? My eyes glazed over when she showed me that list. I had thought, "Old book, ancient list, what *ever*."

But it didn't look familiar.

"What do you think, Fraoch? Is it the one from your childhood?"

"Explain it tae me again — I could hae seen it in the year 1717, and then m'father might hae hidden it away? And now someone, somewhere, has activated it, and turned it on in every time period? Anyone who finds it is in danger of jumpin'?"

"Exactly."

"Why haena anyone found it yet?"

"I don't know."

"Och, I guess we must go in and find it ourselves."

"Does it bother you that this involves your mother? That this is a secret you are figuring out, that your father kept from you?"

He shook his head. "Nae. I am only worried about the vessels and the danger they pose tae m'family: ye and Archie and Isla and m'brother Og Maggy. I am serious, Hayley, when I say tae ye, I daena care about the connection tae my ancestors. They are nae here now. I lived with them for a time, I married, I lived a life, but when I left home I truly left. I am nae regretful on it."

"Good, I'm glad you feel that way, it's how I hoped you'd feel." We rode quietly for a moment. "Do you think, since Lady Mairead knows her, that they might be adversaries?"

"I daena ken."

"And if that's the case... what side would you end up on? What side would I have to be on then? I do not like the idea of being on Lady Mairead's side—"

"But Lady Mairead's side is Og Maggy's side." He straightened his back. "I daena ken if m'mother and Lady Mairead hae bad blood between them, tis nae matter tae me. The only thing I must concern m'self with is the bad blood between m'wife and Lady Mairead. And keeping ye safe from her ire."

"What if she did something to your mother, though? What if *that's* what happened to your mother — that Lady Mairead did something to her? If so, don't you have to do something to avenge it? For your honor?"

He shook his head. "Nae, not really. Tis nae my fight. M'mother passed on when I was verra young, I daena remember her. I canna fight for her honor and I hae nae need tae fight for mine. With Lady Mairead I hae tae trust Og Maggy's judgment and ken that she had many chances tae kill or conquer me and I am still here, livin' with her son. If ye think on it, if she wanted tae keep me far away from Og Maggy's throne, she has nae been verra good at the plan, for I am as close as could be. She is lucky I hae nae need for the crown."

"Good, I wouldn't want you to feel torn between your ancestral family and our current family. It would be difficult to balance."

"And ye arna thinking on it right, m'bhean ghlan. Ye are thinking too modern about it. This is the eighteenth century in the lands of Scotland. M'ancestors are Scottish, Magnus's ancestors are Scottish, we are all one people, ye ken, and my father was a poor man who lived in a small village and died..." He paused then said, "Och, I hadna thought of it."

"What?"

"He died just afore I was approached by Roderick tae kill Og Maggy. I hadna thought on the coincidence and now I daena like the..." He shook his head. "I am relieved Og Maggy killed him."

He exhaled. "But that is m'point, Hayley, m'family was poor. Living in Glencoe I had nothing, now I am part of a family that is rich and powerful and Og Maggy is a king. This is m'family now, my clan, I would nae trade it." He smiled, rain dripping from the front of the hood pulled over his head. "Besides, Og Maggy's family has the better food."

"Hell yeah. Okay, good, that all makes sense." I looked around. Our horses were plodding along, splashing on the wet trail, not wanting to near the epicenter of the storm.

Finally Fraoch said, "We should tie our horses up, they won't want to get closer."

We dropped down into the mud.

ELEVEN - HAYLEY

We walked into the storm, trying to get as close to the center as possible, triangulating with the monitor to find where the vessel was hidden. Ahead of us was a small stone chapel with a slate roof and beside it some very simple graves, ancient-looking, worn and covered in moss. The stone markers tilted in different directions, a gnarled tree stood beside — just then, lightning sparked from the sky to the ground, illuminating the graveyard and setting my teeth on edge.

Fraoch and I crouched a distance away, watching, but with a storm this fierce there was no way we could get closer. It was clear that the vessel was there, on the grounds of the church.

"We can't get closer!" I yelled to be heard over the storm. "We have to wait for it to stop!"

A loud boom of thunder, a flash of lightning — way too close.

Fraoch jumped up, grasped my hand, and we retreated to the horses, who were tied a safe enough distance away. There we sat under a tree with our hoods pulled down over our faces against the rain, waiting out the storm.

Suddenly, a last loud boom and the storm clouds rose quickly then dissipated into nothingness and clear skies.

I looked at Fraoch with wide eyes.

"Are ye ready, Hayley? We must go intae the graveyard where mischief is afoot."

I groaned and checked my gun. "Do you think someone might have arrived?"

"I daena ken."

We raced back to the church, cautiously watching from a distance, and then deciding it was all clear, scrambling over the fence into the graveyard. The ground was soggy wet. Some of the graves were mounded or eerily sunken, roots had broken through the earth, headstones leaned and some had tipped all the way. I sloshed across the muddy ground headed to the gnarled tree where I found a gravestone face down. A large root lay under it, having been instrumental in raising it from its foundation.

It was evening, growing dark and cold, and having been wet through, I was beginning to shiver. I called over to Fraoch, who was searching near the far wall, "Find anything?"

"Nae, not yet."

I pulled futilely at the corner of the gravestone and then I dug some mud away and peered underneath — something shiny, metallic.

"Fraoch! I think I see the vessel!"

He splashed across the graveyard.

I had barely budged the stone marker, but then Fraoch pulled it up, and flipped it over, making it look easy.

I joked, "I loosened it first."

"Och, ye want me tae think yer wee-lassie arms are strong." He crouched down beside the vessel and I watched his brow furrow, then he scowled.

"What?"

ELEVEN - HAYLEY

Fraoch said, "Tis where m'mother's grave will be. I had forgotten the placement of it."

"But she's not dead."

"Aye, they lied tae me about it. They put the vessel in the earth under a gravestone and when I was young I believed they buried her here. It does nae seem fair tae place a headstone above naethin' and tae tell the son that there lies his mother."

I hugged an arm around him. "You're right, it doesn't seem fair."

He asked, "Tell me again how the vessel is here in this time?"

"Because it's been activated, it's in this spot in every time, anyone can find it. It's very dangerous right now."

"Aye."

"Speaking of which, don't touch it, Kaitlyn grabbed one just like this and it dragged her off."

"But this one is nae on, tis off. Tis safe enough tae—"

"No, I don't agree — but fine, if you're going to touch it, I will at least hold onto you the whole time."

"Och, I am nae going tae touch it. I am nae an idjit." He looked around. "Hold here, Hayley, I will be back." He rushed away to the horses while I waited inside that very little graveyard in the middle of... *where was I?*

Suddenly it was lonely and quiet and I was reminded of those first days when Fraoch was rescuing me.

TWELVE - MAGNUS

That night Madame Sophie asked if we wanted tae meet upon the walls tae look through her telescope.

We met there after dark, with drinks in hand, gathered around her telescope set upon a stand. Kaitlyn said, "Fun! It's like a cocktail party I went to once back in..." She glanced at Sophie and finished, "back home."

Sophie adjusted the scope and then declared it ready. She said tae the bairns, "Ye will see the moon!"

One at a time, each bairn looked through the scope and for the cousins twas verra remarkable what they were seeing, but for Archie and Ben, twas verra commonplace. They came tae where Kaitlyn and I were leaned upon the wall drinkin' a dram of whisky, and Archie muttered, "Seen better on Guardians of the Galaxy."

Kaitlyn whispered, "Shh, Archie, we aren't to talk about that, plus, this is good for you to see. Madame Sophie has been studying with her telescope for a long time against great constraints, she was almost charged with witchcraft for it. You must honor her courage, even though you have seen more in your life."

I said, "I agree, how about ye both go thank her for allowin' ye tae look through the scope?"

The boys ran off.

Kaitlyn drank a shot of whisky down and hiccuped. "This is going to be tricky, raising a son who knows more than most. How will we keep him from being cocky?"

I drank m'own shot and chuckled. "Och nae, he will be good and humble like his father, the greatest king Riaghalbane ever kent." I took her by the hand and drew her toward the telescope for our turn lookin' at the skies.

Kaitlyn played her part well, I kent she had seen the stars and moon verra close before, much better than this telescope, but she marveled at the sight and said, "Magnus! Look!"

I pressed my eye tae the end. "Och, tis beautiful," I waved up, "Hello little man!"

Madame Sophie laughed. "A little man, on the moon?"

"Aye, I hope someday. Can ye imagine it, Madame Sophie, if man could see a way tae sail there in a ship?"

She had her hands on her hips looking up at the sky. "So far! But it is a wonderful thing tae imagine!"

Lizbeth came up. "Madame Sophie, I am verra glad tae see your telescope set up. I hae been looking forward tae having ye shew me the face of the moon. Of course, Liam disagrees with me on it, he thinks there might be a mischief tae see it, but he has said I *may*, and I do look forward tae it."

"I promise nae mischief, Madame Lizbeth, tae look through the telescope is verra wondrous. Tis nae magic, or mystery. Ye might tell Master Liam that tae map the skies is important for navigation, even the church has agreed on the importance of it. Or so m'late husband has told me." She showed Lizbeth where to look and took a moment to describe what she was seeing.

Lizbeth said, "Och, tis wonderful. Can ye remind me the name of yer late husband?"

"I was married tae John Milne, had ye heard of him?"

Lizbeth asked, while her eye was pressed to the eyepiece, "I do believe I heard of him when I was last in Edinburgh."

Sophie nodded. "He was well known at the university. His findings were celebrated."

Lizbeth cocked her head. "Yet ye were left without money or land?"

Sophie exhaled. "Aye, he was important and learned, yet lived a humble life, and has left me without a living."

Lizbeth shook her head. "Och, then ye will need a husband verra fast." She sighed and straightened. "Was he a good husband?"

Sophie laughed. "He was nae kind or good, but made up for it by being always with his telescopes and nae botherin' me much. I assisted him while he was studyin', but then he left me tae study on m'own."

Lizbeth said, "If he must be unkind, ye came up with a verra good arrangement for yerself."

Sophie said, "And please daena think poorly of me for this, but some nights I was able tae overhear his dinner conversations. There were many lively discussions with other men of science. I only listened because I had naught else tae do."

Lizbeth patted the back of her hand. "It sounds as if ye made the most of yer situation. A learned husband, who is unkind, is a troublesome thing. There are many a woman who must listen at doors tae understand the meaning of their world. I would never hold it against ye."

Sophie nodded.

Lizbeth looked through the telescope again and then stood up and sighed, looking up at the stars with her naked eye. "So John Milne kent of the universe, but was nae wise enough tae provide for his widow? Tis a shame the men who gain learning, daena ken tae take care of their household. Tis why I like my Liam, he daena pretend tae be learned. He lives tae be in service tae his family: his brothers, his wife, his bairns, his nephews.

TWELVE - MAGNUS

Now this is a man I prefer over a learned, but destitute and unkind man."

∼

The followin' day, I was in m'office, reading through a contract for flour, when James walked in followed by Quentin.

"A word, Magnus?"

My brow drew down. "What means this serious look?"

James said, "I have decided to marry Madame Sophie."

I laughed. "Och I believed ye were telling me bad news. But this... Master Cook, ye..." I shook my head. "Has Quentin told ye about the way of the widows? Ye arna forced tae marry them, ye ken? Ye may negotiate a favorable outcome for yerself, with some precautions, and ye daena need tae worry on it much."

"I don't think so, I sat with her most of last night. She was left with nothing. She has nowhere to live, no one to take care of her. She's really smart, it's dangerous for her and I could change her life in a second, just by deciding to. I've made up my mind, I want to marry her."

"Och." I looked at Quentin. "What dost ye think?"

"I think he's lost his mind, I think the lack of modern women has caused him to get confused all up in his head. I think it's the dumbest thing I ever heard."

James moaned. "I'm standing right here. You should say that shit behind my back like a good friend. I won't let you disparage her character."

"I'm not saying anything about her — she seems nice enough. You've known her for how long? Like three days?"

"I know it sounds crazy, but I asked her and she said yes. I talked to Sean about it—"

I chuckled. "What did Sean say?"

"He said he kent she would be a good match. He said she was a fine girl, demure and godly. He said a bunch of shit about how she would obey me properly. Don't tell Kaitlyn, she would throw a fit. And he said you should welcome the match."

Quentin said, "He also said you were too old to have never been married."

"Yes, he called into question my age, and my mental stability, but he was all for it other than that."

I said, "I daena believe Kaitlyn trusts Sean in matters of the heart."

"Well, I know what I want and it's Madame Sophie."

I shook my head. "Och, it looks as if I canna talk ye from it. There is no dowry. Ye daena expect anything from her?"

"No, but that's okay, I don't need it."

"I suppose it will be okay for a while, as we are going tae be living here for a time, but daena ye think she will be surprised if ye are time traveling around? Are ye nae worried she will be confused that ye are from a different time?"

He shrugged. "I'll cross that bridge when I get there. Quentin did it with Beaty, she hasn't been any trouble."

I chuckled. "Och, Madame Beaty has been a terrible amount of trouble, though I daena think Quentin would change anything about it."

"Exactly, that's what I'm saying, it'll be worth it."

THIRTEEN - HAYLEY

When I saw Fraoch again I was so relieved I almost burst into tears, not really almost, I kind of did a little.

"What, ye canna be apart without thinkin' one of us will die?"

"When you put it that way it does seem idiotic, but yeah, one of us will die, Fraoch. If I don't see you, you might as well be dead. It's not really all that healthy, but I'm calling it a trauma response. Every time you're out of my sight some crazy shit goes down."

"I ken, I feel it too, but here we are and we are solvin' a problem."

He took a thick leather rope-cinched sack and spread it out wide, then he and I both crouched beside the vessel. I held onto his arm, while he used the leather sack a little like a dog scooping bag, to quickly grab the vessel, maneuver it into the sack, jostle it to the bottom, and toss it away. We scrambled in the opposite direction.

"Och, twas scary."

"True that." I was still clinging to his arm.

We stared over at the lifeless sack lying in a mud puddle.

He said, "Next I hae tae get the sack intae this box."

Quentin had sent a lead-lined safe box. We had no idea if the vessel would activate from within it, because we hadn't been activating vessels or testing hypotheses. We knew vessel activation was a good way to be tracked and not being tracked was our only mission right now.

"To do that we need to be close, right?"

"Right ye are."

We both took in a deep breath and approached the sack. We crouched down beside it and I held onto Fraoch's arm again.

He scooped up the dripping, muddy sack and dropped it into the box, slammed the lid, and locked it with the combo lock.

We both backed away from it again, standing near a far fence, watching the chest.

I asked in a whisper, "Now what?"

"Now I am goin' tae put it in this larger sack and tie it tae the saddle on Thor."

We timidly approached the box.

I held the top of the large sack open.

Fraoch was about to use his foot to kick the box into the sack, when I said, "Wait! I have to hold your hand!"

"I daena think kicking a chest with a vessel inside is how we are meant tae time travel."

"True, but there is literally *always* a first time with these things."

I held one side of the sack in my teeth, the other side with my outstretched right hand, held Fraoch's hand with my left hand, and mumbled, "Go."

He kicked the heavy, muddy chest into the sack. Then grasped the ends of the rope and drew it closed. It lay limp in the mud and we stared down on it.

I said, "Well, now it just seems kinda like we were overreacting."

"Aye."

He said, "We ought tae load it ontae the horse and begin tae head back I think. I am nae sure when it will begin again."

"If it starts, you cut it loose from your horse. If a storm rises above us, you cut it loose. If you hear it making a sound, if you feel it vibrating, you cut it loose."

"Aye. I will carry m'sword in my teeth like this so tis at the ready." He put his dirk in his teeth.

"Oh my god, Fraoch, I am swooning! You look like a pirate, and that is *seriously* a fantasy of mine, possibly because of Johnny Depp, a super sexy guy who acted like a pirate once in a movie."

He sheathed his dirk again and pulled the sack to his back kinda like Santa Claus. "I hae nae idea what ye are talking about, but it sounds funny for ye tae hae a fantasy about a man with a dirk in his teeth — what is he tae do with the dirk? It sounds dangerous."

"It is. I guess that's part of the fantasy."

"Och, I canna understand women. I tell ye, Hayley, if ye hae a man come toward ye with a dirk in his teeth, ye run the other direction, or ye shoot him. Daena wonder if he is a movie man, Johnny the Dip, first, ye run."

I laughed as we trudged through the mud to the horses.

We strapped the sack to the side of his horse and mounted. "Dost ye want tae see m'village where I grew up?"

"Hell yeah I want to see where little Frookie was born, you bet I do."

We rode further into the valley. Because the sky had cleared, villagers had emerged from their homes and headed out to their fields to get the day's work done while the sun still shone. They were slogging through puddles, turning the animals out to graze, and gathering in groups to stare up at the sky, wondering if there would be... could be... more storms.

Fraoch and I continued on until we came to a cluster of

homes near the village center. It was there that he said, "Hayley, that was where I once lived."

The house was a low building with a wide thatched roof. There was an old woman sitting on a bench in front of the door.

I said, "Go ask her who lives here, maybe it's your grandfather. She might be your grandmother."

Fraoch looked from me up to the house and back to me, and then begrudgingly climbed down from his horse. I wasn't forcing him to do anything, yet he was irritated at having to do it. I understood his mood, it was how I talked myself into hard things all the time. Step one: Get irritated at the person giving you the pep talk.

He said, "Here's the dirk, if you have to cut the sack free from the horse."

"Oh, I almost forgot about that." I sat in an uncomfortable position with a blade close to the rope, ready to cut if necessary, while he trudged up to the croft.

A moment later an old man came around the corner to speak to him, then men crossed from the fields, gathering around Fraoch in discussion. Another man arrived until there were eight men in all.

The men were all much like Fraoch, wide shouldered, barrel chested, with ruddy complexions and red hair. Because of their size it was a little like a linebacker convention.

Their conversation lasted for so long that I lost feeling in my left leg and grew pretty irritable myself.

He returned to the horse after a while. "Och I am sorry, m'bhean ghlan, I hae just met m'grandfather. I couldna think straight. I was surrounded by ancestors, men I hadna seen before, though they were verra familiar. The auld man looked much like my grandfather, though he was my great-great grandfather, m'grandfather was younger than m'self."

He swung up on his horse.

"Are we going to stay longer? Spend some time...?"

"Nae, I daena need tae. They are strangers, Hayley. Twas fun

THIRTEEN - HAYLEY

tae see them, but that was enough, besides they want tae work while the sun shines." He rode his horse along the trail between the crofts. "Look, there, Hayley, this is where I used tae chase m'brother, up and down through the fields. And there," he pointed. "There is the edge of the loch, where a young Fraoch, years from now, will tie his skiff tae the shore. Then he will carry his string of fish in tae shew his father in that verra house."

He shielded his eyes and looked back at the house. Then out over the loch, his back straight, his gaze sure. I let him be quiet and think on things for a moment.

The loch was gorgeous, deep blue surrounded by deep green grass on both sides, the deep moisture-laden colors of a land right after a drenching rain. Florida looked like this often, color wise, but the undulating hills and mountains were nothing like Florida.

Finally he broke his trance. "Och, m'bhean, twas good tae bring ye here, do ye see it, where I come from?"

I said, "Aye."

FOURTEEN - KAITLYN

I asked, "So what the hell is going on?"
James was quiet and awkward.
Magnus said, "Master Cook plans tae marry Madame Sophie."
"What the... *seriously*? James, have you lost your mind?"
Quentin laughed. "That's what I said."
James said, "Go ahead, get it out of your system. She's coming downstairs in a minute to eat and you need to be done insulting me."
I sputtered with my hands out. "But... what the... don't you... Hayley has to... what the hell dude...."
"Nice, eloquent, done now?"
"James, *listen*, she's from the eighteenth century, right? She's different, less modern, more religious, she will 'obey' you and it won't be ironically."
James said, "Beaty is a modern woman."
I huffed. "Beaty is an anomaly."
Quentin said, "I'm not sure I'm down with everyone using Beaty as the best and worst case scenarios. Beaty and I have been married now for years and she's a part of this family and y'all need to shut up about it."

FOURTEEN - KAITLYN

I frowned. "I'm truly sorry Quentin, I was just painting a picture. I love Beaty and intend no insult toward her. She was just young and it could have been so hard to bring her into the family. The fact that she fit so well is a testament to her personality."

James said, "Madame Sophie has an excellent personality, she's a lady of science."

I scoffed, "Like you've noticed over her bosom."

He grinned.

"I do want you to know, you're going faster with her than I did with Magnus."

"Sure, and as a friend I told you that you were making a mistake, but I also butted out of it."

"Yeah, but by marrying her you're bringing her into our girl group. Me and Hayley and Emma and Beaty are going to have to like her. Do you know how hard it is to get four women to agree about a fifth woman?"

He joked, "That sounds like a personal problem."

I said, "The other thing I hate to mention, that means your wedding would be two days after my anniversary, can I not have a single celebration that isn't usurped by someone else in the family?"

"Hey, I'm about to put my wedding anniversary on the greatest, most patriotic celebration of the year, you don't see me complaining."

"You're just thinking how cool it will be to blow off fireworks on your wedding day."

"Can you imagine how amazed she will be?"

FIFTEEN - HAYLEY

We had to spend the night out again. We chose a nice secluded spot, leaving the sack covered with leaves a few hundred feet away. We were wary that it would come alive again, a storm right above us, that it might grab us and jump us, so we kept it as far away as possible.

I said, "Weird, huh, that the last person to touch this was your father? That it belonged to your mother?"

"Aye, and before that a man in the year 1557 perhaps, there is a deep history about the thing," he said, totally missing the point.

I loved that he wasn't sentimental about his ancestors but it also drove me crazy. I had been thinking about it on our ride — I thought, because we weren't going to have children, that it made our ancestry more important, that the branches on our family tree were above us, shading us. We had decided to prune our family back, but didn't that make the rest of the family doubly important?

But Fraoch had a whole other opinion — that we could be content in the now, not worrying about who came before us, a bunch of unimportant arseholes. But the fact that no one came after us, because I was still committed to this... didn't that make us all alone?

Except for Katie and Magnus and Archie and Isla and Ben and... I was being ridiculous.

Nothing happened with the vessel.

We put up the tent and I was exhausted and ready for sleep, but Fraoch felt the need to stay up and guard.

I never understood how he did that, stand guard after a long day. Possibly he slept in quick naps or something, but when I asked, he just shrugged, "Only the wee need tae sleep."

The next morning we loaded up the tent and horses and then rode over to the sack, tied it to Fraoch's horse again, and took off toward home. We barely spoke, our ride was lovely, horse hooves plodding on an easily passable terrain. We enjoyed the view.

∽

Then, a couple of hours into the ride, Fraoch startled. "Och!" His horse pulled in a circle. "Tis hummin'!"

"Shit shit shit, get it off Fraoch, get it off!" He carved frantically at the rope with his dirk as a storm grew above us, sawing and sawing—

"Get it off!"

"I'm trying!"

"Hurry!" I tried to turn my horse toward him, to get close enough to put my arm on his shoulder, but I couldn't get my horse to go towards his because by now there was a full blown storm happening and then the knife loosed the last strands of rope and the sack fell to the ground.

Fraoch turned his horse, I pulled my horse around and galloped away with Fraoch just behind.

We made it to the outer edge of the storm, dismounted our

horses, and watched the bank of clouds towering over the hillside where the sack lay.

"Shit. Looks like we'll have to wait it out."

Fraoch said, "Aye, we will hae tae wait til the storm clouds clear again." He tied our horses to a tree, while I tried to get Quentin on the walkie-talkie.

We weren't close enough yet.

Fraoch pulled a gun from his satchel, and sat under a tree facing that direction. I remained standing. "That was so scary. My heart is racing."

He said, "Sit down, we are safe now."

"Are we? I mean, someone could come in the storm, someone might come up behind us... I'm going to watch behind us, like this..." I climbed onto his lap and sat down, straddling him. "Is this comfortable?"

"Aye, but tis nae the usual guarding position."

My chin rested on his shoulder, my arms under his, chest to chest. I joked, "You and Quentin don't sit like this on guard duty?"

He chuckled. "Nae, he is too large, but we tried somethin' like it one night when we were usin' the Trailblazer, because twas so cold."

I kissed the side of his neck. "So what do we do now?"

"We guard and we wait."

∽

It took about six hours for the storm to clear. We were farther away from the loch, this storm was less wet, but more electrical, lightning sparked everywhere. It was more dangerous feeling and we were closer to it, more on edge.

We had moved the vessel — someone was looking for it right? Turning it on to locate it? If so, had we just brought it further out into the open?

I asked, my voice loud to be heard over the storm, "Will someone come for it now?"

Fraoch said, "I daena ken, but perhaps nae one is tracking it, maybe tis only turning on, or... I daena ken the word, ye ken the word... ye used it for the Xbox once."

"I don't know... what...? And I love that you're in the eighteenth century thinking on the Xbox."

"I miss it, twas braw tae play Mario Kart with Archie and Ben. But when the Xbox wouldna work — ye ken the word..."

"Glitch?"

"Aye, glitch, perhaps the vessel is glitchin'."

"Will they do that?"

"I daena ken, we daena ken half of what we ought tae ken of them considerin' we be ridin' them."

He passed me his gun. "Hold this." He dug through his satchel.

"What are you looking for?"

"M'whet stone." I held the gun while he sharpened his dirk. We waited for the storm to pass.

***

Fraoch had actually fallen asleep for a time, his mouth hanging open with a bit of a snore. So I took over watch. Then he woke back up and just returned to his sharpening. Then sheathed his dirk and watched the storm alongside me.

Until it abruptly stopped about three hours later.

My legs were so stiff I had to shake them out. We mounted our horses and rode back to the sack, lying lifeless in the middle of the trail, once a dry path now a wet puddle. He dismounted, and using another rope wrapped it around the top of the sack and tied it to his horse again.

"Now we head home," he said.

. . .

Close to Kilchurn we were able tae make contact with Quentin who told us tae meet him directly at the cave on Ben Cruachan, so we rode our horses there. We arrived just as Quentin and Magnus rode up.

It took all three men to roll the stone away from the door, exposing the tunnel opening. It was small, having been a cave Magnus and Sean had found when they were young.

Magnus took off his sporran to begin the crawl into the cave when Quentin gestured with his head. "*Hayley.*"

My eyes went wide. "What?"

"You're the smallest person here, why don't you save Magnus the trouble?"

Magnus said, "Och, tis okay, Quentin, I can do it, I just hae tae stretch first."

I asked, "You want me to go into the small cave? Dark and with spiders?"

Magnus said, "I daena think the spiders will bother ye, they daena come out in the day."

"How will they know? It's dark!"

Quentin, without waiting for a response, pulled a headlamp from a saddlebag and passed it to me.

I said, "Okay, fine, sure, I'm doing this."

Quentin said, "All of us have done it more than once, it is your turn." He switched on the lamp.

"What do I do?" I stared at the dark maw of the tunnel, trying to psyche myself into going in. "How long is the tunnel?"

Magnus said, "Nae long enough tae get wedged."

"Wait, is there a chance of getting wedged?" I circled my neck and stretched my shoulders doing circles.

"You're going to drag the sack into the cave, take the vessel out, note the markings on this notebook, here's a pen, then put the vessel inside one of the lock boxes. The code is—"

Magnus said, "Och nae, daena tell her the code."

"Why not? It's Hayley."

"I hae already told four people, each person makes the location less safe." He put out his hand for the headlamp so I passed it to him.

Quentin said, "I'll go then, Boss."

"Nae, I got this Quentin. They're my vessels, I ought tae be the one tae put them in the small, dark, spider-infested cave."

He crouched down and dragged himself into the opening and then pulled his legs in with a grunt, the sack following behind. There was a shifting noise and then a thud as he dropped into the cave.

Quentin called in, "Don't forget to note the markings!"

Magnus's voice came from deep in the cave, "I winna!"

We waited a few moments then Quentin called in, "How ye doing, Boss?"

"Good!"

Quentin clutched his chest. "That's a relief, I didn't know what would happen, what if he didn't answer?"

It took a while and then there were scuffling noises, and grunts as Magnus heaved himself back through the tunnel. He stood up and stretched his back. He passed the notebook to Quentin. "It's in the fifth lockbox."

Quentin asked, "Did you count the vessels?"

"Aye, with the ones we ken are out, we hae twenty-four now with the one from Glencoe it makes twenty-five, and there is the odd machine, we daena ken what it does—"

"I hate not knowing that, what if it's a do over button, or like a... fix the world button?"

Fraoch said, "I daena think ye should work a machine when ye daena ken what it does. What if ye make the little men angry?"

Magnus asked, "What little men?"

"The wee men who work the magic within the machines, ye ken, ye must treat them well or they are full of mischief."

Magnus chuckled, "We hae a strange machine chock full of mischievous wee men, and, we hae the metal chest we canna get the lock open, tis likely tae be full of wee men as well."

"But the vessels, that's the right amount, right?"

"I believe so."

Then the three men shoved and rolled the giant boulder back in front of the door.

We all rode back down the mountainside. By this time the day had grown long, the sunlight was dimming. Magnus and Fraoch rode on ahead while I rode beside Quentin and told him more about the trip. Then I asked, "Why didn't James come?"

"Kind of a crazy story, James is going to marry Madame Sophie on the Fourth of July."

"Are you serious? Wait... what? Did no one try to talk him out of it?"

Quentin said, "Katie gave it a valiant effort, but I think he is following Sean's advice on it."

"I knew that meeting the men of the eighteenth century was going to mess with his head."

"Well, if you think about it, he's never had a stable long term relationship, maybe this is how he has to do it."

"The high school quarterback has to marry an eighteenth century widow to be stable?" I added, "I guess it's not the craziest thing we've seen lately."

Quentin said, "And stranger things have worked. Look at you and Fraoch."

"Fraoch and I have the most normal relationship of *any* of us, he's literally a good ol' Georgia boy. Freaking Katie married a king."

Quentin laughed. "Good point." We rode up to the gates of the castle.

SIXTEEN - KAITLYN

I was on my knees over Magnus, he was awake, he was always awake, but his arm was over his eyes, pretending to be asleep.

"Wake up love, it's our anniversary!" We were in a tent, on the shore of the loch, within sight of the castle, but hidden behind a tree so it could seem like we had 'gotten away'. I had picked this as my anniversary present, to go camping with my husband, because it was my favorite part of our year away. The only part of that time that had been worth it — the deep alone time I had gotten to spend with him.

"Och, so early in the morn?"

I laughed. "Do you want chocolate? I stole it from the storeroom."

He opened one eye. "Nae, ye can hae it."

I popped the chocolate piece in my mouth and moaned with pleasure. Then I began licking each finger clean of it and Magnus's eyes grew wide. He lumbered up, pushed me back, climbed onto me, and kissed me. "Ye taste like chocolate."

I licked his lips and he nibbled my bottom lip and then his mouth traveled over to the side of my neck and sucked there for a moment and my legs wrapped around him, pulling him close.

He tugged my shift up to my waist and entered me with the most delicious exhale against my skin, a warm rush through my insides as he held me and pushed and pulled against me, our mouths against each other's ears. It was a lovely, lovely oh god oh and—

Suddenly we could hear Isla's cry and it was coming closer.

He whispered, "Och, the bairn has terrible timin'."

"Oh my God, she's coming to the tent."

He held my leg up near his shoulder and tried to continue.

"Hurry, she's coming closer."

"Wheesht, I'm trying to concentrate."

Beaty's voice was trying to console Isla as she carried her toward us on the path.

I whispered, "Go fast."

And he did go fast, a very very fast fuck that ended with a rush just as Isla's wails made it to the tent.

Beaty called in, "Queen Kaitlyn, Isla was wantin' ye and she would nae listen tae reason on it."

Magnus blew out a breath against my skin.

"Hold on a moment!" I said in my most singsong voice. "We just woke up, let me get up, hold on." I giggled as I tried to get my shift down to my feet. My husband lumbered off me to cover himself in the bedding properly.

I opened the tent and Isla dove in. "Mama!" She grinned. "Mama tent!"

Beaty said, "I am so sorry, Queen Kaitlyn, I kent ye were celebratin', she was havin' a fit, and I couldna get her tae calm down."

"No worries, Beaty, you can leave her with us. Actually, if you see Archie will you tell him to come too? That would be a nice way to celebrate our anniversary."

Beaty left and Magnus went out and built a fire while I gathered the breakfast we had brought: bread, butter, and jellies. We heated coffee over the fire and as we were eating, Archie arrived. "Hello!"

SIXTEEN - KAITLYN

Magnus said, "Hello Wee Man, ye want some breakfast?"

And so the four of us sat around the fire on the edge of the shore, a comfortable morning full of 'telling the kids about when we camped' and talking about when we camped in the snow all of us together right before we came here. Then Archie and Magnus walked over to the field and picked flowers for me and Archie gave them to me in his fist with the pronouncement, "Happy Anniversary!"

And when Magnus asked me if I wanted to stay there for the whole day I said, "You know what? This morning was perfect. I love you, thank you. Let's go back home."

Archie helped us take down the tent and we left a small pile of gear there for one of the young men to come get with a cart as the four of us walked back to the castle. A lovely anniversary, one of my favorites of all time.

∼

James was honestly going to marry this lady. She was lovely, but as Hayley kept saying, "What the hell?"

Whenever we needed him he was sitting beside her, on the wall, as she fiddled with her telescope and made notes in her book or they were gone on long walks. She didn't ride much, having grown up in the city of Edinburgh, so walking was what they did.

He asked us about sharing a light with her, and after the group had conferred and then given him permission, we would see them up on the walls, him holding a flashlight and taking notes, while she looked up at the stars.

Then he asked if he could go home and get her a telescope, a new one, one to blow her mind.

Magnus said, "Nae, not now, it might be too dangerous."

"To travel? But we need supplies soon, right?"

"Nae, not tae travel, it might be too dangerous tae shew her what the skies hold out there. Ye daena want tae frighten her, I recommend ye go slow."

He nodded, but I could tell he wanted to get her one. And that it was hard to hold his excitement.

She was very pretty, with her high ginger coloring, so we could see why he would like her, yet Hayley, Emma, and I kept whispering in hallways. "Is he serious with this?"

Hayley's theory went like this, "There is *no way* he's doing it. This is one big game of chicken, you'll see, as soon as he catches a whiff of the church he's going to back out of there. He'll be a cattle reiver with Rob Roy again in no time."

My issue with her was that she was smart and inquisitive and committed to astronomy, a science nerd, even if her science was based on knowledge from three hundred years ago. I was confused that James, my old boyfriend, liked her: he'd been a player most of his life. She did not fit his mold at all. Also, though she seemed to laugh easily, she was eighteenth century raised: demure, obedient, devout.

We whispered suspicions though that some of her piety was a cover to protect herself from accusations of witchcraft. We couldn't blame her for being guarded.

And we were all guarded, too. It wasn't that we didn't like her, it was that we had to hide so much from her, that our conversations were stilted and weird. We had to check our stories and jokes, and pretend not to be modern. We weren't sure how to behave.

This was why getting to know her seemed difficult.

Lizbeth and Sean took all of us in stride, they understood that there were things we had that were frightening, but also useful and convenient. They purposely didn't ask questions, and simply chalked it up to 'Magnus's kingdom'. Sean assumed it was within the same time period. Lizbeth knew something else was going on.

Maggie, Sean's wife, ignored all of it, thinking us odd, and

SIXTEEN - KAITLYN

misunderstanding our behavior as 'foreign' and as Magnus told me, "She takes comfort in that she prays for ye, but she daena go as far as believin' ye wicked, she likes her shoes and her mattress too much for that."

I said, "I love that she doesn't think you're wicked, just the women."

He chuckled. "Aye, she believes all the men of the castle tae be verra proper, tis the women she worries on, ye might corrupt us with yer wicked ways."

"Och," I joked, "it makes me furious on the one hand, but oh well, she might as well pray about me, I can use all the help I can get."

∽

The night before the wedding, we had a light dinner together saving the effort of a large meal for the feast the following day.

Zach stood in the middle of the Great Hall during the meal acting incredulous, saying, "So we're seriously going to have a wedding tomorrow? With hotdogs for the meal? What the hell is going on?" Then he said, "Nah, I'm just joking, I'm psyched you boys brought the meat sticks. I've been so sick and tired of cooking every damn thing from scratch — takes all the fucking fun out of cooking I tell you."

Emma laughed. "You don't do all the cooking, you know. Eamag does most of it."

"Yeah, I'm mostly organizational at this point, she has pointed out that I add too many spices, and she's not having any of it." He grinned wickedly. "Wait until she tastes Dijon mustard tomorrow. Sweet ketchup. Potato chips, am I right, Quentin?"

"Hell yeah, we brought Doritos too."

Zach kissed his fingertips. "Delicioso! I'm tempted to kick her out of the kitchen and serve the meal making her wonder how the hell I made it all."

Emma said, "You would never kick her out of the kitchen, you love arguing with her about cooking."

"True, that old broad is like my best friend."

We all laughed.

SEVENTEEN - KAITLYN

*L*izbeth knocked on my room door. "Kaitlyn, I am headed tae Madame Sophie's room, ye said ye wanted tae help with her hair and dress?"

I was again reminded how much I wished for a coffee maker in my room. I got dressed as fast as I could and rushed to Madame Sophie's room, arriving just before Hayley.

Sophie was sitting on a stool in her shift, with Lizbeth and Emma working on her hair. We sent a maid down for food and then we all talked and teased while she dressed.

Hayley asked, "What was your first husband like?"

She said, "He was a man like most others: auld, resolute, and firm."

Hayley joked, "Well, firm is good, I suppose."

I said, "Hayley, she is going to think you're wicked."

Hayley said, "God-fearing Christian women want a firm man in the bedroom just like anyone else."

Sophie's eyes went wide.

I said, "Don't mind Hayley, she has a mouth on her, it's a travesty." I stuck my tongue out at Hayley and pulled Sophie's laces tighter. "This is a beautiful dress."

"Aye, I had it made just before my husband passed."

Lizbeth said, "How come ye daena hae any bairns?"

She said, "I daena ken... None will come."

Lizbeth said, "Were ye yer husband's first wife?"

"Nae, he had another..."

"Did he hae a bairn with his first wife?"

Sophie's chin trembled. "He had three sons, they were all older than I."

Lizbeth arranged a curl on her forehead. "So ye are barren — does Master James ken it?"

Her face grew so flushed I thought she might faint away. "He kens I... I told him I daena hae a bairn... I daena..."

I said, "If you told James you were married before and that you don't have children now, I'm sure he understands what you mean by that." I said it though I wasn't sure he actually *would* know what that means in a world of no birth control.

I wondered, *did James want children?* But it might not have been Sophie, it might have been the husband. He had been old, whatever that meant.

Lizbeth said, "Never mind ye then, I am sure, as Kaitlyn said, that Master Cook understands."

Tears welled up in Sophie's eyes. She said, "I am so worried on it. I hae nae dowry or contract, what if I canna perform m'wifely duty? What if he daena like me?" She began to really weep.

Hayley said, "Honey, take it from me, if you want kids you can figure it out, there's adoption, there are fertility clinics—"

I shot Hayley a 'shut up' look, and said to Sophie, "This conversation is too practical: dowries and bairns and duties, and it's too late. This is not what you should be thinking about right now. James wants to marry you." I squeezed her arm. "He wants to marry you more than anything. I don't think he's given a thought to contracts or duties."

Madame Sophie began to ugly cry. "But what if he changes his mind? What if he decides he wants a contract, I hae nothing. What if he sends me away? I hae naewhere tae go! I daena ken

SEVENTEEN - KAITLYN

what I would do! They would hae me tried as a witch without a friend tae stand for me!"

Lizbeth stepped away with her hands up. "Och, Madame Sophie, I daena believe I hae the sensibility tae help a bride dress. I am too practical. Ye must ken, if a man plans tae meet ye at the church, tis enough. He will bind his life tae yours and however that unfolds, tis God's plan for ye. Ye canna cry over it, the chapel is beckoning."

I dabbed at Sophie's eyes with a handkerchief and said, "And the truth is I think every bride cries on her wedding day."

Hayley joked, "Not me, I didn't cry, it rained torrents, and I didn't cry at all."

I said, "Hayley, you get my point, it's *frightening*. We all go through it, but he's waiting for you in front of the altar. *That's what you focus on*."

Lizbeth said, "Och, ye young women marry for love, us auld women hae tae marry with contracts and our father deciding it all."

I said, "First off, you are not so old, Lizbeth. Second, don't listen to Lizbeth, Sophie. Lizbeth married her Liam because she greatly liked the look of him, and he made her flush red when he looked at her across the room. I saw it with my own eyes."

Lizbeth said, "Kaitlyn is correct in this — I married my Liam because I wanted tae and dinna worry much on anything else. I kent he liked me and I kent he would be true tae his word. Ye must trust Master Cook tae honor his word tae ye." She brushed Sophie's shoulders. "Ye desperately need a husband, and ye hae found one." She cocked her head tae the side. "If a woman is clever, and a man is honorable, it can be acceptable for them tae form a marriage without dowries or contracts, right, Kaitlyn?"

"Absolutely."

Lizbeth said, "And ye are verra clever, Madame Sophie, ye are a woman who studies the stars. I think ye will ken what ye want upon the earth. And I hae seen James look upon ye, with a gleam in his eye. Ye hae given him a purpose and ye shouldna worry on anything else. Now wipe yer tears, Madame Sophie, and let us look ye over."

We all stood back.

I said, "You look really beautiful, right, Lizbeth?"

"Aye, she looks beautiful and wise. James is going tae be a verra fortunate man."

We all led Madame Sophie down to the family chapel.

∽

James met us in the courtyard and took both of her hands. "You look gorgeous, Sophie, I am a lucky man."

Hayley and I nudged each other with wide eyes.

"Thank ye." She lowered her eyes demurely and we all went into the church.

EIGHTEEN - KAITLYN

This was much like Quentin's wedding, except different in some key ways — Beaty had been young and silly. Quentin had been caught unaware by the need for marriage, but had stepped up and done it. There had been negotiations for her dowry by the older men of the castle, and while the actual marriage had begun as protection, Quentin took Beaty under his wing, becoming her husband and guardian in a way. Then, from that arrangement, they grew the friendship they now had, full of fist-bumping good humor and a deep abiding loyalty on both their parts. A partnership that spanned centuries and didn't look at all like Magnus's and my marriage, but still seemed right.

I sat down in a pew beside Magnus with Hayley on the other side of me.

Come to think of it, Hayley and Fraoch's marriage was different from mine, too. She and Fraoch had fallen in love and had, without any input from anyone else in the world, decided to join forces together. They weren't planning to have children. They were completely content to live hand in hand together, a perfect union in a way, because it was just the two of them without all the stresses that the larger commitment of family brought. They were the perfect aunt and uncle, devoted and true and fun, because they could do what they wanted to do without consideration of all the people that counted on them.

Though they didn't mind being counted on.

Then there was Zach and Emma's marriage, fully modern, a loving partnership and friendship that had grown over many years. They had overturned some of the roles, but had made a classic, traditional marriage with kids that they doted on. I remembered him standing up and saying she and Ben were the greatest thing that had ever happened to him, and tears welled up a little. Then I chuckled to myself at how irritated Zach would be to know I thought his was a traditional marriage. I glanced at where he was sitting farther down the pew, holding Emma's hand, his tattooed arm exposed.

Emma smiled at me with a look that said, 'I'm thinking about all our weddings too...'

And then there was Magnus and I.

We were all of these things and more. We had fallen in love and our marriage was arranged. We had mutually rescued each other and had logically partnered. He protected me, and I took care of him too. We had grown a family and friendships and he guarded over an extended family and a kingdom and... our commitments were huge.

Again, like always, there was one word to describe it, entwined.

James and Sophie had something different. He was very handsome there at the altar, that hot quarterback I had once loved more than anything. What my young self wouldn't have given for James Cook to stand beside me at the front of a church. He had been so cruel to me, but in the ensuing years he had grown, I thought, settled down a bit. And when I considered it, he didn't want a partnership so much as something more traditional. He wanted a woman to be his wife.

I had always been a little too independent, a little too strong. Or maybe I had grown into that too.

I had once wanted to be a 'wife' in the sense of a picture-perfect marriage, but it took Magnus, a man not afraid of my personality with all my faults and exuberant modern-ness, to take me on as an equal and to love me as a partner, and to ask me for advisement as a friend.

God I loved him. He took my hand and we smiled at each other as the wedding began.

James held Sophie's hands and smiled down into her eyes as he repeated the vows. He looked nervous, his hands shaking. He kept flipping his head to get his hair back from his eyes. Hayley held my other hand. She whispered. "I can't believe the boys didn't fix his hair for him."

I chuckled.

She added, "And I can't believe he's freaking doing this."

I whispered, "Me either, but here he goes, marrying a poor widow astronomer in the eighteenth century. You owe me five bucks by the way. He did not back out of the church."

She said, "Remember when this would have been all your dreams come true?"

I shook my head. "I was just thinking that, but no, that young girl seems a million years ago."

Sophie said her vows, and I said, "This is amazing to watch. It's like my brain doesn't believe my eyes."

Quentin leaned over to whisper, "Our boy is doing it." He wiped his eyes with a chuckle.

There was a long sermon, then a great deal of follow up prayers. The one thing we had learned living here, was that though our family church was presided over by a kindly, open minded man, he did very much like to hear himself talk.

Magnus exhaled long and low.

I knew prayer was important to him. He visited the altar here every day that he could, but even *he* grew tired of listening, and his exhale caused me to giggle quietly. He looked at me and smiled, his brow raising, that lovely crinkle at the edge of his eyes.

I read his look — it was saying, *Och, this is going long, and m'arse is pained, but listening is the least I can do,*

and so he did.

And then the minister pronounced James and Sophie man and wife and they turned around to the congregation, their smiles wide.

We gathered in the courtyard, hugging and kissing James, and welcoming Sophie to the family. Quentin pretended to cry, and it quickly crossed over into an actual tear rolling down his cheek.

James said, "Dude, you crying?"

"Hell yeah I'm crying, you got married, you're all grown up."

Fraoch laughed. "Daena get me started, I winna be able tae stop."

NINETEEN - KAITLYN

After the morning wedding we all gathered in the courtyard where Zach had grills set up over an open fire. Eamag was ordering the kitchen staff to bring out plates of hotdogs to be grilled. We were going to feast on hotdogs in buns with ketchup, mustard, relish, onions, and on the side, piles of potato chips, which Zach had taught Eamag how to fry. They had been working on them for hours to have enough for all.

It was funny watching Eamag, an old Scottish woman, proudly beaming beside Zach the young American man, covered in tattoos, a curse word always on his breath, as they presented the feast they had managed together.

In the kitchen Zach was often full of "Dammit, stir it, stir it!" And Eamag was often, "Och! Ye are a waste, how are ye going tae cook like that? Ye daena hae any sense!" But somehow they got our meals out. Today they stood over it proudly, and then he made Eamag a hotdog, put the mustard on it, the relish, some onion, placed on a paper plate, with a pile of potato chips and said, "Ready, Eamag, you old wonderful hag?"

She laughed. "Och, ye are a bumpty! Are ye goin' tae force me tae eat this terrible meal ye hae made?"

"Aye, you have to eat it or you'll break my heart, Eamag. We have been in the fucking trenches over this meal. You can't leave me out here to plant the flag by myself. Or some such shit. Take a bite." He held the hotdog out for her.

She shook her head and then wiped her face in her apron and opened her mouth for a tiny bite. Then while we all watched she chewed, her face twisted up comically, then she nodded and smiled, "Tis verra good!"

Zach thrust the plate in her hand and cheered, "Eamag likes hotdogs! I knew it! " And then, "Let the meal begin! Line forms around here!"

In the afternoon, we were all sitting around the courtyard, when James dropped a big duffel bag at his feet, and held up a tankard of beer. "My friends, I want to make a toast to Sophie, who walked into my life when I least expected her—"

Sean held up his glass, "Why nae? Ye're an auld man!"

James laughed. "Aye, I'm an auld man, not expecting to find her here, now, but there she is—" He put his hand over his heart. "And what a beauty, am I right?" He grinned. "I'm a lucky man to have these friends around me. I'm luckier still to have you enter my life and join my family, thank you."

She smiled and he leaned over her chair and kissed her sweetly. Then he said, "And because this is *our* day, I get to pick whatever I want to do, and I pick this!" He pulled a kickball from the duffel bag. "Who wants a game?"

We decided to, in the name of wedding day, make the game men against women. And all ages could play. Quentin and James placed bases out in a wide diamond in the courtyard and then James strutted in front of us all explaining the rules, but then Quentin got a chant going, "Let us play! Let us play!" Because none of the eighteenth century people understood what he was explaining and they needed practical experience instead.

So we played.

On the men's team:

Magnus was hilarious as he kicked and raced around the bases.

Fraoch danced and preened jokingly through the whole thing.

Sean took to the showmanship quickly, he was yelling at everyone to do better.

Liam took it very seriously.

James coached us all.

Quentin kept strategizing how to win.

On the women's team we were laughing a lot, because we couldn't take it seriously in our long skirts and tight bodices. We tried, oh we tried, but we couldn't compete so we just had to have fun, because when it was our time to kick...

Sophie, for instance, had never in her life kicked a ball, and when she rushed up she missed as the ball rolled right into her skirts.

James yelled, "That's okay, Sophie!" Clapping he said, "You got this, go again."

Quentin rolled the ball very slowly and Sophie's kick was a slight tap that barely nudged it away from her feet. Then James and Quentin conspired to go really slow so she made it to first base.

Then Beaty kicked.

Quentin beamed. She had played before. She tucked the back of her skirt up into her belt and when he rolled the ball she rushed forward and kicked it fast and far. All the little boy cousins and Archie buzzed around trying to retrieve the ball as she raced to first base. At the same time, James was trying to explain to Sophie that she needed to run to second base.

Then it was Lizbeth's turn.

She said, "Och, tis nae a proper sensible thing tae—" The ball rolled toward her and she jogged forward, meeting it almost halfway, too far away from home base but no one complained.

She kicked it right to Liam who looked surprised and then not at all like he wanted to chase her with it as she made it to first base.

Then it was my turn.

I joked, "Quentin, looky here, you've got the bases loaded with eighteenth century women — looks like if I make this kick and kick it well, I can, at the very least, get the bride home." To Hayley I said, "What do you think girlfriend? You think I can get one, two, three runs on this kick?"

Hayley laughed, "I don't know, depends on how fast they run!"

Zach laughed, "You ladies are strategizing, but look at how many men are in this outfield, there are at least thirty men out here."

I laughed. "Yeah, but through sheer grit and determination I managed to get a teammate on every base, pure skill baby, like *Olympic* level."

I hitched up my skirt.

Quentin started to roll but I stopped him, "Wait! Let me talk to my teammates for a second."

To all the ladies on bases, I said, "I just want to make sure — you all know what to do — you run, right? Sophie, as soon as my foot connects to the ball you run to this base." I pointed. "Got me? Run fast! Beaty, you know what to do. Lizbeth, you're going to where Beaty is standing and if you can keep going, just keep running, following Beaty, got me?"

They all agreed.

I said to Quentin, "Okay..." I hitched up my skirt even higher and looked out at the field, every square inch covered by my opponents. The only weak link, Liam, because he was confused by the whole game. But there was James, infield, grinning — he was the *groom*.

The ball rolled toward me, I swung my foot back, connected, expertly, and slammed it into James's hands.

He said, "Shit, I have the ball!"

I raced toward first.

Lizbeth jogged to second, and Liam, following her, asked, "Och, twas where ye were tae go?"

"Aye, tis what Kaitlyn said."

I turned around and saw James pretend he couldn't get Madame Sophie out as she crossed home base, then he threw the ball to Quentin who pretended to chase Beaty as she crossed home base, and then Magnus ran alongside Lizbeth coaching, "Run that way, tae the base, ye must touch it! Keep going!" While Liam ran alongside her thinking that was his job, and then Quentin threw the ball to Magnus as my foot stepped on third base.

I picked up speed with Magnus in hot pursuit, his footsteps close behind, as I sprinted, one, two, three — I dove for home base as Magnus tagged me with the ball a half second too late.

I was covered with the dust and dirt of the courtyard, and sat up spitting and coughing, everyone laughing. Archie threw his arms around my neck, "You got a home run!"

Magnus held out a hand to help me up.

After that the men didn't 'let' us win, but they also didn't kick our arse, and most of the women dropped out from playing because our dresses made unfortunate athletic uniforms. We switched around our teams, filling in with men, until after a couple of hours our teams were more like me, Magnus, Zach, Emma, Quentin, and Sean, against James, Hayley, Fraoch, and Liam with some of the cousins and a few of the guards joined in. It was a freaking amazing afternoon with our large extended family.

And whenever we needed more to eat there was Eamag at the grill with yet more hotdogs and potato chips.

Sophie came over when I was putting ketchup on a hotdog for Isla, "Do ye need any help, Queen Kaitlyn? Ought I tae help ye with the bairns?"

I laughed, balancing three paper plates for Isla, Archie, and Ben. "Am I looking that incompetent?" I passed Isla the hotdog and a second later she had a smear of ketchup on her face. "Besides, it's your wedding day, you don't need to help me with the children. Enjoy yourself."

She said, "Och, I thought..."

"You thought what...?"

Isla squirmed away from me as I tried to wipe her face clean.

"I was told tae help ye."

"Ugh, you don't have to help me, I'm an old married lady. No one will mind if you don't offer to help on your wedding day, so don't worry about it."

She looked flustered.

Isla pulled on my skirts. "Want chips!"

"Who told you to help me?"

"Everyone, they said I ought tae do m'best tae keep ye happy."

"To keep me happy... why? Is it because I had a relationship with James back in the day? Because you don't need to worry about it — that was nothing. You are a part of his family now, which makes you a part of *our* whole family."

Tears welled up in her eyes.

"Madame Sophie, what is it?"

"Ye had relations with James, what dost ye mean?"

"Oh! I mean, no, not really, not anything to worry about... I'm so sorry I said anything, Sophie, boy, open mouth insert foot." I watched the kids eat. "I'm really sorry about that, do you need a napkin?"

"Aye." She dabbed at her eyes. "I am sorry, I hae been overwhelmed t'day."

"It is your wedding day, you're allowed to be emotional." I asked, "So why did everyone say you needed to make me happy?"

"Because ye are a queen."

"Och." I grimaced. "Yeah, that is... confusingly simple and a perfectly good reason." I saw James standing across the way. "Can you hold on for a moment?"

I rushed to where he stood. "Okay, I screwed up, I told her we had a relationship and God only knows what that means inside of her head."

"What the hell, Katie?"

"I *know*. I am so sorry about that — go talk to her."

I pushed him toward where she stood with a forlorn expression, staring out at the crowd in the courtyard.

TWENTY - KAITLYN

The games wound down, though drinking followed in earnest like at any good wedding, and then continued into the growing darkness.

Kids were, as Beaty said, "Cranking out all over the place," but James had more festivities planned. He and Quentin and Zach brought out a big leather bag and we followed them out of the gates in a meandering procession, everyone except the few men left guarding the castle.

We went down the causeway to the low grassy beach near the edge of the lock.

James said, "I know you might have seen fireworks before, but these are new and improved, are you ready for some fireworks y'all?"

Hayley got a cheer going up. "Fi-re-works! Fi-re-works!"

We sat in the grass, Isla on my lap, Archie, Magnus, Ben, Emma, and wee Zoe, and all around the women and men of the castle about to have their minds freaking *blown* by modern pyrotechnics.

Hayley grinned. "This is going to be so freaking cool."

"True that."

The show started — thousands of dollars of fireworks. The

TWENTY - KAITLYN

audience gasped and cheered, the kids covered their ears, and even those of us who had been around fireworks our whole lives cheered and applauded.

Liam and Sean stood beside James, Quentin, and Zach 'helping' to light the fuses, setting up the mortars, Magnus and Fraoch having seen it before, ooohed and ahhhed anyway.

They had the fireworks that blew up like giant umbrellas, some looked like daisies popping up in a wide black sky, but the favorites were the ones that made sounds, the spiraling screamers, and the fizzing spots.

It was a lovely, wonderful night.

Fireworks echoed through the valley, messengers having been sent around to all the villagers telling them that lord Magnus Campbell was putting on a show and to enjoy and giving them casks of ale and some chickens for their trouble.

After the show we walked back to the castle following James and Sophie holding hands.

I wrapped my arm through Magnus's and he kissed my forehead. "Twas a grand night," he said, "a good wedding day, a proper Fourth of July party."

"I totally agree."

The next day, full of patriotic fervor and a bit of a hangover, Quentin called another vote. "I'm calling it because I think it's high time. We've been here for a few months. The weather is good, we could be training and planning. I want a vote: 'Nae' if you want to stay here and do this, live like this. 'Aye' if you want to fight for the kingdom and come up with a plan for returning home to Florida. All right?"

I glanced at Magnus, he nodded.

Quentin said, "All those in favor of fighting for the kingdom say, 'Aye'."

He, Beaty, and Fraoch said, "Aye."

He glared at James. "What the hell? No vote?"

James shrugged, "I just got married, I need to stick around."

Quentin groaned. "All right, everyone else. If you want to stay here, live here, say 'nae'."

Zach and Emma, Magnus and I, and Hayley and James said, "Nae."

Quentin said, "What about you, Hayley, you're going to split your vote with your husband? Why don't you come over to our side?"

Hayley said, "Why doesn't he come over to my side?"

Fraoch laughed, "I daena hae tae. I get tae vote how I want tae vote. I ken how democracy works now Quenny has explained it tae me."

TWENTY-ONE - KAITLYN

It was the day before Lughnasadh, Magnus's favorite day, the harvest festival, and for the past week Zach and Eamag had been baking a ton of bread for the villagers as part of our thank you to the whole freaking region for being so cool.

The people of the area needed all the extra food and help they could get: there had been an economic downturn and the weather was shite, cold and wet. There was barely any harvest so Magnus was spending time over his books, arranging payments, shipments, trades, and gifts.

But tomorrow we would be feasting, which was necessary, because the baking meant that the meals had been sparse and plain, or as Hayley put it over breakfast, "The output from the kitchen is so super sucky right now that I'm about to straight up eat a leather saddle."

Zach, who I had long suspected was actually *purposefully* putting flour on his face before he came out of the kitchens to see us so he could complain about all the work, put his hands on his hips and said, "Did you seriously just call the food sucky?"

"Hell yeah I did, *super* sucky."

Fraoch was sitting in a chair between them, indulging in his new hobby, knitting, working on oddly shaped socks for Magnus, after having made an overly long, awkwardly stitched scarf for Quentin. He had his left ankle on his right knee, with a ball of multicolored yarn in his lap, his knitting needles clicking while Hayley and Zach bantered. Then he put his knitting needles down and said, "The food is kinda shite."

Zach looked incredulous. "What the... what? I just baked hundreds of loaves of—"

Magnus laughed. "I ken ye baked bread, Chef Zach we hae been hearin' on it for weeks, but the dinner last night was verra bland."

Zach waved his hands at Magnus causing a flop of flour to sail across the space and land on Magnus's cheek. He brushed it off laughing.

Zach said, "Look, this is the deal around this fucking place, if the food is good, it is because of me, if it's bland, it's Eamag. She fights me on *everything*. If I so much as pick up the salt shaker she rushes over and stands glowering over my shoulder. I think I broke her with the taco night a few months ago — they weren't even spicy! Not really! Fuck, that auld lady drives me crazy. God love her. Hey, did I tell you what she told me about Lady Mairead?"

"No, but tell us, I want to know, dish dish!" Hayley rolled her hand.

Zach pulled out a chair, turned it around and sat on it. "Eamag told me that when Lady Mairead was really young—"

Hayley said, "I can't believe Eamag was around at the same time."

"Why not, she's old as hell! She is an eye witness to the fact that Lady Mairead ran off with a boy, a local farmer."

Hayley said, "Uh uh, no way!"

Zach said, "Magnus, you ever heard this?"

"Nae, I heard she was a wanton woman, the boys taunted me with it. I beat Jimmy fairly for sayin' it and it wasna said again."

Zach laughed and held up his hands. "Don't beat me, I'm just telling it. I don't think it's anything disparaging. I think it's astonishing to find out she's a real human who wasn't always deviously scheming."

Magnus asked, "What did Eamag say on it?"

"That Lady Mairead was found in an old croft with the boy and brought back to Balloch, locked up, and then quickly married to Sean's father."

Hayley asked, "What happened to the boy?"

"He *died* from 'falling off a horse.' I swear Eamag meant there to be air-quotes around the 'falling off a horse'."

Magnus said, "Och, I hadna heard it."

Hayley said, "No fair! I wanted to hear fun dish, now I feel sorry for her."

Zach said, "You don't have to feel *too* sorry for her, I mean, she's still mean as hell, just because something awful happened to her thirty years ago doesn't mean she shouldn't be nicer."

I said, "So she was married to Sean's dad and..." I squinted my eyes. "Maybe don't tell this story in front of Sean."

"Oh, because he might be... oh!"

"Yeah, this is probably best kept to ourselves."

Magnus said, "Aye, I agree." He paused then said, "Did Eamag ken who it was who found her with the boy?"

"Yep, it was the Earl."

Magnus sneered. "Och, the man has always been reprehensible, I am glad tae hae taken Lady Mairead's side in their arguments through the years."

∼

The following day we woke to a day of festivities: first a church day with the blessing of the bread, then a harvest fair and games that began with traditional games, including, excitingly enough, my first chance to introduce all my friends to my skill at archery.

I had three bows made for the day and we had bales with

targets on them. We ran heats and I was gosh darn glorious. There had been a moment when I had been worried because Sophie, when asked, had said she had competed in archery before. I tried really hard to shake it off and be cool with the idea that I might get beaten at the best thing, competition-wise, that I had ever done.

It had been something that had been important to me in that long year away from my family, something I really wanted to show off about, but *whatever*, I was a grown up.

If Sophie beat me it would be fine.

But then she didn't. I came in first, fair and square, and everyone was impressed with my skill, because Sophie came in second but well down in the score, like not even close.

The men competed in a caber toss and then a big game where they lifted giant stones.

I was standing beside Magnus, watching Sean lift, "Master Magnus you are crowing like a rooster, I see, preening like one, too, all because you can carry a big rock."

He joked, "Och, ye were verra proud of yerself as well with the little stick flying through the air."

"Ha! Well, you're right, I was very proud of myself."

"I was proud of ye as well."

"Now go lift another rock, I want to see more leg."

He laughed and got up for his turn. Fraoch was the one to beat, but it was fun to watch all the other men try, some jokingly, like Chef Zach, who could barely budge it, and Magnus, of course, coming very, very close and giving me a bit of a thrill. Fraoch took the prize, but all the men posed as if they were bodybuilders.

Then to round out the day we taught the whole castle soccer.

It was lovely at the end of the long day, to watch some of the boys and most of the men playing soccer out on the grass. Then

TWENTY-ONE - KAITLYN

because of the exertion a few of the men, specifically James, Quentin, and Magnus, took their shirts off and it was like, epic.

Hayley called, "Fraoch! Take off your shirt!"

He grinned and put his hand behind his ear, "Och, I canna hear, is m'wife asking me tae take off m'skirt?"

We all laughed.

I glanced at Sophie's face, she was blushing, as her eyes followed her husband chasing the ball down the field.

I said, "What do you think, Madame Sophie, do you like soccer?"

She said, "Soccer, what is soccer?"

Hayley said, "The game they're playing with the ball!"

A sly smile tugged at the side of her mouth and she said, "Och, are they playin' a game? I hadna noticed, I was watching m' husband with nae shirt upon his chest."

Hayley burst out laughing. "Awesome, you are our kind of girl." Then we all, including Sophie, spent the evening cheering on our teams, advising and coaching from the sidelines.

Sean was running down field and yelled to James, "Tis verra fun that ye hae taught us tae play with a ball."

James joked, "Next week I'm going to teach you American style football."

TWENTY-TWO - KAITLYN

A few weeks later, Lizbeth and Sean and their families had to return to Balloch for the winter. They wanted to get ahead of the winter weather, because really from then on, it was totally foul, cold, and poured rain all the time.

We had some celebrations here and there, like Samhain, but by the time we were celebrating autumn holidays we had already been living through such crappy weather that it was hard to believe we had even more coming.

And it was only November 1st.

Fraoch made the Samhain celebration pretty great though. He gathered all the kids around and told ghost and evil fairy stories and regaled them with a long story about living in a swamp surrounded by monsters and finding Magnus washed up on shore. He stood and told all about saving Magnus from certain death at the teeth of the beast.

Magnus said, "Tis nae how I remember it at all, the monster was big, aye, but I think ye told me tae roll away from him and I did."

Fraoch said, "But twas how I told it tae ye, I said ye must roll away from the monster or he will eat ye."

TWENTY-TWO - KAITLYN

Ben asked, "Uncle Fraoch, did you have to push Uncle Magnus?"

Fraoch said, "Why yes I did. Here, let me show ye!" He made Archie lie down and got Ben to roll Archie across the floor of the Great Hall. "Now ye reminded me, Ben, twas just like this — yer Uncle Magnus layin' in the swamp, wailin' and begging me tae save his life, and I rolled him over and over."

I raised my hand from where I was sitting on the ground with Isla in my lap watching Fraoch's storytelling. "I think seeing Ben push Archie is just not *quite* good enough for my imagination, can we actually *see* Uncle Fraoch roll Uncle Magnus? And now that I think about it, could Zach pretend to be the alligator monster too? Just so we have it clear in our minds how it went?"

Applause went up, with urging from everyone.

Magnus laughed. "Och, it sounds as if everyone wants tae see it."

Zach got down on his stomach on the ground and gnashed his teeth. "They make a roaring noise, from down in their stomachs!" He roared again.

Fraoch said, "Og Maggy, ye must get down there, lay down beside him."

Magnus pretended to be afraid. "I daena want tae, he is verra frightening."

Ben and Archie yelled, "It's okay, it's just a play!"

And Isla joined in, "Play play!"

So Magnus lay down beside Zach and said, "Och, I am near death and verra close tae the log, and tis dark and I canna see his teeth."

Zach gnashed his teeth.

Fraoch feigned surprise, "Och, who is this wee man lying here in the swamp?"

The kids all laughed uproariously.

Fraoch said, "The wee man is goin' tae be eaten by the beast if I daena save his life." He showed off his muscles and then set to work rolling Magnus across the floor. "Ye see, Og Maggy, ye are too verra weak tae save yerself, tis up tae me tae do it." And rolled him all across the floor to the far door.

The kids were falling all around laughing and then for a while we had rolling-time until it devolved into bed time.

TWENTY-THREE - KAITLYN

The weather continued to suck.

Magnus and Quentin ran daily exercises among all the men: guarding, fighting, protecting. They target practiced, they fenced, they sparred.

Three times a week the women were run through exercises too. We trained in marksmanship, hand to hand combat, daggers.

Quentin, becoming very bored during these long cold days, invented long elaborate training exercises and ran the whole castle through them. More elaborate than fire drills, we knew we couldn't predict what might happen, but we tried to come up with some examples anyway — like drone army attacks from the woods, or mounted army attacks from over the mountain.

One day, after going through exercises, a few of us had been battling in the Great Hall and Hayley scrambled up on the big long wood table, facing me, and drew her wooden blade. "Draw!"

"Shit, that's cool, it's like Harry Potter."

She said again, "Draw!"

"Okay," I climbed up on the table and we stood across from each other, our wooden blades up.

She said, "Damn, this *is* really cool, we look just like we're in Harry Potter, we need robes, and I wish I could remember what they say."

"Snape says something awesome, definitely." I put my hands on my hips. "But you know what really bothers me?"

She shook her head.

"That it took so long to climb up here, that was just embarrassing." I climbed off the table. "What we need is to practice getting up onto a table fast, and sliding down, or rolling across, all these are *highly* necessary skills."

"True, every movie has to have a lunge-across." She climbed off the table.

I said, "Hold my blade so I don't poke my eye out." By now the rest of the women and a few of the boys had joined us.

I pushed a heavy chair up beside the table and grinned at Archie and Ben. "For the shorties."

I stepped back, positioned myself, raced forward, slammed my hand down on the table, propelled myself up to the chair, swung myself around, and slid forward on the table by about one inch.

"Okay, that sucked, but you get my point, let's all try it..." A line formed behind me and we spent a few hours that day and many days after, teaching each other how to do a stunt-slide down the table. Like we were in a movie.

This was how bored we were.

∼

Quentin ran through the courtyard.

Hayley said, "Uh oh, here we go, another drill."

I put my hands on my hips. "Crap, they really scare the kids."

"Necessary though, want to beat our last time?"

"You're on."

He began ringing the bell, clang, clang, clang. Men raced

toward the gate to close it. More men rushed up the steps to the high walls.

Magnus's voice on my walkie-talkie, "Are ye with the bairns?"

"Not yet, headed that way."

Hayley and I raced to the armory, jumped ahead in line, and were passed guns.

Then her job was to race up the far steps to the Great Hall to see if there were any women or children stragglers, while my job was to run up the front stairs picking up women as I went, and getting them to the nursery. We would meet Emma and Beaty there, and help corral the children into the back room.

When Hayley arrived we were to build a barricade against the door, calm the children, and wait.

She called over her shoulder, "First one to the nursery, wins!"

I took off like a bolt. I passed one of the maids on the steps, "Come on, come on! We have to beat Madame Hayley."

She raced after me to the floor and then we rushed along the hall, but could see Hayley running from the opposite direction, holding the hand of one kid, urging on one of the maids. My hand touched the doorframe first. "Me!"

She laughed, as we all pushed through the door.

Beaty pushed Isla into my arms and I rushed through to the back room where Archie and Ben and Emma with Zoe in her arms were sitting with about twenty other kids along the walls. Beaty and Hayley and a few of the younger maids helped push chairs and tables in front of the door and then we all sat down on the ground.

I called Magnus on the walkie-talkie. "Done."

He said, "Och, ye went fast this time."

Hayley, armed, standing near the door, called over. "Tell him it's our personal best."

I said, into the walkie-talkie, "Tell Quentin that was our personal best and we want extra dessert tonight."

"Aye."

I looked over at Archie and Ben, their eyes wide. "But also tell him the kids are frightened, that he can't keep doing this."

"I will tell him, but ye ken we need tae practice."

I sighed. "I know, I know. Just tell him we get extra dessert." I put out my arm for Archie to tuck under while we waited for the guards to come collect us from our hiding place.

∽

Isla had a swing outside. Every day she would center her hands on my face, look into my eyes, and say, "Swing?"

I would say, "It's too freaking cold outside, Isla, too cold and raining."

Sometimes she would frown, sometimes she would cry, most of the time she would wriggle down off my lap, "Go find da!"

And would toddle away. I would peek from the stairwell to see her on the swing in the courtyard with Magnus pushing it, frosty puffs forming with every breath. It would last for about two minutes before she would say, "Cold!" and Magnus would bring her inside.

I asked Magnus why he agreed to go out there with her if he knew it would be too cold and he said, "Och, tis just a wee bit of weather."

And he had his own way of beating the boredom now, puzzling.

Emma, having guessed we would grow bored, had asked Quentin for jigsaw puzzles last time they traveled, and he and James had brought her three, big ones, with thousands of pieces. She spilled one out on one end of a long board table in the corner of the Great Hall and sat there when the light was good during the day, picking up pieces and figuring out where to place them. It was a puzzle with a picture of a castle on a green hill.

On the second day, Magnus sat down at the table across from her. "How do I do it?"

She looked surprised. "I thought you were watching yesterday!"

"Aye, but I canna make sense of it."

"So first you find the flat edge pieces and you try to build the edges, that's what I'm doing now." She slid about fifteen pieces toward him. "These are all edges and they're all blue for the sky, so put those together."

Magnus tried to smash two together. Emma giggled. "That's not quite right."

"Aye, they daena fit." He grinned. "I might need m'dirk tae force them."

"That is not how it works, try those two."

He moved both of them around five different ways before getting the pieces together, then said, "Och, it fits, I see it now."

After that he was there for at least an hour a day as long as the light was good, sitting across from Emma putting together puzzles, until he was pulled away to run through military exercises, or do the other duties that we needed the lord to do.

But sometimes I would tease him, when he was in other parts of the castle, doing other things, and I'd see he was distracted, his mind wandering, and I would ask, "Are you thinking about your puzzle?"

"Och aye, ye ken, tis verra complicated, and we are close tae finishin'. I hae tae get back tae the Great Hall or else they will finish it without me."

The puzzling corner was often crowded with people watching the puzzlers puzzle. Or joining them to chat while they worked on their own hobbies. Fraoch would often sit beside Emma and Magnus, with his knitting needles click-clacking. Hayley had taken to spinning yarn, so she pushed her spinning wheel beside their puzzling table and with clatters and whirs would spin skeins for Fraoch.

Quentin and James sat and watched one day and James asked, "Are you sure, really sure, that I can't plug in an Xbox? I mean, we have the electricity from the pump, right? Just one plug? We could have it up in Quentin's room."

Magnus pressed a puzzle piece in position. "Nae, we talked on it, we can hear the buzzin', everyone would ken and where would it end?"

Quentin said, "I agree with Boss, believe me, I want electricity too, but one day in we'd all be there, on the couch, staring at the screen. Ben and Archie would be there, too. There's no way to keep it hidden. Then the guards would hear about it and then the outer villages and then the king and then there would *have* to be an invasion. The king of Spain for sure wants to play Xbox. Then Wikipedia has a post about it, the Xbox Wars of 1706, and guess what...? We are found."

James said, "Fine. I think we could win the Xbox Wars of 1706 though, just saying, and if they're coming we ought to practice by playing more Xbox."

My hobby was drawing. I sat beside the puzzle station and drew the scene, the people, their hands, an eye, one of the sleeping dogs, anything that caught my fancy, with a pencil set that Quentin had brought. The only downside was that I could never sit there for too long before one of the bairns would need me.

∽

Zach planned a Thanksgiving dinner for all of us, but he was surly and irritated because he didn't have some of our traditional foods with us, like cranberry sauce, or pecans for pie. We had enough food on hand, it just wasn't special, but no one wanted to risk time traveling for 'special'.

Zach also complained endlessly about Eamag, that kind of obsessive coworker complaining. He would not stop bitching about her — Eamag bossed him around too much. Eamag

TWENTY-THREE - KAITLYN

wouldn't leave him alone to cook. Eamag didn't like any of his ideas.

I sat down beside Emma at the puzzle end of the table. She had little Zoe in the sling, and blew her bangs from her forehead. "What the heck, my husband is going to drive me crazy." She wrapped her Fraoch-knitted scarf tight around her shoulders.

"Eamag?"

"How'd you guess?"

"He was just here telling us that she burned some sauce. I stopped listening because it's so common." I puffed breath on my fingers. "Man, it's cold as shit in here. How are you doing puzzles? This is our life now? Just a cold dark dank castle. We need central heat and your husband needs his own kitchen where he's the boss."

"He needs her though, he doesn't want to cook for seventy-five people or however many there are, he wants to cook for ten, with no one else telling him what to do."

She sighed.

I sighed.

Magnus came up and sat down, his eyes admiring the half-done puzzle, three thousand pieces, with every single marvel superhero. He rubbed his hands together gleefully. "Madame Emma, what hae ye done so far?"

"Not much Magnus, my fingers are cold."

He blew on his fingers. "I was thinking on Captain America's shield, that red, I think I ought tae be able tae find it easy enough..."

I said, "We need Fraoch to knit us mittens."

TWENTY-FOUR - KAITLYN

I was asleep on my bed when Isla came in my room, climbed up, and got her face within an inch of mine. "Mama come down."

"For breakfast, is it time already, sweet pea? It seems like it's still dark out." I was being silly, the daylight shone across my comforter.

She said, "Come down."

"Ugh," I pulled myself up, "You're so mean."

She giggled.

"You're always making me do things I don't want to do." I collapsed on her and gave her little tickles on her sides. She giggled maniacally.

"Mama has surprise."

"What?" I looked at her. "What surprise? Oh! Is it my *birthday?*"

She nodded solemnly.

"It's a good thing you didn't tell me, you kept a good surprise."

"Presents!" She squealed.

"I better get ready then!" I scrambled from the bed. "Do you want to watch me get dressed?"

She sat down, this time for only about one minute, then climbed off the bed, "Go tell dada!" She toddled out of the room.

I asked my maid, "Is there a surprise birthday party for me?"

She smiled. "I wouldna ken..."

I said, "Awesome. I really love surprises. But you would tell me, right? Is it big? Tell me, nevermind, don't tell me, I like the excitement." I looked at my reflection as she pulled my laces on my bodice. "Probably."

By the time I got downstairs there was nothing, no sound from the Great Hall except a little bit of a rustle and a giggle. I opened the door, looked around... and, "Surprise!!!"

All my family and friends jumped out from corners and behind furniture and surprised the heck out of me although I had totally seen it coming.

I was served doughnuts and vanilla coffee with cream and sugar. "Where did it come from?"

Zach said, "I've been saving it for just this occasion."

"You have? So you've been thinking about my birthday for longer than a few hours?" I grinned. "That might be the best thing ever."

Magnus said, "We hae presents as well."

I wiped my glaze-covered fingers off on my apron and demanded, "Bring em on!"

There were three presents.

My heart rejoiced. They were all wrapped in blue cloth and tied with yellow rope.

I unwrapped the first, a small, square box. Inside was a Celtic knot, shaped like a heart, carved of wood, with a long piece of blue ribbon tied through it.

I asked Magnus, "Did you make this?"

"I did, I carved it while I was on watch."

"You did?" I turned it over and over, it was the size of my

palms together, and intricate and glorious, it smelled like birch and wax, and had a polished sheen. "I love it so much."

"I thought ye might hang it—"

"In our room, I know just the place." I hugged it to my chest.

Archie said, "Open mine next!"

I wiped my misty eyes and opened the box he thrust into my hands.

I pulled away the cloth to find a rudimentary wooden box. "Archie, did you make this?"

"Aye, tis special. Da helped me."

"It is so freaking special." I pulled the lid open and inside was a rock, shaped like a heart.

"I found it."

"I love this so much."

Then I looked around the room. "Well, I don't know if I need anything else, that is amazing."

Isla said, "Open this one!"

I opened the last one and inside the wrapping was a piece of paper that said, "Go out to the courtyard."

Everyone got up, bundled up in their wraps, and went out to the courtyard to find some hand tools and wood. I squinted. "What is this?"

Magnus said, "We will use clay tae make bricks, and each brick will hae a handprint in them, from all in the family and we will use them tae decorate the courtyard."

"Holy castle-awesomesauce, that is perfect." I beamed at the tools and supplies needed for the big coming project, and pulled my tartan around my shoulders against the cold. "Like today, right — *today* we're going to make them?"

"We hae the first day with nae rain in weeks, tis cold, but aye, we will do it taeday."

I looked around at everyone. "I declare this the best birthday I ever had."

TWENTY-FIVE - KAITLYN

By the time New Year's Eve and Hogmanay came around the weather had been so bleak for so long I really wondered why the hell we had ever chosen to do this.

And the longer we did it, the more we were aware that it could be for longer yet, and that we couldn't take a minute more.

We celebrated Hogmanay with some feasting, but everyone had grown pretty damn testy.

The kids were all tucked away in the nursery with the fire blazing to keep the small space as warm as possible. The grownups were drinking in the sitting room of Magnus's office because it was easier to heat. We were still bundled in our warmest gear.

The men left the room, without their coats, to return a second after midnight, the traditional First Footing.

When they knocked, Emma opened the door, and they stamped in, hilariously drunk, and cold through from the chilly hallway.

Zach said, "I was away from the fire for one minute and I'm frozen like a popsicle."

Everyone got a shot of whisky to celebrate and we went back to huddling near the fire.

Zach said, "Well, that was fucking fun."

Fraoch raised his glass, "We need tae plan another trip tae see if the problem is solved."

Quentin raised his glass, "I agree, we need another reconnaissance mission." He glanced at Sophie beside James, "to um, the kingdom, to check on things."

"How? How would things be solved? I agree on going for supplies, but how is anything solved at this point?" asked James.

Quentin said, "Possibly, I don't know — maybe it just figured itself out? Maybe we needed to settle into this castle and *now* Florida sorted itself? All I know is it's too freaking cold and I'm sick of it being night all the damn time. I want to go home."

I glanced at Sophie, her brow pulled down.

Fraoch said, "I miss Florida."

"Hear hear!" We all raised our glasses.

Quentin said, "While we're all here..."

Everyone laughed.

James said, "We know! You want another vote!"

"Hell yeah, I want another vote, this has been the bleakest coldest winter and I'm ready to get the hell out. All those that want to fight... say, 'Aye'."

Quentin, Beaty, Fraoch, and Zach all said, "Aye."

Magnus said, "All right, I think twould be good tae go see, I would take two men with me and—"

A look passed between Quentin and James.

Quentin said, "Nah Boss, I'll go, you stay here, guard the castle. James can go with me, right? We're the guys who do it, it's our job."

"Why daena ye want me tae go?"

"I don't know, you seem a little winded still, like you need more rest."

"Och, aye." Magnus's face was drawn down in thought.

Hayley said, "I think I'm too jealous, how come you get to

go, James? Why can't Fraoch and I go too? We all have to stay here in the freezing cold? I think we should *all* go."

Magnus said, "Too dangerous."

Quentin said, "Okay forget it — let's wait until February. We have enough supplies, right? That way Magnus will be better."

Magnus said, "A moment ago ye wanted tae go right away."

Quentin said, "I got carried away. We'll put it off until we need supplies. Yeah, it'll be good — in the meantime we've got a new year on us." We all raised our glasses though our mood had turned pretty dour.

TWENTY-SIX - KAITLYN

Come February, Magnus didn't go, neither did Hayley, because they were overruled. It was only Quentin and James and they were gone for three weeks, to make it make sense for Sophie, though somehow she just took it in stride. I could see the confused look on her face though, sometimes, and the way she would shake her head when things we said didn't make sense. And how could any of it make sense?

She asked me, "The kingdom is much farther than Edinburgh, yet they can return in mere weeks?"

"Their vessel is very fast." I changed the subject.

When they returned they had a very large pile of supplies along for the ride.

Seeing the pile of supplies, this time, made me, uncharacteristically and also illogically, furious.

I said to Hayley and Emma, "How come they get to go to Florida and get Starbucks? How come they get to go to the grocery store?"

TWENTY-SIX - KAITLYN

Hayley said, "*Exactly*, and take a proper shower, with suds that come from shampoo that you haven't been rationing."

Quentin said, "We brought shampoo!"

Hayley said, "Great, thank you, blah blah, you're the best. How was the hotel?"

"God, it was amazing!"

Hayley pretended to lunge at him to punch him, I pretended to hold her back.

Magnus said, "How was Riaghalbane?"

"The same — still a violent cesspit of horrible."

"Och."

We helped carry all the things into store rooms, to divide up the loot. And it was freezing outside with a blustering wind. We were bundled and shivering and working really hard.

I caught Hayley asking James, "What was the temperature?"

"Highs in the seventies."

She groaned.

Finally, after all the work was done, Quentin found me alone in the hall. "How is Magnus?"

I scrutinized his face. "Why? The same."

He lowered his voice and looked around. "That's what I'm afraid of, he's the *same*. James and I were talking about it — he's not getting stronger."

I chewed my lip, because I couldn't argue. He was right. "What am I going to do? I want him to go see a doctor but he won't hear of it."

"I don't know, but I wanted to make sure you were on the same page about it."

"I am, but he's unyielding."

Hayley walked up, "Whatcha talking about?"

"Nothing, how much we all want to go home."

"It's the lack of sun. When was the last time we saw a sunny day, no rain, not cold?"

Quentin grinned.

Hayley said, "I am so furious at you, next time *I* get to go to Florida."

Emma walked up then. "Florida? Will you promise to take Zachary with you next time? I am so worried about him."

I asked, "What do you mean?"

"I mean he and Eamag are about this close," she put her finger and thumb together, "to killing each other. They are both too ornery and there are too many knives down there in the kitchen."

TWENTY-SEVEN - MAGNUS

Quentin called for a meeting in the Great Hall asking for James tae come without Sophie so we could speak freely. We made a loose circle of chairs and I leaned against the table.

Quentin said, "James and I discovered that the menace is still at large."

Hayley said, "You sound like an old movie."

I said, "Och, I miss movies, but especially the ones where the cats are falling off the tables."

Everyone laughed.

Fraoch, his ball of yarn in his lap, his knitting needles clicking, asked, "What are we goin' tae do on it?"

Quentin said, "Well, we need to do something different."

I said, "We are hidden well and we are safe, we canna discount that. We hae found peace while I recovered."

I caught a glance passed between Quentin and James. I kent they had been discussin' my health amongst themselves. I tried tae hide m'breathlessness on the stairs, or the weakness of m'arms when I was needin' tae be strong, but I dinna hide it well enough.

Quentin said, "So, now that you have recovered, we need to fight."

I asked, "How would we do such a thing?"

Fraoch pulled a long length of yarn from the ball causing it to roll off his lap and across the floor, and one of the storeroom cats raced up to check what it was. "Och wee boy, ye daena want the yarn, twould taste terrible." He scooped the ball up and said in answer tae me, "Ye could challenge Sir Padraig tae a fight in the arena. Ye would need tae train first, but ye could recover the throne that way."

"True, there are mechanisms in place tae make the challenge legitimate and the running of the fight fair, though Sir Padraig would hae the upper hand. There is a chance I would lose." I looked down and noticed I was rubbing my left hand again. I ran my hand through my hair.

James said, "You have more vessels. You'd be able to surprise him, arrive, challenge, and you'd be able to leave if anything was amiss. We jumped in and out of the arena once, right? We could come up with a plan to keep you safe — possibly."

Quentin said, "Nope, I hate this idea. What we need to do is fight on a larger scale. We need to surprise attack and take down his military capabilities. Damn, I wish Hammond was still there."

I said, "Aye, me as well."

We all stared off into space while Quentin looked around at us pointedly.

I chuckled. "What dost ye want?"

Quentin said, "Don't pretend like you don't know what I want, Boss, we need another vote."

"Och, yer votes are goin' tae be the death of me."

Quentin said, "Only an authoritarian dictator would say such a thing,"

I joked, "Or a king."

"True, but you're committed to being more modern than that. Think of yourself as the king with the pesky parliament.

We keep voting on what we are going to do, while you pretend to rule with an iron fist."

"Tis a blade of steel."

"Yeah, and on that ominous note we're going to vote on whether we agree with the king or not. 'Ayes' are to blah blah blah. 'Naes' are to do nothing in the darkest coldest part of Scotland."

I joked, "All of Scotland is the darkest and coldest."

Quentin stood and asked the group, "Who thinks we need a new plan?"

James joked, "Can you explain the rules again, Quenny? I can't figure out what the 'aye' or 'nae' mean."

His eyes went wide. "Argh! I have gone over this — 'aye' for Florida, sandy beaches, good food, 'nae' for staying here!"

I said, "I think the 'aye for Florida' is quite a bit more. Twould be an 'aye' for war. There could be losses. Twould nae be easy."

"It's not just war though. It's coming up with a plan and making something happen. If you agree, I have like one hundred and seventy-eight different plans we can start talking about. Some of them are shite, but some are probably workable. So everyone — 'aye' for plans."

Quentin, Beaty, Fraoch, and Zach all said, "aye," and then Kaitlyn said it as well, all by herself. "Aye."

I said, "Och, Kaitlyn, ye are goin' tae vote against me as well?"

She raised her chin. "I think we should consider, with proper caution, that there might be a solution we haven't figured out yet. Maybe we just need to jiggle the handle, do something different, cause something to happen. I think it might be good."

I exhaled. "Kaitlyn, once ye set yer mind on somethin' ye are verra difficult tae turn and ye are settin' it against me?"

"My mind isn't set, my mind is open to all possibilities — I won't hound you, I just think you should consider it. 'Consider' is a very forgiving word."

I said, "All right, I will consider it, but I am still goin' tae disagree, I believe the risk is too great."

Fraoch said, "In the meantime, reivers stole some coos this week. James, I ken ye just returned, but would ye ride with me out tae speak tae Rob Roy?"

James grinned, "I'd love to, haven't seen the good ol' boy since I got married!"

I said, "I will send money with ye for his payment. Try tae get m'coos returned, tell him I daena like payin' for his services *and* losing m'cattle."

TWENTY-EIGHT - KAITLYN

After breakfast, a week later, when Fraoch and James had gone off to intervene on cattle business, I was enjoying a sit and sigh with Hayley.

Today we had less interesting things to sigh about because her husband had been gone for a whole week.

She said, "What am I supposed to do when my husband isn't here? He's off gallivanting around." She wrapped one of his awkwardly long scarves around her neck.

I pretended to be Fraoch. "I daena gallivant."

She pulled it up over her mouth and inhaled. "I miss his smell — don't tell him I said that, I prefer to have him doing his best." She laughed. "He better get the cows back, he better come home soon. My bed is cold and he needs to be keeping me warm."

"You're just pissed you didn't get to go."

"Yeah! Why didn't I get to go?"

"Because cattle-thief negotiations are no place for a lady?"

"And why not?"

I sighed.

Beaty rushed up. "Excuse me, Queen Kaitlyn and Madame Hayley." Her face had a pallor.

Hayley asked, "What is it? Did ye see a ghost?"

"Nae, but the one I do often see in the upper hall was there last night, hae ye seen it? The woman who washes the stone walls?"

Hayley's eyes went wide. "A ghost! Now this is interesting. What — is she floating or pale or...?"

I said, "We have plenty of time to talk ghosts, Hayley, it looked like, before she got sidetracked, Beaty was going to tell us something important."

"She inna who she says she is."

"Who?"

It was like stepping out into the street about to cross and a truck had wheeled down upon me and forced me to step back.

"Madame Sophie."

"What do you mean? You know it?"

"Aye. I ken it, with certainty."

My eyes went wide. "They have been married for almost nine months, these are serious charges. What is your evidence?"

"I was in the nursery with her and I started the kids on a nursery rhyme, a poem I heard many times when I was a bairn, and she dinna ken the words. Twas odd tae me, but I thought twas because she is from a different part of Scotland. Edinburgh is a many day ride from m'village, ye ken."

Hayley said, "That's not that far, Beaty, I think nursery rhymes travel farther than that, don't they? I mean, do they? They do, right?"

"I daena ken, but I thought she *ought* tae ken it. So I waited for a few moments, we played something else, and then I asked her tae recite a nursery rhyme for the children. She said she dinna ken one. I said, and twas a lie tae say it, 'Dost ye ken the one from m'youth, Twinkle Twinkle Little Star?' And she said, 'Aye,' and recited it for the kids. I said, 'Did James teach it tae ye?' And she said, 'Nae, I learned it from m'mother when I was verra wee.'"

She looked at us wide-eyed.

TWENTY-EIGHT - KAITLYN

I said, "Well, that's a very old poem right? Like as old as things get?"

"Nae, Emma taught it tae me, and when I asked where it came from we looked it up on the Google back at home, twas from the year 1806 — a hundred years from now."

Hayley said, "Maybe she forgot that James taught it to her?"

I said, "You think her husband James taught her a poem about the stars and she forgot and gave credit to her mother?"

Hayley said, "Yeah, bullshit, you're right, no way."

I asked Beaty, "Will you go to the nursery, make sure Isla and Archie are—"

"I am already on m'way."

∽

I rushed out to the hall. To the guard I said, "Will ye please watch over Madame Sophie? Keep her from the nursery?"

The main guardsman said, "Of course, Queen Kaitlyn, we will add some guardsmen tae her."

"Okay, thank you. And King Magnus is on the walls?"

"Aye."

I took the stairs two at a time and found Quentin and Magnus on watch together. My husband had binoculars to his eyes, pointed in the direction of Ben Cruachan and the cave where the vessels were kept.

Quentin said, "You look like you've seen a ghost."

"That's what I just said to Beaty and of course, she had seen one," I panted, "but I'm totally panicked." I pulled my bodice trying to get in air. "Beaty said Madame Sophie isn't who she said she is and told me her proof, and I just panicked. I think she's a time traveler." I doubled over. "Fuck."

Quentin said, "Beaty said so? I asked her to keep her eyes open, something... I couldn't put my finger on it."

Magnus said, "Madame Sophie daena hae a vessel on her, how can she be a traveler?" He huffed. "She married intae the family, she haena given us any reason nae tae trust her. Ye saw something, Quentin?"

"Just a hunch, a lack of questions... I don't know."

Magnus said, "Master James inna here, he will be furious when he finds out we are suspicious about his wife during his absence."

I said, "I get all of that, but also, Beaty is scared — shouldn't Sophie be locked up?"

I looked at their faces.

"Why not, because she's a woman, a wife? Because she is a lovely woman with all her batting eyelashes and soft smooth skin? And she hid it so well? For nine months! I'll remind you of one thing, Magnus, your mother is a lovely woman. And the fact that she hid it so well for nine months is *exactly* the reason why she needs to be locked up. As far as I'm concerned Madame Sophie goes to her room right now, guards are stationed at her door."

Magnus said, "Och," and circled his fingers in the air as if to say, 'round 'em up' to the men. Quentin whistled and began calling up and down the walls.

The men gathered and Quentin commanded them down to arrest Madame Sophie.

The whole thing gave me pause because it felt very much like something Lady Mairead would do.

TWENTY-NINE - KAITLYN

*H*er eyes followed me as I entered in front of Hayley and Quentin and we all sat down in James and Sophie's small sitting room.

Sophie asked, "Why hae ye locked me within? I daena understand, Queen Kaitlyn. There must be a mistake!"

Hayley said, "I don't think so. You understand that we have to be cautious, there is a king and his children here, and it has come to our attention that we don't know your full story. It's *troubling*."

She sank down on the settee. "Why? What did I do? And I am without James or m'telescope." She dabbed at her eyes, sniffling.

I was so scared my hands were trembling, yet I was conflicted. She seemed honestly forlorn and it made me feel like the bad guy. I was wondering why I offered to come and talk to her in the first place. "I'm trying to protect my family."

"Och, they are my family too, what hae I done tae hae ye mistrust me so? I daena understand!"

"It's not that we… we have trusted you… very much, you are a member of our family — but there are some discrepancies and I have to protect my children…" I felt on the verge of tears myself, so I straightened my back and folded my hands in my lap.

Hayley saw I was struggling, so she asked, "Why don't you tell us why you are truly here."

"I had nae where tae go! Nae family, nae friends! They were goin' tae try me for witchcraft! I remembered afore I was married, m'guardian was a cousin of the Campbells of Breadalbane, I had heard mention of Lizbeth and Sean Campbell, I asked if I might come tae visit. Tis all!" She clasped her hands pleadingly.

I said, "I know that is the story, that's how it goes, but Lizbeth didn't know of you before you arrived. I know there have been long months with no trouble, but—"

"I hae nae idea what ye are speaking about. I daena understand why I am locked away, but I will tell ye anything ye need tae ken."

I squinted my eyes and looked at her. "Here's a question, are you using your telescope to look for storms?"

She shook her head, "I daena ken what ye are... m'telescope is for looking at the stars and the moon."

Hayley said, "Look, this is only until we figure out who you really are, what you're doing here, and who sent you — that shouldn't be that hard, right? You tell us the year you were born for instance, and that will get us started right off."

"I was born in the year 1682."

Hayley snapped her fingers. "That makes you what? I have the hardest time with age math... like twenty-five, right? When you arrived you told us about the storms in Glencoe. Did you really just hear about them in your travels or did you have some business there?"

"Nae! I daena ken what ye are accusing me of, I am telling the truth!" She sobbed even harder.

Hayley said, "Och, this is not going well."

Quentin and I exchanged glances. He said, "Look, this is our family. You understand we want to keep our family safe?"

She sniffled. "They're my family too."

"Beaty heard you say something that if you were from, um... here, you couldn't have known—"

"I am nae from here! I am from Edinburgh! Tis verra far away!"

Quentin went quiet.

I said, "This is true, but... I mean, the only conclusion I can draw is that you are here to make us less safe. Please, be honest with me, let me know what is happening, we can come to an agreement. Who sent you?"

"I would never want to cause harm to you, or to your son and daughter, Queen Kaitlyn. I..." She clutched her hands. "Queen Kaitlyn, I would never want tae harm your sweet bairns."

I sighed. "I'm sorry we have to keep you locked up, truly I am. I think the world of you." I dug through the bag I kept at my waist. I pulled out my Burt's Bees tinted lip balm and passed it to her without a word. "You understand that I'm just worried about my children. That's all this is. I'm just worried."

She nodded, holding the stick of lip balm in her hands.

I passed her a compact mirror. She flipped the mirror open, pulled the top off the lip balm, twisted it up, and smeared some on her lips. I glanced at Hayley sitting open-mouthed.

I smiled. "You look very pretty. Has James given you some lip balm, does he use it?"

"No, I daena think he does, why?"

"He doesn't carry some in his pocket to share with you?"

She shook her head.

"Then I'll leave this one for you."

"Tis verra kind of ye."

"We're going to step out in the hall to discuss for a moment."

Quentin and Hayley followed me from the room. In the hall outside he said, "I don't know how much longer we can keep her..."

"Bullshit, we can keep her as long as we want, she's a time traveler, we just have to figure out from where."

∼

I joined my husband up on the freezing cold walls.

He was checking the mountain with the binoculars while I wrapped my arm around his and rested my chin on his shoulder.

"Madame Sophie is a time traveler, but she's not fessing up."

"Och. I hae been watching the woods and the mountain, yet here she is within our walls.

"Are there any vessels anywhere?"

"There is naething on the monitor."

"I'm glad we have plenty of weapons."

"Aye, me too."

He sat quietly for a moment.

I asked, "Anything happening on the mountainside?"

"Nae, but I check all the same, I was waiting for ye tae come from your discussion, then Quentin and I are going tae ride up there tae check them."

"No one knows they are there, right? No one told Madame Sophie about them?"

He shrugged and looked down at the binoculars. "She has lived with us for nine months. We were verra relaxed. We talked of Florida and m'kingdom at times, and some here call me a king. She may well ken about the cave, and though I daena ken how, she might be reportin' tae someone about us."

"I don't know. I don't talk about the vessels. I don't think James would…"

"She might just suspect. She might hae seen us ride that direction, day after day —we daena ken. I felt safe because the vessels are hidden and they daena shew on any monitor, but she might hae advised someone exactly where they are."

"I thought they were safe too. Just yesterday I was teasing you about checking them so often."

"Aye, nae matter how hidden, I still check." He kissed my head. "The kids are safe?"

"Yeah, in the nursery."

"So why are ye here?"

"I don't know, I missed you. I wanted to touch base."

He leaned against the wall so that I could fold up in his arms on his chest. Held by him. I said, "This is so complicated you know?"

"Nae, tis nae complicated, mo reul-iuil."

I looked up at his face. "What do you mean?"

"We are naething but an exiled king and queen in their grand highland castle. We are surrounded by our family and so far it has been a good life here. How long since we moved in?"

"Almost ten months."

"It has been better than I ever thought twould be, daena ye agree?"

"Except for the dark and the rain, the long boring winter indoors — besides that, I do. It's been far better than I expected."

"And I am getting stronger."

"Are you?"

He nodded, his lips pressed against my forehead. It was the lack of voice to it that kind of freaked me out.

When I would lie awake at night, I thought he deserved to be 'tired'. He had lived the lives of three men. He had been a hero and had fought and done more than... but also, there was something *very* tired about him. Exhausted. Depleted. I knew he needed to rest, to recuperate, but it nagged at me more and more. We needed to take him to a doctor.

But I kept that to myself, though it was getting way past time to do it.

"We haven't talked about it much, about the fact that the kingdom is still overthrown, that it's ruled by Sir Padraig. What is there left to do? How do we solve it? You know how in the middle of the night I lie awake and stare at the ceiling?"

"Aye, right after I hae gotten up tae guard the walls."

"I've been cycling through worries: the future looks exactly as it did when we crash-rescued you, full of war and mayhem and Isla and Archie are in big danger. Or, it's a bleak wasteland of nothingness, because you stopped that from happening, but nothing has been written over yet. Or your kingdom is how it was before Paddy attacked, but it's without its king…" I snuggled into his chest. "And without its king, who knows what will happen."

"It's just for a time," he said. "Soon enough we will figure out the solution. I will fight for my throne, and we will end Sir Padraig's reign of fear."

∼

I went to nursery to see the bairns.

There was a raucous, roaring kid-brouhaha happening, Archie and Ben had created a full blown free-for-all. I stopped Archie as they raced by. "Hey little man, kiss!"

He kissed me very fast.

"Where you going?"

"Playing dragon break, gotta go mammy, they running."

"Okay, okay, but not out of the walls, okay? Stay in the castle today."

"Okay mammy!" He raced away.

I used my walkie-talkie to tell Magnus.

His low voice answered, "Hello."

"The boys are in a full run, headed toward the courtyard. Make sure the gate knows they aren't to go out."

"Aye, they are running by right now. I will hae security alerted tae the dangers."

Isla was sweetly toddling around the room, but I could see she was on the verge of a meltdown. "What's up with your eyes, wee Isla? They are glassy. Are you a little on the silly wee sleepy side?"

She grabbed a cloth doll from the hand of one of the other kids. "Want doll!" Then the kid grabbed the doll back and Isla wailed, "Mine!" as if her heart was breaking for having had the doll stolen from her though she had clearly stolen it first.

So I tried to come up with a solution. Then Beaty tried to help to no avail and so all I could do was pick Isla up and move her away from the other kids since she was definitely swinging at them, yelling, "Mine! Mine!" She was shrieking and bending backwards and struggling until I got her onto my lap where she cried desperately as if her world was crashing around her. I rocked her and shushed her and she was hitch breathing, in gasps and fits, and then thirty-seconds later she was fast asleep.

Beaty said, "Och, she has a temper, Queen Kaitlyn."

I sighed. "Well, she's going to need it. The world is going to try to beat her down and we're going to need her to be a terrible arse."

Beaty said, "Tis true."

THIRTY - MAGNUS

*J*ames and Fraoch returned and James was incredulous. He stormed into m'office where I was speaking with Quentin, with Fraoch following.

"What the hell is goin' on?"

I said, "We felt Madame Sophie needed tae be locked up while we ascertained her true purpose."

"What the fuck, Mags, you're saying... what? She's a bad guy? That's my wife! Who's she working for?"

"I hae nae idea."

"Then how come you know she's a bad guy?"

Quentin said, "It's a hunch. Beaty figured it out."

"Beaty? Beaty figured it out? You're going to take her word for it? From here it seems like you got rid of me, sent me on an errand, and then locked up my wife. I won't stand for it. You're taking Beaty's word over mine?"

Quentin squinted his eyes. "Why *wouldn't* I? Beaty is from this century. She's a woman. She knows enough to be able to trip someone up. She tripped her up. Sophie is not who she says she is."

Beaty knocked on the door and then entered.

Quentin said, "Beaty, tell James what it was she said that made you realize it?"

"This morn, she recited a poem that has nae been written yet — Twinkle Twinkle Little Star. Did ye teach it tae her?"

James said, "No, I didn't. I totally forgot about it."

I shook my head, "We canna mess about here, Master Cook. I ken she is yer wife, but tis nae secure tae hae someone under our roof when we daena ken her business. Ye ken we must keep the—"

James interrupted, "I know, we have to keep the kids safe. But this is my wife. Nine months, Magnus, and not one suspicion—"

Magnus said, "She never said anything tae give ye pause? How would she ken the poem?"

"I have no idea, I know she grew up in Edinburgh, I…"

I said, "Why are ye pausing?"

James groaned. "I'm sure there's a reasonable explanation, I just... she calls her family in Edinburgh her 'guardians'. I didn't think it was important."

I nodded. "Now it seems too important tae hae overlooked it."

THIRTY-ONE - KAITLYN

I was sitting beside Hayley, drawing to get my mind off my worries. The scene: the fire glowing on Hayley's cheek as she sat at her spinning wheel. I rubbed a section to blend a shadow. "Why do you like spinning?"

"I don't like it, I *love* it."

"Really?" I blew on the paper to get some eraser bits off.

Her wheel went whizz, whirr, whizz, whirr. We were talking about nothing important because we were both worried about Sophie and waiting for Magnus to break the news to James about Sophie.

I asked, "Why do you love it so much?"

"Because I'm good at it, I mean, look. Cool huh?" Whizz, whirr, whizz, whirr. "It's relaxing, and contrary to what you think, *not* boring."

I brushed across the paper and then looked up at Hayley. I had her ear out of proportion. I erased a line and said, "Plus Fraoch knits from it."

"Yep, it's very satisfying that when I'm done spinning yarn, my husband takes it up and knits outrageously odd scarves and hats to give as gifts. But perhaps most *importantly*, spinning is something I can do alone with no one talking to me."

"Sorry." I laughed.

"No worries, I need the company today, I've got stuff on my mind." Whizz, whirr. "But the best part, it makes me look busy and productive, while not being that important. No one will die because I didn't make enough yarn."

"I can see that. But now that you've said the quiet part out loud, I'm onto you. Next time I'm in charge of assigning chores, you're going to regret it."

"Miss Drawing-a-picture is going to judge Miss Spinning-wheel?"

"True, and I agree, there are a lot of jobs around here that if done poorly or not at all, someone might die. Like food production. It gives me anxiety just thinking about it."

"That's why I spin. My best days, Fraoch knits beside me, not talking, just enjoying the quiet of each other, and the warmth of the fire."

"You glad to have him home?"

"Hell yeah, of course they're in meetings right now, I am glad I don't have to be the one to tell James we locked up Sophie—"

Quentin and Fraoch walked up right then and Hayley let her wheel slow so she could jump up and kiss Fraoch hello.

Quentin was wearing an oddly shaped beanie, it fit snuggly but the top was bulbous.

I said, "Nice hat."

"Prized possession, a gift from Fraoch, I love it. It's totally weird."

"It's definitely that…"

Fraoch said, "The extra on top is for all my admiration, he can store it up there."

Quentin chuckled, then his face went serious again. "I'm gathering us all up, we need to go talk to Madame Sophie, James loaded up a plate with food and went straight up there."

Fraoch said, "He's sulking."

I said, "You think? I mean we did accuse his wife of traitorous lying." I exhaled.

Hayley said, "Remember when Reyes attached himself to me? It was awful that I not only got lied to, but that I put everyone in so much danger. James must be really freaked out."

Quentin said, "Yeah, but he needs to remember it's family first and all. She might be a danger to the kids." He shook his head. "Plus it's his turn at guard duty and he's not there, like he knows if he doesn't go, Magnus will have to take over, and Magnus guards too much, we all know this."

I said, "Magnus is going to work himself to death."

"Yep, if they weren't married, if Sophie was some dude, James would be pissed. He'd be talking about kill first, ask questions later."

Hayley said, "Jesus Christ, listen to you all bad ass — kill first? Did you learn that in a movie?"

"Hell yeah, it's just common sense, right?"

Fraoch said, "I daena ken if murder is ever common sense. Tis nae common sense if ye hae tae pray tae God for forgiveness after."

Quentin said, "I stand corrected. We should ask a lot of questions first, but if she has any and I mean *any* connection to Sir Paddy-whack, we might have to kill her."

Fraoch said, "Unless she has information about Sir Paddy-whack and then we ask her tae tell us."

Quentin said, "Damn, so the eighteenth century dude is going to be more civilized than me? I'm going to sound like the arsehole? Fine, I can see that no one really agrees, but living out here in the highlands with evil afoot and an enemy in our midst makes me feel all kind of good-vs-evil and anyone who comes with an association to Sir Paddy is evil. They just are."

I said, "So we all need to go talk to Madame Sophie."

∼

THIRTY-ONE - KAITLYN

The guard let us into James and Sophie's room where they were sitting on the settee waiting for us.

Quentin said, "James, it's your turn up on the walls for your guard shift. Magnus is filling in for you. We agreed not to make him take our shifts, what the hell?"

"No one wants me to be a guard, I'm not feeling that guardian like."

"Screw that, you know why we need guards, none of that has changed. Actually it's worse now that your wife is involved, she might have led people here."

Sophie's eyes were terrified.

I started to speak, but Hayley interrupted by asking, "Are you working with Lady Mairead?"

"Nae, who is Lady Mairead?"

Hayley said, "Jesus Christ, *seriously*, you need to fess up—"

I said, "Hayley, chill a little, will you?"

"Fine." She sank back in a chair. "It's just been a long time without proper coffee and I'm irritated."

I said, "Madame Sophie, one thing I've realized, is that I can have all the normal, relaxing days in the world, and everything will seem fine on my timeline, but then enemies time jump here and all hell breaks loose. For instance, if someone knows you're here, they might actually be on their way, we have had armies at our castle walls before, it is not funny. Time travel sucks."

She blinked her eyes.

I held my hands out toward her. "James, do you see?"

"See what?"

"I just used the terms 'time jump,' 'timeline,' and 'time travel,' and she doesn't have one question about it, she's just sitting there."

James humphed.

Sophie said, "I hae heard ye use many of those words before, Queen Kaitlyn. I am always overhearing ye say things I daena understand. At first twas verra shocking, but I am tae be shocked by what ye say now? I daena understand what ye mean by any of this, but I ken this is my home—"

Hayley said, "But can we trust you?"

James said, "Careful, Hayley."

"Ye ken ye can trust me! I am nae a witch! Ye hae me on trial for witchcraft and hae me caught in a trap — am I tae say I daena ken what ye mean, tis tae be unintelligent. Do ye want me tae lie? If I lie and go against God, then I am sinful and bad and perhaps that is what makes me a danger. I can only tell the truth tae ye, Madame Hayley. I hae lived here for many months and I ken ye are talking about travel a great deal and ye are from a great distance away in Magnus's kingdom. How am I tae answer yer charges, if I daena ken what I daena ken?"

I said, "I passed you a tube of lip balm yesterday, you put it right on. It hasn't been invented yet."

"It haena been invented, but it exists in Queen Kaitlyn's hands? Ye hae conjured something that inna real? I daena understand how I can be the one at fault if I hae seen what is in the world, that I ken is true."

Hayley huffed. "That is not the point, the point is, where have you seen one?"

She sniffled. "I daena ken, twas a verra, verra long time ago."

Hayley said, "Now we're getting somewhere. Explain what you mean. Who would you have been around a long time ago that would have been using a lipstick tube?"

"My mother gave me one, when I was verra young. I kept it for a verra long time and once I ran out I tried verra resolutely tae get more wax and mint intae the tube but I couldna get it right."

I asked, "Why didn't she just give you another?"

"I dinna see her again, I was taken and raised by another family."

I asked, "So you don't know where she got it from?"

"She just had it, tis all I ken."

James turned and took both her hands in his, "Sophie,

please. Haley and Katie are right and as Quentin pointed out I need to be on guard duty, now more than ever. If your being here has made the castle less safe, you have to tell us. Think about Isla and Archie, you love those kids. You have to help us protect them. We are on high alert, are you a time traveler?"

She raised her chin. "I am nae a time traveler, James. I daena understand what ye mean by it. I hae never left Scotland, tae come here was the first time I left Edinburgh."

He asked, "What about the rhyme you knew, Twinkle Twinkle Little Star, where did you hear that?"

"Twas also m'mother, I daena remember much but this was something she sang tae me every night."

Hayley banged her hands on the arm of her chair. "Yes! Now we're getting somewhere. Who is your mother and your father and all that stuff?"

"I daena ken m'mother' name, I daena remember it, but I remember there was a man and a woman, they frightened her terribly, and..." Her chin trembled. "I was told tae be verra quiet and tae hide, tae nae let them ken I was there — I was given tae m'guardians, and told tae never speak of where I came from. I never saw her again."

Hayley leaned forward. "Well shit, that sucks, and then you were raised by someone else?"

James said, "Your guardians, right? In Edinburgh?"

She nodded.

I asked Sophie, "How old were you when it happened?"

"I was verra young."

Hayley said, "Wait… let me go get Magnus and everyone, this seems important." She rushed from the room.

I pulled my walkie-talkie from my bag and called Magnus and told him to come to James's apartment and if he passed Hayley to tell her that she's got a two-way radio in her pocket too and to stop being a dumb ass.

THIRTY-TWO - KAITLYN

A few minutes later, Hayley, Magnus, Zach, Emma, and Fraoch entered James's apartment.

Hayley's face was flushed from the unnecessary racing around. "Can you tell us again, what you just told us?"

Sophie said, "I am nae sure...?"

Hayley waved her hand. "About your mother, about the guardians."

"One night when I was verra young, m'mother was verra frightened. She had me hide, she told me tae be verra quiet, she put me in... I daena ken what it was, twas dark, and loud, then she gave me tae the Campbells in Edinburgh and she left and I haena seen her again. I was told tae keep it all a secret."

Magnus said, "Och, so the Campbells in Edinburgh are nae yer relations, we daena ken who yer true parents are?"

Her brow furrowed. "Nae. I wish I could tell ye more, but I..."

Hayley said, "You said, 'dark and loud,' was it like a storm... what happened between that moment and when you were given to the Campbells?"

She shook her head. "I daena ken, twas a stormy night and then... I daena remember after."

We all met eyes.

I said, "So there was a storm, you might be the child of a time traveler. We don't know — you could be from any year, you might be any age."

"How could I? I am a woman who has lived most of m'life in Edinburgh."

I sighed. "That's not really how time travel works, sadly. It's just twists and turns and nothing makes sense, not in the normal way. Do you remember anything about her?"

Sophie shook her head. "I daena ken anything of her, all I remember are these bits and pieces — I was about the same age as Archie when I was left with m'guardian, John Campbell, and then he married me tae Master Milne. Ye hae tae understand. I dinna ken anythin' about m'mother nae even her name—"

Magnus said, "Tis nae an accident — that ye hae come tae be here."

She addressed him, "It wasna an accident, but I dinna understand how it happened. After Master Milne died, when I was accused of witchcraft, I received a letter — it told me of a connection I had tae the Campbells living at Kilchurn castle."

Quentin said, "Where is this letter?"

"I hae been told tae keep it hidden from..." Her eyes went to Magnus.

Magnus said, "From me, ye were told tae keep it from myself?"

"Aye, but I... I will get it for ye."

She stood, her back very straight, went to her desk, pilfered through the back of the drawer, and returned with a folded up piece of what looked like modern paper.

James said, "Great, secret letters, just great."

She passed the letter to James and he read out loud:

Dear Sophie,

I wish to remind you of your connections to the Campbells

currently residing in Kilchurn, including your cousins, Sean and Lizbeth Campbell. As you are in dire straights, you ought to reaffirm your connections to them.

I will warn you, you must be wary, it would be dangerous for King Magnus to learn of this letter, you must keep it hidden from him.

Once you are there and settled I will send you further instructions.

Yours,

R.

James put down the paper. "I wish you would have told me about this before."

Magnus stood. "Hae ye received further instructions from this person? Do you hae any idea who they are? Hae ye been in contact with them?"

"Nae! Never! I ken tis an odd letter, and I daena ken who it was from, but twas helpful and I desperately needed the assistance. I contacted Sean Campbell and was invited tae come." She looked down at her hands in her lap. "I hae never heard from this person again. I ken tis suspicious, but twas also *necessary* and I dinna understand most of it — King Magnus, I hope ye ken, this letter caused me tae be afeared of ye, but once I met ye, I kent twas nae true. Once I lived here and became a part of the family, what was in the letter dinna matter tae me anymore."

I squinted my eyes, "You never heard your mother speak about Magnus?"

"Nae, I only hae a vague memory of a man telling me a story about a King Magnus, and how he had stolen his throne — in the story, tae exact revenge, the bairns of King Magnus were murdered, twas terrifying tae me. I remember the man saying, 'daena forget this story of King Magnus.' I believed it tae be a fairytale, it could nae be about the flesh and blood king I hae met."

She removed her hand from James's and used it to smooth back her hair. "I hae one more memory. I daena ken if it will help."

Zach said, "Anything will help."

"M'mother told me the names of the man and woman who were followin' us. She told me I must hide from them. I feel as if I hae heard ye say his name before, Padraig, but tis likely someone..."

Quentin and Magnus met eyes.

Quentin said, "And her name?"

"Agnie. M'mother was verra frightened of them both."

I said, "Shit, I think your mother was afraid of Sir Padraig Stuart and Agnie MacLeod." I looked at Magnus. "Do we know if Sir Padraig and Agnie are friends?"

Magnus shrugged. "Wherever I turn, Agnie MacLeod has been conspiring with m'enemies, I am nae surprised Sir Paddy would be one of them."

Magnus asked Sophie, "And ye hae never had a vessel?"

"Nae, and I daena understand what ye mean by 'vessel'. I honestly daena ken what ye are talking on. I hae never meant ye any harm, King Magnus. I married James Cook, became a part of your family, I would never do anything tae put your life in danger."

Magnus exhaled. "Ye might hae, we may be in grave danger. The person who wrote this letter, kens ye are living with my family. These are dangerous people. Your mother was right tae be frightened of them."

"I only came because I had naewhere else tae go."

Magnus said, "And what did ye learn about King Magnus while ye were living here in m'castle?"

She said, "That ye are nae some dangerous—"

Magnus interrupted. "This is nae the right answer, Madame

Sophie. I fought for m'throne — this letter is tellin' the truth, I am verra dangerous if crossed." Magnus shook his head. "I believe I hae been doin' what is necessary, but ye will need tae be clear-eyed. If ye hold me infallible, ye will be easily swayed against me. In matters of thrones ye must be clear with whom ye are aligned."

Madame Sophie said, "I promise ye, I had nae idea that the letter was so dangerous. I am clear on alignin' with ye." She ran her hands down her face. "I dinna want tae hide it, I hae been so worried about it all."

Magnus said, "Sir Padraig is conspiring tae do terrible things tae my family. He is the reason why we are in hiding here. It sounds as if he is the reason ye hae been in hiding as well." He shook his head. "I wish ye would hae told us of the letter, had told us of yer past. It would hae warned us and now it has been almost ten months. We might hae been readying ourselves." While he spoke he massaged his left hand.

Quentin asked, "This is what I don't understand, why hasn't Agnie MacLeod or Sir Paddy-whack come looking for you? Why hasn't the writer of this letter sent another?"

She said, "I daena ken."

James said, "Knowing what we know, we ought to let her go, she hasn't been a time traveler."

Magnus nodded. "I agree, Madame Sophie is free tae go."

James said, "Oh. I had a whole argument. Are you letting her go with exceptions? If everyone is suspicious of her, maybe we should just go off on our own."

"Tis nae necessary, I am nae suspicious of her. She is free tae go with my deepest apologies and I hae nae exceptions." He added, "Do ye accept m'apology, Madame Sophie?"

"Aye. Thank ye, King Magnus."

James said, "Okay, but why? What made you decide?"

"Because I was thinkin' on it, if she was a time traveler," he smiled at Sophie, "M'apologies, for what I am about tae say, but wouldna she hae a much stronger telescope? When I am on guard duty sometimes she has allowed me tae look through the eyepiece of her telescope. She is a lady of science, if she had seen the stars Kaitlyn has described tae me, I daena think she would be content tae be lookin' through a telescope that can barely see the moon."

Kaitlyn said, "This is such a good point."

"Aye."

Sophie said, "There are better telescopes?"

Magnus answered, "Aye, Madame Sophie, I hae heard of wondrous telescopes that travel themselves in space and they can see farther than we hae ever imagined."

"Och, I would like tae see it."

Magnus said, "Maybe someday ye will. I am sure James would like tae shew ye, and I believe the rest of us would like tae be there when ye see it for the first time."

Sophie asked, "I am welcome tae stay?"

I said, "Yes, of course, you're welcome to stay."

Magnus brought his hands down on his knees and then stood. "We ought tae stay vigilant though, we need all able-bodied men back on the walls taenight."

He left the room.

THIRTY-THREE - MAGNUS

Kaitlyn followed me out tae the hall and pulled my hand tae the side tae speak. "So do you think she's related to you?"

I considered for a moment. "Aye. I believe she must be… I daena ken how, but we should move forward with that idea in mind."

"I agree. What if she's a… what if… could it have been Isla?"

"Perhaps. Or even farther along, we daena ken… or she could be a cousin five times removed. We hae nae way to ken." I added, "But I think we ought tae be quiet on our suspicions. Until we ken who she is, tae talk of it would be a mistake."

I climbed the stairs tae the walls tae commence m'guarding. It had begun tae rain so Fraoch and I stood beside each other with our raincoat hoods pulled over our heads. "Ye think we must be vigilant?"

"Aye, dost ye feel it? I feel a charge in the air, somethin' is comin' this way."

Fraoch said, "Somethin' has been comin' for ten months."

I said, "Somethin' is always comin', but this time tis serious."

THIRTY-THREE - MAGNUS

I asked, "What dost ye think of this, about yer mother sidin' with Sir Paddy, frightenin' the young Sophie?"

"Och, I daena ken, if she is spendin' time with Sir Paddy she sounds a terrible person. I do appreciate that she has proven me right. Hayley thought she might be a fine woman, and that I would need tae rescue her from troubles caused by Lady Mairead."

"She sounds more trouble than Lady Mairead."

Fraoch laughed. "Hayley daena like the idea of it."

"Ye can tell her what I hae heard Quentin say before, that, 'both those things may be true.' Tis possible that Lady Mairead is a verra troublesome person and that Agnie MacLeod is also a verra troublesome person, and tis extremely possible that Donnan was pure evil."

Fraoch chuckled. "How did we turn out so fine?"

"I daena ken, I hae tae give a whole lot of credit tae m'sister, Lizbeth."

"She is a fine woman, another example of a fine person comin' from a suspect lineage. I notice ye dinna mention Sean?"

I joked, "Och, Sean, he is nae needing credit. Tis more likely he was tryin' tae help me turn out wrong than right."

"When do they come for the summer?"

"They should arrive in the next couple of weeks."

The downpour became torrential, so twas difficult tae hear over it. I pulled m'hood farther down over my face.

Fraoch cupped his hands out in the rain and they quickly filled with water. He drank from his hands. "Scottish rain, tis spicier than Florida rain."

I said, "Aye, Florida rain has a sweetness tae it."

I watched the drips sliding down the front edge of my rubber coat. "Ye hae been a good friend tae me Fraoch, I am relieved our families haena gotten in the way."

"I feel the same, yet I had grown used tae thinkin' of m'family as being gone and away from m'mind. Tae discover m'mother has been conspiring with yer enemies sets m'teeth on edge."

"Och, especially with Sir Padraig, the man is vile, but we will deal with him soon enough and then perhaps she will come around."

"I winna count on it."

"Why nae?"

"I daena, I am fiercely loyal and I daena give up on things once I hae decided they are worth doin'. I probably got the trait from someone, and m'father, the one I was raised by, was kent for bein' a changeable mind. Did I tell ye he could be headed tae the field, needin' the crop tae come in for the day, and all ye would hae tae say is, 'Auld John, want tae fish?' And he would change his mind on it."

I laughed. "Ye daena sound that far from him, Fraoch!"

"Och, nae at all — I winna allow m'self tae be turned tae go fishing, I go fishin' first." He tapped the side of his head. "I will never give up on fishin'."

"Tis why ye winna give up on Master Cook?"

"Aye, because he has a verra fine boat."

Later, after the rain had passed, I left the walls, passin' Madame Sophie in a walkway. She was with Master Cook, headed tae the Great Hall.

I bowed. "Madame Sophie, it has turned intae a fine day outside, ye might want a turn on the grounds after yer meal."

"Thank ye king Magnus, tis lovely tae see the rain has passed."

I nodded and they passed and continued on their way.

∽

That evening, Madame Sophie set her telescope up on the walls and once more invited us all tae come look at the skies.

THIRTY-THREE - MAGNUS

We stayed long, talking tae her about the moon and stars, twas a truce we had called, one of tentative steps intae the world of trusting again.

We drank a great deal and long stories were told. Fraoch sang a sea shanty and James and Sophie sang Twinkle Twinkle Little Star, and we all sang along as a way of saying we are all taegether in this family.

I kent I had made the right decision, Madame Sophie was one of our own, whatever her past had been. Her connection tae Agnie MacLeod and Sir Padraig gave me pause, but her connection tae James was a stronger one. And I couldna shake the feelin' that she had a stronger connection tae m'own family, nae just through marriage tae a friend, but that she might be an ancestor, needin' harbor from a storm.

At the end of the night we carried the sleepin' bairns down tae the nursery and then climbed the stair tae our rooms.

Near the top of the last stair I became verra breathless, my heart pounding — I gripped the rail and held on for a moment. Kaitlyn's voice comin' through the fog tae my ears, "Magnus, are you okay?"

I managed an, "Aye," and gained m'senses enough tae pull myself tae the next step and then up tae our floor, one step more, then I was able tae walk tae our rooms.

I smiled. "Tis naething, mo reul-iuil, the food disagreed with me."

"That seems to happen a lot," she said, "must be Eamag's fault." Her voice was curt and clipped as if she was upset.

THIRTY-FOUR - MAGNUS

We got intae our room and she was quiet as she undressed for bed. I sat on the edge of the bed with m'back tae her, takin' off my shoes and kilt tae climb under the covers. I did it quickly because twas verra cold in our rooms.

She undressed tae her shift and quietly climbed under the covers and then shifted closer against me, her arms around my head, her leg upon m'side. She held my face against her breast and clung tae me, and then I felt her body tremble and there was a catch in her throat.

"Och, Kaitlyn, are ye cryin'?"

She nodded.

"Why are ye sad?"

"I'm not, I'm mad, I'm so mad at you — right now, you are going to die. You're going to leave me and the kids and die, in this godforsaken castle in the middle of the eighteenth century, and you'll have done it without one single thought for me."

I pulled myself away. "What are ye sayin'?"

"That you are wasting away... becoming weaker. Your heart is not growing stronger. I think this mountain, the hoard of vessels, it's changing you. You're not fixing this motherfucking mess, you're just content to die, and I don't know why."

THIRTY-FOUR - MAGNUS

"Ye ken why. I canna fight, Kaitlyn, nae when I am winded on the stairs. Tis nae fair tae say this tae me."

"I want to take you to a doctor. I want to take you to a doctor first thing tomorrow morning. I demand that you let me take you to a doctor."

"Tis easy tae say, mo reul-iuil. Where is this doctor, when?"

"I don't know, perhaps we go to the year 2025. We go to New York and I drive you straight to the hospital. We worry about everything else after that."

"Ye ken we will be found."

"See, you're going to tell me no. You're going to act like I'm being unreasonable, but it's not unreasonable to say, Magnus. You have a whole lot of people who rely on you and you need to stay alive for us. You might not be able to swing a sword right now, but you can damn sure go to a doctor and see what they can do to help your heart."

I let out a long low exhale then flung the covers off and sat up. "M'heart is fine, I daena need a doctor. I ken ye mean well, but ye are making demands of me that would put our family in danger."

Kaitlyn said, "Then what do we need to do to this fucking world so we don't have to hide anymore? Tell me what it is, what are we going to do? Wait for your heart to get better and then... what?"

"I daena ken."

"Growing up we used to play a game called Hide-and-Seek. Do you know it?"

"Aye, I played it with the boys and Fraoch last summer."

"Who was left hiding at the end?"

"Fraoch, we couldna find him for the longest time."

"It's not a fun game when you're the last one hiding. It's not fun at all. It totally sucks. I hate that part of the game. And I forget that I hate it, I get into the hiding place full of excitement that I've picked the best one, and then a while later I've grown paranoid and fearful. I'm startling at sounds. I was in control, I was the hider, and then I became the hunted. I hate that part."

Kaitlyn pulled the covers up to her chin against the cold. "And then when you're hiding you can try to get to home base, but that's complicated. You can't see home base. You don't know if someone has stopped hunting for you and is just sitting there waiting for you to give up your hiding place. That's the exact same situation we find ourselves in now."

"What dost ye propose we do?"

"We run to home base. We can do it by stealth or we can wave our arms and scream but we need to go to home base."

I said, "Kaitlyn, when we came up with this plan, we decided it taegether. We talked it through."

"I know, and I make mistakes all the time — this is one of them. I made a mistake. Hiding here was not the best idea. My husband is ill and I'm fucking worried I will be burying him on the hillside and I—"

I stood up and flicked the covers down. "I am going tae the walls, I canna listen tae this."

"Then tell me I am wrong! Tell me that you aren't going to die, that I'm worried over nothing."

"I winna play along with this game, Kaitlyn, where ye are tae tell me what tae do because ye are afraid of life and death and I am supposed tae jump tae where ye tell me tae go. I hae tae keep an entire castle of people safe. Ye are being verra unfair tae me."

"I'm scared."

"I ken ye are scared, I am doin' the best I can tae keep ye safe."

"I don't want you to keep me safe. I want you to take one damn moment and stop thinking about everyone in your life and for once think of yourself, keep yourself safe, do *that* for me. That's what I want."

I shook my head. "Ye are asking me tae give up our safe house, tae expose ourselves tae Sir Padraig's wrath. I winna do it. When the time is right I will fight for m'kingdom, until then I winna allow ye tae steer me from m'course. This is what I must do."

"What if you're wrong, Magnus? I know it's rare, but what if you're wrong? What if you're miscalculating with your life?"

I exhaled.

She said, "It's too great a risk."

"Tis a risk I will hae tae take. Ye will hae tae ken, Kaitlyn, that I hae done this because I believed twas what I needed tae do. I hae always put ye first, the bairns first. Always. Ye ken it, right?"

She nodded. "I do."

"Good. I daena need a doctor. When I do need one I promise I will go without argument."

"Thank you, I'm sorry I pushed you."

"I'm sorry I got so upset." I looked around the room. "I am goin' tae dress, I daena think I can sleep now. I will go ahead and take a turn on the walls."

She said, "I love you."

"I love ye too, mo reul-iuil. Sleep tight." I leaned over and kissed her goodnight.

THIRTY-FIVE - KAITLYN

My night was spent thinking, round and round, about our argument, and his health, and about how Madame Sophie was the daughter of a time traveler, and yet, there was a mystery, an anonymous letter, and Sir Padraig hadn't caused any trouble in nine months. I worried about how to protect my family from all these unknowns.

Once I had thought of the Hide-and-Seek analogy it was really hard to un-think it. We were in a hiding place, and we had no way to know if the seeker was looking for us, or waiting at home base to catch us when we grew impatient. Or maybe he had even given up, was carrying on with other conquests and games, leaving us to our self-defeat.

I didn't like self-defeat.

I didn't at all like seeing Magnus defeated and weakened.

And I felt — he needed a doctor. I knew he hated such a thing but he still needed to go, and I needed to figure out how to solve all of this.

And I barely slept.

At all.

Until the morning, when I woke up and he was lying in bed beside me, fast asleep, exhausted by his night guarding over me.

I kissed his shoulder and looked at the door of the room as Isla was toddling in. I gestured, *shhhhh*, and got up, scooping her into my arms, and carried her into our sitting room.

"Da is sleeping, let me get dressed, and we'll go to breakfast."

∽

Magnus met us in the Great Hall. I got up from my seat, rushed up, and threw my arms around him. "I'm sorry about our fight last night. So sorry about it."

"I am too, mo reul-iuil. I couldna think of anything else. I ken ye are worried on me, I ken it, but ye hae tae accept that I am goin' tae be fine. I need ye tae restore yer faith in me. I can remedy this. I am better when ye ken I am capable, please daena lose sight of it."

I looked up at his sad smile.

"If ye daena believe I can do it, who will?"

I said, "Ah, love of my life, it's not that I don't believe in you. It's that I think you need a doctor. Those two things are not the same. You have a human body, they need help sometimes."

"I ken." He kissed my forehead.

I said, "I just want you to be alive to see your children grow up."

"Aye. I hae seen Archie as a grown man, but I haena seen Isla. I wouldna want tae miss it."

My eyes traveled over to the bench where Isla was standing wiggling her hips, laughing, and making her brother roll his eyes. Ben was laughing, too.

"Promise me you won't."

"I promise."

I glanced at him, standing here at the head of the room, lookin' out over his family, he had a look about him, one of watching. I didn't know how to put to words how it made me feel, the way he was being, but it felt like he had grown outside of us, becoming a part of the outer wall, the guard on the tower, the stone gargoyle looking down on us. While we all lived and participated in living.

I knew it wasn't true... I thought back to our camping trip on my anniversary, and my birthday, when he made the handprint stones. But there were many many days where he was just our guard, up on the walls, watching the mountain. It felt very removed from the man he used to be.

And I wanted to save him from it, more than anything.

I had voted that we should do something, and since then it had become more imperative. I didn't know what, but something...

THIRTY-SIX - KAITLYN

*J*ust after breakfast I went downstairs. The courtyard was full, lots of people working, bringing supplies and wares, delivering for the kitchens and store rooms. A woman pulling a cart said quietly, startling me, "Ma'am Campbell, I hae a message for ye."

"Oh, um, for me?"

"Aye, I be told tae give it tae ye directly. Tae make sure ye dinna shew it tae anyone." She passed me a sealed letter. I looked at the back, there was a wax seal, with M, pressed into it.

I gave her a coin, glancing around to make sure I wasn't seen.

It was easy to be unseen. It was one of my biggest complaints about the castle. I missed a wide open house in Florida. Coming downstairs and seeing most of my family in the main room, adjoining the kitchen, or through the glass doors out on the back deck. How I missed seeing my loved ones through the rooms, out on the deck, with the ocean breeze in their hair.

It washed over me suddenly how homesick I was, standing in a crowded, smelly, courtyard, being jostled as I made my way toward a corner nook to read my message.

I broke open the seal and read:

. . .

Dear Kaitlyn,

I ken tis irregular tae receive a missive from myself, I am unaccustomed to asking for help, but in this instance I fear I must. I hae come tae a determination — there is a point in my timeline, when I was returning the Trailblazer tae Sir Padraig after having used it tae rescue ye, where I made a mistake. Tis a moment I can now see has spread confusion.

I believe I hae looped upon myself, more than once, without memory of it, and within that error I hae lost control of the timeline.

Since Magnus has gathered all the vessels, the timeline has become stationary, but still Sir Padraig has control of the future. I wish tae relieve him of his upper hand, but I canna, as I was there already.

Thus I need your help.

I have considered all aspects and canna figure out who else but ye would be able tae help me.

I need ye tae meet me in the kirkyard at Glenorchy. It should take ye a couple of hours travel, ye must come alone. Daena tell anyone that ye are going. Magnus canna come, as he will only be a hindrance tae it.

Please bring yer weapons. We may need them.

I ken ye winna want tae be without yer bairns, I do not intend tae see ye separated from them again. I will see tae it ye are returned within a couple of days.

Sincerely yours,
Lady Mairead

I turned the letter twice trying to see if there was more on either side. *What the...?* I was supposed to meet her in a secret place without telling anyone where I was going? I would literally be the biggest dumbass in the world to even consider it.

But there was something about her tone.

She needed me. She had never 'needed' me before. Plus this

THIRTY-SIX - KAITLYN

was about Sir Paddy — she had an idea. She was trying to figure this out. While we were living in Scotland, she was still working the problem...

She had created the problem, but still.

Ugh, *why was I considering it?*

But what if I could solve this with Lady Mairead? What if we could go back to Florida? What if Magnus's kingdom were restored to him?

What if I could solve this and make Magnus safe?

I had just been wishing for something to do.

What if I could solve this whole thing?

I folded the letter up small. Then stood looking down at my hands, considering.

How had no one noticed Lady Mairead was nearby? Why hadn't our monitor picked her up?

We were on fucking high alert. My husband was constantly on guard and his bitch mother just sent me a letter.

Wasn't that as good a sign as any that we were exposed, and not protected well enough at all?

"Mama!" Across the way, Isla was holding onto her swing, the saddest sight in the world, a little girl too short to get onto a swing by herself.

I walked over and she demanded, "Swing! Swing!"

"Where's your da?"

"He too tiwed. He said nae."

I pulled her up and pushed her on the swing. "Oh he did did he? Where did you see him? I thought he was going up to the walls."

"He sit down." My heart dropped, that too-common-these-days worried feeling dragging me down.

"Where? His office?"

"Aye."

"Oh."

I pushed her for a few moments, then she said, "I go find Ben."

I held the swing still while she slid down. Then I hugged her and held her little pudgy face in my hands. "Do you know how much I love you?"

"So fweaky much."

"Exactly."

"Go see Archie and Ben." I let go of her and she took off toward the stairs to climb to the nursery.

I stood still, watching where she had gone, considering: Archie was playing. Isla would be with him. Beaty would watch over them. Emma and Hayley could run the house. The men would guard over Magnus while he guarded the vessels.

He wasn't even on the walls right now, he was in his office, too tired. He wouldn't see me go. I could leave, I could meet with Lady Mairead and as she said, I could be back in a day or two, *probably*.

I took a deep breath.

I remembered that I was never, ever, *ever* supposed to talk to Lady Mairead without Magnus nearby.

I also remembered her expression when she saw Isla.

I crossed the courtyard to the stair and climbed it for my room. I kept saying to myself, if someone stops me, I will stay. If no one notices me, I will go.

I grabbed a leather satchel, and pulled the wooden heart that Magnus had carved for me off the wall, put it in the bag, and slung the bag over my shoulder.

Then I returned downstairs to the rooms, repeating: if I see someone I won't go. I got to the room where the armaments were kept and asked for, "Two guns, modern, please."

The guard peered at me. "Who's it for?"

"I was sent to get them," I said and he took that to mean, of course, 'I was just a woman and not ever planning to use the guns myself.' He passed them to me along with bullets and a holster.

I placed it all inside the satchel and strode toward the gate.

THIRTY-SIX - KAITLYN

Near it I saw Beaty, with three baby chicks on her arm, and Mookie at her feet.

"Where ye goin', Queen Kaitlyn?"

"I have to run an errand, Beaty. I will be gone for a time, can I ask you to please keep a secret for me? It's a very important secret?"

"Ye ken I would do anything for ye, except I canna lie, twould be against God. I canna do it."

"Well this is going to be a conundrum for you then, and I understand, Beaty, I truly do. But I need you to keep this quiet, that you saw me. I need you to wait until after the midday meal before you tell anyone that you saw me leave. Then, if Magnus asks where I am you tell him that I went to go see Lady Mairead. Say that I am fine and I will be back soon. Tell him not to be worried."

"I daena think ye are supposed tae see Lady Mairead without an escort or protection of some kind."

"This is true, but this time it's to protect Isla, so I'm making an exception."

"What if she sends ye back in time again?"

"She won't, she has no need to, because she knows my importance," I lied. "She knows I'm necessary."

I rummaged through my pocket for the letter.

"After the midday meal, you give this letter to Magnus, so he knows. Okay?"

She nodded and put the letter in her pocket. "If something happens tae ye, Queen Kaitlyn, twill be my fault for nae stopping ye. They will blame me for it and I winna be able tae forgive myself."

I gulped, and drew in a deep breath. "Well, I will have to make sure nothing happens to me, because I love you and I would hate for that to happen. You tell them you tried to stop me." I faltered. "But I still went anyway because this is our only last shot to save us."

I turned to go then added, "Remember how when Magnus went to the past-past to get all the vessels and we didn't know if it was going to work. It was dangerous, and I was mad at him for going, but he went anyway? This is like that, dangerous, and necessary. I have to go. Lady Mairead needs my help."

I left through the gate and mixed in with the tradespeople coming and going along the causeway to the shore of Loch Awe where I would walk the few miles to the small village chapel and my meeting with the worst fucking person in the world.

THIRTY-SEVEN - KAITLYN

I didn't see her outside so I ventured inside the old chapel, looking around for anyone, and growing more and more nervous. "Hello?" I went down the aisle to the small altar. "Hello?" I whispered, "Lady Mairead, hello?"

Lady Mairead stepped from behind a darkened wall.

"Oh!" I clutched my chest and tried to get my breathing under control. "You scared the shit out of me."

"Where is your weapon, Kaitlyn?"

I gasped for air and pulled my bodice. I pointed at the holster, the guns on both hips, and then between my breasts, "Sgian-dubh, here." Then I patted the dirk strapped to my upper thigh. "Dirk, here."

There was a glimpse of an approving look in her eye. "Next time have yer gun drawn, ye canna allow yerself tae be overtaken."

"What am I doing here?"

"I have a plan, I am going tae intervene with Sir Padraig Stuart." She dropped her bag to the bench and began to dig through it. "Hold this." She passed me a vessel. "I would do it on m'own, but I hae been there before, and I fear I hae looped upon myself too many times. I hae made the situation unreasonable." She stood and slung the bag across her chest.

She continued, "If ye are there, ye could do it for me. Ye haena been tae Los Angeles in the year 1926?"

"I don't think so..."

Her eyes widened, "Ye daena think so?"

"I was joking, I haven't."

She looked stern.

"I am certain I haven't."

She said, "We daena hae time for joking, yer daughter's future hangs in the balance. I am asking ye because I feel ye are in the best position tae help me — ye are smart and are driven by a mother's desire tae protect her bairns, but if ye want me tae ask someone else I will do it."

She stalked toward the door of the church and out to the churchyard.

"No, that's not necessary." I followed her. "You think I'm smart?"

She twisted the vessel. "I think ye are a great pain in my arse, and if ye were smarter ye would try nae tae be such a great pain in my arse."

A storm grew above us.

"I don't remember saying, 'yes, I will do it.'"

"I daena hae time for ye tae consider it. Your husband has probably seen this vessel. He has likely sounded the alarm that ye are missing, and Sir Padraig grows stronger with each passing moment. Would ye like me tae wait here while ye make an endless decision?" She made her voice higher to mimic me, "'I daena ken what tae do? What would m'husband want me tae do?' Or would ye hold ontae my arm and come save yer daughter?"

"That second one," I muttered as I grabbed hold of her sleeve and the vessel yanked me away from the time that held everyone I cared about.

THIRTY-EIGHT - KAITLYN

I pulled myself to consciousness from deep depths to see Lady Mairead sitting beside me, on a bench, reading a book. I groaned and sat up, holding my head in my hands. "I supposed you're fine, you've got a golden string, right?"

"Of course I do." She flipped a page. "I wouldna travel without it."

I watched her read, nonchalantly, while my body was wracked in pain and misery.

Once the pain began to subside, I asked, "What are you reading?"

"Poirot Investigates, by Agatha Christie, my favorite author."

I looked around, we were on a bleak, parched, weed and dirt landscape. "Are we in California?" The sun was beating down on my wool-wrapped body and it felt like I was baking in an oven.

"Aye, Los Angeles."

"Where are all the buildings? What is this place?" There was a round, familiar sort of structure farther down the hill.

"We are above the town. This below us is the Hollywood Bowl. It has excellent concerts." She closed her book, and dropped it in her bag. "First we need tae go tae my hotel and get ye a change of clothes."

We walked what felt like a mile or so... leaving the barren hillside for a bustling town. The streets were lined with buildings, many people moving about. I didn't want to complain, but man, I was complaining inside. I was hot, thirsty, and everything ached. I trudged along beside my mother-in-law wondering if my senses had left me long ago.

We came to the intersection of Hollywood and Highland. It was a big wide street with rails running down the middle for streetcars, and so many old cars chugging up and down, weaving in and out. Terrible traffic and no discernible rules. People were walking everywhere on the sidewalks, but also crossing the street wherever, stepping into traffic and risking their lives. Beeping horns created a cacophony. The whole place looked like a wreck about to happen.

This whole idea was a wreck.

And it came to me, what if my mother-in-law was delivering me to Sir Padraig? What if she was trading me? *Oh god.* I stopped in my tracks on the corner of a bustling Hollywood and Highland in the year 1926 and felt a little like the heat and thirst might bring me to my knees.

Lady Mairead was about to step into the street when she turned tae see me. "What on earth is happening tae ye, Kaitlyn? Ye hae the pallor of a ghost!"

"Are you going to trade me to him? Are you going to... are you going to do something awful to me?"

"Why would ye think I would trade my son's wife tae a madman?"

"I don't like how you're answering a question, a panicked question, with more questions." I took a step back. "You have the only vessel — what have I done? What are you going to do to me?"

"Firstly, I do not appreciate yer tone. Secondly, I am nae tae trade ye tae the madman — what kind of person do ye think I am?"

"The kind of person who had me kidnapped in the eighteenth century." A well-dressed man pushed between us, headed somewhere in a hurry. "The kind of person who put poisoned flowers on my bed. The kind of person who put that godforsaken gold band around my throat, and beat Magnus half to death. The kind of person who would sign away her granddaughter to that madman. So yeah, I want to know — are you about to trade me to the madman for the contract? What are you about to do?"

She huffed. "There is a logical explanation for *every* one of those things. The kidnapping was because ye were unruly and had broken yer contra— ye ken, I daena hae tae answer tae ye. I asked ye here tae keep Magnus and Isla alive, tae protect Isla and Archie. If ye daena want tae help, I will do it myself."

"I want to help. But I also am not sure you have answered my question directly enough. I feel like you are the kind of person who finds permission in the in-between. Like I will tell you, 'I do not want to be murdered,' and you will say, 'I will not murder you,' but then someone will kidnap me and you will be all, 'I dinna say I wouldna kidnap ye.'"

She laughed. "I suppose that *does* sound a bit like me."

I said, "I don't know if I've ever heard you laugh before, maybe that one time."

"When would that hae been, tis highly specific?"

"You laughed when I showed you the video when I scratched Braden's face."

"Well, twas the most humorous thing ye ever did." She said, "I will not murder ye, or kidnap ye, or cause ye harm. I hae nae given up on the idea of my son being king. I daena accept that he has lost the kingdom, and I hae an idea tae get his kingdom restored, but I need yer help. I will not trade ye tae the madman."

"Okay. Fine. Thank you. But I am trusting you, please don't make me regret it."

"Aye, ye hae been verra brave tae come with me, I winna break yer trust."

"Okay, now, I am practically on fire, where's the hotel?"

"Just across the street." Three cars careened by, honking furiously. "If we daena survive the crossing tis nae my fault."

THIRTY-NINE - HAYLEY

Magnus was staring down at the letter Beaty had dutifully passed him.

He was telling us what it said as he read it, not nearly fast enough.

I said, "She is going to help Lady *Mairead*? She... she fucking knows better than to do that!"

Magnus said, "Aye."

I said, "She would leave Isla again? Archie?"

Emma said, "She wouldn't have, unless she thought this was very important. She was talking to me about Isla just this morning, it must have been really important. I know she didn't think this was a tenable situation. She was worried that we weren't solving the problem, we weren't keeping Isla safe enough. I think she thought this was what she had to do."

I said, "I think you're being awfully kind, I think Katie needs an ass kicking."

Beaty said, "I want tae ask King Magnus, dost ye think I am tae blame? Please daena blame me for her leaving, I did m'best tae make her stay."

Magnus said, "I daena blame ye Beaty, Kaitlyn kens her own mind." He folded the letter up and placed it in his sporran.

He was chewing his lip, and looked upset, but said simply, "I expect her home within the next two days, then we will ken."

I said, "You're not going after her? What the hell?"

Fraoch said, "Hayley, wheesht."

"No, I won't, he should go after her."

"I canna, I daena ken where she is." He was massaging his left hand, something I had noticed he did all the time now.

"Great, well how about me? I'll go!"

Magnus said, "Nae, where are ye tae go? When? Nae one should go runnin' off lookin' for her, we are tae remain here until she returns."

I huffed.

Magnus said, "If ye want something tae do, perhaps ye could take over some of Kaitlyn's duties for the day."

"Fine," I stormed out of the room and waited for Fraoch in the hall and then when he came following me said, "What the hell, Fraoch, why didn't you back me up in there?"

"I winna, cause ye are wrong, and I dinna want tae take yer side in it."

I waved my arms incredulously. "You didn't want to take my side! You have to always take my side, I'm your wife!"

His brow drew down. "Nae, I daena think that's how it works."

I crossed my arm and tapped my foot. "How about you tell me how it works, Mister I-side-with-Mags?"

"Ye ken Og Maggy will always go after Kaitlyn, hae ye ever seen him stay behind? He daena ken where she is!"

"That's never stopped him before."

"Aye, but he must calculate: his family, his throne, the vessels, he canna risk all of it for one person—"

"She ought to be the most important person."

"Ye ken she is the most important person, but he has tae calculate all the same — and, m'bhean ghlan, she daena want tae be followed. She made Beaty wait tae tell Og Maggy. I think if she is the most important person tae ye, ye ought tae honor her decision."

I rolled my eyes, jokingly, finding it hard to stay mad.

He chuckled. "Ye hae been practicin' yer battling with Kaitlyn, hae ye nae?"

I nodded.

"If yer friend has chosen a battle, has ridden off tae meet it, and has left ye behind on purpose, what are ye tae do?"

"I don't know, when Katie went off to college I kind of just threw myself into work and drinking too much."

"Och, maybe nae whisky, twill end poorly, but ye might want tae find something tae do. And when ye are worried, ye can go up on the walls and stand beside Magnus and watch the horizon. He will be up there, m'bhean ghlan, he is always up there."

I nodded. "Yeah, you're right. I'm not furious anymore. I forgive you for not taking my side. I forgive Mags for not going after her. I am still mad at Kaitlyn, but that's mostly because I'm worried."

"I ken."

I smiled. "And I'm mostly mad because she left me with her chores. She is off on a jaunt with Lady Mairead while I have to go to the nursery? It's not fair."

Fraoch pulled me into his arms and gave me a big long hug, and being held by him made our whole argument slip away.

"Thank you for talking me down."

"Ye are welcome."

FORTY - KAITLYN

The hotel was lavish, chandeliers in the lobby, bellhops bustling around, Lady Mairead waltzing through, telling the concierge to, "Send for Rodolfo, I need something fitted."

She ushered me up the grand stair and then down a long hallway to our rooms, a suite with two bedrooms. It was an odd decor, vintage, by my point of reference, modern by the standards of the day, everything covered in fancy fabrics.

She said, I am sure ye are ready for a bath, ye may do that now."

"I am very hungry actually." My mouth was watering at the idea of eating modern cuisine, restaurant food.

"I will have room service brought up while ye bathe, ye are a frightful stench."

"Oh, great." I went through to the bathroom and took the most delightful bath in a claw foot tub. There was a small table with a pitcher of water for drinking. I was light headed with hunger but as soon as I got finished with the luxurious soak I put on the robe and room service had arrived with food. I ate ravenously in my own room.

I felt content and happy, but also guilty as hell, like a mom who took a vacation from her family, except this wasn't a vacation, it was a business trip, a necessary job with my mother-in-law. But also — that bath had been really decadent after so much time without big tubs and ample sweet smelling soaps. I had gotten towels for Magnus but one washing at Kilchurn castle and they had sucked. I was deeply conflicted about enjoying this luxury.

∾

Rodolfo arrived in Lady Mairead's room to fit me for an outfit. The dress Lady Mairead picked out for me was a sequined, crepe-romaine, black dress, knee-length, in a flapper style. "It's beautiful!" I said as it was brought down over my arms. It was at once weightless compared to the dress I had just removed, but also a bit heavy from the beading and sequins that draped at my waist.

Lady Mairead said, "It ought tae be beautiful, tis a Chanel. Coco has given it tae me herself." She walked around me appraising the back. "Ye will fill the actresses with jealousy that ye hae one already, tis only now in the magazines, but ye will also gain their respect."

I was given silk stockings to cover my legs, thankfully, because my leg hair was 'wild-hippie-love-child-long,' as Hayley would say. My shoes were silver with a little heel. To top the dress off I had a wrap of fur, and a diamond necklace. Lady Mairead said, "Ye will be dining with Clara, daena listen tae her, she is an insipid little girl. She drives me tae distraction, but she is on the verge of stardom so ye must spend time nodding and smiling in her direction. Then there is Marion, she has gone through an ordeal. She does not have the standing she once did, so she will nod and smile at Clara the most. The men are vastly unimportant."

Pins were placed up the side of my dress and one stuck me in the side. "Ouch."

Lady Mairead sneered. "Daena be a bairn."

"So what exactly am I doing?"

"Ye are going tae go tae dinner with some of m'dearest friends. I will introduce ye, then I will be called away, because someone I canna see is going to arrive." She shifted her eyes toward Rodolfo to show me she couldn't speak freely in front of him. He didn't seem to speak English, but one could never tell.

"Ugh, I feel like a lot could go wrong."

"Aye, it already has."

"Sir Padraig will be at this dinner?"

"Aye, he will arrive next, and will be sitting at the end of the table beside Marion, ye must keep yer eye on him. But daena let him guess who ye are. This is an important dinner, I hae the Trailblazer tae return tae him, the contract is between us. He has the upper hand. After we eat, he will take me tae a back room and this is the moment where I have lost the game. He will take the Trailblazer and I will hae lost the kingdom for Magnus. Tis the moment I hae been trying tae undo."

"Sounds easy," I joked. I took a big bite of a pastry.

She said, "Daena get crumbs on the dress, tis verra expensive."

"What do you care, seriously, you can just get another one?"

She spoke in fluent Italian, mockingly towards me, to the tailor, who laughed.

I rolled my eyes and frankly felt petulant.

I asked, "So you're going to leave, but then the other Lady Mairead is going to arrive? Will the other Lady M have the gold band around her neck?"

She nodded. "Yes, tis how he has gotten me tae sign the contract in exchange for the Trailblazer, and how he has assured that I will return it. I will hae the band around my neck. I am effectively under his control."

My fingers went to my throat instinctively.

I said, " I hated you so much for that."

"I ken."

FORTY - KAITLYN

She appraised me, "Ye look verra beautiful, Kaitlyn, what can we do with your hair?"

"I can do a French Twist?"

"Good, that would work, I believe ye will blend in verra nicely." She told Rodolfo that I was done and sent him from the room.

Then she said to me, "Sir Padraig kens he has the band around my throat so he believes I am under his control. He gets up, before the meal is ordered, tae go tae the kitchen and speak tae the chef about the meal. In that moment, I want ye tae undo the band from the other Lady Mairead's neck, verra quickly, and then ye tell her tae go tae Elmwood. The other Lady Mairead will ken what ye mean—"

"What do I mean? What is Elmwood?"

"Elmwood Mansion is m'house, ye ken, in the Upper East Side."

"I have never heard you mention it."

"I am sure ye hae, we have a safe in the closet for keeping our effects and sending messages. I plan tae pass it down tae my granddaughter... *Elmwood*."

She searched my face while I shook my head, then she shrugged.

"Well, now ye ken, tell the other Lady Mairead tae go tae Elmwood." She stood in front of me and adjusted my wrap. "What did I just tell ye tae say?"

"I'm to take the band off the other Lady Mairead's neck and tell her she's to go to Elmwood."

"Aye. Now, it has happened before that Sir Padraig has already taken the Trailblazer from me. But it will happen at the table and ye will notice it if it happens. Tis why ye must pay attention. Either way, once the other Lady Mairead runs away, and before Sir Padraig returns, I will sit down at the table, wearing the exact same dress." She waved her hand down to show off her clothes. "So that he winna expect, and I will deal with him."

"I will have weapons though, I could just kill him."

"I will kill him, I hae been wanting tae for years. He has caused me a great deal of grief."

She dropped a gun intae her bag. "But if I miss... ye will kill him. He is nae allowed tae leave the restaurant alive. Once he is dead ye will scrounge through his pockets. If ye find anymore vessels or Trailblazers ye must take them."

She looked at her gold watch. "We hae three hours, twill be just enough time for ye tae get yer makeup done so ye will be presentable."

"Was that a complaint about my looks?"

"Ye will need tae do something about yer eyebrows Kaitlyn, ye canna go out like an eighteenth century barbarian. And yer nails, ye must apply yerself, these are actresses!"

∽

I did apply myself. I put on makeup, painted my nails, put my hair up, paced, and felt ill from worry. I nervously took off makeup and reapplied it. I was ready really early, but still somehow, full of apprehension, had to rush at the end.

As soon as I saw her next I asked, "We won't get separated though, right? If we shoot someone in the middle of a restaurant there's sure to be police involved."

She waved her hand. "This is practically the Wild West and as soon as we shoot him we will leave."

"But you won't be able to return, you'll be...okay, please explain it to me again."

"Ye will enter the restaurant. I will introduce ye tae the actresses. Then I will step away and the other Lady Mairead will arrive a few minutes later. Offer her the empty chair. She will be confused by your presence, but I think it winna be that difficult tae figure out. Ye will sit halfway down the left side, nearest the door. Make sure there is an empty seat beside ye. Ye will make lively conversation with the actresses as if ye hae kent them yer whole life. Dost ye ken anything about film?"

"1920s film? No, not really. Black and white, right?"

She rolled her eyes. "How dost I ken more than ye do on the time period?"

"I have never visited this time before. Give me a break. So I will be there before Sir Paddy?"

"Aye. Your only job is tae enjoy the dinner and convince me tae run from the restaurant as soon as there is a moment. I will be waiting outside and will—"

"This sounds an awful lot like looping… I looped over and over on myself when I was trying to get to my grandmother before she passed and every time I tried her life got shorter and shorter. You have to make sure you aren't looping or it could—"

"I hae looped before, I ken what happens."

"When?"

"I tried tae intervene in a death from my youth." Her eyes went faraway. "My Fionn passed away many years in the past, but I was lonely, and I wondered if I could intervene in it. I tried tae loop tae save him. I was nae thinking of the implications, the possible dangers, I simply wanted tae keep him alive."

"Did it work?"

"Nae, of course not, I tried, then I grew desperate, and with each loop I lost days — twas devastatin'. I lost the time when I told him he was tae become a father and he died without knowing. Twas a heartbreak I will never wish tae live again."

"I heard about Fionn a few months ago actually, I'm really sorry."

She shrugged. "Well, tongues will wag. Twas centuries ago. I was tae be a farmer's wife and hae many bairns and live a life of drudgery and hardship and now see what I hae gained instead?"

"A lot of freaking hardship. A constant need to carry a weapon."

"True, but also a son who is a king. Tis nae something tae be dismissive of — in the history of the world how many women have had their sons elevated tae kings? And of those women how many had sons who deserved the honor? As ye ken, Magnus is a good king, one tae be proud of, and I consider it an honor." She brushed some lint off my shoulder and appraised me. "We are nae tae interfere with the normal life and death of our world, only tae ride along as lives unfold. I ken it is sometimes melancholic but it can also be wonderful tae be the most powerful women in the world."

I chuckled. "I have never been included in your power before."

She scoffed. "What am I, the mother? Ye are the Queen. Ye hae murdered the former king and then murdered the king's mistress. Ye have adopted the heir tae the throne, and birthed a princess, and the king listens tae ye in everything. Ye hae much more power than me."

I felt shocked by her statement.

Then she added, "Tis why I hae decided ye are worth keeping around. I haena liked ye much, but I was proud of ye when ye killed Bella, twas the first time I saw strength in ye."

"You know, I have saved Magnus's life more than once. I have raised two beautiful children. I have made Magnus very happy..."

"Och, all those things are for yer own benefit. Killing Bella was the first thing ye did that was for Archie, tae put Magnus's son on the throne. I consider that something ye hae done directly for my own bloodline."

"Oh."

"And ye arna tae tell anyone of the truth about Sean's father. I ken many people suspect, but I daena want tae admit tae it."

"You're right, people do suspect it, but I will keep it quiet."

"So do ye hae anymore questions?" She took a perfume atomizer from her dressing table and sprayed a cloud of Shalimar all around me.

"Yes, you never finished after 'waiting outside and...'"

"I will come in, I will kill Sir Padraig, you and I will leave the restaurant and reconvene here at the hotel where the vessel will be in the safe. We will jump back to Scotland, 1707, two days after we left. Now repeat the plan back to me."

"I'm just supposed to get along with everyone at the table. As soon as the other Lady M arrives, I'm to convince her I'm there for legitimate reasons. As soon as Padraig arrives, I'm to convince him I'm not there for nefarious reasons. As soon as he goes to the kitchen, I release Lady Mairead from the neckband and tell her to run. Then I continue in my seat as you arrive. You're sure one of us shouldn't have a vessel?"

"Nae, it might be taken from us, then I would hae tae get the other."

"You have another? Maybe I should know where, just in case."

"I hae a vessel hidden at Elmwood, but ye would hae tae get from here tae there, we ought tae make sure we daena lose the vessel here. I will leave it in the safe."

I gulped. "Then, in a crowded restaurant we..."

"Nae we, I — I will kill the man."

We gathered up our bags and filled them with cosmetics. I placed my wooden carved heart into mine. I had a knife sheathed on my thigh and a gun hidden on my other thigh.

It wasn't easy to keep them hidden in the flow of my little black dress. I loved this dress so much. It swished when I moved. My legs looked delightful in the hose. I wore a bejeweled silk ribbon tied around my hair and my makeup was excellent.

I would have enjoyed going to dinner with actresses in Hollywood if it were not for my mother-in-law, and the impending shoot out at a restaurant in 1920s California.

One of my worries, a simple one: I had just gotten here, I didn't really know the lay of the land.

Note to self, *pay attention as you go to the restaurant — no getting lost.*

Also, *Probably don't drink, you need to have your wits.*

Lastly, *don't die, Kaitlyn, your whole family needs you.*

The panic attack settled in my chest causing me to feel breathless. I had run away. What if something happened to me? What if I was lost or killed a million miles and years from my family and hadn't said goodbye? What had been the last thing I said to Magnus?

Had I told him I loved him?

Would Isla know I didn't mean to leave a second time — I had to, to protect her. Would she understand?

The truth was, I had to survive.

No dying.

Lady Mairead gathered a handkerchief, stuffed it intae her handbag, and said, "Are ye ready tae go Kaitlyn?"

I nodded, finding it hard to speak.

FORTY-ONE - KAITLYN

We walked down the ornately designed hotel hallway to the grand entrance stair, and descended to the lobby. Lady Mairead walked through as if she owned the place.

"I hae the something tae put in the safe, Harvey, I will return for it verra soon." She placed a stack of bills in front of him.

He pocketed the cash, opened the safe, and brought out a drawer. She placed a vessel into the middle. "I will return for it after I hae eaten dinner."

"Of course, Lady Mairead, we will be waiting for you, as usual."

"If I am nae here tae retrieve it after dinner, ye may give it tae m'daughter-in-law, Kaitlyn."

"Of course."

I whispered, "I might be here by myself?"

"We ought tae be prepared for every eventuality."

Uniformed bellhops and footmen bowed as we sashayed by, our dresses swishing around our knees. Lady Mairead was wearing a dress in silver, with beading in stripes, she looked very sophisticated, and as always had a way of carrying her head, that said, 'important.' No matter how I tried, her look made me seem like her personal assistant.

I said, "I'm nervous, this is all... you're sure you know what you're doing?"

"Of course I ken what I am doing, I mean, I haena killed anyone before but—"

"You haven't?"

"Nae. I am nae practiced in the art of it as ye are. How many people hae ye killed?"

"At least two close up."

She smirked, "And ye are thinking *I* am nae tae be trusted."

It had grown dark, the streets were crowded with restaurant goers and people moving in and out of clubs. Street lamps lined the street, but the pools of lights were dimmer than modern day.

Cars, very old fashioned cars, slid up to curbs and fabulous people stepped out. I noticed people looking at us as we passed.

As we came to the door Lady Mairead saw the friends we were there to meet.

"Clara! Marion!"

There were four people, two women, two men, everyone in finery, smoking, standing at the door of the restaurant.

As we walked up Lady Mairead said, "I hae never seen them outside the restaurant before."

Her brow furrowed. "I will introduce ye, but perhaps I will nae go in. Ye must keep an empty seat, so that..."

"I know I know, the plan is already falling apart."

I was introduced to Clara Bow and Marion Davies and the men, Percy Marmont, and B.P. Schulberg, both much older than the women. Percy Marmont had his hair slicked back and was tall and distinguished with a British accent. B.P. was younger and seemed to want to make sure everyone was happy. Every position they held was like a pose. A crowd began to form around them.

Lady Mairead expertly started a conversation between me and Clara Bow who had very big eyes and batted her eyelids incessantly. She was young, younger than Beaty it seemed, and twice as silly.

I was asking her about her dress when Lady Mairead leaned in and said loudly, "Hold a chair for me. I must run back tae the hotel. I will return in a moment."

She was gone.

It was just me, making small talk with the ladies who were living long before I was even born. The press showed up, a reporter commanded, "Clara Bow! Smile!"

Her smile was dazzling. The two men in our circle preened. Percy, in particular, looked at once irritated and also grateful for having been photographed. Flashes went off around us and the maître d' rushed out to the sidewalk to usher us into the restaurant.

"My apologies to keep you waiting! Follow me, we had a private room set up, last minute..." and other things I probably should have taken note of.

FORTY-TWO - KAITLYN

The restaurant was crowded and dark, wood booths with red vinyl cushions, the waiters were wearing red coats as they buzzed around the room. The maître d' wove around tables making sure everyone in the bar noticed the new guests. Clara giggled happily and twittered loudly, waving greetings toward no one sitting in the corner.

B.P. asked, "Are we not sitting at our usual table?"

We wove past the bar, the entertainment, a woman singing accompanied by a piano.

"No, you have a private dining room tonight, Mr Schulberg."

"I did not ask for one," he muttered.

The maître d' said, "Sir Padraig arranged for it."

I stopped dead in my tracks.

B.P. put out his elbow, assuming I had lost my way as my group serpentined through the hall. I put my hand into it and tried to ask the maître d' casually, "Sir Padraig Stuart is already here?"

"Yes, he's expecting your party." He put out his arm, gesturing us into the room.

. . .

FORTY-TWO - KAITLYN

The key point in all of this was that I was undercover.

No one was supposed to know me except Lady Mairead, but as soon as the door closed behind us, as the group I was with appraised the room, my eyes met the other Lady Mairead, who was shocked that I was there. Her eyes flitted from me to the man whose arm I was holding as if trying to understand the situation.

I let go of his arm.

There were two other women there. A young pretty woman who was pregnant and looked frightened and a woman who looked highly amused by the whole thing.

The man who must have been Sir Padraig said to the young pregnant woman, "Get up and go sit at that corner table." He pointed at a dark chair. She got up, gave a quick, submissive bow, and went to sit in the corner.

Sir Padraig, stood and bowed low, "Thank you for attending my soirée here, welcome."

His eyes raised and looked directly at me. "Welcome especially, to you, Kaitlyn Campbell, I don't believe we've met."

Fuck.

He had a glisten in his eye, as if he found the whole thing funny as hell.

The other woman, pale, beautiful, and well dressed, was sneering at me, knowingly. A woman in on a secret with an evil man, these were not endearing qualities.

All the Hollywood types sat in their seats unaware.

Sir Padraig approached around the table. "You won't mind, Kaitlyn Campbell, if I check you for weapons."

"I do mind, frankly."

He pulled up behind me, way too close. I shoved his hand away.

He chuckled. His stale breath in my ear. "You carrying something?"

Percy laughed. "Of course she's not carrying any—"

He stopped short when Sir Padraig said, "Aha!" as he patted my thigh.

I pushed his hand away again, but it was too late, he wrestled out the gun and tossed it to the table.

Lady Mairead's eyes were wide. The gold band around her neck glistened in the low lamplight.

"More?" He whispered in my ear.

"Of course not, why would I—?" I tried to squirm away, but he expertly held my arm while grabbing my blade from its sheath on my other thigh.

Great.

The plan had been shitty, but even shitty plans don't usually have everything go exactly the wrong way.

He dropped my knife on the table beside my gun and returned to his seat.

Everyone was looking from him to me, and it freaked me out.

Lady Mairead jerked her head ever so slightly at the young woman in the corner. Her eyes wide.

I glanced at her, the young woman was watching but trying not to, and a certainty settled in my stomach, I didn't know her, but she was familiar — she was *family*.

He gestured toward the chair. "Sit sit! You must sit down, you came all this way. I have your meal ordered for you already." He drew my weapons toward himself.

My voice shook as I said, "How do I know you?"

The lady to his left laughed. "How does she know you? Priceless!"

"You don't know me? After all I've done to you? I'm personally offended."

Percy said, "Oh come, come, Sir Padraig, you've got to be more courteous than this, first you accost her, now you argue with her. You know the phrase goes, after all I've done *for* you.'" He laughed. "She is lovely, our new friend, though she carries more arms than a civilized lady might. Marion, dear, it's a good

FORTY-TWO - KAITLYN

thing William isn't here, he would be smitten with the well-armed lady, wanting to take her on safari in Africa."

Marion rolled her eyes. "He does love to shoot things."

A waiter moved around the table pouring wine into our glasses.

I wasn't close enough to Lady Mairead to get the band off her neck.

Sir Padraig didn't look like he was going to leave the table.

I was unarmed.

Sir Padraig grinned. "How's your husband?"

I figured I would try to dispute it all. "I don't know who you're—"

"Stupid bitch, doesn't think I know all there is to know?"

Percy said, "Sir Padraig, watch your language in front of the ladies!"

The woman beside Sir Padraig said, "He's just calling her what she is, isn't that right, Lady Mairead?"

Lady Mairead shook her head but refused to answer.

I narrowed my eyes. "And who the *hell* are you?"

"I'm Agnie MacLeod." She leaned forward to address Lady Mairead again, "I'm just a little know nothing farm girl from the village, isn't that what you called me that one time?"

Lady Mairead raised her chin. "I hae never considered ye important enough tae talk on much less pass judgments upon. Ye are nothing important enough tae waste m'time."

Sir Padraig chuckled, maliciously. "I do like you, Lady Mairead, you are a real prize. It's been great doing business with you."

Our dinners were brought to the room and there was a bustling and moving around of plates and utensils and bowls as we got our meals. I stared straight ahead trying to figure out how to get out of this situation.

Sir Padraig leaned back as if relaxed, staring directly at my face.

As all the plates were placed and the waiter bowed from the

room, he reached across and removed my utensils from me, sliding them to his plate. "My apologies, Queen Kaitlyn, you look like someone who can figure out how to make a spoon into a weapon."

"How am I to eat the steak you ordered for me?"

"Maybe you don't get to eat." He said to the other guests, "But you, of course, eat up!"

I reached for a slice of bread, trying to imagine how to sharpen it into a shiv.

He smiled. "Aw, sweet Kaitlyn, you look worried."

I tore the bread in half and ignored him.

"I truly believed you to be more interesting than this."

I shrugged, put a hunk of bread in my mouth, and chewed.

He leaned forward and spoke to the table.

"You see, Kaitlyn Campbell here, is a *queen*."

I chewed and chewed.

"Did she tell you? Her husband, Magnus I, is king of Riaghalbane. Have you heard of it?"

Everyone agreed that they hadn't, but there was a rising estimation of me at the table: backs straightened, smiles widened, faces turned toward me. I went from starlet want-to-be in a nice dress to someone that everyone was 'aware of'.

B.P. laughed, "So instead of you, Sir Padraig, I should be asking Queen Kaitlyn to urge her husband, the king, to produce my next film?"

He had just been joking, everyone chuckled, but Sir Padraig dropped his fork and knife to the plate with a clatter. "Why would you do that?"

"What? It was to be humorous, Sir Padraig, I—"

"Why would you say that, about asking King Magnus instead of myself, are you saying he is more important than me?"

"No, that's not what I meant, I was joking. It's not—"

"You owe me an apology."

B.P. said, "For what, for joking about asking a king to back my next film? I..."

FORTY-TWO - KAITLYN

Sir Padraig glared at him, a stare that sent a shiver down my spine. Then his face broke into a sinister smile. "Now I'm just being humorous. Magnus is nothing to me, to borrow Lady Mairead's insult from earlier, I don't think about him at all."

I chewed and swallowed and staring at the wall over Lady Mairead's head, said, "Bullshit."

His brow raised. "What — bullshit? What are you saying to me?"

"I'm saying bullshit. My husband is the king of Riaghalbane arguably the most powerful throne in the history of the world. He has ruled as a benevolent king, admired by most, and it is very clear to me that, despite your protestations, you think about him all the time. He lives in your fucking head. Jealousy eats away at your black heart and your obsession with him is going to be your downfall. That is a promise, from Magnus through me."

He chuckled and said to Agnie Macleod, "Told you she had a bitch mouth on her."

I glanced at the actresses, all with their mouths open.

Clara Bow said, "My word, that was a chilling speech! You are both ruining a lovely dinner!"

Sir Padraig asked her, "Do you not like your meal, Clara?"

"I like the meal, but the conversation is excessively impolite!"

He took a bite of his steak and chewed and swallowed, then tossed his napkin down and leaned back. "You didn't answer me, Kaitlyn, how is your husband? I haven't seen him in a while." He grinned a wide slithery grin. "How's his heart?"

I felt a chill pass through me.

FORTY-THREE - MAGNUS

I asked Quentin and Fraoch tae go with me up the mountain tae the cave.

Sometimes I went alone, I just needed tae see with m'own eyes that the boulder was there, as it should be. I might hae gone alone again today, as I had a great deal tae think on, but I kent Quentin and Fraoch would be quiet enough for me tae think, as well as being witty enough tae keep m'mind off Kaitlyn's leaving, and tae advise me when I needed it.

Quentin asked as we went up the trail that I had been traveling for so many days now without fail, "Why do you go so often? You have the binoculars. If the safe boxes are moved it would set an alarm. We would know."

"I am the guardian, I hae tae inspect it. Tis like the guard on the walls, ye hae tae walk the walls, ye ken, tae make sure they are safe."

Quentin said, "I suppose that's true."

"I ken, logically, that there is a security system in place, but I hae tae lay eyes upon them. I must see the trail has nae footprints, I hae tae ken the sky daena hold a storm, I must check the boulder. If there is a branch fallen I must ken it, move it, deal with it. I hae tae make it safe."

FORTY-THREE - MAGNUS

Quentin joked, "I kind of thought the security system on the safe boxes would help you relax."

I joked, "I am verra relaxed, tis why I daena sleep up here in a tent in front of the cave."

Fraoch asked, "You're worried about Kaitlyn?"

"Aye. I hae never kent her tae run off before."

Quentin chuckled, "Yeah, that sounds more like *your* style, Boss."

I laughed. "Aye, I suppose ye are right."

"Yep, you are often taking off to go set things right or fix what's wrong and Katie is usually the one wondering where the hell you are."

"Aye, tis a good way tae think on it."

"Difference: with you left behind there's a lot less crying."

I joked, "I will remember tae continue tae hide m'crying so I can be admired for handling desertion better than my wife."

"I'll never forget that first time, during your wedding reception, when you left and I had to keep her company. That was a long bleak time."

"Well, I daena ken if I feel better, but I am sure I think about it differently. I was feeling verra put upon that m'wife left without a word goodbye but tis good tae be reminded, I hae had tae do it before."

Quentin said, "She wouldn't have gone, if she didn't think she needed to. Not after that year away. She did it because she felt she had to."

We rode in silence for a time.

Then Fraoch asked, "How are ye feelin' about living here?"

"I tell ye, I am nae enjoying the weather. This day is the first clear day since when… last summer? And I am enjoyin' some things, such as ridin' m'horse on the hills. I am glad tae hae my family around. How about ye?"

"Tis nice tae hae the loch beside me, but I do miss good modern food."

"Aye."

We were quiet again, my horse rocking under me as it climbed a steep pass. A hawk swooped overhead on the hunt for its next meal.

I watched it fly, then said, "I believe I made a mistake."

Fraoch said, "What dost ye mean?"

"Kaitlyn has argued with me, and I fought her about it but now I am thinking on it... I am worried I hae backed up against the wall. I hae never lost a battle afore, but I ken one thing, m'uncle Baldie always told me, 'Daena let them back ye up,' tae do it would be tae chance losin' yer footin', ye ken?"

"Aye, if ye are pushed tae the wall ye canna get away, there is nothing left but tae fight back or fall tae the ground."

Quentin said, "Retreat to a castle is a terrible idea in modern warfare, especially when we can fight from the sky — it's a fortress of course, but also, it becomes a waiting game. The inhabitants of the castle might be protected but if the enemy lays siege then the inhabitants could starve or worse."

Fraoch said, "Och, daena say it, starvation is m'biggest fear."

I said, "Mine as well." I joked, "And ye are supposed tae be m'advisor, Colonel Quentin. I daena remember ye saying ye were worried we might starve in Kilchurn."

"I think I said exactly that, but basically we had no other choice but hold up in the castle while we figured out the next step."

"How are inhabitants of a castle victorious, does it ever happen?"

"Sometimes, I suppose. Army sieges don't always last forever. One way to shorten a siege is to draw out the inhabitants, to create a distraction, or—"

"Like tae tell the Queen that she is needed somewhere else, so that she leaves and the rest of the inhabitants are left nae knowing what tae do."

"Yeah, kind of exactly like that."

We drew near the cave, dropped down from our horses, and the three of us pushed the boulder tae the side.

FORTY-THREE - MAGNUS

I climbed through the tunnel tae the cave, a tight fit, but short enough that I wasna too worried on it, but I had tae grunt and groan with the effort so that Fraoch called intae the cave, "Ye are a big wailin' bairn."

"Och, ye daena ken what ye are talkin' on, tis a tight fit. Yer girth is too big else ye would be here with me."

He said, "This is why I need more food, I am afeared I will waste away and ye will make me go inside the hole."

Quentin climbed in after me and then he and I went through the chests, counting and replacing, like we did every time we came tae take stock. The vessels were all there, I kent it because I kept the records. Before, the world had seemed made of competing strands of time, pushing and pulling against each other, but now it all felt stable.

The rock of the mountain, Ben Cruachan, held the vessels, guardin' them well. I lived at the base being watchful. It all felt safe.

My advisor, Quentin, felt so too.

Fraoch, guarding the cave while we counted, believed it as well.

I had stabilized our history and had thus made our present safer, but I hadna fixed the future, and that was where all the difficulties lay.

Quentin said, "I want a vessel."

"We hae the one down at the castle. Ye daena think tis enough?"

He shook his head. "With Sophie's history, and the anonymous letter, and with Katie gone, we need vessels at the castle. I don't think we're safe anymore. Kaitlyn made a good point, once something goes time-twisty, it all follows fast, and I don't know if we'll have enough time to get back here if we need to get away."

I considered it for a moment.

Then I called up out of the cave, "Do ye need a vessel as well, Fraoch?"

His voice called down, "Aye, I would like one."

I said, "I suppose if there are three at the castle, we ought tae be able tae save everyone, and we can go in different directions if need be." I tossed a vessel to Quentin, one of the older ones, marked it as missing on the list, and carried another out of the cave tae Fraoch.

FORTY-FOUR - KAITLYN

"What do you know about my husband's heart?" I tried to sound casual.

He said, "I've met him, I've seen his weakness." He grinned at Lady Mairead. "Do you think of your son as weak?"

"Of course nae. He is much stronger than ye, and he is verra dangerous when he is angry and I canna think of anything that will anger him more than that ye hae his wife here, holdin' her against her—"

"What?" He held his hands up. "Who's holding her? I'm feeding her dinner. She's a guest!"

Everyone at the table laughed.

Lady Mairead said, "Then allow her tae leave. Ye daena need her for our negotiations. She is young and impetuous. Her incautious behavior will only cause trouble for ye."

"And that is why you didn't get a meal, Lady Mairead." He shook his head slowly. "Do you hear this, Kaitlyn? How your mother-in-law thinks of you?"

I said, "I'm very aware of her feelings about me. It doesn't change the fact that you're an ass and you need to take that fucking necklace off her throat."

He took out a small box, no bigger than a ring box, and

pressed his finger to the surface. Lady Mairead began to choke and cough. She scratched at the surface of the band.

The actresses shrieked and all the guests jumped from their chairs. B.P. said, "What are you doing, Sir Padraig?"

Sir Padraig took his finger from the box and Lady Mairead all but collapsed on the table.

He stood and put his napkin beside his plate. "I want everyone to go." He gestured toward the door. "The exit is through there."

The actors and producers about fell over each other, gathering their wraps and bags, and trying to get out of the room first.

Sir Padraig slumped into his chair and said to Agnie MacLeod. "Told you this would be fun."

"I think you should kill her, Sir Padraig. She and her husband have killed everyone I ever cared about — Reyes, Donnan—"

I said, "You have fucking horrible taste in men."

The table was covered with half-finished meals, forks and knives tossed down, napkins all over the floor, chairs pulled out in every direction. I glanced beside me, a knife was within reach.

He reached across the table, grabbed all the utensils and pulled them toward himself. He wore a shit-eating grin, his hand on my gun.

"Your husband..." He slowly shook his head. "I can't believe he let you come here by yourself. I rather wanted to meet him again, I'd love to talk to him more about his children."

"Don't you dare talk about my kids."

In the corner the young woman glanced over at us, then went back to looking down at the table.

I said, "Who's the lady in the corner?"

He smirked, "Who? Rebecca? She's no one." He chuckled and took a bite of his steak and chewed slowly.

Then he swallowed. "You know, I've seen his medical records."

I narrowed my eyes but refused to answer.

"You're not interested in knowing?" He turned to Agnie MacLeod, "She doesn't want to know."

I said, "Know what, you tepid bag of moldy fish stew?"

He laughed, a laugh like a cackle. Then stopped cold. "That many years ago, back before my time, another king had him under his care. That king discovered that Magnus has a weakened heart, it's congenital. He got it from his mother probably, but whatever — he had a heart attack, now there is scarring. He is weak, weak, terribly weak." He raised his glass and sneered at Lady Mairead.

"There is nothing weak about my husband, you are making that shit up."

"Oh I am? You're a liar. You know this, when he was there with me, I saw it. I had him checked. He's defective. Broken. He won't last another few years. He won't be able to keep a throne, rule a kingdom. His own heart will bring him to his knees."

He shrugged. "Of course this is pretty convenient for me. That whole time you've been living at Kilchurn he's been dealing with it." He tsk-tsked. "So far away from any modern hospitals. No matter how you cut it, I won this game. I don't even have to do anything, he will just topple without my help."

He pressed his finger on the small box again and Lady Mairead began to gasp and claw at the band.

The young pregnant woman shrieked from the corner, "Stop it! You're going to kill her!"

He took his finger off the box and Lady Mairead collapsed back on the table. Then he turned in his chair and said, "What do you care? Do you want me to come back there?"

She shook her head.

Then he looked at his watch. "Ah yes, it's begun."

FORTY-FIVE - MAGNUS

The afternoon was spent up on the walls, appreciating the sun, a wide sky with a high breeze blowing tufts of clouds across it. There was warmth on m'skin, but I had tae pull the wool around tae keep the wind from cutting through.

The day continued, and having lengthened a bit, the wind grew stronger, until twas almost a gale. We sat low on the parapet, blocking the wind, watching the area in the woods where our clearin' was. It was close enough that when we saw storms we could get there in time, but Fraoch and James had been waiting there most of the day in case Kaitlyn arrived.

Then they returned tae the castle and Quentin and I rode out tae sit and wait — especially as the cold night descended upon us. If Kaitlyn returned someone had tae be there tae protect her until she awoke.

Quentin said, "What if she doesn't return today, what if she doesn't return tomorrow? I know it's a terrible thing to think of, but what will you do?"

"I believe she has gone tae be a part of a meeting between Lady Mairead and Sir Padraig, I daena remember the date, but twas in the year 1926, in Los Angeles."

"So you would just wait there for her?"

"Aye, I ken the restaurant, Twould nae be so difficult."

"Maybe you don't think so, but it sounds arduous to me."

I chuckled. "It could be that their meeting is January 2nd, it might be easy. I've done far worse than visitin' every day in a year."

"I suppose you have."

"Also we hae the meetin' places: Lady Mairead has the safe deposit box at C Hoare and Company Bank in London, another in the Bank of New York where messages can be placed. We hae a house on the Upper East Side, Lady Mairead bought it in the 1920s when she was friends with the Whitneys, there is a safe in a back closet of that home. Tis like a mailbox passed through time."

"Weird, you never mentioned that before."

"I haena?"

"Nope, in all the years we have been trying to communicate with each other, we haven't had a safe in a closet in New York, that's new."

"Och. Tis a long time since I thought the timeline was confused."

"Well, if that is a new addition, at least it's a good one."

"Aye. I suppose tis." We sat quietly.

Then I asked, "Hae I mentioned the home on the Cape?"

"No, how many houses do you own? Mister I-was-renting-a-house-in-Florida!"

"At least seven, but I think they hae always been m'houses?"

"Dude, no, they haven't always been your houses. Your mom's been buying real estate this go around. Next you'll tell me you own a plane, please, God, own a plane."

"Of course I own a plane."

"Really?"

"Nae. But I hae ridden on one once, as ye ken, so I daena need tae fly anymore." I shivered.

"You time travel all the time, at great risk, but a plane is too much?"

"I also daena think Kaitlyn wants tae own one because she worries about the air."

"The air danger or the air pollution?"

"Pollution."

We both looked up. The wispy tufts of clouds that had been racing across the sky were billowing, higher and higher. There was a dark edge tae it and then the sunlight darkened as banks of clouds covered the sun.

"Och, there is a storm, but it inna here."

"It's in the direction of the castle!" We both jumped on our horses and rode that way.

∼

As we emerged from the woods we could see a spiraling storm right above the castle, as if twas centered inside the courtyard. This was somethin' we had never dared tae do and only a few times had been tried, during the battle for the walls, years ago, when the army of Uncle Samuel had fought against the Campbells. It had been too dangerous tae even consider for the convenience of it.

Wind was whipping debris into a tornado within the castle. The slates from the roof were projectiles. Rubble spun. Quentin and I pushed our horses forward, he yelling, "Go go go!"

We raced down the causeway, forcing the horses faster, until, as we neared, they reared and balked at the wind. A thick branch whipped past us tae the water.

I checked the walls but could see no men and as I gained on the front gate, an explosive arc of lightning sparked down on the tower house, electrifying the castle, with a thunderous boom, but more terrifying, an explosion — matter up intae the sky, a cloud of smoke, and then yelling from the castle, everywhere men running back and forth. We made it intae the gate, tae see chaos.

Men were running toward an area of wall that had fallen. A fire had started there with wind whipping the flames higher. It had gone from a lightning spark tae a castle fire in mere seconds.

We tied our horses near the armory. The guard was nae there, men were grabbing guns, but they were nae our men. Quentin began firing, hidin' behind a post, shootin' towards the armory, I saw more men running up the stairs tae the nursery.

Zach came running up from the kitchens. "There's a fire! Fuck! We need to go get the kids from the nursery."

The wind was ferocious. With my gun drawn, and an arm up tae block the buffeting blasts, we skirted the courtyard tae the closest stair.

I killed a man going up, and another in the hallway. There were three men attempting tae barge in through the nursery door. I found Fraoch there, in the far stairwell, his gun sighted on them, the closest shot, but men were coming up from behind. James jumped out and shot one of the men advancing, while Fraoch and I shot at the men at the door. Zach came running up, "Are all the kids in the nursery?"

More of my guards, hearing the battle, joined us, and from inside the nursery came screams and wailin' from the bairns. Fraoch was fighting men as they rushed up the stair behind him and I raced past him tae the door, shooting, killing all three men and bangin'— "Tis me, Magnus! Open the door!"

From inside, the sounds of bairns cryin' and large furniture being pushed across the floor. Then Hayley threw the door open and inside was a barricade, now in disarray, but built as we had planned, with women and children cowerin' in the room beyond.

James and I pushed more of the barricade away and passed Hayley and Emma guns. "Are all the bairns accounted for?"

Hayley said, "Yes! I counted heads."

"Everyone!" James yelled, "Line up here! We need you holding onto the person in front of you, we've got to leave!"

I led the way, with Zach standing at the wall, ushering all of them through, James at the rear. I spoke tae Quentin on the walk-n-talk, "We are movin'!"

"Alright Boss, I've cleared the south stairwell."

Smoke billowed from the far end of the hall, fire was racing along the balustrade.

Zach was telling everyone, "Cover your nose and mouth, hold onto the shirt in front of you!" I led the train of women and children along the hallway and down the stairs tae the courtyard, where Quentin held the door.

I glanced up, battles were happening on every floor. "Tae the chapel!" I yelled.

Hayley led down the short distance, rushin' while clinging tae the walls. We urged them along, yelling, "Go go go!" Isla was carried by Beaty, screaming and trying tae reach me. Mookie was on a leash pulled along behind. Archie met my eyes, I said, "I will see ye soon, wee man."

And he was pushed along, toward the chapel with Madame Sophie holdin' ontae him and Ben. Tears streamed down her face, she looked terrified. I said tae Zach and James, "Help them barricade, protect the doors!"

I turned tae see Quentin, calling me tae follow.

I yelled tae Fraoch. "Head tae the cave! I'll come as soon as I ken they are safe!"

Fraoch left across the courtyard in the direction of the gate. Everywhere around us were the sounds of gunshots and explosions.

I met Quentin and we took two stairs at a time. As soon as we emerged from the stairwell there was crossfire from the far walls. The storm was behavin' verra different from how we expected them tae behave. It was still churning, the wind was fierce, Quentin yelled tae be heard over it, as lightning struck again, and again, "They must be jumpin' one at a time to keep this storm lasting for so long!"

My hair was lashin' my face, my kilt whipped against m'legs, twas difficult tae keep tae my feet in the blasts of wind. Twas frightenin' tae be buffeted up on the walls of the castle, and we were exposed under the flashes of lightning and rumbling thunder. "How would they have so many vessels?"

FORTY-SIX - KAITLYN

"What has begun, you creep?"

"The final assault on Kilchurn castle, and a storm of destruction to cover — I can tell you this, because you aren't there to stop it, the storm will cover us while we take all the vessels from the cave on Ben Cruachan. Did you know that in the twenty-first century there is a hydroelectric power station there?"

My mind was gone — flooded by fear.

I was here, brought here by Lady Mairead, the sort-of-helpful one, who was nowhere to be seen, while her big plan of grandiose ideas, fell apart around me. Not one of her ideas was in play.

Then there was a second Lady Mairead, not helpful, weakened and useless. She had nothing to offer to the situation, but I couldn't run away. If she was left behind she would be killed.

And there was the young woman in the corner. I couldn't leave her here.

I wished I had a weapon.

I wished I could punch that sneering woman sitting beside Sir Paddy.

I was literally in all the worst case scenarios.

FORTY-SIX - KAITLYN

But I had been told to tell Lady Mairead one thing.

I interrupted Sir Padraig's monologue to say, "Lady Mairead."

"What?" She sounded dazed — surprised I had spoken to her.

"I was told to tell you to run to Elmwood. Do you understand?"

She met my eyes and nodded.

Sir Padraig spluttered. "What are you talking about, you bitch? You aren't in *any* position to be advising anyone. Look at you, alone, unarmed, by now I have all the vessels. I have this machine, right here." He pulled the Trailblazer from his pocket. "By now I have the kingdom of Riaghalbane under my control, made certain by the death of your family, one by one, including the former King of Riaghalbane, whose heart fails as the last life blood squeezes from it. Death will be slow, but he is awfully young, that will be the poetry of it."

He kissed his fingers, like a chef's kiss, a motherfucking chef's kiss, like he was some fucking two-bit mobster in a movie, *acting* how he thought a mobster would act. He was in this old Hollywood restaurant, pretending he was going to take my life, my children's lives, pretending he was going to kill Magnus.

Rage filled my heart.

I hadn't had this kind of rage in me in a long time, but like an old familiar friend, I welcomed it. Let it fill me — blood coursing, heat and energy, like a goddamn exploding star.

I was the motherfucking matriarch.

Lady Mairead wasn't the matriarch, she was taking my orders.

It was me.

And this piece of shit was talking about killing my children? Killing Magnus?

Time slowed down. The man continued to talk, crowing about what he was going to do to me — my sight focused.

I thought about what Magnus had taught me through the

years: calm down, pay attention, watch your opponent, look for their weakness.

And boy did this dude have a weakness.

He had a way of talking that had him stretched back in his seat. That condescending, bullshit-talking, mansplaining kind of relaxed. His head was tilted back, so he was looking down his nose at me. He had a habit of gesturing with his left hand.

I looked at how his hand settled near my gun, but then lifted as he gestured, his neck exposed, his head turned. A pattern. I had found his weakness.

I said, "The crazy thing about this situation, if you think about it, is you've beaten us in literally every timeline, you're unstoppable. That's what Magnus was just saying to me the other day."

His head tilted, he nodded approvingly. He said, "Now, *that* is the first intelligent thing you've said this whole..."

His hand gestured

and I leapt.

My left hand on the table.

My hip crashed down on the plates, but I was fast, had caught him unawares,

I swung, the claw of my hand ripped down his cheek.

Fucking classic Katie temper there, fellas.

As Magnus had said back in the day, "What *that* tiny scratch?"

This was not a tiny scratch, this was talons, this was scarring — he was off balance, shocked, and I was right there, over him, above him. I had grabbed my gun from right in front of him.

He reached for it, tried to fight me, but I pushed his hands away with my left hand and fired with my right, right at his smug-ass evil psychopath face, and with a spray of blood and gore, Sir Padraig Stuart, the man who had been traumatizing and brutalizing my family was dead in a chair in front of me.

FORTY-SEVEN - MAGNUS

Quentin and I both turned tae look up on the mountain — above it a shelf of clouds, reachin' tae the heavens, gale force winds gyrating above the peak, wide and full and brutal. The storms spread in every direction, seeming tae cover the miles between the cave where the vessels were stored, and this castle where I stood powerless tae fight it.

I felt the blood rush from my head, m'vision disappeared tae pinpoints, a sharp pain as my knee hit the stone, and I collapsed forward tae the ground. I struggled tae right m'self — the kids were nae safe, I had tae protect them — Kaitlyn was nae here, *where was she?*

I looked up at the sky as the storm clouds suddenly rolled back upon themselves, and then 3,2,1... they were gone. Nae more wind, nae thunder or lightning, just the smell of fire and a black cloud of smoke replacin' the storm clouds as they retreated.

I grabbed m'chest and lost consciousness.

FORTY-EIGHT - KAITLYN

My heart pounded in my chest. A shrieking noise filled my ears, it came from myself but was matched by the young woman in the corner.

Lady Mairead, always the wiser, started going through his pockets, grabbing everything he was carrying and shoving it into her bag.

Agnie MacLeod tried to push Lady Mairead away and I aimed my gun at her. "Want a piece of me?" I said, because it was cool.

People were screaming outside the door. I climbed off the table, grabbed Agnie MacLeod, and held the gun to her head.

"Come with me," I said, repeating it over and over, trying to be soothing, but not for her, for me. I was trying to calm myself down. Blood was splashed all over me, making me feel nauseous and anxious. A memory slammed into me of that day, years ago, when I had killed Donnan in a horror bloodbath. " It's going to be okay, just come with me, this is fine," I held the gun to Agnie's head. "You're going to be fine, this is just a tragedy, I'm not usually like this. This isn't what I do. I'm a mom..."

I backed us from the room.

FORTY-EIGHT - KAITLYN

Rebecca rushed up to Lady Mairead and said, "Let me take off your choker."

Lady Mairead pulled up her hair and exposed the back of her neck. "Thank ye, dear."

I dragged Agnie to the exit as Lady Mairead and the young pregnant stranger named Rebecca ran past me out the door. Lady Mairead called over her shoulder, "We are goin' tae Elmwood, Kaitlyn, be safe!" as they burst out of the back door and raced down the dark back alley.

I made it out of the restaurant and shoved Agnie MacLeod down to the ground and pointed the gun at her. "Don't follow me!"

I turned and ran through the dark night. I was following Lady Mairead's shadow but she got to the end of the alley and turned right.

Not toward the hotel.

I heard old-timey style sirens wailing down the street. My feet pounded, my heart raced, or was it the freaking opposite? As I ran, I glanced down to see the gun still in my hand. I broke stride and kicked it behind a pile of disgusting smelling debris, then I ran again. I came around the corner and out onto a street full of people, all looking shocked, gawking at the sirens and the commotion — some turned to stare.

I said, "Oh my! There was a shooting! Down at the restaurant! I barely escaped with my life! Back that direction!"

The crowd cleared for me, stepped out of my way. I kept repeating, "Someone was shot! Over there! Down the street! I barely escaped!" I shoved my way through the crowd, aiming for the hotel, sure I would find the Original Lady Mairead here, there, somewhere.

I made it to the hotel. The doorman stepped in front of me, "What is...?"

"I'm a guest, room #310!"

"Lady Mai—"

"Yes! There was a shooting over at the restaurant! I was just there!"

He stepped back to let me pass saying something that I couldn't hear, couldn't understand, and didn't process. I staggered to the front desk, having forgotten the name of the man there that was supposed to give and take my things from the safe, whoever he was, I managed, "I need my things — Lady Mairead, I was just here."

He gestured me behind the desk, to hide my clothes, and opened the safe while I was mentally repeating, *faster, faster, faster, faster.*

He whispered, "Is Lady Mairead all right?"

"She's not here?" I looked dazedly around the grand lobby. "She was supposed to meet me here. Maybe she got detained. We were in the restaurant. There was a shooting."

"Hollywood has gone downhill with all these new people moving in here." He pulled a drawer from the safe. *Faster faster faster...* The tray hit the counter and I grabbed the vessel.

He said, "Lady Mairead won't tell me what it is..."

"Oh, this? It's just a... um..." I tried to think of the history of the twentieth century and what might have been invented in 1926 but I was incapable of any coherent thoughts, so I said, as I backed around the counter, "One of those thingies, you know, that does the blink-blinks?"

He looked at me blankly as I backed toward the front door.

"You know, it goes spinny, you know, one of those things."

"I have no idea what you are talking about."

I made it to the front doors. Surprised that Lady Mairead, the one that had persuaded me to do this bullshit errand, or the one that had been at the dinner — *neither* were here to meet me, to tell me what to do next, to join me in my escape.

But that's the thing about an escape, if they weren't in the getaway car when it was time to get away, they would miss the whole thing.

FORTY-EIGHT - KAITLYN

The doorman opened the door for me and I rushed out into the dark night in front of the hotel. It was barely lit, and cool for Los Angeles, I had forgotten my wrap. I rushed down the street to the corner and up a half block and freaking spun that vessel, reciting the numbers to myself, going to Kilchurn, the clearing, and hoping to get there to help with whatever was happening. What had dickwad said — something big was happening?

Well, guess what.

It wasn't that big, not anymore. Now he was dead. How big could his plan be when he died in the middle of it?

I would have cackled in evil mastermind laughter if I hadn't been so freaking scared.

FORTY-NINE - MAGNUS

꧁꧂

I opened my eyes to see Quentin crouched over me, yelling over his shoulder, "Get the kids! Everyone out to the field!"

Over his head the billowin' smoke of our castle, our home on fire, but nothing else. Nae explosions or wind or gunfire, just silence except for the sounds of men shouting from one tae the other instructions for the fire, or getting tae safety.

I grasped Quentin's shirt. "Are we under attack?"

"Nah, Boss, it stopped, out of nowhere, it just freaking stopped."

I tried tae sit up, but he pushed me back. "Lay your ass down, Boss, you are in no condition."

"I can, I can move." I tried tae move, but stopped as pain shot down my arms and everything grew dark.

∼

I rose out of blackness tae hear the voices, one of them, General Hammond, m'eyes fluttered open, trying tae see, "Tis Hammie?"

His face swam intae focus. "Yes, King Magnus, I have been

looking for you for a while, found you now, near dead on a castle wall that's about to burn to the ground."

"I thought ye were dead."

"Yep, nearly, we were hunkered down, a military onslaught that was impossible to live through, then it just ended. I lived to see another year, this one is when...?"

Quentin said, "1707."

"Great, really a great year, looks to be a ruin already."

Smoke drifted across overhead. I managed tae say, "Twas a lovely castle just hours ago. Has anyone seen Kaitlyn?"

Quentin shook his head, "Not back yet, and we got to get you out of here, you need a doctor." He stood, talking to someone on his radio.

"Where are the bairns?"

Hayley's face swam intae view. "Safe, ready to jump."

Quentin asked, "What year are we going to? I have Fraoch on the radio I need to let him know."

Hammond said, "You should bring Magnus to the kingdom, the physician can see him there."

"It's not rubble?"

"The palace is still standing, the infirmary is in operation. The attack ended, we don't know how or why. Luckily they weren't around long enough to do much damage."

Hayley asked, "How long have we been gone?"

"About two weeks."

Quentin groaned, "This time shit is crazy."

James rushed up, doubled over, out of breath. "They took Sophie! She's gone! Someone grabbed her and they disappeared in the storm!"

Quentin leapt tae his feet, "From here on the walls?"

James nodded.

Quentin said, "We need a headcount of everyone here, make sure no one else is missing."

He squeezed James's shoulder. "We'll figure it out."

James asked, "Where's Fraoch?"

Quentin said, "I just spoke to him by radio, he went tae guard the caves. He said he'd stay behind. I'll come back for him once we know how safe it is."

I managed tae say, weakly, "I daena want tae leave without..."

The last thing I heard was Hayley asking, "Is it okay to move him so far?" Before I went under again.

FIFTY - KAITLYN

Ugh. I was face down in leaves, damp, chilled leaves. I groaned and forced myself onto my side. I ached everywhere.

I needed some electrolytes.

I sighed and looked at my arm, splattered in dried blood.

I looked like a zombie, or some other terrifying remnant of a horror story gone wrong.

What had I done? I killed Sir Padraig. Like, *totally* dead.

Shit, my Dead Count was staggering considering I was some YouTuber from Florida.

It was practically serial.

And what had I done — had I stopped his plan? What if he was later life Sir Padraig? What if he already took over the kingdom, traumatized a grown Isla, killed a grown Archie?

But also, he had called Magnus a king, he wouldn't have called him that if he had overthrown him.

I had to believe he hadn't gotten past the first part of his plan to overthrow Magnus.

Unless...

I flipped onto my back and stared up at the sky, a bright blue, a chilly air.

I listened with everything I had, for any sound, any fighting. Nothing.

He had looked at his watch and said, 'It's begun.' Had he meant a battle?

Maybe not, but if not, why wasn't anyone here to meet me?

I sat straight up.

Why wasn't anyone here?

Shit shit shit. I lumbered to my feet and stretched and groaned from the pain of the jump. It felt like every square inch was aflame, but also, the air smelt like smoke.

My heart dropped.

I began to stagger in the direction of the castle.

There were people there, but I didn't see anyone important and I knew that sounded a shite thing to think but it was true. There were no guards up on the walls. A big plume of black smoke rose into the air, carts and horses were standing on the grass along the shore of Loch Awe, and there was a pile of discarded furniture and other things laying all over the grass.

I went to the edge of the loch and washed my arms and face in ice cold water, scrubbing off the blood and trying to get presentable, but I was in a dress from the wrong century. A Chanel design that was black, sequined, and smaller than a shift.

A woman rushed up with a wrap. "Och! Queen Kaitlyn! Ye are nae covered!"

"I know, thank you." I wrapped the tartan around my shoulders and tucked the edges in to keep it around. "Have you seen King Magnus?"

"I daena ken, Queen Kaitlyn, there was a terrible fightin', a battle, there was a storm and then a fire." She wiped her face with her apron. "I canna believe we survived."

"Did everyone survive? Where are my bairns? Archie and Isla?" She shook her head, no help at all.

I saw Eamag up in the grass, unloading cloth from a cart. I raced over and asked, "Chef Zach? Where is he?"

FIFTY - KAITLYN

"I daena ken, Queen Kaitlyn, I daena ken where anyone has gone."

I rushed up the causeway toward the smoldering castle, a long hike, especially when I was in pain all over, and walked across the courtyard, calling, "Quentin? James! Zach!"

I knew Magnus wasn't here. He would have been on a horse in the clearing when I returned, or up on the walls watching for me, in lieu of that, he would have been... on the mountain?

I looked in on the armory, the guns were gone, all that was left were empty shelves. I would have gone upstairs but there was smoke billowing out of windows on the second and third floors. I couldn't risk it though the fire seemed to have done its worst. There were black streaks up the wall, and over windows. A part of the roof over the kitchen was gone.

Zach must be bummed wherever he was.

I left the castle and walked back down the causeway to the outer stables and called inside, "I need a horse!"

Timmy emerged from the back.

I asked, "Where's Magnus? His horse, Cynric, is here, you haven't seen him?"

"Nae, daena ken."

"Anyone? Fraoch? Master James or Master Quentin? "

He shook his head.

"Okay then, well, I still need a horse." He brought me one of the gentle mares and tried to talk me into letting him accompany me.

He didn't need to. I thought I had been proving over and over again — I was plenty capable of whatever anyone needed me to do. I didn't need help, I had killed a man. I could do this alone.

I rode from the stable to the trail that led up to the cave on the side of Ben Cruachan.

∽

About a mile up the trail I wondered why the hell I was out here all by myself. That had been a whole lot of stuff happening back there, a battle, and... I probably ought to have had a chaperone. Why hadn't I brought that gun?

I continued to ride, I was exhausted but running on fumes. There was brown caked blood on my legs. The wrap didn't cover enough of me. It was too cold for what I was wearing and there was a catch-22: if I was in the sun the breeze was ice cold, if I was out of the wind the tree shade chilled me down.

I huddled on the horse and let it lead me up the trail.

Close to the cave, Fraoch waved from where he was sitting on a log, a small fire burning in front of him. "Och, ye are found!"

I neared and dropped down from my horse. "Oh my god! Thank God, Fraoch! I thought I had lost everyone again and I kinda thought I should stay put... but no one was here and it was eerie as hell — what happened, where are my kids, where's Magnus?" I shivered.

"Here, I hae a wrap for ye, ye look cold." He passed me up a blanket. "Why is there blood on ye?"

I looked down at my legs. "Um... apparently I murdered Sir Padraig. He totally had it coming though, so yeah..."

He squinted up at me. "Ye killed him? Is that why the battle ended so abruptly?"

"It abruptly ended, *really*?"

He nodded. "Aye, there was a battle, then it just ended."

"But then where is Magnus?"

"Och, he is nae well, Kaitlyn. Quentin told me on the radio. They hae taken him tae the kingdom tae see a physician. Tis the last thing I heard."

My heart sank. "What the hell is going on Fraoch? Everyone is alive, right? *Everyone?*"

"Aye, all are alive and accounted for, even General Hammond."

FIFTY - KAITLYN

My head reeled as I tied my horse to a tree beside his.

"Hammond is alive? I think you need to explain this all to me like I'm a child."

Fraoch launched into the story — there had been a huge attack, a multi-storm attack, on the castle and this cave, and then the castle had caught fire and in the melee Magnus had fallen unconscious.

I was so scared for him, but also a little pissed off. "I knew it, I knew he was still weak and I was right. He should have gone to the doctor, a doctor would have fixed him..." I sat down on the rock on the other side of the fire.

"What doctor would ye hae taken him tae? One in Florida? I daena think it would hae been smart, he is a king—"

"I guess that's true... but I can't believe he was so sick and—"

"And so ye killed Sir Padraig and then twas safe for Og Maggy tae go tae see the physician. If ye think on it, ye are both right."

I chuckled. "Where did you learn to do that 'you're both right' nonsense?"

"M'fine wife taught me tae agree tae us both being right, else she will always win."

"Sounds like her." I looked down at a spot of blood on the back of my hand and tried to wipe it with the edge of my wrap. "I'm the one who solved all of it, by shooting Sir Padraig?"

"I daena ken, but it sounds as if twas the cause. General Hammond shewed up soon after, I think, I daena ken for sure — Sadly, my walkie-talkie has nae juice anymore, but then there's nae one left tae talk tae."

"So that's a good question, where is Hayley?" The blanket he had given me to wrap around myself smelled like horse and dust.

"I offered tae stay here tae guard the cave, so she evacuated with the rest." I noticed a small puddle of something beside him.

I gestured with my head toward the boulder. "And everything is inside, it's all there, safe?"

He turned to look over his shoulder. I noticed a bit of a

wince as he did. "I daena ken, I canna push the boulder by m'self. I am guardin' it in faith."

"So what's that — are you bleeding, Fraoch? Are you wounded?"

He glanced down. "Och nae, I ken, tis naething." He opened the blanket and showed me a wound on his side. It was bleeding pretty good.

"That's not good, Fraoch, you need a doctor too, like now."

"Nae, this will heal well enough."

My eyes went wide. "First, Magnus, now you. You need a stitch, an antibiotic. I might have a kit back in the castle, but it might have caught on fire. Shit."

"I daena need a physician, and I need tae stay here, by the cave, tae make sure tis safe. Og Maggy would be guarding it if he could, tis up tae me."

I took a deep breath. "So I need to jump to the kingdom, the kids are there, too, right?"

"Aye, everyone went taegether, General Hammond said twas safe enough for them."

"Good, because last we saw it was a shitshow, am I right?"

"Aye, twas a steamin' pile of shite on a rocky shore of a polluted river."

"So modern of you to be an environmentalist."

"Now I hae seen different centuries, I am more cautious in how I would use something." He poked a stick in the fire. "Warm your hands and hae a drink with me. Ye are in nae condition tae jump yet, ye need tae rest first."

I warmed my hands over the fire.

He asked, "Hae ye ever thought about how ye, Kaitlyn, might take a shite, here in this castle and bury it under a tree, and then in another century ye might dig it up and say, that there is m'shite from hundreds of years ago?"

I grinned. "I think it would have been long decomposed by then, turned into something else."

"Like what?"

"Well, like nutrients for the tree, so like it's carbon, right? All living matter is made up of carbon, and so once shitted, or shat, or shited, however you say it, into the hole, it decomposes into dirt and nutrients. Then the tree drinks it up to grow. Therefore the carbon from inside of you turns to shite and then becomes part of the tree."

He passed me a hunk of bannock and I realized I was famished. I stuffed some of it in my mouth and while chewing said, "Here's something else. So say the tree is an apple tree, you pluck an apple off, you eat it, seeds and all—"

"Of course, the middle is the best part."

"You think? I'm not so sure..."

"Aye, the rest of the apple is just sweet and soft, if ye eat the middle there are different flavors and textures. Tis better when ye hae both."

"I never thought of it that way, you are probably right. And once you've eaten the whole apple, then you poop it out, seeds and all, and then your poop grows the tree and feeds the tree and you get more apples."

"Och," He looked up at the tree and joked, "That tree, right there, is m'child."

I laughed. "That is definitely one way to look at it. And that is called the circle of life."

"Aye, like the song in the lion movie. The bairns shewed me."

"Exactly like that." He pushed the stick around in the fire.

"I said, you're cool with not having kids right? I know Hayley is hardline about it, but... she loves you a lot, and—"

"I am all right on it, Kaitlyn, I ken her reasons and I share them. We are content tae be Aunt Hayley and Uncle Fraoch. Tis somethin' that suits us, and we would do anythin' for Archie and Isla, and for Ben and Zoe as well."

"I am so grateful for that, thank you." I took another bite of bread. "One thing I need to say, and this is awkward, but I met your mom."

He scowled. "Who, the lady by the name of Agnie Macleod, who sometimes goes by the name Jeanne Smith? Seems tae be all anyone can talk about these days."

"Yeah, she was with Sir Padraig, and... she was kind of a bitch. She lived through the encounter."

He snarled, "Och, I daena like tae ken I am the son of terrible person."

"Magnus too, you can commiserate with him. And the good thing is, you're not terrible, you turned out great."

He chuckled, "I turned out 'great' despite the fact I had terrible parents, because I am a great person, ask anyone." He grinned.

"True, everyone agrees. You've saved all our lives more than once." I finished off my bread. "So you should come with me, right?"

"Nae, I should guard, ye go on, tell Quentin tae come, bring some strong backs for the boulder, a small man for the dark cave. We might need tae move the vessels, I daena ken."

I stood. "I think you're right about the rest, but I'm too desperate to see Magnus and make sure he's okay. I'll tell Quentin you're here — tomorrow morning so that there's no looping, sound good?"

He nodded.

"I hate to leave you."

"Och, I am a Scottish man on the side of a ben. Ye canna worry on leavin' me here, tis m'natural habitat.

FIFTY-ONE - KAITLYN

I moved off to a clearing that had trees bent, broken, and uprooted, fallen to the ground. The destruction of the woods looked fresh as if it had been destroyed by a recent storm. From my view I could see Kilchurn, my home until just a few days ago. The castle, now with a destroyed roof and one wall crumbling, looking more like the ruin it would someday become, instead of the home I had loved — and had also grown so tired of.

I wondered if my things were gone? I was wearing my jewelry, but had anything else been retrieved from my rooms?

Or was it all left, to disintegrate into the ground around the castle, beaten down by time?

I looked over my shoulder at Fraoch, also left, the last guard of the hoard of vessels. His back rounded as he sat on the rock, a blanket wrapped around his shoulders, a wince in his eyes, he had been trying to hide it but I had seen it clearly. He was injured and in pain.

There was something very melancholy and desolate about the way he looked and I wished I was better at convincing people to go to the freaking doctor.

I waved and he waved back.

. . .

I twisted the vessel to go not a reasonable amount of far but a whole lot of too far. Right to the kingdom of Riaghalbane, right to the rooftop where the king was allowed to jump in and out, last time I had been there it had been a lost cause.

This was definitely a leap of faith.

What or who would meet me once I was there?

FIFTY-TWO - KAITLYN

I woke up on the tarmac as voices above me said, "One two three — lift." It was night, stars above, partially obliterated by the spotlights on the rooftop.

My body was lifted up, weightless-like, and then I was deposited on a stretcher. I made eye contact with one of the soldiers. "Friends?"

Another voice said, "Queen Kaitlyn, I am here."

I looked up to see General Hammond smiling down at me as my stretcher was pushed through the wide doors leading into the palace hallway, once a place full of art plunder and now bare.

I said, "I'm so glad you're alive, I don't know if Magnus told you, but he needed you desperately."

"I am glad tae be alive as well and the king did not mention his desperation for me, but I assure you the feeling was mutual."

I laughed and then moaned, because everywhere was pained. "I can get up, I think. I can walk. I need to go see Magnus."

"We know, we're taking you to the infirmary. I don't think you can see him until you've been checked, there's dried blood all over—"

"It's not *my* blood, it's the brains of my enemy."

The soldier to my right chuckled.

I joked, "You liked that?"

"Yes, Your Highness."

Hammond said, "I can see the pain of the jump has worn off, if you can joke —who is the enemy you're speaking of?"

"Not 'is', *was,* it was Sir Padraig Stuart, now nothing but a horrible memory."

"You did this?"

"Hell yeah. Lady Mairead planned it. Is she here by the way?"

"No, not yet."

"Well, she'll probably want to make an entrance."

Walls were busted and doors were broken down. The business of the kingdom was being run while the inhabitants were clearing out the rubble of the last siege.

God I hoped this was *definitely* the last siege.

I was wheeled into the infirmary through the long hallway with rooms on either side and there were family and friends waiting in the waiting room with my children. Isla pushed out of Beaty's arms and ran toward me, "Mama! Mama!"

I swung my legs off the stretcher and about leapt off it in mid-motion and caught Isla as she ran into my arms and then Archie held onto me and I fell back onto my butt but it was better down there on the ground being hugged. "Were you scared?"

Archie said, "I was so worried something happened to you!"

"I didn't mean to scare you, I had to handle something. I'm so sorry I wasn't there when the big—"

Isla looked at me with her big doe-eyes. "Big fire."

"I heard, did it scare you?"

She shook her head.

Archie said, "She was really scared."

"I'm so grateful you are both here."

FIFTY-TWO - KAITLYN

Hayley said, "Yeah, well, what the hell, Katie, *seriously*? You just disappeared."

"I had to handle something, I knew it was something I had to do and I didn't have time to talk first—"

"You always have time, you just have to make it — you're a time traveler."

I sighed. "You know that's not true, I have had emergencies. I have had accidents, and though I know, I one hundred percent know I need to always let someone know where I'm going, there are exceptions. I had to break the rules this time."

She huffed. "I'm irritated with you, but glad you're home. But still irritated with you."

"I get it, I truly do, but I would do it again."

"Well, you're wrong about—" Our maid came in just then and interrupted Hayley and me, asking if I needed food.

I said, "I am so hungry, it's like I haven't eaten since the twentieth century. Though there was a wee bit of bannock in the eighteenth century with Fraoch." I said to Hayley, "*That's* why you should be nicer to me, I bring you word from your loving husband."

She humphed. "Thank god, you're finally doing something helpful. Did he send sweet messages? We're going to go get him as soon as the supplies are gathered."

"I hate to say it, he's injured and it doesn't look great, but he would not come with me to go to a doctor."

Hayley said, "Fine, I forgive you. It was really bad?"

"I don't know. But you need to go get him. And we need a plan for the vessels so he will actually leave that cave."

Quentin said, "Did you happen to see Madame Sophie?"

"Wait... what?" I glanced over at James by himself leaning against the wall. "James, where's Sophie?"

"She disappeared into the storm, someone grabbed her, right as it stopped — she was gone."

"I didn't see her when I was there. I'm so sorry."

Quentin said, "Hammond and I will come up with a plan

for picking up Fraoch and moving the vessels, once Magnus is out of surgery he can give us orders."

James said, "Maybe Sophie is there again. I'll go with you, maybe we'll find her."

Quentin met my eyes, he was worried of course, a missing person in time was a real worry. It was heartbreaking to wait for them to return, impossible to follow if you didn't know exactly where they were, because where was she? When? And she had never time traveled before. I said, "Yeah, maybe she's there, probably she is."

I looked up at Beaty and around at all my friends. "Thank you for getting Magnus, Archie, and Isla here safely."

I lumbered achingly to my feet while groaning a lot. Zoe was asleep in Emma's lap but the rest of the kids were all there, wide awake, listening, "Hey, all you guys, cover your ears and close your eyes. You too Ben."

Archie, Isla, and Ben all covered their eyes.

I whispered for all the adults, "So I killed Sir Padraig."

They all looked astonished.

Quentin asked, "Where? When?"

"In a restaurant in Hollywood, in the year 1926. It's going to be one of those gruesome stories that will give the restaurant a reason to have historical murder-tours for the next century."

Quentin said, "That's why the battle stopped in its tracks?"

"I guess so?"

Zach said, "It was crazy, the storm disappeared and the people were just gone, no more warriors, no more anything—"

James said, "No more Sophie."

"Yeah, she got caught in the withdrawal of the troops. But if it wasn't for that, or the fire, we might have been able to go about our business."

"Weird."

"Yeah, weird."

We told the kids they could uncover their ears and eyes.

FIFTY-THREE - KAITLYN

Then I asked, "So Magnus is in one of these rooms?"

General Hammond said, "Yes, Queen Kaitlyn, he's here."

He gestured down the hall. "You'll need to go wash up first."

I crouched down and kissed Archie and Isla. "I'm going to go talk to your da. I will be back in a moment."

I went through to the bathroom and washed my arms and my face, rubbing my skin raw practically, to get the murder and centuries of filth off me. There were a pair of scrubs stacked on the counter, and like years ago, under a different king, in totally different circumstances, I dressed to go to my husband's bedside. I tossed the 1920's-style dress off, peeled off the torn stockings, and pulled on the scrubs. Because the lights were dimmed, giving the hospital an air of hushed sleeping-time, I tiptoed to the door of Magnus's room.

His room was dark, a four poster bed, luxurious bedding, but with machines beside it, a bag of liquids going into his arm. I did not like seeing him hooked up to machines again.

He said, "M'heart is nae workin' again, mo reul-iuil."

I pushed a chair up to the bed and sat beside him holding

his hand. "I learned something while I was in Los Angeles, you have something wrong with your heart, it's hereditary."

"Och, I heard it. The physician saw it on the records and on the images. It caused m'heart attack and now there are scars upon m'heart. None had ever mentioned it before — how would ye ken it?"

"Sir Padraig told me, he read it in your medical records..."

He dropped his head back on the pillow. "Ye were with Sir Padraig Stuart?"

"I killed him."

"Och, are ye all right?"

"Yes," I said it but tears welled up in my eyes all the same.

I wrapped my fingers around his.

He said, "Tell me about it."

"Your mother asked me to come help her, she had been looping, so it was all out of control."

"She is lucky she dinna get herself killed."

"Yeah, she was in deep. She had this whole plan, for me to go to dinner, and that I would disrupt the meeting, cause it to go differently, but guess what?"

His voice was quiet. "He kent ye were comin'?"

"Exactly, and he was awful, totally malicious, just like you said. He took my weapons and he was being all cocky and—"

"Ye never allow a man tae be cocky without breakin' him down — did ye cause him cry?"

"No, but I did cause him to be dead. You would have been so proud of me, I watched him until I found his weakness."

"The movement he makes with his hand when he is talking?"

"I saw it and counted on it and then I lunged across the table and clawed his face. I was able to grab my gun and without thinking I pulled the trigger. Killed him dead."

"Good."

I looked down at his hand, the structure of it, thick and strong, the veins running through it. The skin soft on the back, so rough on the front. I kissed it.

FIFTY-THREE - KAITLYN

"Och, Kaitlyn, they are goin' tae cut me open."

I pulled his hand closer and wrapped up around it.

"They tell me they are goin' tae cut through m'artery and go up through m'groin, and clean out the scar tissue from m'heart attack. My heart was weakened and now tis full of scars. They said tis called a heart rejuvenation."

I said, "That sounds not so bad, right? How will they do it?"

He gave me a sad smile. "Twill be robots, Kaitlyn, I will hae robots inside of me. A man from the eighteenth century with robots in his heart."

"That is the perfect use of robots, if you think about it." I rested my cheek on his hand. "And what did the physician say — would it be easy to accomplish?"

"Och nae, tis robots, Kaitlyn. I daena think robots are ever easy."

"Well, the good news is that *then* you'll be able to recover. It's been a long time without being able to recover. And now we know. We can make you strong again. That will be good, right?"

"Aye."

"You don't have to be scared."

"Och, I am nae scared, I am never scared."

I pushed some hair off his forehead and smoothed it back.

"I'm not scared either." I kissed him. "This is great news, your heart is strong. You have just been trying to work against something you were born with, and now we can fix it."

The physician entered the room. "Queen Kaitlyn, the king will need to go in for the surgery now."

I sighed and kissed Magnus again. "I love you, don't be scared."

He gave me a weak smile. "What hae I got tae be scared of? M'wife is a terrible arse, she has fought m'enemy and won. I hae my kingdom once more. This is just something I hae tae go through and then I will rule."

"True, and you'll be through it in no time. Did you already tell the children you love them?"

"I did, they ken. Do ye ken it?"

"I do, my love, I ken it everywhere. I haven't ever got any doubt about it." I smoothed his hair again, and patted his chest. "I'll see you on the other side my love."

The physician said, "King Magnus, Your Majesty, we are taking you in now."

My husband was moved from the bed to a stretcher and wheeled into the operating room. I stood and watched the swinging door, where he had gone away.

FIFTY-FOUR - KAITLYN

I returned to the sitting room, sat on a couch and my kids curled up on and beside me. I kissed both their foreheads and held them close.

"What are we going to do about Da?" asked Archie.

"There is nothing to do but wait. He has to have surgery and while he does, we are going to hold onto each other and be gentle with each other because we might be scared. We might cry, we might feel angry, and we will pray that he will be all better when it's over. Does that sound good?"

"Aye," he said. Then he said, "I'm hungry."

"Me too." There were trays of food on a table at the side of the sitting room. Plain white bread sandwiches and cut veggies and dips for the kids, plus plain potato chips.

Zach grumbled, "It tastes like food from the eighteenth century, I wanted something special."

Emma said, "Like what?"

"I don't know, a cookie bar, or like, spaghetti carbonara, or... could've been ice cream."

Quentin had his head back on the couch. "Can't have ice cream until Magnus is out of surgery."

I asked, "Hayley, when are you and Quentin going to leave?"

"Hammond is gathering supplies. I want to go, but he told us to eat something and get some rest while he's organizing our supplies for the trip."

Beaty went to the table and returned to the couch with a cola poured into a glass with ice. "I am verra excited tae drink this, but remember when I was verra sick from it? The first time I ever jumped?"

I said, "I remember it so well, you drank that whole gigantic Coke and then you heaved all over and—"

Beaty clapped a hand over her mouth. "Daena say it, Queen Kaitlyn, ye will get me started again and it has been a long time with nae good food. I want tae keep it all inside."

"Did you bring Mookie? Is he okay?"

"Aye, we were able tae bring him with us. He was terribly frightened but he is goin' tae be fine now. They winna allow me tae bring him in the hospital though, tis a shame, I am sure ye want tae see him."

"I do desperately."

I watched the door, it would probably be hours before we knew anything, at least two. Ben was spider-monkey-asleep on Zach's lap. Zoe was asleep in Emma's arms.

Beaty was beside me cross-legged, a plate of food in front of her. James at the end of the couch, staring into space, his eyebrows knit, deep thinking.

"How you doing, James?"

"Not good, she was pulled away from me, I didn't... I keep reliving it."

"There are so many moments like that. I'm sorry."

I looked down at Archie, rubbing his eyes trying to stay awake, and Isla tucked against my side, her mouth open, deep sleeping, drooling.

I whispered, "We have our apartments. You could all go up there, it's just a different floor."

James said, "You forgot we blew out a whole section of the building with the helicopter when we were rescuing Magnus."

FIFTY-FOUR - KAITLYN

"Oh shit. That feels like a long time ago. It still happened?"

He said, "Yes indeed."

"I'm sure there are a ton of other guest rooms though, with the royal residence exploded and the recent war, I doubt there are many visitors."

Emma said, "We don't need a room, not yet. I can't leave this room until I know how Magnus is."

"Thank you... as soon as I offered I kind of regretted it. I don't really want to be alone."

Emma said, "That's the thing about having a big family, you're never alone."

"True." I leaned my head back on the pillows. "But oh man, I was so alone in Los Angeles..." I glanced down to see that Archie was sleeping and then I told them the story again, more, longer and detailed. I told them about the hotel and Lady Mairead's rooms, and her well-laid plan that had been a pile of horse poop *before* I even walked into the restaurant. I had to answer Zach's questions about the restaurant and the food, and then the play-by-play of what went wrong: everything, literally everything went wrong. Then finally about how I killed Sir Padraig and rescued Lady Mairead and the young pregnant woman and then escaped through the streets of Hollywood. By then almost everyone was asleep except Zach, Emma, Hayley, James, and Quentin — we were whispering in the darkened room.

James said, "And you never saw Lady Mairead, the first or the second one, again?"

"I don't know where she went. I took her vessel. She said she had one in New York—"

Quentin said, "Did she say it was in a closet in a house on the Upper East Side?"

"Yeah, I never heard of it before, how did you know?"

"Magnus started talking about it the other day."

I shrugged. "Looks like I've got more real estate. What's worrisome though is I've got a Lady Mairead situation, possibly two of them." I stared off into space. "Unless... unless she knew she was dangerously looping, she did seem very cavalier about it. Maybe she purposely left so there wasn't a chance of looping with herself."

Hayley said, "She left you stranded?"

"Nah, she left me with a pisspoor plan, a terrible situation, and barely a chance of survival, but she didn't leave me stranded. She told me exactly where the vessel was."

James shook his head. "That lady is something else."

"True."

Quentin said, "I can't believe you shot Sir Padraig."

"I scratched his face too. Wish there had been a YouTube video of *that* one, I was pretty proud of it. Magnus taught me what to look for; I saw my moment and took it. And Hayley, I even used that jump-on-the-table move we practiced."

Hayley said, "That is so badass, I forgive you for everything."

"Yeah, if ever a murder deserved a complete wipe-clean of all the bad I've done, it would be that one."

James said, "That shit was self-defense. And I can't believe you scratched his face. I always said, don't cross Katie."

I said, "That mofo crossed me *hard*." We all chuckled.

James said, "I need to go, I need to be doing something productive. Mind if I head down to help Hammond?"

Quentin said, "That's probably a good idea."

James left.

Hayley said, "How is he going to find her?"

I said, "I don't know. Maybe she can get us a message somehow... but would she even know how to do that? Or why?"

I stared off considering impossibilities. "You would have to understand the future to know how to send a message, I don't think she'd be able to, we just have to find her, make lists of possible places."

Hayley said, "Hope she stays put and waits."

"Yep."

Emma said, "Maybe if we research from here, look for her."

FIFTY-FOUR - KAITLYN

There weren't shifting images on these walls, because it was a hospital waiting room, but... "All I have to do is ask."

One of the shifting images projected on the far wall, almost as if it read my mind. "Yes, Queen Kaitlyn?"

"I need to find someone, a Sophie Cook, Scotland in 1707."

"I have a wedding record for Sophie Cook, married to James Cook in 1706."

"Do you have any other record of Sophie Cook, after 1706?"

A moment later, "No, there is no record of Sophie Cook after 1706."

"What about before 1706, like between 1552 and 1710?"

"There is no record of a Sophie Cook between those years, Sophie was formerly named Sophie Campbell and then Sophie Milne, wife of the Astronomer—"

"Yeah yeah, that's not that helpful." I sighed. "We don't know what her name would be, or what... wait, what is her birthdate? That would help."

"I have no birthdate for Sophie Campbell later Milne and then Cook. Usually this is because of poor record keeping in those centuries."

I grumbled, "True, or she was born in a different century, and you're not being smart enough."

Beaty, her eyes wide, said, "She could be from any century if ye think on it."

Hayley said, "Yes, that's a whole consideration—"

Beaty said, "What if she is related tae one of us?"

Quentin said, "She might be, but more likely she isn't, there are a lot of people in the world."

She nodded. "Aye, but nae time travelers. I daena think there are many of those."

Emma said, "I'll start looking tomorrow."

Zach said, "Now we're here, I really hope we can go back to Florida. I missed it."

Quentin acted incredulous. "I've been running votes for

months, and you wouldn't vote with me. We might have done this earlier."

Zach said, "But that would have meant going against the boss. I'm not going against Magnus."

We all looked at each other and sighed.

I said, "He's going to be fine, right? I mean, what happened? Same as before?"

Quentin said, "Yeah, the same as before, but also, there was something really scary about it, like — I don't know if we noticed how weak he had gotten. Before it was as if a healthy man had his heart stop, now it was like he was weak and it was just ending for him."

Zach said, "It was chilling."

I said, "We had a horrible fight about it just a few nights ago. I wanted to do something, he was worried about all of us. I wasn't okay with that, I felt desperate. Then Lady Mairead sent the the message and I just had to go try something else."

Hayley joked, "Once you set your mind to something..."

"Yep, I'm relentless. It's one of my biggest failings. Everyone knows it. But also, I killed that guy who was menacing us."

Quentin chuckled. "Are you going to say that all the time?"

"I might get it printed on a T-shirt. Maybe a new family motto. It could be a coat of arms. It could say 'Campbell' with sea grass and a sword, maybe a heart, the word 'time' in Gaelic, what would that be, Beaty?"

Beaty said, "It would be ùine, but ye might want tae hae it say Tempus Omegas, like the vessels."

"Ooh, that's a good idea. Then under it a motto: 'I killed that guy who was menacing us.'"

Hayley said, "I like it, nice and threatening like all good family shields should be, but maybe a little too serial killer sounding, maybe it should be like time jumping."

I said, "Or 'entangled'."

I took another bite of my sandwich. "But he is going to be okay, right?"

FIFTY-FOUR - KAITLYN

Zach said, "Of course he is. He's at the royal hospital, the royal physicians are working on him. He's going to be fine."

A look passed between him and Quentin and my heart sank to my toes.

Zach joked, "I miss Eamag already."

Emma laughed. "That was one of our more interesting friendships in our year in the past."

"Who would have thought I'd have so much in common with an old lady who was born mid-seventeenth century?"

Emma asked, "Did you have a lot in common with her? From my standpoint, it looked like a lot of arguing."

He said, "True, there was a lot of arguing. I really miss having a fucking kitchen all to myself."

We had a long pause.

I adjusted Archie because he was heavy on my side, but the good kind. I had been without him enough of my life that I never begrudged his sleeping against me. Soon enough it would be gone, he would have grown out of it.

Tears welled up in my eyes. "What would I do without Magnus?"

"You don't have to think about it, it's not going to happen," said Quentin. Then he joked, "Who am I kidding though, I can't live without him, either."

Zach said, "He's the greatest goddamn thing that ever happened to me."

"More than Emma?"

"If it hadn't been for Magnus, Emma would have left me years ago. It was that stability, the fact that someone trusted me the way Magnus did, that got me to grow up."

Quentin said, "Yeah, me too. I would probably be mall security right now, riding around on a Segway, harassing kids for gathering in groups of more than three."

The house manager, Marie, entered, "Your Highness, I have some guest rooms made up, enough for everyone, I think."

"Thank you. Can you find some changes of clothes? I know we need to be fresher than this to be in a hospital."

"I'll see what I can find." She bowed out of the room, something I would need to get used to again.

∽

Hammond and James returned.

"I have the supplies ready for your trip. There are plenty of weapons, I urge you to remain on guard, and to go fast, once the vessels are out of the cave anything could happen, you ought to have an army with you, but that in itself would be dangerous."

Quentin said, "We'll go fast."

Hayley jumped from her seat. "We'll definitely go fast."

To me she said, "I'm going to go get Fraoch, we'll be back tomorrow. Sorry I won't be here right now."

I said, "I understand, you need to go get him, I'll see you tomorrow."

She air kissed us all since there were so many sleeping people in the group. Then they left. Quentin saying, "Tell Boss as soon as he wakes up that I won the vote, I knew I would eventually."

And then Hayley, Quentin, and James left to go look for Sophie and relieve Fraoch from his watch.

FIFTY-FIVE - KAITLYN

*E*ventually, a doctor came out to tell me that the surgery was more complicated than they thought and it would take longer and...

Emma startled awake when he entered and moved to sit beside me on the couch with her arm around me while I listened.

Magnus's situation was 'complicated'. The doctor stood with his hands behind his back, head down. He had the sound of someone delivering 'news' and trying for it not to sound positive or negative and, like any human, that made me try to guess what he was hiding. My brain was whirring and I couldn't make out all he was saying: performing a minimally-invasive heart surgery... usually... would take a few hours... but... more difficult... he guessed... it would be longer... before we knew.

He would let me know.

Images flashed in my mind: Magnus on his back, surgeons cutting into him.

I was shaky and very very afraid, and as soon as the physician walked out of the room the tears began to flow.

Emma held on around my shoulders and passed me tissues until I was able to regain my composure.

But I couldn't talk, or think, nothing coherent. I was flooded in fear, riding it like a whitewater rapid. It was one ongoing mid-level panic attack and my coping skills were shite.

I just stared into space as hour after hour passed by.

Then the doctor re-entered the room. "Your Highness, the surgery is done, the king has come through very well. We were able to clean out the scar tissue. The arteries are like new. We believe there will be a full recovery."

Zach and Emma cheered, quietly, but still it was enough commotion to wake the kids. Isla began to cry, of course, because that's how she would do.

"Thank you, thank you so much, I'm so relieved," I said.

"He's sleeping now, he should sleep until the morning. I recommend everyone go get some rest in real beds."

He left down the hall and I hugged everyone and then we lifted kids off couches and the house manager led us down the hall. I dropped Zach and Emma and their kids off in the Green Suite, Beaty in the Silver Suite, and then carried Isla and led Archie into the Gold Suite, the nicest guest room we had since the royal apartment was a ruin.

I dropped Isla into the middle of the bed. She asked, "Da sleepy?"

"Yes sweetie, he's sleeping. We'll get to see him in the morning."

Archie threw his arms around my waist and I held onto him. "You heard the physician? He's good."

"I ken," he said, nodding.

I leaned down and kissed the top of his head. "Climb up in bed, you're pretty filthy, but we'll have to do a proper wash tomorrow."

He climbed under the covers beside his sister. While I went to the bathroom and took a shower, washing every crack and crevice three times, shampooing and conditioning, then I dried off in a towel remembering how much Magnus had missed towels.

And thinking, 'He was right, freshly laundered, soft towels *are* the pinnacle of human existence.' I wrapped a towel in my hair, pulled on a robe, and climbed into bed too, with sparkle and shine and hope for tomorrow.

I was out of bed at dawn. It had only been a couple of hours of sleep but I made up for it in excitement. And coffee in my freaking room.

Emma and Beaty came to help Archie and Isla get cleaned up while I ate a couple of bites of a delicious pastry, but not much because my stomach was empty, but churning with dread. Everyone else was moaning in ecstasy over the food while the kids splashed in the bathtub.

I kissed them goodbye and left for the infirmary. Emma and Beaty would bring the kids as soon as Magnus was officially awake and ready to see them.

I was so thankful for the help, I couldn't be a good enough mom right now, I was too busy being a barely-hanging-in-there wife.

The hallways of the palace were full of people and activity, especially workers, builders, renovators. It was a little like when Balloch castle was being built centuries ago. People nodded and bowed as I walked by, "Your Highness," they said, or "Good morning," and, "Welcome back."

But then the doors to the infirmary opened and it was quiet, dark, and desolate. I gulped. I was definitely feeling a mood.

I passed through the waiting room to his room, and in the middle of the four poster bed, Magnus was still asleep.

FIFTY-SIX - MAGNUS

Waking up in the infirmary was difficult. Twas as if I was comin' up from a swim, much like when I had almost drowned outside of the fort in St Augustine. There was a long time where I could nae focus, and went in and out of sleep. Then I was finally able tae open m'eyes and take in the room: twas a dim light, a comfortable bed, a good temperature, a lack of smell as if twas clean, unlike the castle in the eighteenth century that had every kind of smell at once. Then as I awoke I felt sharp pain shootin' through my body, from all over, but an uncentered ache. It caused me tae focus, and cleared m'head of sleep.

My eyes traveled across the room tae the window, darkened by drapes, but standing there, my Kaitlyn. She held the edge of the drapes open, staring out the window, a slight line of sunlight across her pensive face. She looked beautiful and I felt calm rush over me, a feeling that I was goin' tae be a'right.

She noticed I was awake and turned tae smile upon me, her face gone from downhearted tae pleased in a moment of time — just a breath from sadness tae seeing me.

Yes.

Aye.

FIFTY-SIX - MAGNUS

"Hi you."

My voice was a croak. "Hello, mo reul-iuil."

She neared my bed. "What were you thinking about just then?"

"How fine tis tae hae ye tae wake up tae."

"That's nice of you to say, but is it really true?"

"Aye, that and that my whole body is in fiery pain."

She sat down on the edge of the bed and pushed buttons for the nurse. "I think we can solve this. There are enough bells and whistles and tubes sticking out of your body. There should be a way to put pain relief in."

"Tis like that first time I returned from time travel."

"Yes, it is, except this hospital room is a lot more luxurious, and I'm an old mom of two now."

"Och, ye are as young and beautiful as the first time I laid m'eyes upon ye,"

She smiled. "When I was hungover, driving you around in the Prius?"

I said, "Aye, twas a merry sight, I kent I had seen yer bare arse just hours before."

"Ha. Tell me more. I missed you and I was worried that you were not going to come out of the surgery and I was really scared."

"Sounds like ye might hae been worried ye had unsaid things for me tae hear."

"You are a smart man." She took my hand.

The nurse came bustling in. "How are you feeling, Your Majesty?"

"Terrible."

She said, "Good, you're awake and ready for more medicine, so that's how you *should* feel." She took my temperature and a few other vitals and adjusted the flow of the tube running into m'arm, then she left.

I felt my body relax.

Kaitlyn said, "I wanted you to know you're my whole life and I love you."

I said, "Ye should be closer when ye say these nice things tae me."

She lay down beside me and held my hand and wrapped around my arm. "Is that better?"

I placed my hand between her thighs "Aye, I can hear ye better when yer gardens are pressed against me. Ye ken tis where the hearing happens."

She laughed. "I think you might be feeling the pain meds."

"Nae, but if ye think on it, tis m'manliness where all m'thoughts are happening, so if ye want tae speak tae me ye should be verra verra close."

"It's your manliness where your hearing is?"

"Aye, m'whole brain, everything is right there." I waved m'hand around my middle.

She laughed again. "And here I thought it was in your ears where you heard things."

"Nae, I am a highlander from the eighteenth century — nae, I was born in the seventeenth century. I was born in 1681, did ye ken?"

"I did ken."

I said, "And in 1681 we dinna hae ears yet, twas all about our swords."

"This is such an interesting thing to learn. So what you're saying is that whenever I speak to you, all this time, it's been your cock that is the one listening?"

"Aye, m'cock, he hears what ye are saying first, and then m'cock decides what tae do with it."

She whispered in m'ear, "But what if I tell you something like this. You're sure it's not your ear that hears?"

I patted m'cock. "Nae, see, the whispering got my cock coming tae attention. I canna believe ye dinna ken this, Kaitlyn, m'cock is the center of all of me, ye ken it, ye hae been married tae me."

"I do, now that you mention it, I really do."

"Good, I am glad ye ken it." I yawned long and loud.

"You sleepy again?"

"Nae. I just woke up, I might go up on the walls tae do guard duty if the physician would follow m'orders. I told him twas a command..." I kissed her forehead. "He would nae listen... what was I saying?"

"I have no idea, but I am so glad you are doing so..."

I couldna stay awake any longer.

FIFTY-SEVEN - HAYLEY

"Quentin! Why isn't he here? Did he not see the storms?"

"I don't know, maybe he's just waiting at the cave. Maybe he doesn't want to leave it."

James was already up looking through binoculars in the direction of the castle. Sweeping them along the hillside.

"I don't know, that sucks, I thought he would be here, and it's freaking me out that he isn't. Let's go!"

We had two ATVs, James hopped on one. "I'm headed to the castle. Got your walkie-talkie?"

Quentin and I hopped on the second ATV with a trailer hitched to the back for loading up the vessels and jumping them to the castle. We had landed north of the castle instead of the clearing to the south, so we would be closer to the caves.

This whole time, whenever I was nervous about Fraoch, Quentin would say, "He's fine, we're going to go get him."

Now he looked nervous. It was not at all a good sign that Fraoch hadn't come to meet us. Quentin raced us up the hill following a lightly traveled foot path until we came to the cave.

Fraoch was on the ground on his side.

Quentin slammed the ATV to a stop and I leapt off the side. "Fraoch! Fraoch!"

FIFTY-SEVEN - HAYLEY

He moaned.

"Fraoch!" I crouched beside him. "Honey, what's going on?" I looked down in his face. "What's happening?"

He muttered something but it sounded more like a groan.

I patted all around him, he was wrapped in a wool blanket, his roll of yarn sitting on a rock, his knitting lay in the dirt. He had been walking to the woods and had fallen down and hadn't gotten back up.

I pulled his shirt away and saw the wound on his abdomen. "Quentin!"

He said, "Crap, that looks bad. Let me grab the medic kit."

I said, "We should dress it, right? What should we do?"

"We gotta get him to a hospital, antibiotics, he needs them fast." He pulled out his two way radio. "James, we have a situation... Fraoch is not good... we gotta get him back." Quentin looked over his shoulder at me beside Fraoch. "We gotta do it now."

James's voice through the radio, "Fuck!"

"I know, just come back, we'll figure the rest of it out."

Quentin gave a weak try pushing the boulder, of course it didn't budge.

We could hear James's ATV coming closer. Finally he pulled up in the clearing and said, "Fraoch, what's up man? You do not look good."

Fraoch groaned.

"He doesn't sound good either. We moving this boulder?"

I jumped up to help and the three of us heaved it aside.

Quentin said, "Okay, look, I'm going into the cave, I'll pass out the vessels to you."

He passed me a gun. "Hold this weapon, you're standing guard while we get the chests from the cave."

I stood over Fraoch with my gun drawn. "Hold on, hold on, sweetie, it's an infection, just hold on," while Quentin crawled through the tunnel.

A few moments later James was quickly pulling out the safe

boxes, then the metal chest, then another safe box, and then a small stack of books.

Quentin climbed out of the cave and brushed off his pants. It was clear Quentin had parked the trailer too far away.

James ran with a chest jostling to the trailer. "Dude, crappy parking job."

"I see that. What am I going to do, take the time to move it? You're almost done." Quentin picked up the books and ran them to the trailer.

James rushed past, lugging another crate.

I grabbed a chest and yelled, "Less talking, go faster!"

As James lugged one more crate, Quentin padlocked a strap over it all. Then, James, full of angst driven energy, grabbed Fraoch under the arms, Quentin grabbed his legs, and they lugged him to the trailer. I gathered up all of Fraoch's knitting.

Quentin talked to him, "You cool man? You cool, right? You should have told us you were injured — we didn't know. Why ya gotta go being a hero?"

They placed Fraoch right beside the trailer.

James said, "I don't have time to look for Sophie, right? What am I going to do?"

"You can stay here. It'll give you a chance to take all these supplies to the castle. Find out what they need. I'll come back for you tomorrow. Then we'll do some supply runs for them."

James said, "Okay, that sounds good. Come tomorrow." He climbed on his ATV.

Quentin said, "Shit, I do not like leaving any man behind."

I said, "Me neither. But we don't have time, we need to go."

Quentin sat on the lockbox on the trailer and we held hands while he twisted the vessel. "Next stop the landing pad in Riaghlabane," and time-jumped us back to the future future.

∽

FIFTY-SEVEN - HAYLEY

Quentin was on top of me, climbing up, groaning from the pain.

"Get off me." It was hard to tell where I ended and all the other bodies began and the problem was Fraoch was heavy, hard, and still. "Shit shit, get up!"

Hammond's voice, "What is going on with Fraoch MacLeod?" He put his fingers on Fraoch's neck, then freaked me out by saying loudly, "We need a stretcher and life support, now!"

Paramedics descended on Fraoch, while I pushed myself away so I wouldn't interfere, curled up around my knees, my eyes pressed against my kneecaps, so I wouldn't have to see.

He was taken away, up on a stretcher, and rushed down the hallway toward the infirmary with men around him trying to save his life.

I stood wringing my hands.

Quentin said, "How you doing Hayley?"

"Not good, kind of..." My voice trailed off without knowing how to finish the sentence.

He said, "You can follow them. Me and Hammond need to get these crates down to the safe."

I stared at the door. "Yeah."

He and Hammond pulled the heavy trailer away from the ATV and rolled it toward the doors to the castle.

Quentin called back, "Come on Hayley, come inside, you need to go to the infirmary."

I asked, "What if I went back earlier?"

"You can't, we left yesterday — we came back today. It was just too late in the day, but there's no way to fix it. You'd be looping on yourself, and don't worry, we're in the year 2387, there are royal physicians here. You'll be fine, this is good."

"I think I need to try. Katie said he was talking to her, just the evening before, he was lucid. She should have made him come with her."

"He was guarding the vessels, Hayley, we were attacked. He was trying to keep them safe. He was doing it for Magnus, his brother. It was what he had to do. How was Katie going to talk him out of that?"

"I might need to try though, what if I could get just a few hours earlier?"

"How though? You know we don't know how to do that, we land on the day, our timing is unplanned, you know this—"

I rushed up to the trailer and yanked on the lock.

"What the hell are you doing?"

"I'm taking a vessel!"

He put his hand over the lock. "No you're not, because guess what? I'm not giving you a vessel. You don't get to try."

"You are not the boss of me." I tried to grab the lock.

He pushed my hands away. "Hell yeah I am, I'm Colonel Quentin Peters, I'm in charge of all of you. I get my orders direct from the king and if I tell you you aren't allowed to time jump I mean it, now you need to be a good soldier and get in that infirmary and let Hammond and I get our work done. What would Fraoch do if your situations were reversed?"

"He'd pray."

"Well you better get going then."

I brushed off my clothes. "Fine. Okay."

And I walked through the doors to the castle hallways.

∾

This was the worst moment of my life. I was different from Katie in that I couldn't handle this. She was always crying or carrying on, but that was her way of dealing with trouble. Though she *seemed* weak she also managed to keep us all together, around her, and she drew strength from it. When I thought about all the things she had been through, and how she managed to build this family and keep all these people safe, I was floored by what she could do.

But then there was me — different. I wasn't strong. I had always been kind of alone. I couldn't count on other people, so I had to do things on my own. Some thought that made me the stronger of the two, but as I walked that lonely hallway I thought they would be wrong to think it.

Katie had an extended family, I just had Fraoch. He was all of it.

My mother was a drunk, living in Sarasota. My dad was a drunk, living in Charlotte now. Neither cared much about what I was up to. It was only Fraoch.

Katie was, of course, my best friend, the only family I ever had, which was why I kept in touch, pushed my presence on her, even when she had gone away. I kept on being her friend despite her absence, until she finally came back. But when it came down to it, Fraoch was all I had that was all for *me*.

He loved me exactly as I needed to be loved, completely and selflessly.

I came to the infirmary door.

Please Lord, in your infinite care, protect and hold Fraoch as he undergoes this treatment... Then I opened the door.

FIFTY-EIGHT - MAGNUS

I pulled out of my unconscious again tae a quiet empty room. I looked around and rang the bell.

A nurse came in. "Ah, you're up!" She began checking my 'bells and whistles' as Kaitlyn would say.

"Where is Kaitlyn?"

"The queen? She is in the waiting room consoling Madame Hayley."

"Och, what has happened tae Madame Hayley?"

"Her husband, Fraoch MacLeod, is in intensive care, sire, he is in a very dire situation."

"Am I allowed tae get up?"

"Let me call in the physician to give you a check. We might be able to let you up for a short visit."

I was told that I could be wheeled out to see them in a chair, so that I wouldna put weight upon m'leg, since it was where the robots had entered me. The physicians spoke about it verra scientifically but I got him tae explain it in robot terms because I liked the idea of it and looked forward tae telling Archie about having robots inside my body.

FIFTY-EIGHT - MAGNUS

Getting up from bed was an exertion and then shifting myself over tae the chair with the help of the nurse, was embarrassin'. She was small and I was verra large compared, but she was strong enough tae heft me up and over. She pulled along some of the drippin' bags and wheeled me through tae the waiting room.

There was Kaitlyn, her face lightin' up when she saw me. She had her arm around Madame Hayley who looked verra frightened. The nurse wheeled me right in front of them. Kaitlyn kissed me. "So glad you're up."

"Thank ye. I am glad tae be up."

"You're more lucid too, remind me to tell you what craziness you were talking earlier. You were saying that your cock is how you listen to me."

"Tis nae crazy tis true." I took Hayley's hand and held it on m'knee. "How are ye?"

"Not good."

"I am sorry, Madame Hayley, what do they say on his health?"

She dabbed at her eyes and sniffled. "They say they don't know yet. They say he's got a blood infection."

"Och, it daena sound like something ye want, but he is a strong man. I daena think we should consider it hopeless, I believe he is strong enough tae fight it."

Madame Hayley nodded.

"Would ye pray with me, Madame Hayley?"

She nodded again so I bowed my head and prayed while she silently cried.

Then we sat quietly for a moment. "When will ye ken more news?"

"The doctor said he'd know more in the afternoon."

"Then we hae some time tae waste, and the nurse might allow me tae remain here for a short time. I tell ye, Madame Hayley, she daena listen tae a word I say, forgettin' I am a king."

"Maybe we should tell stories about Fraoch," said Kaitlyn.

I said, "Och I hae one, did he tell ye about the fish we tried tae catch one day on Loch Awe?"

Hayley said, "I think so, but I can hear it again."

"There was a fish, the biggest fish in Loch Awe. He weighed at least two stone, we named him Iasg Mor."

"What does that mean?"

"Big fish." I grinned. "And so on this day in August we took Archie and Ben and went out on the loch tae search for him. Iasg Mor was last spotted at Fraoch Eilean—"

Kaitlyn asked, "And what is Fraoch Eilean?"

"The island Fraoch named after himself — did ye hear of it before?"

She shook her head.

"When he wakes ye should ask him tae sing ye the song he wrote for it. Tis an ode tae Fraoch Eilean, tis where he finds the best fish. He said if he wasna at the castle I could always find him at Fraoch Eilean."

"I'll definitely ask him to sing me the song."

"So we went tae a wee inlet, surrounded by rocks. Fraoch and I had our rods and the sun was just coming up. Fraoch told the boys he was goin' tae 'try tae surprise the fish with a mornin' snack and catch him for our dinner.'"

Kaitlyn said, "I don't remember eating the biggest fish from the loch any time last year, so I'm thinking there's an unhappy ending to this."

"There is a funny ending because we got tae the inlet and Fraoch was verra wound up tae catch him. He was talking tae the fish the whole time and the boys thought twas verra funny. 'Here Master Fish, where are ye Master Fish....?' Then he spotted Iasg Mor and yelled, 'Och! I hae ye now, Iasg Mor, ye will come home with me tae feed m'nephews.'" He leapt from the boat tae the rock and crouched low tryin' tae pick him up from the water. The fish swam away. The boys were laughin' verra hard at their Uncle.

"But then Fraoch said, 'He thinks I am a man and I can be

tricked. He daena ken I am really a bear.' He dropped intae the water, twas verra cold. He stood shiverin' and declared, 'Now I will stand here verra still and be a bear, and he will come by me and I will grab him.'

"He was whispering as if twas a secret and he went verra still. I laughed and asked him, 'Fraoch, ye might do better with a rod and reel?' He was shiverin'. His teeth chatterin', 'Nae, I daena need anythin'.'

"I said, 'But tis verra cold.' He answered, 'Tis all part of m'plan, he winna expect me tae be in water this cold, tis how I will trick him.' He tapped the side of his head as if he was outsmartin' the fish. Whenever the boys asked him how it was goin' he'd say in a whisper, 'Wheesht! Ye are ruining the plan!'

"He looked down in the water and after a long few moments he said, 'I canna feel my dinglewhilly anymore, but tis okay, I will warm up when I am cooking the fish.' He was grinnin' verra wide."

Hayley said, "This sounds just like him, to put himself in the cold water to feed his nephews."

"Aye, he is a selfless soul, our Fraoch, he has been a friend and guard for a long time."

Kaitlyn asked, "He didn't catch the fish?"

"He was visibly shivering. I said tae him, 'Fraoch, ye are goin' tae turn intae a popsicle.' He said, 'I canna be a popsicle, I am a bear.' And lookin' intently in the water he said, 'Wheesht!' And from up on the boat I saw Iasg Mor swimmin' past his body. He said, 'I am a bear!' And dove down tae catch the fish and was submerged, thrashing in the water, as if there was a mighty struggle between them and when he finally came up, fully drenched, a bit blue in the face from the cold, he said, 'Och, I missed him.'

"The boys and I laughed verra hard as we helped him into the boat. I said, 'It looked like you were in a big battle!' And he laughed and said, 'Nae, I never touched him.' And he just laughed and laughed. 'He was too smart for me, boys, I might be a bear, but I am a dumb bear, and he is a smart fish,' and so we turned around and came home."

Magnus smiled at Hayley. "Dost ye ken the best part?"

"What?"

"The boys were beginning tae think fishin' was the most boring thing tae do, but after our day at Fraoch Eilean they loved going out with Fraoch on the boat. They always wanted tae go look for Iasg Mor. If ye think on it, the hearts of the nephews was what Fraoch wanted tae catch all along."

Hayley dabbed at her misting eyes. "The man does love to fish."

"Aye, a man who loves something that much canna leave the earth, he has too much to live for."

"I think I might play some part in it."

"Ye might, I believe he loves ye a great deal more than fishing."

"Thank you, Magnus." She got up and hugged me in my chair and clung around my neck for a moment then she sat back on the couch.

Kaitlyn asked me, "Are you able to see the kids? You look pretty fresh."

"I feel verra fresh, I am missin' them. Can ye send them in?"

Kaitlyn left the room and Madame Hayley and I sat in companionable silence, until it was broken by the door opening and the bairns rushing in, Isla toddlin' and Archie comin' up timid. He seemed reserved, but I put out an arm. "The physician says I am good, wee'un, ye daena need tae worry." He climbed in my lap with his arms around me with his face buried in my shoulder tae hide his tears.

Kaitlyn said, "Is that comfortable?"

"Aye, tis fine." Isla climbed up on my other side, too young tae understand what I had been through, she asked, "What this, Da?"

I said, "These are m'tubes, and did ye ken, wee'un, there was a tube inside m'body and a robot went right through it, up intae my chest, and it worked upon m'heart? Did ye ken it?"

Isla shook her head solemnly.

I said, "The robots hae reported back that tis all verra good about m'heart now, and I hear that in a few weeks we winna ken any difference, I will be well and m'heart will be strong and I will be able tae play all the games where we kick the ball and chase it and your mother winna need tae worry on me anymore. Winna it be a good thing?"

Archie said, "What about Uncle Fraoch?"

"Well, we need to keep prayin' for him. He is nae well yet."

Isla said, "Frookie, Frookie, Frookie."

Kaitlyn sat down beside Hayley again and they held hands and I held the bairns, until Isla said, "Go see Ben."

Kaitlyn said, "Archie, will you take Isla back to Beaty?"

He dutifully took his wee sister's hand and I said, "Archie, if ye want tae come back tae see me, ye can, even if I am in m'room. I like tae hae yer company."

"I will Da."

FIFTY-NINE - MAGNUS

Soon after I was verra tired, so I was wheeled back tae m'room and hefted back intae m'bed. And I was close tae sleep when Archie came in. "Ma is with Isla."

"Good."

He stood awkwardly.

I said, "Do ye want tae come up on the bed?"

"It won't hurt?"

I shook my head. He scrambled up on the bed. The lights were dim he plumped up a pillow and lay down with an arm cocked behind his head in such a way that he reminded me of Sean when he was verra young.

I asked, "How are ye feelin' about the battle?"

"Was scary."

"I ken, twas for me as well. What did ye see when I was down?"

"I saw you on the ground and then Quentin and James were carrying you."

"Och I am too big for them tae carry." I scoffed, then added, "But I am sorry ye saw me like that, I dinna want tae frighten ye."

He nodded.

I said, "The truth is tae be a man ye will hae tae get used tae seein' things that frighten ye, and ye must be courageous and do what needs tae be done though ye are afraid. What did ye do once ye saw me bein' carried?"

"I held Isla's hand, because mammy wasn't there and I told her twould be okay."

"Good, that is exactly what needed tae be done. That is verra good, I am proud of ye."

He said, "Ben was scared too."

"Well, it was verra scary, his father was afraid. Quentin was frightened. I ken James was frightened as well. We all were doin' our best."

"It doesn't seem like it, it seems like they are not afraid."

"They are, they just daena shew it. Tis how we help each other be strong, by doin' what needs tae be done so we can get through it taegether. Someday ye will be grown and a king and ye will hae tae always do what must be done, but ken that if ye hae good men around ye, ye will be able tae do it."

"Like Ben."

"Aye, he will be your best friend. Isla will be verra brave too, like her mother, and ye will hae other friends and family as well, and aunts and uncles tae take care of ye."

"I am worried about Uncle Fraoch."

"Me too." I yawned. "I need tae go tae sleep I think, I am having trouble keeping my eyes open."

"Is it okay if I sleep here?"

"I would like that, tis too quiet in this room with nae one else breathin'. I get verra lonely."

And slowly I fell asleep tae the soft sounds of m'son sleeping beside me.

∽

Middle of the night Kaitlyn came in. She whispered tae Archie, "This is where you are?"

"Da needed the company."

"Ah, I see, do you want your own bed?"

"I think he will be lonely if I go."

"I see." She kissed him on the forehead and helped him get under the covers. "Sweet dreams."

She came over and kissed me, "Good night love, I'm going to sleep in the waiting room with Hayley."

I nodded and fell back tae sleep.

SIXTY - HAYLEY

I was asked if I wanted to see him. It was a quiet request and gave my heart a tug to hear it. I followed the nurse to his room, a bed, in the dimness of a hospital. He was sleeping, a tube from a bag into his arm. I went and sat beside the bed.

"Hey you big lug, what the heck are you doing?" I sat down.

"This here is not what you're supposed to do. You are supposed to love me forever, and it has not been forever yet, and so I won't let you leave me. You aren't allowed. And you have to listen to me because, as you know, I'm the boss. I do not like this. At all."

I sighed. He didn't move.

"Here's the thing, if you leave me, I will be all alone. I know it doesn't seem like it, I have Katie and Mags and their children, of course, but if you leave me with them I will just be Aunt Hayley and I'm not that good at it. I'm better at it when I'm with you. We are the aunt and uncle, we are a team. So what I'm saying is you are not allowed to do this. You have to get better."

I looked over at the machines hooked up to him. "And not just broken alive, you need to be the same alive, because our world has been shit for a long time. I just want you and me to have some normal life together, with the nephews and our nieces and our friends, and maybe Beaty will have kids... I don't know. What I'm saying, Fraoch, is we have to get you up and out of here, you're too important to me."

It was late, and I was exhausted. I watched him sleep for a little while, but then my eyes were heavy so I dropped my head down on his bed and fell asleep. Then I got a neck crick and woke up because of it. I leaned back in the chair and slept the uncomfortable yet exhausted sleep of people who are very worried at hospital bedsides.

SIXTY-ONE - MAGNUS

*T*was morning and I was in the wheelchair once more. I was fine tae walk. I told the nurse I was fine tae walk, and she said she dinna care what I thought, I was on medications that might cause me tae fall and she asked, "Do you want to fall, the king, to fall on the ground, and then it will be my fault, is that what you want to have happen?"

I got into the wheelchair, though I felt much better. Almost well enough tae walk, though I did feel a bit faint when I was up tae relieve m'self, when I had tae lean on her shoulder tae steady m'self as I walked, so I believed she was correct in her demand.

I was alone as Kaitlyn was with the bairns, and so I wheeled toward Fraoch's room.

Hayley came out. "I need to use the bathroom. Can you sit with him while I go get my clothes changed and freshen up?"

"Aye."

She left the infirmary and I sat looking at the once virile and powerful Fraoch, lying flat upon his back in a bed.

"Och we are a mess are we nae?"

He dinna answer.

"Twas a terrible battle, they were aimin' tae take the upper hand. The castle was burned. Twas a tragedy. The people scattered tae return tae the villages. Those that live in the castle will hae much tae do tae make it livable." I shook my head. "I am sendin' money and supplies for them tae rebuild, but twill take a great deal of work for them."

I watched him.

"How are ye doin', Fraoch? I daena remember if ye ken how much we need ye in our family — ye hae become our strongest guard. Ye must nae evade yer duties. And what of fishing? Who will I go fishin' with? It canna be James, he is too serious about it. Ye must continue tae fish or else I winna get tae do it anymore."

I stared out the window. "Twould be a travesty."

I watched the machine drippin' the medicine intae his veins.

"Did I ever tell ye how grateful I am that ye saved my life that day long ago in the swamp? If ye hadna saved me I wouldna have gotten tae ken m'son. I wouldna hae had Isla. I wouldna have had these years with Kaitlyn. Last year when we spent the year in the past, twas a long trying time, but one I wouldna trade. And then ye guarded the mountain for me, and the vessels I—"

His hand twitched on the bedding.

"Fraoch, are ye waking?"

He mumbled, "Aye."

"Och, ye hae given us a fright."

"I ken." His words sounded like a groan.

"Ye caught me sayin' kind things tae ye."

"Is this what ye do, talk tae a man when he is near dyin'?"

I chuckled.

He said, "I heard ye anyway. Ye canna live without me, I am yer hero."

"Tis a good thing ye heard it, cause I winna say it tae ye again."

He asked, "Where am I?"

"You are in the kingdom of Riaghalbane, where we are now safe because Kaitlyn has killed the enemy. I will let her tell the story, but in the meantime, I must call Hayley. This is important for Hayley, she needs ye tae be all right."

I pushed the intercom button and an image projected upon the wall. "Yes?"

"Master Fraoch is wakening."

"I will be right there."

Fraoch asked, "Why are ye in the chair?"

"I hae had a surgery on m'heart. Come tae find out, twas all I needed tae be well. All the talk of 'Magnus ye need tae rest,' was nae correct."

"Och, who wants tae rest — tis a boring man who rests."

The nurse entered the room, followed by the physician, and while I rolled away from Fraoch's bed they set about testing and checking him.

Hayley came in a moment later.

She whispered, "What is happening?

"He is awake, briefly, they are checking him. But he sounds good, Madame Hayley."

We both clung tae the wall tae stay out of their way while they began tae examine him. I patted her hand. "I will give ye some privacy," and I rolled back tae my own room.

∽

Quentin, followed by Hammond and Chef Zach, came intae my room. Zach asked, "We're still meeting in hospital rooms, aren't you free yet?"

I said, "They winna allow me tae leave until I am well. Tis a travesty."

He asked, "How ya feel though?"

"Good, I feel as if I am healed. I had forgotten how weak I had become, or I dinna realize. Now I am strong, my hands work." I clenched my fists. "I feel energetic. I could fight, if I must."

Zach said, "Or dance, probably a better thing to do."

They all sat down in chairs in front of the window of my hospital room. I asked, "You retrieved the vessels?"

Quentin said, "About that... yeah, they're all accounted for, mostly. We have the monitors, the metal chest that we can't figure out how to get into, that other machine that makes no sense, and the vessels. Except a few are missing—"

"How many are a few, three?"

"A few more than that."

"How many more?"

"We have twenty-three vessels."

"Tis including Lady Mairead's? The same amount as before?"

"Yes."

"I feel I hae taken one step forward tae end up in the same spot. What of the Trailblazer?"

Quentin shook his head.

"Och, nae. And has Master Cook returned from searching for Madame Sophie?"

"Aye, this morning, he's in his rooms. He searched the castle, asked around the villages. Nae one has seen her since the battle."

I shook m'head, I had been in this situation before with Kaitlyn, but then I had a path tae find her. Madame Sophie wasna a time traveler. I couldna think of a way tae advise Master Cook. "What is he tae do tae find her?"

"I don't know, he left messages with villagers. He left a letter at the cave. There is a letter in your office at Kilchurn and he even left a letter at Balloch, with messages for Lizbeth and Sean as well. They asked after you, he told them you were doing much better and that you would visit soon."

I thought for a long moment. "What do ye think, Colonel Quentin? I ken she has been abducted but tae what end? What dost ye think her captors want from us?"

"I have no idea. There must be something, but until we have some kind of message, there's nothing we can do but look for her and wait." He looked down at his hands and shook his head. "We have nothing to go on."

SIXTY-ONE - MAGNUS

"I will talk tae James later today. She was from Edinburgh. Next time he might search there. Perhaps I will be well enough tae travel with him. We should also check with Rob Roy."

"Sounds good. Until then we need to keep our eyes open, looking for messages."

Hammond said, "I will send men to check the caves on Ben Cruachan, regularly."

Zach said, "Check the stones of the castle, too."

I said, "Aye, tis how I got a message tae Kaitlyn once."

SIXTY-TWO - KAITLYN

I walked into the infirmary to pick up Magnus. He was undergoing his last check before he was allowed to leave, something that had been a point of contention for many days.

Fraoch was up in a wheelchair, still very weak, but growing stronger. Hayley sat beside him holding a skein of yarn while he was attempting to knit a pair of hilariously big socks, but he complained of headaches. "They cause me tae lose m'countin'."

I asked, "Who are the socks for, Bigfoot?"

"Nae, they are for Magnus, because he has big feet."

He held up the socks that were more in the shape of a hat, or possibly a dog's sleeping bag. We all laughed a little, but it was good natured, and I truly imagined that once given them, Magnus would wear them everywhere, possibly with garters.

I said to Magnus, "You ready, love of my life?"

"Tae leave this godforsaken hospital, och aye." He stood from sitting on the edge of the bed. He was dressed in his uniform, his medals upon his chest, his hair trimmed and cleaned, healthy curls springing around his strong jawline, his color returned, and whoa nelly, his virility. I really liked the way he looked in that coat. He straightened it, smoothing the front and said, "Ye look verra beautiful."

I was wearing a long blue filmy dress, sort of a tea dress, with heels, which I was out of practice wearing, but I liked being in them. I was taller, more impressive, and more importantly, I felt pretty, clean and fresh, civilized, in my makeup and perfume. "I was told to look like a queen."

"I hae seen a queen — hae ye seen Elizabeth I? I daena think ye look like a queen, ye look like a beauty."

"Well, that is a lovely thing to say." I kissed him.

"Tis time tae see the people." To Fraoch he said, "Master Fraoch, I am released from this dungeon, I will send back messages and food."

Fraoch weakly said, "I want the food, I am famished. They daena feed us well enough in here."

Hayley said, "They feed you plenty. You had a huge lunch just moments ago."

"Och then why is m'stomach so empty? If tis meant tae be filling there is nae enough cheese in it."

Magnus said, "This is true, but ye will only be here for another week, Fraoch. Twill nae be that hard."

"I will be a shell of a human, all that will be left of me is a ball of yarn and a skeleton." He stuck his tongue out and pretended to slump over in his chair.

Hayley batted him on the arm.

Hand in hand Magnus and I left the infirmary for the castle halls.

The workers and staff of the castle lined the hallways to see him. He shook hands with every person there and asked them about their health and their work. He listened to stories about the battle against Sir Padraig, and about their work restoring Riaghalbane. General Hammond and Colonel Quentin followed along behind us, Hammond introducing the staff to Magnus, and whispering reminders.

Magnus, more than once, said, "I thank ye for yer service tae the crown, Master…" To be reminded of the soldier's name. "I ken I had forgotten, but ye must forgive me, the hospital stay has caused me tae hae a foggy mind."

And they did forgive him. You could see it in their faces as one by one they were addressed by the king, and then the queen of Riaghalbane. It was my job to say, "It is wonderful to see you again," and, "It is my pleasure," and, "How have you fared since the war?" and after hearing one tragic story from a widow of a fallen hero, "My deepest condolences, would you come to see me tomorrow afternoon? I would like to hear the full story of his heroism."

It took us a few hours to get through the entire receiving line, and though Magnus looked tired it was the tired of having been bedridden for a time and not the tired of a poor heart.

It was like a breath of fresh air filling my lungs and giving me the energy to carry on.

SIXTY-THREE - KAITLYN

We made it to his office and closed the door behind us. I leaned against the door. "Phew!"

He stood stock still in the middle of the room and looked around at all the things. "I dinna think I would see it all again — the fancy photos from the coronation tae prove I am a king. The war hammer tae look as if I am ready tae kill though tis on a desk tae prove I am judicious at who I choose tae murder. The drawing by Archie, tae remind me I am a father first and foremost." He turned a frame with a drawing by Archie of a stick figure man on a stick horse.

He leaned casually on the desk in his hot uniform, his shiny shoes crossed one over the other, laidback and a slow smile spread across his face, crinkling the corner of his eyes. "Dost ye ken what I think we must do?"

I had an idea, but the way he was looking at me was making me feel kind of breathless, so I asked, "What must we do... Master Magnus?"

He put his hand on his heart. "Och, ye ken it. The Madame Campbell can read m'mind."

I ran my hand through my hair, and flipped it a bit. "Not sure I know what you're talking about...?"

His delicious chest rose and fell with a deep breath while his eyes looked like they might devour me.

He undid the buttons on the front of his coat and spread it open, relaxed, and casual. "Ye ken, I was watching ye on the line just now, as ye greeted and spoke tae all the people and I thought tae myself, I must share her now, but twill be just a few moments more before she will be all my own again."

"I think I am always your own, Master Magnus, it was in my vows."

"Ye ken I hae kent it since I married ye, but still sometimes I catch a sight of ye across the room, and still I hope that ye might be mine. I forget ye are *easy*, is what I am saying."

I laughed. "I'm so glad." I walked closer and ran my finger along the back of a chair. "So what I'm gathering is that you like the look of me and you're thinking you might like to...?"

"Perhaps I hae been in the hospital, Madame Campbell, and before that twas a long time of needing tae rest, and now I feel, I daena ken how tae say it..."

I said, "But you really need to say it..."

"I feel as if I would like tae take ye right here, just because I want tae, because I am the king and I like the look of ye. And ye ought tae submit."

"Now this is interesting... But what about our bed? Perhaps we should be wearing pajamas? We might need to—"

He strode toward me and swept me into this arms and pressed his lips to mine in a delicious deep roughness that had me breathless and wanting in one hot moment and then he lifted me from where I stood and carried me to the edge of his desk and sat me on it, with a small nudge, pushing his war hammer aside. He ran his hands down my legs and pulled off my shoes dropping them by his feet, then he bunched up my skirts and gently pulled my panties off my legs and dropped them to the floor beside my shoes, and parted my legs and kneeled in front of me and buried his face inside the folds and licked and nibbled and sucked between my legs and pulled my hips closer, and then after a few moments of *oh god, oh god, oh god, ooooooooooh,* he rose up in front of me and unzipped his pants and dropped them to his feet and there he was in his full glory. "Ye might hae tae kneel before me."

"Holy shit, yes, I might, that is..." Words escaped me.

I dropped off the desk to my knees and took the length of him in my mouth and held and sucked while he held my head to steady it and I held on around his hips until in a near frenzy of desire he pulled away from me, pulled me up, and pushed me back on the desk and laid upon me and shoved his way into me. His fingers gripping roughly in my hair. His lips wet on my cheek. His hips banging against my open thighs. His moans desperate and intense, and so freaking hard and big and strong and I was lying all the way back as he rose up, a hand wrapped around each of my knees, holding me tight and close, he drove and drove into me again and again while my moans grew meeting his and with a last wave of intensity I raised my hips and he met me on the wave and our moans raised along with our movements — a pummeling and thrashing and all the fun fucking things until he reached his climax and continued to stand holding me close and himself deep as he came — panting from the effort. He relaxed his hold on my legs and slowly softened.

He put his hands flat on his desk as he slid from inside my body, and I wrapped my legs around his waist, holding him close though we were past the connection. I stretched my arms out almost knocking a pen holder off the side. He chuckled.

"A moment ago twas the sexiest thing in the world, now tis verra uncomfortable."

"True, how does that happen so fast?"

"I daena ken, I was a king conquering the queen on his desk and now I am a husband with his wife on a hard surface."

I giggled and wrapped my arms around his neck. We kissed, slow and sultry and very sensuously.

"That was awesome."

"Aye, Madame Campbell, and it has been a long time. I canna make promises but I am already thinkin' upon the next time, so maybe if ye continue with the dress that goes tae here," he kissed me on my cleavage, "in the fabric that feels like skin tae the touch, and the shoes that make yer arse go like that," his hand slid under my body and he grabbed my ass and squeezed it.

"Jesus Christ Magnus, this is so freaking hot, I will continue with it. I will continue with all of it. I do like the idea of next time, are we talking tomorrow?"

He turned his face to look at mine. "Nae, I am hopin' tae get back to it after a snack."

I laughed. "It's a deal. A high-protein snack—"

"Nae, I think I need the carbs."

I laughed again. "That's so modern of you." His hand massaged around my ass while his other hand dove in through the side of my dress and grasped my breast and caressed it. Then he kissed me luxuriously with his tongue licking and then nibbling my lips. I teased, "The carbs indeed, are we talking granola, maybe some fruit?"

He pretended to wretch. "Granola and fruit? Has the Madame Campbell met her husband, Master Magnus?"

"I have, I have met him very much, and I will meet him again and again."

His mouth traveled down my neck to the edge of my throat, where he sucked along the edge, with the other hand on my breast and a hand on my arse and so many hands — my hands up under his shirt, running up and down over his tight form, his angles and hard lines, his taut muscles and hard planes while he caressed and fondled my softnesses...? And oh my and oh whoa he was...

His voice near my ear he asked, "Are ye comfortable enough?"

"What...? I don't... yes...."

He was kissing and... and... and his hands between my legs

and I held onto him, bringing him back to hardness and power after some diligent foreplay of all the best kinds, he said, "Och, I dinna need the snack."

I giggled. "I didn't even need to put the shoes back on."

He stood back up over me and entered me again, and this time it took longer. We had fun. We undressed during it. His shirt came off. He stepped from his pants and kicked off his shoes. I turned over and bent over the desk and he unzipped my dress and pulled it off over my head while entering me from behind, over and over his hands caressing me. Our clothes were strewn around his office and we were completely naked coupling in the middle of the room, in all the best ways, taking our time, enjoying the second round, until finally with my excitement building and expanding and roaring me home, with his soft breaths in my ear, he reached his climax and collapsed down on me, "Och."

I whispered, "I know."

"Twas excellent tae go twice."

My legs shook from the effort. "I might be so spent I have to take a nap."

He drew away with kisses down my front. Then ran his hand through his hair. "Do ye want tae take a shower?"

"Okay, but I can only clean from the neck down. I can't wet my hair, I'm supposed to be in this dress for the rest of the day's events."

He laughed, "Och, ye are a mess."

"You are too!"

"Tis okay for me."

"This is so true, you could go just like this and they would be fine with it."

He put his hands on his hips, "Like this? With m'willy hanging out, and the smell of m'wife upon m'groin?"

"Ha! I meant, *dressed*, but with your hair a little mussed, but yeah, you could go naked and no one would mention it. You've heard the tale of the emperor who wore no clothes?"

"I hae, I think tae see my manliness out in the halls might give people a startle, and since tis m'first day at work since the war, I might nae want tae startle them."

I went in to use the shower to clean everywhere from the neck down, and then to try to right myself as much as possible with the little makeup I had in my purse, because the next part of the day was to be, 'meetings with the household staff.'

SIXTY-FOUR - HAYLEY

"We're ready to get out of here, huh?"

"Aye," he was sitting on the edge of the bed. I stood in front of him watching him wiggle his toes.

I kneeled down to help him put on his shoes, trainers, in some future brand I hadn't heard of before. Which seemed kind of lame, seeing how as time travelers we could go back and get a pair of $4,000 Air Jordans or something.

He hefted himself up onto his two feet.

"Do you need a wheelchair to leave?"

"Och nae, I am nae sittin' in one of those again. I am a free man."

"You sound like Magnus, so much complaining!"

He looked stiff and kind of hobbled as we walked to the door. He said, "First thing I want tae do, is tae go fishin'. Magnus promised me I could."

On the chair by the door was a very large pile of his knitting. I asked, "What on earth are we going to do with all of this?"

He chuckled. "Tis most of it a scarf tae wear." He pulled an end from the middle and wrapped it up on his shoulder then wound it around his neck, drawing it from the pile, around and around and around, until he had wound about twenty-four feet of knitted scarf around him.

"You look like a tiny little gopher peeking up from a hole in the ground."

He grinned, "Tis m'favorite animal! I will put it upon my crest, tae guide me."

"Ha! I would think the alligator would be your animal."

"Och nae, gators are always sneakin' up on ye, tis nae my style. But first—"

"Fishing."

I lifted up the bundle of knitted things and led him out to the hall to show him to our room. "And after fishing...?"

"I changed my mind. First, a meal, the largest meal I can find."

"I felt like your list might be out of order."

At the end of the hall I led him into the elevator. "How many elevators have you been in before?"

"Tis m'first, I hae always wanted tae do it."

I pointed. "Push the button for the floor under the crown."

He jabbed the button. "Now hold on while it lifts us."

He pressed to the wall and held on. "Och, it left m'stomach below us."

As the doors slid open, he watched them intently. Then he investigated the buttons, and the crack between the elevator and the shaft. "I always wondered what is the point of it, if ye could just take the stairs — now I see the point of it is fun. Maybe Archie and Ben will ride it with me later."

I chuckled as I lugged his knitting down the hall to our door and pushed it open. "Our room!"

"Tis luxurious, the king gets rooms such as this?"

"His is better. He is the king after all. But this is very grand. Wait until you try out the bed, hint hint."

He grinned, "Och aye, first, I want tae bed ye."

I strode to the sitting room and dropped the knitting on the closest chair then raced back and jumped into his arms. "I thought you would never ask."

He carried me to the bed and we fell onto it and laughed, kissing while struggling out of our clothes. He got his pants off, but had forgotten his shoes. "I forgot how tae do it."

I gasped with laughter as I had pulled my shirt over m head without bothering to unbutton it, and it was stuck on my ears. "Me too!" I pulled the shirt. "I'm going to tear the buttons, crap."

He reached around me to unlatch my bra but I was still trying to get my shirt off while he was also trying to kick off his pants, socks, shoes in one tight wad around his feet. Finally we stopped and just clung to each other laughing.

His big booming voice, "We are stuck."

"It's the most embarrassing thing in the world, but also the most silly." I rolled onto my front while he fumbled with the button on my shirt and pulled it away from my arms. We got my bra off with a wee bit more respectability. Then I pulled his shoes off, his socks, and let him, with dignity, kick his pants off. Then I leaned back on my arms. "Now take my pants down!"

"Och ye are excited!"

"This was my 'first thing' and so I'm feeling pretty happy about the order we are going in. I beat fishing and a big meal."

"Ye were always going tae, I was just teasin' ye." He pulled my pants and panties down and started to drop them on the floor but then folded them in half and tossed them to the chair like a good boy.

Then he climbed back onto the bed and wrapped his big strong arms around me, holding me the way he was supposed to, the way I needed. I clung to him as he kissed me, his beard rough against my lips, and his hands caressing me, stroking up and down my back.

I said, "I missed you so much."

"Aye, m'bhean ghlan, I missed ye as well." His voice deep

and rumbling in my ear. His body big and heavy and warm and furry in all the best places. The weight of him, a pressing insistence, he was here, he was alive, on me and then in me and around me and there was no denying, no fear — he wasn't lost to me. He was alive.

SIXTY-FIVE - MAGNUS

Dinner was tae be a state dinner, a grand affair tae prove my largesse though my kingdom remained in shambles and m'palace, Caisteal Morag, was a half-broken ruin. I had tae prove that I was back, home, and ready tae rule and that the kingdom was strong and powerful like the king.

I had not been ready and available tae fight for many long years, but I felt my old self again, and I hadna realized how weakened I had become. I had m'kingdom, most of the vessels in the safe, my wife and bairns safe, our family and friends close under the same roof. Chef Zach, though, was verra bored and Master Cook was agitated. He would leave on the morrow tae look for Madame Sophie again.

Kaitlyn stood beside me, and read my mind as she often did. "I worry about James. He misses her so much."

"Aye, when yer wife is absent, a husband feels a powerful pull tae go get her, but if she is lost tis verra difficult."

Zach and Emma walked up, he said, "What the hell is with this monkey suit?"

Magnus grinned, "Ye look quite fine, Chef Zach."

"I wore a suit at my wedding, I was promised that was the end of it, and now look."

Kaitlyn said, "It's worth it though, so Emma can get dressed, right? I mean look at her, she's beautiful."

"That is true." He leaned over and kissed her.

Fraoch and Hayley arrived and joined us. Fraoch said, "How are we tae wear these for the whole night? Are ye mad, Og Maggy?"

I said, "Aye, ye must wear them the whole night, with all buttons buttoned. We must look respectable, tis the price we pay for the six course meal we are about tae be served."

"If I am tae eat six courses, I will hae tae unlatch the belt."

A round of wine was delivered tae us and I raised m'glass tae say, "Tae the women we are surrounded by, Madame Beaty, Madame Emma, Madame Hayley and Queen Kaitlyn, ye all look verra beautiful."

Kaitlyn raised her glass, "And to the beautiful men, in your dignified suits."

James walked up, "Were you guys talking about me in this monkey suit?"

Emma said, "You look very handsome, James, I wish Lady Sophie were here to see it."

He tugged at the collar. "Yep, me too, I'm wracking my brain trying to figure out where there might be a sign or a message. How would she know where to leave one? *Would* she know?"

Everyone's face was pensive. Kaitlyn asked, "You've gone back to Balloch? You sent men to Kilchurn — how many times now?"

James nodded. "Yes and yes, three times already, again tomorrow." He held up his drink.

I said, "I will send more men with ye on the morrow—"

Kaitlyn said, "I can't believe I'm about to say this, but I'm worried about Lady Mairead. She should be back by now, too."

I said, "I will send men to look for Lady Mairead as well, but for now we celebrate the might of the Kingdom of Riaghalbane." Kaitlyn's brow raised with an amused smile.

SIXTY-FIVE - MAGNUS

I glanced across the room at a circle of officers, all basking in the glory of our win, though ultimately Kaitlyn had won it in a restaurant all alone. I tugged her closer and kissed her forehead. She would nae get the glory, not from these men, but she assured me she dinna want it, saying, "It wasn't tactical. It wasn't a military strategy. I didn't win the war through waging it. What if we think of me as the spy who infiltrated the enemy lines and murdered the king, like, I did it, I deserve kisses and hugs for it, but as a spy I don't really want my name to get out there, you know? I feel like it might put a target on my back." She had grinned and said, "And if everyone knows I'm so lethal and amazing my cover would be blown and I wouldn't be able to be a spy again, that would suck."

I had said, "Aye, that would suck."

∽

The company at the state dinner filled the dining hall. Long tables with six courses, beginning with a cream of cauliflower soup, followed with smoked scallops and mushrooms on couscous, and Champagne sorbet, then roast duck a l'orange that Chef Zach declared delicious. After that we were served a salad of roasted endive and pear, followed by a wheel of sharp cheddar and then lastly a layered ice cream torte with assorted crisp cookies. We had a selection of single malts and wine flowing. And after, the party was led down the halls tae the ballroom, only used once since I had become king.

Kaitlyn leaned in, "I am tipsy! Am I supposed to be tipsy? Hayley! Do you want to dance?"

"Maybe in a little while, not feeling this rock band." She squinted at the orchestra.

I said, "I think ye will find tis nae that kind of dancing."

Kaitlyn asked, "What kind of dancing do you think we are going to do?"

I laughed. "The wrigglin' kind, as if ye are a worm on a

hook. This is tae be the borin' kind — the men winna even kick their legs, we hae tae be orderly throughout it."

The dancing began, ballroom style, Kaitlyn said, "Man, I wish you could just king it, go out in the middle and kick your legs a lot."

I smiled and lifted my brow. "Tis yer definition of kingin' it?"

"Hell yeah," she took a sip of her drink. "I mean, what is more king-like than making the band change music, mid-song and dancing in a totally different way? It would be totally badass. You know what? The queen will give you a special Master Magnus hello-good-morning if you do it."

"Och, a Master Magnus hello-good-morn? The special one?"

She laughed, "Aye."

SIXTY-SIX - KAITLYN

Magnus raised his hand and circled his finger around drawing the attention of our friends. He strode out into the middle of the ballroom as the band clanged and crashed to a trailing stop. Dancers stepped out of his way. He raised an arm with the other hand on his hip and his foot crossed over the other.

The conductor asked, "What song, Your Highness?"

"A Scottish jig." To the men he said, "Take yer places, the Queen has asked us tae dance."

Fraoch, Quentin, Zach, James, and Hammond and a few of the other men all gathered around Magnus and got into the same position.

The music began.

The men danced, jumping on one foot, kicking the other and spinning. It was almost in unison, but more from 'trying' than 'practicing'. The overall effect of them turning and kicking and laughing and watching each other for what to do next was very comical. Only Fraoch and Magnus were able to do it well, so slowly the other men left the floor and joined us to clap and cheer, leaving the two Scottish Highlanders dancing in the middle of the floor, and when they were done and all came back to where we were standing, I said, "Well *that* was not boring."

He grinned and said, "Aye, what say ye Fraoch, twas a braw dance?"

"Aye, we shewed the men how tae truly be manly."

Hayley kissed him happily.

Magnus said, "Tis good tae be released from the hellish hospital."

Quentin laughed, "You really don't like that place do you?"

"Hae ye been in one, Colonel Quentin? They daena feed ye well, they are always poking and prodding ye, tellin' ye tae sleep when ye daena want tae, and wakin' ye up tae see if ye are comfortable. And then when ye tell them tae leave ye alone a'ready they winna let ye decide it — they hae tae tell ye when ye are well." He scowled. "Tis nae my taste."

I said, "They did fix your heart and you are dancing and healthy. I think you ought to be grateful."

He said, "Och, I am verra grateful but it daena mean I hae tae like it."

He and Fraoch raised their glasses. Fraoch said, "Tae the hospital, the worst place in the world, but I am grateful for it."

A round of drinks was delivered. Quentin and Beaty danced, and then after a look from Emma, Zach led her out to join them on the dance floor.

Magnus asked, "Would ye like tae dance?"

"No, I do usually, but this time, James standing nearby all sad, you, having already danced the greatest dance I ever witnessed in my life, no. I am content standing beside you looking dignified." Just then Quentin and Beaty spun by, sort of waltzing, kind of line dancing, wiggling their hips. Quentin made a goofy face.

I continued, "Nodding and smiling as your subjects spin elegantly by."

James said, "Uh oh."

We followed his eyes to the ballroom doors where Lady

Mairead dressed in an elegant black ball gown strode into the room and then stood appraising the scene.

Hammond passed us, heading to her side.

Magnus said, "Tis always fun and games until m'mother arrives."

I held my glass to my face to hide my laughter.

SIXTY-SEVEN - KAITLYN

Hammond bowed low over her hand and they spoke for a moment then he led her around the edge of the ballroom to where we stood. "Magnus!"

"Lady Mairead, ye hae returned." He dutifully kissed her cheeks.

She turned to me. "Kaitlyn," she bowed low, "I am relieved tae see ye safely returned."

I huffed. "Your plan was shite as my dear friend's husband likes to say, and I barely escaped with my life."

She stood beside me, her right eyebrow expertly raised. "But ye escaped with yer life, Kaitlyn. Daena be overly dramatic."

My eyes went wide. "You had a terrible plan. You screwed up the timeline. You had looped so many times that the world was in disarray and then you threw me into the middle of it. I had to murder a man to escape!"

"Ye hae murdered more than one. I daena think it should matter that much."

I shot Magnus an exasperated look.

He said, "Lady Mairead, I winna allow ye tae—"

"I ken, I ken. Ye winna allow me tae talk down tae Kaitlyn. Ye

SIXTY-SEVEN - KAITLYN

will use yer brawn tae keep me in line. Well, my dear son, ye winna need tae use yer threats and bluster with me. I daena want tae cause any trouble for Kaitlyn. She has done me an important service, one for which I am verra grateful." She drank a large gulp of her wine.

She added, "Also, by killing Sir Padraig she has restored your throne. Nae, I hae deep gratitude for Kaitlyn's prowess. How did ye do it, Kaitlyn?"

"He exposed his neck, I leapt across the table, scratched his face, grabbed my gun and... you know."

"Tis a boring story. Ye best get better at telling it, if ye daena want the dull-witted officers here tae take the credit for it. M'apologies, Hammond, nae harm meant with the characterization."

"None taken, it is true. If the queen doesn't tell the story, it will become a military tale." He nodded in the direction of one man, built like a tank. "Duckworth there, he's the one who would love to take all the credit."

I said, "I was thinking I would let them take credit. I'm uncomfortable with the idea of being the queen *and* a murderer. I remember having the reputation before, it isn't fun. They can take credit for whatever they want."

Lady Mairead appraised me approvingly. "Tis verra calculating, Kaitlyn. Ye will get much more done if ye daena hae a reputation for bloodshed. Allow yer husband tae hae the honor of having killed Sir Padraig, for having ended the war, and ye can continue tae protect yer family from the shadows."

I was alternately pleased at having been 'seen' and 'approved of' by Lady Mairead and also repulsed that she was pleased with me. Had my actions made her proud? I straightened my back and took in a deep breath to keep from throwing up in my mouth a little bit.

I said, "So, two questions, one, how did you get back after I took the vessel?"

She waved her hand and continued watching the dancers. "I

took a train tae New York, spent some time at Elmwood, enjoying the company of Abby and Flora, then traveled here."

"Second question, who was Rebecca?"

Her eyes flitted to my face, her lips pursed. "She is nae one important."

"She seemed important, she was pregnant, she knew how to get the gold band off your—"

She said, "Rebecca is unimportant, Kaitlyn, please drop it," which made me think she was very very important.

Lady Mairead took a swig of her drink, her brow raised mischievously. "Tae change the subject... how are my grandchildren?"

Magnus said, "They are well, ye may see them in the morn."

She said, "I am surprised ye dinna bring them tae the ball, ye seem tae hae verra many modern ideas about parenting that put ye at odds with what is sensible."

I groaned, "Yes, I do like to have the kids with us, but a state dinner and a ball is not..." I let my voice trail off as she leaned in to speak with Hammond completely ignoring me.

When she was finished talking to him about something, she said, "Ye look verra fine tae night, Colonel Quentin," completely ignoring Beaty all together.

He said, "Thank you, Lady Mairead. You remember my wife, Beaty Peters?"

"Aye, I suppose I do."

She then said to Zach, "Good evening, Chef Zach, Madame Emma, how are ye both?"

Zach said, "Great," while Emma said, "Good," both awkwardly.

"And yer son Ben is well?"

Zach said, "He is, and our daughter, Zoe."

"Ah yes, I remember, you incautiously bore a daughter during all of this excitement."

Magnus glanced around. "Lady Mairead, ye remember m'half-brother, Fraoch, and his wife Hayley?"

SIXTY-SEVEN - KAITLYN

"Aye, of course I do. Fraoch is the son of that horrible, insignificant, conniving woman and Madame Hayley married him."

Hayley flustered.

Magnus sighed. "And ye might remember James Cook? He works for me back in Florida?"

She squinted her eyes. "I hae nae seen him verra often. Ye are well?" She asked absentmindedly but then asked Hammond for another wine. They both scanned the room for a waiter.

James said, "I am as good as can be expected — my wife is missing."

A waiter came by with a tray and Lady Mairead plucked her glass from it.

"Your wife? I dinna realize ye were married."

"I got married back in the eighteenth century, at Kilchurn."

She turned to Magnus, "How was living at Kilchurn, Magnus? It has nae comforts, nae for a king, the privations must hae bothered ye greatly."

"We were comfortable enough, though the food here is better."

Zach said, "Hey, I take offense to that. Eamag and I did the best we could under the circumstances and you know it."

Lady Mairead said, "Eamag? I canna believe ye worked alongside the auld bag, Chef Zach, tis surprising ye survived. She was always unmindful of her recipes. Speaking of, Magnus, ye look thin."

Zach said, "It's not the fault of my cooking, he just got out of the hospital."

All eyes shot to him.

He said, "What?"

Lady Mairead looked shocked, "What were ye in the hospital for, Magnus?"

"I needed heart surgery."

"But there is naething wrong with ye. Who was it that told ye there was something wrong with ye?"

"The physicians, some of the best physicians in the kingdom."

"Word of it dinna get out, did it? It sounds verra weak tae be needing surgery on yer heart. Tis a wonder ye daena hae men lining up tae fight ye for your throne."

"I would like tae see them try. I feel verra good, nae one will be winning my kingdom any time soon."

She muttered, "What could hae possibly happened tae your heart?"

He said, "Twas congenital."

"What on earth...?"

"Meaning, as the physician says, I got it from m'parents."

"Twas nae from me, I assure ye. Ye can put *that* at the feet of Donnan."

She appraised the room, watching the dancers. "This is a fine ball, Magnus, I am thrilled ye are celebrating yer kingdom and yer throne."

"I would like tae return tae Florida as soon as it can be managed."

She groaned, but her eyes also looked delighted. "I suppose ye will want me tae be yer regent again. I am rather busy these days with m'work with Abby Rockefeller, but I would like tae get m'museum ready tae open again."

Magnus's eyes twinkled. "Ye mean *my* museum?"

She waved him away. "Fine, tis your museum."

"I am only teasin' ye. Tis yer museum. We might be able tae hae yer name upon it more prominently."

"Ye would do that for me, why?"

"Because it seems tae me ye are finally acting as if ye are part of the family. The one in which Kaitlyn is the Queen. All I hae ever asked of ye is tae shew her some respect."

She laughed. "All I hae ever said is I would if she did something worthy of respect."

I raised my brow. "You say this to the mother of your grandchildren."

SIXTY-SEVEN - KAITLYN

She said, "Ye hae given yer bloodline tae one of my grandchildren, but I only dispute it, nae tae cause trouble, but tae say twas nae the birth of a child that deems ye worthy of respect in m'eyes. Tis how ye hae seized power and control over the bloodline that was nae yours. That is what has been worthy of respect. I praise ye highly for becoming the head of the bloodline of another woman's son."

Again, I had no idea if I should be thankful or sick to my stomach. I nodded curtly.

Magnus joked, "Well, it was fun getting reacquainted, always a pleasure, mother."

"The pleasure is all mine." She stared off across the room, then turned on James.

"Whatever has happened tae yer wife — ye said she is missing?"

He coughed, having been startled. "Oh yes, my wife, she is missing since there was a battle at Kilchurn. She was ripped away from my arms, time jumped somewhere."

"Well, she could be anywhere." She squinted. "What is her name? Perhaps I've come across her in my travels?"

"Her name is Madame Sophie Cook, formerly married to John Milne."

Lady Mairead's face had gone pale, "Who was her mother, please?"

James said, "She doesn't remember, she was taken from her home, very young. She was raised in Edinburgh."

Lady Mairead went totally pale. "With the Campbells?"

Magnus said, "Aye."

She dropped her glass, shattering it across the floor, startling all of us as she stared blinking into space, as if she was calculating.

Magnus said, "What is going on, Lady Mairead? What do ye ken of her?"

Her eyes scanned the room, nervously. "Nothing, Magnus,

nothing at all. I thought I recognized the name, but tis a common name. Twas nothing."

"We hae determined she was the child of travelers, though she haena traveled herself..."

She cut her eyes to him and whispered. "Magnus, what are ye doing, takin' in all these unknown people? First ye take in Fraoch, a child of Agnie MacLeod—"

"I dinna ken it at the time, he dinna ken it either."

"Fine, but still, now ye are goin' tae take in more strangers?"

"Dost ye ken Sophie Cook? Because ye sound like ye ken who she is."

She humphed, considered, then said, "What I am saying is ye canna trust strangers."

I said, "Sophie remembered meeting Sir Padraig and Agnie MacLeod when she was a child."

Lady Mairead said, "See! Magnus, what are ye thinking? Donnan has children, Sir Padraig has children, ye canna trust anyone."

SIXTY-EIGHT - KAITLYN

Magnus directed us to follow him from the ballroom. The other guests bowed as he walked by, parting to give him a path as we followed along, his face stoic and furious, to the elevator and up a floor and down the hall and into his office.

No sooner had the door closed behind us, when he rounded on Lady Mairead, "Explain this tae me!"

"Ye hae allowed Agnie MacLeod's child, Fraoch, intae yer inner circle! He has a claim tae yer throne, now ye hae another child of a time traveler here, do ye ken if she has a claim tae yer throne? Nae? Agnie MacLeod has another son, Domnall, are ye going tae allow him tae live here as well? Perhaps ye can train him so when he fights ye for the throne ye will be well matched."

Fraoch growled. "I am nae fightin' Og Maggy for the throne."

"Yet."

She huffed and then said, "Ye canna trust her!"

Magnus said, "Sophie has been married tae James for almost a year, I daena think we hae any reason nae tae trust her. She daena ken who her parentage is, how can she hae a claim tae a throne she has never heard of before?"

"You had never heard of your throne when ye were born!"

"Daena be ridiculous, ye told me I was meant tae be a king from the moment I could speak." Magnus glanced at Fraoch, then asked, "Tis true that Agnie MacLeod has another son?"

"Aye, and I want tae go on the record as saying, ye will trust everyone in the world tae yer disadvantage."

"Says the woman who signed a contract with that evil man Sir Padraig."

"Agnie Macleod is just as bad. She was there, was she nae, Kaitlyn — working with Sir Padraig?"

I said, "Yeah, she was there, she is pretty awful."

"Your enemies are like cuckoo birds, Magnus, now ye hae allowed one of yer enemy's bairn intae yer nest, they will begin tae peck and kill yer own—"

Magnus said, "Och, ye are crossin' a line, Lady Mairead, ye are crossin' it verra fast."

"Tis what is at stake here, Magnus! Agnie hates me, she will do anything tae win, includin' findin' yer weakness and insinuatin' her children intae yer family."

Magnus said, "Fraoch, hae ye ever had any dealings with Agnie MacLeod?"

"Nae, she haena insinuated me anywhere."

Magnus asked, "If ye came upon this man... what did ye say her son's name was?"

Lady Mairead said, "Domnall MacLeod."

"Fraoch, if ye came across Domnall and he was tryin' tae harm me or m'bairns, would ye take my side in it?"

"Och aye, ye are m'brother, Og Maggy, I would take yer side, yer son is m'nephew."

Magnus said, "I think ye are forgettin', Lady Mairead, that just because someone is a son daena mean he will take his mother's side. Ye should ken this."

Lady Mairead gave an exasperated huff. "I am nae speaking on Fraoch any longer, he has been a friend tae the family. I believe he has proven himself. I am telling ye tae be cautious. Ye hae invited in this Sophie without properly vetting—"

Magnus asked, "Master James, dost ye trust yer wife?"

James's jaw line was clenched, his face red, he looked to be holding back his anger. "Of course I do and she has never had any dealings with her birth family, whoever they are."

"Och, there are many people who want naething more than tae take this throne." She breathed out. "Can we sit down, we must hae more wine, we must relax. Ye are a king. I am your regent. Ye hae your officers around ye, yer family and friends, let us sit and have a drink."

SIXTY-NINE - KAITLYN

Magnus ordered drinks to be served and we all took places in the sitting room, Zach on the edge of a couch, some sitting on straight back dining chairs, two perched on a chaise. The rest of us on couches and chairs.

Lady Mairead asked, "How did Sophie ken how tae find ye? How did she ken tae meet ye?"

James said, "After her husband died she had nowhere to go, she was accused of witchcraft—"

"Och nae, men can be such barbarians."

James continued, "Then she received an anonymous letter telling her to seek out Magnus's family."

Lady Mairead threw out her arms incredulously, sloshing a bit of wine from her glass in her excitement. "And ye just took her in, James? Ye married a woman with nae lineage, without question?"

James said, "We had plenty of questions. She came from a good family in Edinburgh. Later, any doubts we had, she answered them. She is not caught up in any of this, she is a widow, that's it."

Magnus sighed. "Since we are at a loss how tae find Master

James's wife, do ye hae any ideas? I feel as if ye hae heard of her...?"

I thought Lady Mairead's eyes would pop from her head. "Ye want me tae help ye find a woman I hae warned ye might be a danger? I hae heard everything now."

Magnus asked, "Master James, if Lady Mairead has information do ye require it?"

"I do, I intend to go looking for Sophie first thing tomorrow, but I don't know where to look. It would be very helpful. I would be very grateful for any information, *anything*."

Magnus said, "Master James and Madame Sophie were married in front of God and the church. He made a vow and means tae honor it. If she comes from a competing lineage tae my own, he can deal with that later, for now he must find her."

"Ye are only this relaxed because she is a woman and ye think her harmless, ye are a big brute and ye daena consider any woman tae be a match for ye, but I assure ye tis nae true. She might hae connections that are verra dangerous. Ye must be more cautious."

"Kaitlyn said a similar thing tae me back at Kilchurn, a warning nae tae trust her just because she is a woman."

I groaned, not at all happy with all the comparisons to my mother-in-law. I really was going to need to rethink my whole vibe.

Magnus asked, "Dost ye hae a list, Lady Mairead, of all the bairns of Donnan and Reyes—"

"And Roderick and Samuel and yer cousin, Callum? Aye, I hae a list of most of the bairns. Uilliam Paterson, a second cousin, Scot Hepburn, and Aodh Menzies. Fraoch and his brother Domnall are on my list as well as Ormr, Fraoch's half-brother, and Ian the Troublesome"

"How come I dinna ken of yet another brother of Fraoch? Fraoch did ye ken?"

"Nae, tis new."

Magnus continued, "And how come I haena heard of a

cousin named Ian the Troublesome? I feel these are things I ought tae ken. How come I am only hearing of most of these men now?"

"First, I hae only now been working on the list, but also, why would I hae tae tell ye anything at all? Ye hae been addin' tae yer family without asking my opinion on it."

"I hae just undergone a surgery, and hae a new outlook; I will be more cautious in m'dealings, if ye will be as well. In return I would like ye tae give us all ye ken about the whereabouts of Madame Sophie."

"Will ye promise me ye winna go yerself, Magnus? There are men who desire tae beat ye at any cost. Ye canna just walk in and ask if they ken where Madame Sophie is."

James said, "She has been kidnapped, I don't need anyone to go with me. Wherever she is I'll go get her."

She paused, her eyes on James for a moment. He was pensive, chewing his lip, waiting for her next thought. "I daena ken for sure, but... I hae heard of Sophie Milne. I believe she is from the future. I canna say for sure, as I winna go, on *principle*, tis the future, past what I am comfortable seeing."

She took a sip of her wine. "Did I tell ye that Agnie MacLeod has a grand house in the 20th century, in New York, Magnus? Tis infuriatin' because tis my favorite place, and I bought a home there, and she has nae business buying a house on the—"

Magnus said, "Lady Mairead, I believe ye are off topic."

She dug around in her pocket for a small book, opened it, and flipped pages, occasionally licking her fingers to keep them from sticking. "My point is I must always ken what Agnie MacLeod is up tae. I heard the name Sophie in connection with Agnie's son, Domnall. He had been livin' in a castle, Dunscaith, on Isle of Skye, a guest of Ormr. Really tis a rock with the ocean all around — who in their right mind would ever build a house there?"

Magnus said, "All of us here hae been livin' in a castle on an island in the middle of a loch."

"Tis naething the same. Ormr's castle is built upon a rock in the sea, with a bridge tae cross tae get tae the walls. Tis battered by waves. Tis as if he is a savage instead of a civilized lord."

I asked, "This Ormr... is it the same Ormr you listed as Fraoch's half-brother, someone who might challenge Magnus for the throne?"

Lady Mairead said, "Aye, the cousins are conspirin'."

James asked, "Why would Sophie be there?"

"I daena ken. If ye think on it, twould be a good, private place tae keep someone hidden." She tapped a handwritten entry in the book. "Right here, the year 1589. That is what I heard from an informant I hae on the inside. If it were me I would go in June, but daena let the season fool ye, ye ought tae take a jacket. Ye might find your wife there, but I canna promise it."

"All right, thank you, Lady Mairead."

"Ye are welcome."

She paused. "If ye hae a chance though, Master James, if ye see Domnall or his mother it would be a great service tae me if ye would kill them. I hae nae had a straight shot at Agnie MacLeod or I would hae done it years ago. I should hae done it from the verra first time I kent of her." She took a long drink of wine and then waved the glass asking for more.

Hayley said, "Um, *no*, or Fraoch would not be here."

Lady Mairead exhaled. "True, and he did a service tae me with the Trailblazer, he and Quentin." A playful smile spread across her face as she looked at Fraoch. "I should hae killed yer mother *after* ye were born."

Fraoch laughed.

Magnus said, "Och, ye are diabolical, Lady Mairead."

Fraoch shook his head. "Nae Magnus, she is sensible. Since I daena ken my mother, I will nae mind yer anger with her. I daena ken what she has done tae ye tae make ye hate her so, but I am glad tae be on yer side, and relieved ye daena want me dead."

Magnus said, "Fraoch also saved my life."

Lady Mairead said tipsily, "Then he is doubly safe from my murderous rampages." She laughed happily and took General Hammond's hand.

Magnus's eyes went wide at the sight. Quentin tried to stifle a laugh.

Fraoch asked, "What did Agnie MacLeod do tae ye that made ye hate her so?"

"She has always wanted what belonged tae me. I had another son besides ye and Sean, ye ken?" She turned to Magnus.

Magnus looked shocked. "Nae I never kent it."

"Aye, I had another."

"How come I am only hearin' of him now?"

She shrugged. "Tis mine tae ken, nae yours. I daena talk of him, ever. He was about fourteen years younger than ye, Magnus, how auld are ye now?"

"I daena ken," Magnus chuckled and drank a shot of whisky. "About six hundred years."

Lady Mairead laughed and took another sip of wine. "Twould make me eight hundred years auld, I winna allow it."

"What happened tae him?"

"I tried tae hide him, but he was killed... twas heartbreaking. He was too young tae protect himself." She shook her head. "He would nae hae been in line for the throne. His father was a lowly artist, so I should hae been capable of hidin' him. He should nae hae been at risk."

Magnus asked, "Do ye remember when the men killed Abigall?"

Lady Mairead said simply, "Aye. I think on it often."

He asked, "Do ye think Lizbeth and Sean are in danger?"

"I hae kept verra separate from them, indifferent, in order tae keep them safe, and it has worked. Ye on the other hand..."

"I ken tis true, I hae lived a life of borrowed days."

I was sitting beside him and put my head on his shoulder.

SEVENTY - KAITLYN

*J*ames clapped his hands down on his knees. "So I suppose I will head that way."

Quentin said, "I'll suit up, you'll want a man."

James said, "Sorry, but I'm going to be out of my element, I think I want a not so black man."

Quentin joked, "Are you saying I'm black?"

"Yeah, dude, I hate to tell you, I don't think... what year was it?"

"Dunscaith castle, Isle of Skye, the year 1589," said Lady Mairead, drinking some more. "Ye daena need tae worry much on the blackness of Quentin, tis the women who arna safe. King James will begin the witch hunts that year and nae women will be free from the accusations." Her eyes went distant, "Ye said Sophie was an astronomer?"

Magnus chuckled, "James dinna say it, ye kent it because of some foreknowledge."

She waved her hand at him.

James said, "Yeah, she's an astronomer."

"Och, ye might want tae get her then, she winna be safe."

She drank the last of her wine and then checked her gold watch. "Hammond, will ye escort me tae my rooms?"

"Yes, Lady Mairead." He stood and put out an arm, she was unsteady as she was led to the door.

Then she turned.

"Two things, Magnus. I brought the Trailblazer with me, tis in the vault with the vessels. And James, Dunscaith will be heavily fortified, daena risk your life on walking right up tae the door. My spy is an auld cook in the kitchen."

Zach said, "The kitchen?"

Lady Mairead said, "All the best spies work in the kitchen, tis how they ken all that is going on. Auld Eamag told me *everything* going on at Kilchurn, tis how I kent ye had returned here."

They left the room.

Zach squinted his eyes. "Eamag was a spy for Lady Mairead? What the hell did she tell her?"

Emma said, "Ugh, can you imagine the stories Lady M has about all of us?"

We all laughed.

I said, "I suppose the ball is over since the king left?"

Magnus said, "Och, I think so, and I am in nae mood tae dance." He added, "Well, Master James, ye hae somewhere tae look, daena ye?"

"I do, I'll get some sleep and go in the morning. I'll need some supplies, weapons, perhaps a vehicle... a drone might be useful in a castle like that."

We passed out a round of whisky.

Fraoch said, "What if Hayley and I went with you?"

James said, "Are you in perfect health? Physician approved?"

Hayley looked at Fraoch. "The physician said he is *not* in perfect health. He is *not* approved to time jump into the sixteenth century."

Fraoch said, "But what does he ken? He probably daena want anyone tae jump intae the sixteenth century. He should nae get tae decide military strategy, tis right, Og Maggy?"

"Tis exactly right."

Hayley's eyes went wide. "Fraoch was just a few days ago at

death's door. He literally shouldn't drink whisky probably. He is not cleared to go, period."

"Nae, I am goin', but ye can come as well, m'bhean ghlan. I would like ye tae, we can go help Master Cook rescue his wife, twill be fun."

Hayley said, "Fine. But I want to go on the record and say, really? Just rescuing people all the time? Total danger — this is what I do? Am I a danger junkie?"

James said, "It won't be dangerous because we won't engage the enemy. I learned last time that I am not great at sword fighting. We'll take all the guns I can carry, and keep it safe. I'll jump back if I need more men."

I said, "You'll literally jump back and forth, seven hundred years? You'll wear yourself out."

"It's okay, I can do it. She's been taken into the past, right? So far back, she doesn't know I'm coming for her. She's probably frightened and alone. I can do it."

I said, "Yeah, I remember that feeling, happened to me more than once." I drank from my glass. "I will go with you, if you need me to hold the keys in my pocketbooks, if you need me to drive the getaway car, if you need me to... anything."

Magnus said, "I will go as well. M'mother says nae, but though she believes it, she inna the boss of me." He burped from his drink, and everyone laughed.

James said, "Thank you for the offer, both of you, but I don't think I need the king and queen to help me on this quest. I got this with Fraoch and Hayley and Quentin."

I said, "Man, we needed this drink, this dance, this food, this party, didn't we?"

The whole room said, "Aye."

Magnus said, "I hae been thinking on it, we should return tae Florida. Tis our home, we hae been away long enough."

Beaty clapped her hands, "Yay!"

Zach moaned happily. "I could get back in the kitchen?"

I laughed, "You're literally the only person in the world who can't wait to cook for fourteen people or however many of us there are."

He said, "You don't understand — in Florida I can go shopping, do a few hours prep, cook, then I'm done. Everyone's fed. In Kilchurn I was cooking all fucking day, it was a nightmare. Here I'm not cooking at all but there's nothing else to do. Have you seen the shows? They're so crappy. It's mostly gameshows and soap operas. Weird culture you got here in your kingdom, Magnus."

Magnus shrugged. "I daena ken, tis all the same tae me, hae ye seen the show with the lady with the verra large lips sellin' the cars?"

Quentin said, "Boss, are you talking about a commercial? Advertising?"

"She was stretched out upon the car and then drivin' it on the hills, tis nae a show?"

Everyone laughed.

He shrugged again, "I watched it in the hospital, twas verra boring." Then he grinned. "So are we in agreement? We can go tae Florida?"

I asked, "Can we? Is it time?"

"Aye, m'mother is here. The kids are a wee bit older, let us take a break and go home. Things have gained a kind of normalcy in the kingdom of Riaghalbane. I can do what I want."

Fraoch said, "Och, tis good news, we will go get Sophie and meet ye there."

SEVENTY-ONE - HAYLEY

The men were dressed in kilts, boots, coats, with swords. We wore holsters with guns strapped on us, and more guns in leather satchels. We had horses and enough supplies for a few days. I was wearing the closest thing we had to the time period, a bodice and skirt with a wool wrap, a cloth pinned to my hair.

I checked my gun was loaded for like the third time. "We doing this?" I rolled my head around, stretching my neck. "Yeah, we doing this."

We had a case with a drone inside, a big one with two side drones that all worked in unison, a spying kind of drone with not only a camera but with a weapon or two. Quentin was in charge of that, it was his specialty, or as he said, "It ain't easy to fly this thing without satellites, but I'll try."

James's specialty was exuberance and refusal to 'let this asshole take his wife.' I was there to round out the team, every good plan needed a round team. Fraoch was our Gaelic dude, our sword fighter, our guy that probably knew a lot about castles. He was probably the most important of us all.

We thought so, but then again, this was 140 years before his time too.

I mean, things moved pretty slow back then, but 140 years was a long time.

In my time 140 years would be 1883, the world had changed a lot between 1883 to 2023. "We got it all?" I glanced at Fraoch's face. "You sure you're healthy enough to do this?"

"How long was I in the hospital, Hayley?"

"Couple of weeks, but that's not really an answer."

"Twas enough. Let's go get Sophie."

James had been very quiet.

I said, "You ready?"

"Yep those assholes are going to regret this."

Quentin said, "I appreciate the sentiment, but we are not doing anything drastic, we're just looking for Madame Sophie, right? Like the helicopter thing, blowing up the side of the castle, jumping into the castle while in flight? That's *not* what we're doing this time. Promise me."

I said, "We don't even have a helicopter — maybe we need a helicopter."

Quentin groaned. "I'm going to need everyone to verbally promise me." We all said we promised. "Good, now everyone grab hold of the vessel."

He twisted it and sent us way way way back in time.

SEVENTY-TWO - HAYLEY

"I don't want to get up."

I was face down in peat and pretty sure this was where I would die.

Fraoch groaned to his feet. "Get up, m'bhean ghlan, ye daena want tae be face down in the dirt."

I pushed myself up and spit mud from my mouth.

"I don't want to do it anymore."

Fraoch shrugged. "Tis just something we do."

Quentin said, "Like a job? Hell no, a job is something that doesn't take a decade of your life in a day." He shook, making his mouth go, wubbawubbawubba. He jumped up and brushed off his clothes. "We got this? Everyone ready? It's morning, and my plan is we are not here tomorrow morning."

It was a brisk day for June, terrible weather, the landscape covered in rocky grays and deep greens. Beautiful, except a storm was blowing cold winds off the northern ocean that caused our teeth to chatter. I brought a jacket, we each had one, but still — the wind cut right through us.

James asked, "Whose job was it to check the weather in June, 1589?"

We rode north coming to a small village where Fraoch stopped to ask for any news he could find.

He rejoined us at a brisk gallop. "Och, I tried tae find out what they kent about a woman bein' kept at the castle, but I dinna find anythin'. Now we ought tae move, they hae sent someone tae the castle tae warn them we are asking about them."

Quentin said, "We need to beat them there then." He turned his horse and set it into a fast pace.

∽

We rode north for a couple of hours coming to a rise above the castle, far enough away. We had the fancy binoculars, they had the naked eye.

The castle was perched on a rock, an outer wall, a tower, a drawbridge to it. It looked, swear to god, like something out of Harry Potter, and not in the good way. It was like some dark evil lurked there, like a dungeon was it's only purpose, like a Transylvanian vampire was the main inhabitant.

But there on the top of the tower was a standing telescope.

James said, "She's there, she's definitely there! God I could kiss Lady Mairead! Maybe she'll come out tonight, and we can signal to her." In unison we all looked up at the sky, the gray thick clouds. There was no chance of star viewing.

Quentin said, "There are no bad ideas, let's hear it."

I said, "We call the kitchen staff and ask them to let us talk to Sophie."

Quentin said, "Okay, there are bad ideas. What else?"

Fraoch said, "I will go inside, I will ask questions until they release her tae me, or I will begin shooting until we get away."

Quentin said, "Or if she will come out to the rooftop, we could send a drone to toss a vessel at her feet."

James said, "I don't think she would know how to use it. She has no idea what is happening... she thinks she's all alone. She doesn't know anyone is coming..."

SEVENTY-TWO - HAYLEY

Quentin said, "Okay, so we don't have a good idea yet, but—"

James stood, went to his horse, and climbed on. "I'm going into the castle, give me a walkie-talkie."

Fraoch said, "I a'ready offered tae go — I speak Gaelic, I can—

"No, I'm going. Are you going to give me one, Quentin, or am I going to go without it?"

Quentin passed him one. "James, dude don't be crazy... we need a better plan. What if—"

"As our friend Mags would say, 'Nae', nae to your 'what ifs', Quentin. I'm going in. Fraoch, you and Hayley need to guard Quentin while he mans the drones." He turned his horse to look back at the castle. "You send a drone with the vessel to meet me on the walls. I'll get there, and I'll have Sophie with me — aim for the telescope."

Quentin said, "This is the most fucked up plan I ever heard."

James said, "I have six guns on me, so I'm getting in that castle. I'm going to find her. All you have to do is send down the drones, I'll meet them on the roof."

He rode off down the hill.

Fraoch said, "Och, he has a death wish for sure."

James rode fast, it was exhilarating and spectacular. Quentin watched through the binoculars, giving us the play-by-play. "Okay, he's going, mud is splashing... he's on a path, yep, right up to the gate... holy shit, he's lost his mind... he's crossing the bridge... holy shit, he's going right up... Uh oh, he's talking to some people. Like ten men around him... now he's going inside and... shit, he's gone."

He passed me the binoculars and began frantically opening the drone case and assembling the drones, blowing on his fingers while he worked. "I didn't actually think he'd get in. See anything?"

I looked but it was just a castle. "What did you see? Were they acting like friends or foes?"

"I couldn't tell, looked pretty menacing with ten men standing around, Magnus said the most dangerous thing is the castle gate."

"Well, he's inside now, hopefully he doesn't die in there."

Quentin got three drones placed in front of us. Fraoch was guarding over us with his gun drawn as I watched through the binoculars. Quentin wrapped a vessel to the main drone with duct tape.

I said, "How's he going to work it?"

"He'll have to cut it off."

"With what, his scissors?"

"He's got a dirk, I mean..." Quentin wrapped another strip of duct tape around, his hands shaking. "I mean, him getting to the duct taped drone is an impossibility anyway, right? I think the rest of it is likely to kill him long before he gets there."

He rushed around linking the drones up while I watched the wall, the telescope sitting alone. Then we heard it, faintly: pew pew. Guns were firing in a distance.

I spoke into the walkie-talkie: James! What's happening? James!

No answer.

Quentin grabbed the monitor. And then, "Holy shit! James is up on the walls!"

I was giving the play-by-play as I watched through the binoculars, "He has someone... Sophie, I think... slung over his shoulder. Whoa, that's bad ass, he's firing down the walls! Is she injured?"

The drones rose into the air. Quentin holding the screen, guiding them as they swooped down the hill to the castle. He was chanting, "Come on, come on, you got this, come on..." They were in perfect synchronized formation, the vessel-carrying drone in the middle, the two on either side, firing at the walls.

"Don't shoot him!"

"I'm not going to shoot him. I can see him, plain as day now."

SEVENTY-TWO - HAYLEY

Fraoch came to look over Quentin's shoulder. I put down the binoculars and it was like a television, the drone's eye-view.

"Och, he has got ten men comin' up the — he put Sophie down, she's..."

Men on horseback rode across the bridge aiming for the hill, the path, toward us.

Fraoch climbed on his horse. "They're comin' tae fight. I'll meet them down the path. See ye in a moment." He rode away.

Quentin, concentrating, said, "The drone is right there! They're behind a bulkhead, the drone is right there!"

I put the binoculars up to my eyes, "She's grabbed her telescope. He's jumping for the drone. Lower it! Lower it!"

"I see him, Hayley, shut up, I'm concentrating!"

Then James plucked that drone out of the air, like a quarterback, he tucked it to his side and tried to rip the duct tape. He struggled with it for a moment. Then he must have gotten it off. Sophie threw her arms around him and then a storm rose above the castle.

∽

Fraoch was riding toward us, firing over his shoulder at the advancing men. "Get our vessel ready!"

Quentin dropped everything into the case at his feet. Fraoch leapt off his horse and all but crashed into us, while Quentin was twisting the vessel. We grabbed around each other just as the men from the castle came over the final rise, swords raised — we jumped.

SEVENTY-THREE - MAGNUS

*T*was November 21 in the year 2023.

We landed on a stretch of beach on the south end of the island. Kaitlyn and Emma were tae awaken early, havin' a gold thread upon their necks, because someone needed tae be up with the bairns when they wakened. Wee Zoe was a'ready wailin', along with Isla, now three years auld joinin' in.

I spit sand from m'mouth. The sky was a high blue, a Florida sky, a cool breeze with a warm sun. I looked up to see Kaitlyn, sitting with a crying Isla whimpering in her lap, Archie under her arm looking frightened. I said, "Ye feel it, mo reul-iuil? Tis an autumn day in Florida, we are home."

Archie dove into my arms and I hugged him tae my chest, looking up at the sky as the wind picked up and thunderous clouds built overhead as a new storm arrived. "Och!" I yelled, "Everyone tuck under, someone else is comin' on top of us."

The winds pummeled us, sand bursting like bombs had hit, lightning struck the low trees, sizzling the sand and water.

Zach yelled, "Is everyone here?"

SEVENTY-THREE - MAGNUS

Beaty said, "Aye! And I hae Mookie!"

Emma yelled, "Aye, I have the kids!"

Kaitlyn said, "Me too, Isla, Archie, Magnus is holding my hand."

Zach said, "Can we get off the beach?"

"Nae, too dangerous!"

"Then hold on!" The thunder crashed overhead, now the bairns were truly wailin'.

It lasted for about twenty minutes, long enough tae be verra frightening for the children, but we clasped hands and held on through it. And then the storm parted, the cloud bank rolled away as if twas the ocean slidin' away from the Florida shore.

There was at last some warm rain. The sea turned from deep frothin' green tae a paler blue, sparklin' in the sun.

There were sleeping bodies nearby. I rushed tae Hayley, who was partly under Fraoch and Quentin, and began shovin' them off. Quentin said, "Get off me, man!"

I said, "Ye are the one upon someone else."

"Great," he moaned, and began climbing off the pile.

Fraoch was slower, but sat up, giving Hayley a chance tae complain bitterly that she always landed with a pile of people on top of her.

Tae the side was James, groaning, and Sophie, whimpering and clutching his shirt. I crouched beside them. "Madame Sophie, tis goin' tae be all right." She shrieked and cowered against James, but without opening her eyes.

I said, "Master James, ye need tae arise. Yer wife is sufferin' and frightened."

He groaned again so I shoved his shoulder tae attempt tae bring him alert.

Quentin, head in his hands, with Beaty hovering over him and Mookie snuffling against his cheek, said, "Make sure he's not shot, that was a hell of a firefight."

I said, loudly, "Master James, are ye shot? Any pains?" I shook his shoulder again and visually inspected his shirt and pants.

He said, "Any pains? It feels like I just traveled five centuries — what the hell do you think?"

"I think ye are wailin' like a bairn when all the rest of the bairns are already up and running about in the sand."

He opened an eye as Ben and Archie ran by.

"Stupid kids." He climbed up tae sitting and got Sophie tae put her head in his lap. He patted her shoulder and whispered tae her.

I asked, "Is she all right?"

He nodded.

Zach said, "All right, Quentin, want to go get our trucks?"

"Hell yeah." Quentin clamored up and brushed sand off his pants. "Get my truck! I thought I would never hear such a sweet sweet phrase again. Let's do it."

They trudged across the sand tae the road tae walk tae our house. The house that had been closed up for a long year.

SEVENTY-FOUR - KAITLYN

We moved farther into the shade while we waited for the trucks, while the kids were running in the sand. Sophie huddled against James, whimpering because of the brightness and the loudness. I said, "Sophie, welcome to the twenty-first century."

She turned her head to look at me with tearful eyes. "What?"

"The twenty-first century, this is the year 2023."

She looked up at James. "Tis true?"

He said, "Yep, I just said it like fifteen times."

She sobbed, "I can barely hear ye over the verra loud roar, can ye hear it, tis as if I can hear my heartbeat."

Beaty said, "Och, I remember it. Tis a terrible thing. Twill pass in a few months."

She pulled her earlobes and said, "Och nae, so long? I daena ken if I can live with it."

Magnus said, "What Madame Beaty means is twill pass and ye winna remember it, but for now twill be difficult. What they haena mentioned yet, ye will hae such good food, twill make ye nae mind it so much."

The trucks pulled up at the edge of the sand and we all groaned and stood and began dragging the few bags and weapons to the back of Quentin's truck and tossing them in. James carried Sophie's telescope and Magnus had gathered all the vessels and had them slung in a bag over his shoulder.

I asked, "Did you go inside our house?"

Zach said, "Nope, we should all do it together." We piled into the trucks, sitting on laps and barely fitting as there were fourteen of us and twelve seats, thankfully we only had to go about two miles on empty roads.

～

We drove up to the house.

I said, "I never saw anything so beautiful, have you?"

Everyone agreed, and Fraoch said, "Tis a wonderful thing tae be back home."

Hayley teased, "Wonderful that a guy like you thinks of Florida as home."

"Tis a castle, and inna it braw?"

We climbed out of the trucks and milled about on the driveway.

James said, "Sophie, this is our house." Then he sheepishly corrected himself, "I mean, I have another house, but..."

Magnus joked, "Ye canna go tae it, Master Cook, how will we sleep if ye arna under the same roof? I would lay awake wonderin' how ye were survivin' without us."

James laughed. "Good, I'm glad you feel that way, the guest room here is pretty small, but I think that will be preferable for Sophie than being all by ourselves."

Zach grabbed the extra keys from the garage and went to the front door and unlocked it, "Ready to see the place?"

We cheered as he opened the door.

～

SEVENTY-FOUR - KAITLYN

The house was dark and dusty and cockroaches scurried across the floor.

"Ugh," said Emma, "that's going to take some cleaning."

I said, "I'm putting my foot down — we've been through an ordeal, and this requires a cleaning service. Not me and you, we need a crew."

She said, "Hear hear."

"So what do you think of our house?" I asked Sophie. She was open-mouthed at the room and then we went through to the kitchen, living room, and Magnus strode up to the sliding doors, unlocked them, and opened them wide.

He turned to us, his smile spread across his face. "Smell it wee'uns? Tis Florida!"

Ben and Archie ran around looking for their toys while Isla toddled after them pretending she knew what they were talking about.

I sat down in my favorite chair. "I forgot how amazing these chairs are! So much more comfortable than the past, not as luxurious as the chairs in our palace in Riaghalbane, but I can kick my shoes off." I sighed. "I can curl up in this chair." Magnus lowered himself in front of me on the floor leaning against my shins. Our friends sat on the couches and chairs around the room.

Magnus said, "Master James, tell us the tale of rescuing Madame Sophie."

James had his arm wide on the back of the couch, Sophie leaning against his chest. He said, "First, Sophie needs to tell us what happened."

Magnus said, "Och, ye daena even ken?"

Quentin said, "The whole rescue took about thirty minutes. It was done at top speed."

James grinned broadly, "Haven't had the chance to ask."

Sophie raised her head from his chest. "I was helpin' the

bairns from the castle. Twas so frightenin' but then I remembered I needed tae get m'telescope, tis the most precious thing I own, and I dinna want tae leave it. I am so sorry, Queen Kaitlyn, that I left the bairns tae go back."

"First, I am Katie or Kaitlyn here, not a queen. Please don't stand on ceremony. Also, you know what, thank you, don't be ashamed. You helped get the bairns to safety, but you love your telescope and you believed it to be irreplaceable."

"Tis! Tis irreplaceable."

I said, "Exactly, I understand that feeling. I was frantic once when my wedding ring was lost in the past." I looked down at the simple garnet stone and hugged it to my chest. "So you ran to get the telescope and what next?"

"I was closin' it up tae carry and the storm was terrifyin' and suddenly I was grabbed around m'waist, I dinna ken who. The pain was terrible! Och, it ached me all over. I awoke at Dunscaith Castle."

I shook my head sadly, "That is the literal worst thing in the world to have happen. To time jump by surprise? To end up in a strange time and place? I have the shivers just thinking about it."

Everyone in the room nodded and said, "Aye," or, "Yep."

She asked, "Am I surely in a new time here?"

James said, "Yeah, here it's 2023, when we were in Kilchurn it was 1707, and at Dunscaith it was the year 1589."

Her head dropped back on his arm. "I daena understand it."

Beaty said, "Ye canna understand it. Ye just hae tae roll with it and enjoy the food and the clothes and the music and the art and the..."

Quentin grinned and kissed her forehead, "That's m'girl."

James said, "So what happened next?"

Her voice was very small. "I was surrounded by people I dinna ken. There was a man there, he called himself Ormr, he was the lord of the castle."

"Is that the man I saw?" Asked James.

SEVENTY-FOUR - KAITLYN

"Aye, he is verra frightening. He..." Tears streamed down her cheeks. She covered her face.

James pulled her hand away, "Tell me."

She shook her head.

James said, "You can't keep it from me, whatever it is, you have to tell me. There aren't secrets between us."

She said, "You will hate me, I am afraid tae tell ye."

Zach stood up and quietly left the room. In the kitchen I heard him adding ice cubes to glasses and pouring water.

We were all looking away trying to give the sobbing Sophie some time to recover to finish the story. I kissed Magnus's head and absentmindedly played with a curl by the side of his neck.

James said, "This is going to sound mean, but I order you to tell me."

I said, "James!"

"What? I do. I order her. She is crying. She won't tell me why. I order her to."

Sophie was hitch-sobbing, like Isla would when she was really worked up. Emma crouch-walked over to the end table, passed her a box of Kleenex, and pantomimed drawing one and wiping her nose.

It was enough of a distraction that it seemed to calm Sophie. She asked, "Ye really order me tae, I canna keep it inside?"

"No, you have to tell me."

"Ormr forced me tae marry a man named Domnall. Och, I hae sinned afore God, and ye will forsake me!" Her face went into the tissue.

James looked shocked. "What the hell? How long were you there?"

"I daena ken, I was married tae him and was made tae live with him." She clung to his shirt. "Please forgive me, James, I ken twas sinful but—"

James said, "So he bedded you? He forced himself on you?"

She nodded.

James jumped up and began pacing the room. "Fucking-A,

I'm going to kill him. I saw his face, his smug ass face when I ran by him — right by him, I'll add. I invaded his castle all by myself, fucking loser."

He looked at Magnus. "Can I go back? Can I go back in a rampage and murder him?"

Magnus said, "We will need tae discuss all of this. Were ye by yourself when ye invaded? Where were the others?"

James said, "Quentin was coming up with a plan and I got tired of listening."

Quentin said, "It was just like back in the day when you were quarterbacking, remember what Coach used to say? 'Slow down and make sure everyone knows the play,' but no, you used to run off all halfcocked and if you didn't have someone there to tell you to slow your arse down, you would lose the game for us."

James said, "I repeat, I fucking stormed a castle all by myself, and got Sophie back."

"Yeah, and you almost died — the ultimate losing of the game."

"Well I accomplished what I needed to do, but—"

He shook his head at Sophie.

She wailed, "I couldna stop him!" She sobbed into her hands.

Beaty jumped from her chair to take the kids off to march around into the other rooms.

Sophie said, "You winna want me anymore, ye will send me away! I canna bear it, James, I love ye! Please daena do it!"

He shook his head. "Dammit, I was too late, Magnus. Can I go back? What if I loop earlier, would I get there before it happened?"

Hayley said, "James!"

"What? I wanted to protect her before she got married off to some other dude, before she — did he beat you? Look!" He charged toward her and pushed back her hair to show us a faint bruise on her cheek. "Did he do that to you?"

SEVENTY-FOUR - KAITLYN

She nodded.

"Fuck!"

Magnus, full of practicalities, said, "Even if ye wanted tae, Master James, ye canna loop upon us all like that. Ye hae rescued her, tis done. Ye ought tae sit down. Ye are frightening her."

Hayley said, "Look, James, she's sobbing. You better tell her that it's okay, right now, or I am going to take you out back and kick your ass."

James returned to the seat beside her, "Sophie, this is all okay. I'm sorry. It's just a difficult situation, and I am only asking questions about what I can do, what I should do to help you. It drives me crazy to think of you being hurt by one of those guys. I want to stop it, that's all. I'm not going to leave you. I'm not going to send you away. How would I leave you? You're the most priceless thing in my life. I'd go back for you. I did, as a matter of fact, I ran back. I took the stairs two at a time, racing to get to you. I knew you had gone back for the telescope, and right as I got to the parapet, the storm was so bad I couldn't see anything but a glimpse of you as you disappeared."

Hayley said, "Sophie, this is awful what happened to you, but no one here is going to hold any of that against you. You were kidnapped, it's okay."

I said, "And the marriage thing, it happened a hundred years and some change before your marriage to James, longer than a lifetime, and now we're hundreds of years beyond that. Those men are long dead. He can't hurt you, and you are not married to him any longer,"

She nodded quietly.

Then she said, "I believe they were time travelers though, they might come here, might they not?"

Magnus said, "They might, but they would hae tae find us first, and we hae a monitor tae protect us."

She said, "I met the woman, Agnie MacLeod, she is Domnall and Ormr's mother. She wanted me tae give her information tae help her against Magnus." Her voice dropped to a whisper. "She said she wanted tae conquer King Magnus and his family. She said ye deserved it."

"Och."

I joked, "Well great, Lady Mairead was right, she *is* horrible. I hate it when Lady Mairead is right."

Magnus put a hand onto his shoulder to hold mine. He asked her, "Was there anythin' ye told them that might be used against us?"

She turned a tear-stained face Magnus's way. "Nae, never. This is m'family. Are we truly in a different century? Truly? And they winna be able tae find me? I am in nae danger?"

Magnus said, "Aye, ye are livin' long past yer life, well past where ye were. Tis a difficult thing tae understand, I pray on it all the time. But still, tis true."

She nodded.

Quentin said, "So James, what did you do? How the hell did you invade a castle all by yourself?"

"First, I just rode up and pretended to not speak the language, which was true. They surrounded me, and forced me into the castle, disarmed my sword, of course, and then they took one gun, with a fingerprint sensor — they tried to get it to work, aiming it at each other, being total idiots. Then these two big ass dudes walked up."

Sophie said, "Aye, twas them: Ormr, the lord of the castle, and the other man who was my... Domnall."

James said, "Domnall is a stupid name."

She chuckled, it was the first sign that she might not be devastated.

"And I saw you, across the courtyard, near the stairs — I yelled, 'get your telescope!' And when everyone turned to see who I was yelling at, I drew two of my handguns and started firing."

"How many men?"

"Like five. Others were yelling and getting out of my way. I made it to the staircase and started running up, caught up to

SEVENTY-FOUR - KAITLYN

Sophie, picked her up, threw her over my shoulder, and just kept running. But I could shoot down at them, they couldn't protect themselves. It was way more easy than I thought."

Quentin said, "Easy — was you shooting, while running up a staircase — was it circular?"

"Yep, and you know, built crappy like they do."

"Easy — with Sophie over your shoulder?"

He laughed. "Yeah, then I put Sophie down, plucked that drone out of the sky, ripped through the duct tape, while firing, twisted that vessel, told Sophie to hold on and — easy."

Quentin shook his head. "Well, I am impressed."

Magnus said, "Aye," and raised his glass. We all raised our glasses.

Magnus said, "Tae Master James, and the rescue of Sophie, bringin' her tae the New World. We welcome ye tae our home. Slainte!"

"Thank ye, King Magnus and Queen Kaitlyn, tis a relief tae be here and safe." She tucked back in under James's arm. "I am verra hungry."

SEVENTY-FIVE - KAITLYN

Zach, rubbing his hands together, said, "I'm hungry too, who else?"

Magnus said, "We are all famished, Chef Zach, but ye canna cook, ye hae gone too far this day."

"This is true, I'm exhausted. Who wants me to pick something up — drive-through?"

I said, "Oh my god, Zach, are you offering McDonald's? Did that just happen?"

He grinned. "I fucking just offered to go get McDonald's." He strode to the kitchen drawer, pulled out a notebook and a pen, and brought them to the living room. "Make a list!"

Fraoch and Beaty began jumping up and down. "Yay!" And they got the kids jumping up and down, though for most of the kids the idea of McDonald's was a long forgotten concept.

Sophie asked, "Tis like clan McDonald's?"

The list went around, and the page was full by the time it went around twice. Somehow Beaty was already changed into a pair of shorts and a tiny shirt, barefoot with her feet resting on Mookie as if he was an ottoman.

Zach ran off to get the food.

SEVENTY-FIVE - KAITLYN

While we waited, Emma handed James a pile of clothes: sweatpants and a t-shirt for him, a long skirt, a t-shirt and underwear for Sophie. Emma told her, "You do not *have* to wear a skirt unless you want to. There is one here if you do. I see that Beaty is already dressed as she likes. Katie is probably going to run up and throw on some sweats and a t-shirt. The truth is we traveled a long way. We get to dress comfortably. James will show you."

He led Sophie to their room. We could hear her asking, "Ye would allow me tae wear pants? I daena think..."

Emma turned to me. "Wow, imagine being here from the eighteenth century?"

I smiled at Beaty, "Our Madame Beaty came through very easily."

Beaty said, "I think m'life at home was so mean that when Quenny rescued me twas verra easy tae put it in the past and throw m'arms around the future." She rubbed her fingers on Mookie's chin, saying, "Who is the most braw mucag in the world?"

The pig looked just like it was smiling.

We all went to our rooms to get changed. Magnus lay on the bed for a moment, staring up at the light fixture with the ceiling fan spinning the dust around our room. He said, "Tis as dusty as our Kilchurn bedroom."

I peeled off my future-future clothes, a pantsuit sort of thing, for traveling, by a designer in the kingdom. And took off my expensive jewelry and placed it in the top drawer.

I put on my favorite worn Queen concert shirt that I liked even more now that it was ironic: I *was* a queen. Then I pulled on a pair of tiny panties and because I knew Magnus was watching wiggled for him.

"Och, I like it when ye do that, but... I am so hungry."

"You'll have to prioritize food over me right now, because I'm too hungry too." I pulled sweatpants up. "Now it's gone, you won't be enticed."

"But now I ken tis under there."

He was wearing nice slacks and a dress shirt, dignified traveling clothes. He said, "Ye might hae tae come tae the bed. It might be an emergency."

"Oh really?" I put my hands on my hips and appraised him.

His hand behind his head, a big grin.

I said, "You are looking very cocky."

"I am, I canna help it. I traveled a long way and there is nae danger tae speak of and my wife is right there." He reached for me. "Perhaps ye should come tae the bed..."

"After locking the door of course." I locked the door and strode across the bedroom stripping my pants to the floor while I went so that I arrived undressed from the waist down.

I climbed up on him, and straddled his thighs and unbuttoned his pants and wriggled them down his legs to his knees and said jokingly, "Och, yer kingly splendor."

His brow went up delighted. "Did I tell ye this day how much I admire ye? Ye are a braw wife."

"I am, I am literally one of the braw-est."

"But I am nae a king — in Florida I am simply a man. Tis why it is m'favorite place."

"Well, then, this is a manly splendor." I crawled back over him and with no ceremony whatsoever, settled down on him. I was generally a lover of foreplay, a good long time full of kissing and cuddling was always my purpose, but *occasionally* a bit of 'quick down to business' was also fun, especially because he was so grateful, and there was something grand about being brought to excitement after we had already begun. It was like taking it out of order, like eating dessert first. It kind of made it delicious to build up while already connected in this way. On him, I kissed him, deep and long, and though he tried to move me, I held tight, still, and kissed and kissed him while he played with my breasts and then I held his lip between my teeth, lightly tugging and then began to ride... He groaned low and excitedly.

"Do you like that?"

Aye.

Yes.

"A lot?"

"Ye ken."

I rode him, going faster, building with excitement.

∽

Dinner was a working dinner. The food was spread across the bar. Kids ran by eating and running and eating some more, but playing the most. James sat beside Sophie, now wearing a long skirt and a t-shirt with a daisy on the front, guiding her through her meal. The use of the straw took three tries, as it kept bumping her face whenever she tried to aim it into her mouth.

We warned her to go slow, and she did, but marveled as the rest of us shoveled it away, and admittedly we were kind of showing off, eating too much, too fast, gluttonously, and Hayley was the first to clutch her stomach. "Uh oh, that is not agreeing with…" She jumped up from the table and spent a long time in the bathroom.

Zach cleaned up the kitchen, happily, loud music playing. Emma organized and I made lists and talked over business things with Magnus. Then we went through the mail.

Hayley and Fraoch unpacked bags, while Quentin helped Beaty get Mookie's bed settled, and I said, "James, you know, the top deck would be pretty great for Sophie's telescope."

She picked up her telescope and clutched it to her chest, "I would be able tae see the stars? There are stars here? "

James said, "Yes, there are stars, the world is still the same, but sadly it might be hard to see because we have light pollution.

If it is hard to see we also have really amazing telescopes. We can get you a newer one."

She looked down at hers, blinking. Then they began to climb the stairs.

I called after them, "I just remembered, there's a book on the galaxies up in the office, I'll get it for you."

I ran up the stairs behind them and went into the office for the first time since I'd been back. The book cases were full of books. The embroideries by my grandmother hung on the wall, including one I didn't remember having seen before, a large tree in greens, with a ribbon scroll across it with the name, Campbell. It read: From a tiny seed a family tree grows. There was an initial in the bottom corner, an I. I walked closer and put my hand out and touched the frame, wondering if it was real. A gift from Isla, perhaps, from sometime in the future? It made my breathing calm, to have a message from her — she was going to be okay.

The room felt orderly, responsible, as if it were the kind of place to make plans and hold meetings, and while maybe not as important as the office in Riaghalbane, it still gave the impression of a place where a king might make decisions.

I found the book on the shelf: Earth and Space, and when I turned around my eyes landed on a small stack of envelopes wrapped in a ribbon on the middle of the desk.

Magnus appeared in the doorway, he followed my eyes there.

"I hoped tae remove them afore ye saw."

"Oh." I said, somehow I couldn't take my eyes from them. It looked to be about six, in different sizes, different shades of white, a couple well worn and at least one very new looking. They didn't look pretty. They looked important and powerful and my stomach sank a little thinking that this bundle of letters had been something my husband had brought home with him, but didn't want me to see.

It made them ominous.

"What are they?"

"Challenges, mo reul-iuil. Challenges for m'throne, tis time for me tae train tae fight and finally deal with them."

∼

AFTERWORD - KAITLYN

◈

The following day, I found Sophie on the back deck alone staring out at the beach and beyond it the ocean. "Can I show you something?"

"Aye." She followed me down the walkway and then out over the dunes to the beach.

"What did you think of the donuts this morning?"

"I think they might hae been too sweet."

I laughed and then exaggeratedly sighed. "Fine, yes, they were too sweet, but the thing about donuts is you power through anyway, and decide that they are perfect."

She chuckled. "They were perfect."

"Good answer."

We walked to the water's edge where the shells were plentiful. "How's the noise?"

"Verra loud, and the lights are bright, even with these dark glasses over m'eyes."

"There is a lot to get used to…"

I knelt down and began to sift through the shells. "We're looking for shark teeth."

Her eyes went wide. "Shark teeth, what are shark teeth?"

"They are teeth from big fish, and... we shouldn't dwell on that part of it, their teeth are all over the beach here and it's really fun to find them." I sifted a little, and moved a little further along and then found a very tiny one. "I found one!"

She was crouched beside me, her red hair blowing in the breeze, the dusting of freckles across her nose. "Och, tis a tooth from a beast?"

"Yes, it might be thousands or even millions of years old. If you think about it, you have been in the eighteenth century, then the sixteenth, and now here, in the twenty-first century, and now you're holding a shark tooth from millions of years ago… time travel is a lot, huh?"

She smiled. "Tis. Do ye want the tooth back?"

"No, I have buckets of them at the house." I rested my cheek on my knee. "I wanted you to know, that if you're scared, or worried, or just want to talk — you can talk to me. I might not have been through *exactly* what you've been through, but I have been through many scary and traumatizing things. I've heard and seen a lot, and I am a good listener."

She nodded quietly.

"I know what you went through must have been really hard."

A tear rolled down her cheek. "Twas."

"Yeah, I bet." I reached over and tucked a hair behind her ear. "So, how far along in your pregnancy do you think you are?"

Her chin trembled as she looked down at the shark tooth. "I daena ken."

"Yeah, that's what I thought." I chewed my lip. "How many months were you there?"

"I told him I could count the time in days, but I believe twas about eight months. It breaks m'heart tae hae lied tae him."

"Oh honey, you don't look that far along."

"I ken, I daena ken what I am goin' tae do." I put my arm around her and held her while she cried.

The end.

THANK YOU

Thank you for taking the time to read this book. The world is full of entertainment and I appreciate that you chose to spend some time with Magnus and Kaitlyn. I fell in love with Magnus when I was writing him, and I hope you fell in love a little bit too.

Please leave a review. I'm now writing the next installment and I love the encouragement.

Review The Guardian

And if you're ready for what's next...?
The next book can be pre-ordered here:

Magnus the First (book 15) preorder

I dreamed up the story one day while visiting the town where I grew up, Fernandina Beach. I had taken my four kids (aged between 5 and 16) to the beach and, after frolicking, they joined me in sifting through the sand, searching for sharks teeth.

I remember that day so clearly, my eyes swept the beach: my children, the great loves of my life, the high blue sky, calm ocean, warm sand, gorgeous shells and yes, when I sifted, a wee black triangle.

The idea flooded me. Magnus setting his leather clad foot on the shores of my hometown. And Kaitlyn meeting him there.

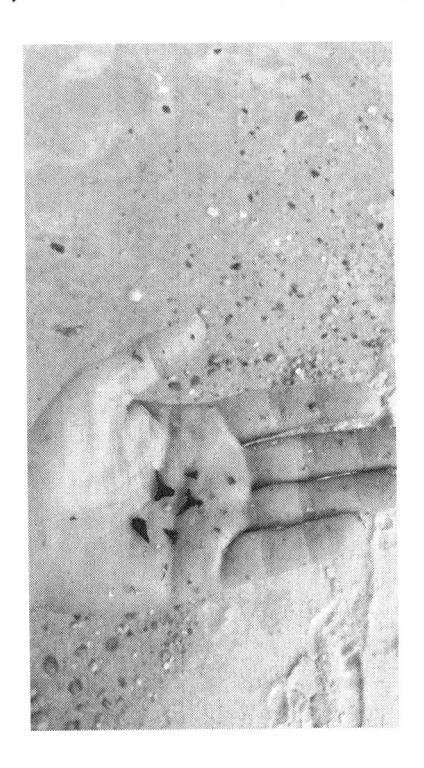

THANK YOU

There are more chapters in Magnus and Kaitlyn's story, coming as fast as I can write them…

∼

If you need help getting through the pauses before the next books, there is a FB group here: Kaitlyn and the Highlander, now at almost 5,000 fans.

And there is a new story too, over on Kindle Vella, Liam and Blakely. It's a romcom and might help to tide you over.

∼

Kaitlyn and the Highlander (Book 1)
Time and Space Between Us (Book 2)
Warrior of My Own (Book 3)
Begin Where We Are (Book 4)
A Missing Entanglement (now a prologue within book 5)
Entangled with You (Book 5)
Magnus and a Love Beyond Words (Book 6)
Under the Same Sky (Book 7)
Nothing But Dust (Book 8)
Again My Love (Book 9)
Our Shared Horizon (Book 10)
Son and Throne (Book 11)
The Wellspring (Book 12)
Lady Mairead (Book 13)
The Guardian (Book 14)
Magnus the First (book 15) preorder

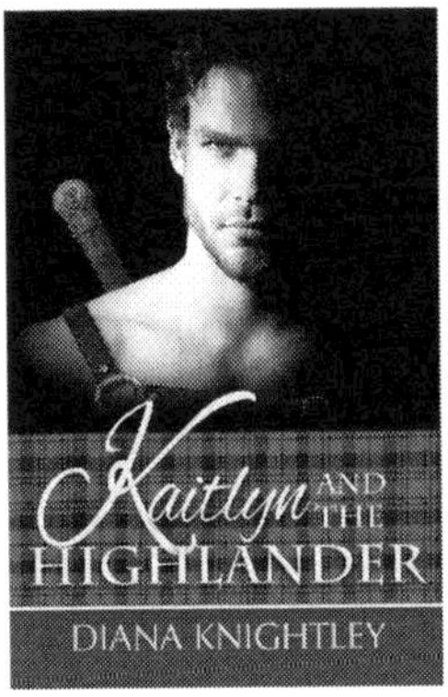
Kaitlyn AND THE
HIGHLANDER
DIANA KNIGHTLEY

Time AND SPACE
BETWEEN US
BOOK 2
KAITLYN AND THE HIGHLANDER
DIANA KNIGHTLEY

Warrior
OF MY OWN
BOOK 3
KAITLYN AND THE HIGHLANDER
DIANA KNIGHTLEY

ALSO BY DIANA KNIGHTLEY

I have a new story called Liam and Blakely.

It's a romcom.

They meet in the Och Nae Pub in a shite town in the middle of nowhere, love ensues.

It is being told in short episodes over on Kindle Vella.

He has a Scottish accent.

He thinks she is verra braw.

Liam and Blakely

SOME THOUGHTS AND RESEARCH...

Characters:

Kaitlyn Maude Sheffield - born December 5, 1993

Magnus Archibald Caelhin Campbell - born August 11, 1681

Baby Archie Colin Campbell - born August 12, 2382

Isla Peace Barbara Campbell - born October 4, 2020

Lady Mairead (Campbell) Delapointe - Magnus's mother, born 1660

Hayley Sherman - Kaitlyn's best friend, now married to Fraoch MacDonald

Quentin Peters - Magnus's security guard/colonel in his future army

Beaty Peters - Quentin's wife, born in the late 1680s

Zach Greene - The chef, married to Emma

Emma Garcia - Household manager, married to Zach

Ben Greene - born May 15, 2018

Zoe Greene - born September 7, 2021

Sean Campbell - Magnus's half-brother

Lizbeth Campbell - Magnus's half-sister

Sean and Lizbeth are the children of Lady Mairead and her first husband.

James Cook - former boyfriend of Kaitlyn. Now friend and frequent traveler. He's a contractor, so it's handy to have him around.

Sophie Milne - wife of James Cook

Bella Florentin - mother of Archie

The Earl of Breadalbane - Lady Mairead's brother

Grandma Barb - Kaitlyn's grandmother

Grandpa Jack - Kaitlyn's grandfather

Fraoch MacDonald - born in 1714, meets Magnus in 1740, and pretends to be a MacLeod after his mother, Agnie MacLeod. His father is also Donnan, which makes him a challenger to Magnus's throne.

Agnie MacLeod - farm girl who hooked up with Donnan. Mother to Fraoch. She has used the alias Jeanne Smith. She has since aligned herself with Reyes and Sir Padraig Stuart, possibly others.

Colonel Hammond Donahoe - Magnus calls him Hammie, come to find out — cousin.

Sir Padraig Stuart - Not the actor. He's from the future-future and continues to wreak havoc. He's a complete arse.

Rebecca - we have no idea who she is.

Ormr and Domnall - half-brothers to Fraoch (not related to Magnus at all) but probably trouble.

∽

The kingdom of Riaghalbane, comes from the name *Riaghladh Albainn*, and like the name Breadalbane (from *Bràghad Albainn*) that was shortened as time went on. I decided it would now be **Riaghalbane.**

∽

The line of kings in Riaghalbane

Donnan the Second - murdered by Kaitlyn Campbell in the year 2381

Samuel - Donnan's brother. Attempted takeover during the transfer of power between Donnan and Magnus, uncrowned. (Killed in the arena by Magnus.)

Magnus the First - crowned August 11, 2382 the day before the birth of his son, Archibald Campbell, next in line for the throne.

∽

Some **Scottish and Gaelic words** that appear within the book series:

Chan eil an t-sìde cho math an-diugh 's a bha e an-dé - The weather's not as good today as it was yesterday.

Tha droch shìde ann - The weather is bad.

Dreich - dull and miserable weather

Turadh - a break in the clouds between showers

Solasta - luminous shining (possible nickname)

Splang - flash, spark, sparkle

Mo reul-iuil - my North Star (nickname)

Tha thu a 'fàileadh mar ghaoith - you have the scent of a breeze.

Osna - a sigh

Rionnag - star

Sollier - bright

Ghrian - the sun

mo ghràidh - my own love

Tha thu breagha - You are beautiful

Mo chridhe - my heart

Corrachag-cagail - dancing and flickering ember flames

Mo reul-iuil, is ann leatsa abhios mo chridhe gu brath - My North Star, my heart belongs to you forever.

Dinna ken - didn't know

A h-uile là sona dhuibh 's gun là idir dona dhuib - May all your days be happy ones.
Tae - to
Winna - won't or will not
Daena - don't
Tis - it is or there is. This is most often a contraction 'tis, but it looked messy and hard to read on the page so I removed the apostrophe. For Magnus it's not a contraction, it's a word.
Och nae - Oh no.
Ken, kent, kens - know, knew, knows
iora rua - a squirrel. (Magnus compares Kaitlyn to this ;o)
scabby-boggin tarriwag - ugly foul-smelling testicles
latha fada - long day
sùgh am gròiseid - juice in the gooseberry
Beinn Labhair - Ben Lawers, the highest mountain in the southern part of the Scottish Highlands. It lies to the north of Loch Tay.

> *"And I will come again, my love, though it were ten thousand mile..." is from the beautiful* **Robert Burns** *poem,* O my Luve's like a red, red rose, *written in 1794 after Magnus's time.*

beannachd leibh - farewell or blessings be with you.

> *"Fra banc to banc, fra wod to wod, I rin, Ourhailit with my feeble fantasie, Lyk til a leif that fallis from a trie..." is from a sonnet by* **Mark Alexander Boyd**. *1563-1601*

breac - trout.
iasg mòr - big fish
uile-bhèist - monster
mucag - is Gaelic for piglet
m'bhean - my wife

m'bhean ghlan - means clean wife, Fraoch's nickname for Hayley.

droch-spiorad - evil spirit

bean Nighe - Described as a form of banshee. Also known as the washer woman. She appears near a stream washing blood from the clothes of people who are about to die.

An uaimh bhinn - 'the melodious cave',

faoileán - sea gulls

Là Naomh Anndrais - St Andrews Day feast

∼

Locations:

Fernandina Beach on Amelia Island, Florida, present day. Their beach house is on the south end of the island.

Magnus's homes in Scotland - **Balloch**. Built in 1552. In early 1800s it was rebuilt as **Taymouth Castle**. (Maybe because of the breach in the walls caused by our siege from the future?) Situated on the south bank of the River Tay, in the heart of the Grampian Mountains. In 2382 it is a ruin.

Kilchurn Castle - Magnus's childhood home, favorite castle of his uncle, Baldie. On an island at the northeastern end of Loch Awe. In the region Argyll. This is where they have been hiding.

The kingdom of Magnus the First, **Riaghalbane**, is in Scotland.

His castle, called, **Caisteal Morag,** is very near Balloch Castle lying on the south bank of the River Tay about a mile from Loch Tay.

Musso & Frank Grill has been a restaurant in Hollywood since 1919. Charlie Chaplin had a special table there.

Dunscaith Castle is a ruined castle on the coast of the Isle of Skye. Originally the castle belonged to a branch of the Clan MacDonald and has also belonged to Clan MacLeod.

Legend has it the castle is featured in Irish mythology as the place where Scáthach the Shadow, a legendary Scottish warrior woman and martial arts teacher, trained heroes. Scáthach's brother was named Domnall. (Note: Ormr means dragon.)

∼

True things that happened:

Clara Bow, Marion Davies, B.P. Schulberg, and Percy Marmont were all real people in the silent film industry. I don't know if they ever met for dinner at Musso & Frank Grill in 1926, but maybe?

At time of press Lady Mairead could not be reached for comment...

SOME THOUGHTS AND RESEARCH... 353

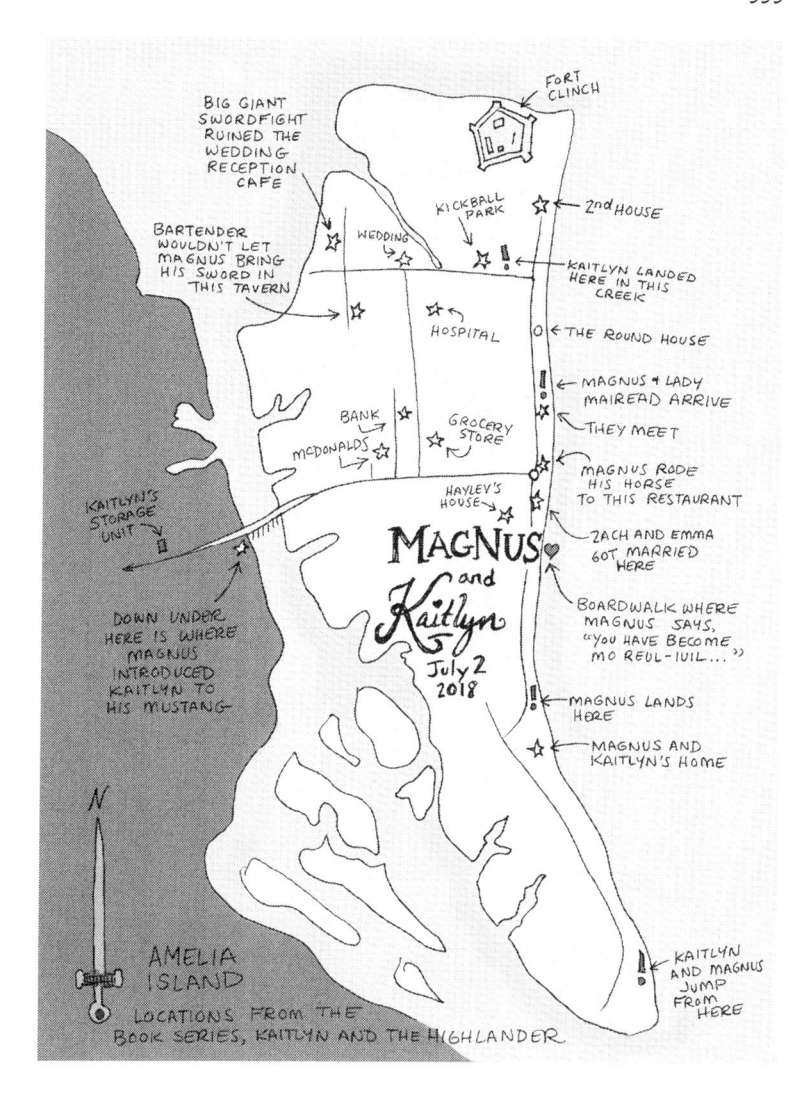

Amelia Island
Locations from the book series, Kaitlyn and the Highlander

- Fort Clinch
- Big giant swordfight ruined the wedding reception cafe
- Bartender wouldn't let Magnus bring his sword in this tavern
- Wedding
- Kickball Park
- 2nd House
- Kaitlyn landed here in this creek
- Hospital
- The Round House
- Magnus & Lady Mairead arrive
- They meet
- Bank
- McDonalds
- Grocery Store
- Hayley's House
- Kaitlyn's Storage Unit
- Down under here is where Magnus introduced Kaitlyn to his Mustang
- Magnus rode his horse to this restaurant
- Zach and Emma got married here
- Boardwalk where Magnus says, "You have become mo reul-iuil..."
- Magnus lands here
- Magnus and Kaitlyn's home
- Kaitlyn and Magnus jump from here

Magnus and Kaitlyn ♥ July 2 2018

N

ACKNOWLEDGMENTS

Thank you so much David for your tireless notes. You are usually the first eyes on the page so you wade through a real mess, asking questions, making points, sometimes I don't know how you can possibly understand what I'm trying to say. Somehow you do, and your notes always make the story so much stronger.

This time, because there were so many characters all in the same place in almost every scene, you were very much like an uncle as we loaded up the car, "Where's Zoe?" Or "Why isn't Fraoch offering to fight?" Or "...surely ask now about Rebecca..." And most importantly, "Why is Lizbeth being so rude?" I fixed it, all of it, you were so right. And thank you also for naming the rooster, Buttnugget; for reminding me that Fraoch might want a ball bath; and the discussion about the drones — you're so freaking good at this.

∼

Thank you to Kristen Schoenmann De Haan for your notes this go around. You started with "What a surprising ride! Especially the wildness in the 20s! Man, I loved that!" You found so many points and issues that you really helped me get some things decided. These were some of my favorites:

"I rose out of the blackness tae hear the voices, one of them, General Hammond..."

YES!!!!

"Where did you learn to do that 'you're both right' nonsense?"

Hahaha

"I didn't need help, I had killed a man..."

Hell, she'd killed 3!

"...ye might did it up and say, that there is m'shite from hundreds of years ago..."

OMG!! How has no one done this?!!?

I appreciate your notes and your enthusiasm for this story so much. Thank you.

∼

A huge thank you to Heather Hawkes for reading again and still being with me after all these years. You wrote, "This was another great story!!! I love all the day to day life going on at the castle. That is always my favorite stuff!"

Mine too!

And you compared Katie to Black Widow, saying, "She was a bad ass!" Which totally gained my undying gratitude (as if you didn't have it already) and you used all the caps, and tons of exclamation points and described the end as heartbreaking, and told me you love the series. So I feel pretty good about it. Thank you.

∼

Thank you to Jessica Fox for all the notes. I loved them and am quoting you here:

You said, *"Wow, this volume is different while still staying true to the roots of the series. I really liked the change of pace in the first half of the book, I think I needed that normalcy for a bit after so much suspense, change and adventure."*

And, *"What I don't understand is why I had to wait until I was 46% into the book to 'see' Mookie? I may be the only one of your readers that was wondering about the pig while everything else was going on..."*

And you added, *"As always, I totally appreciate the comic relief throughout the story. It's healthy to get the unexpected laugh to lower some of the tension from knowing that shit could hit the fan at any moment. Example of a LOL that woke all of my pets up, 'Do ye see we are without coffee yet we are in a family meeting? I worry about our priorities', and, 'So ye decided ye must talk about whose turn tis tae kick the rooster?', and, 'That tree, right there, is m'child.'"*

Thank you for those thoughts, you weren't the only one who would've been worried about Mookie, I put him in a rooting box in the Great Hall for all the kids to parade by because I got worried about him too!

∼

Thank you so much Cynthia Tyler, for being the final eyes on the prize, for your bountiful notes, and your proofing all the faults in the end. Thank you for noting that it would be a Scottish jig for Magnus's dancing, not a reel, that there would be a lot of cars on Hollywood roads in 1926 not just a very few like I had at the beginning, and the discussion about the dress, the Coco Chanel number. I finally decided to put it on Kaitlyn, after we went back and forth.

From music, to food, to fashion, to architecture, and of course, your blessed ability to know when the heck to use lay vs lie, you are amazing.

And thank you for designing the six course dinner. You gave me three to choose from, included here, in your lovely handwriting.

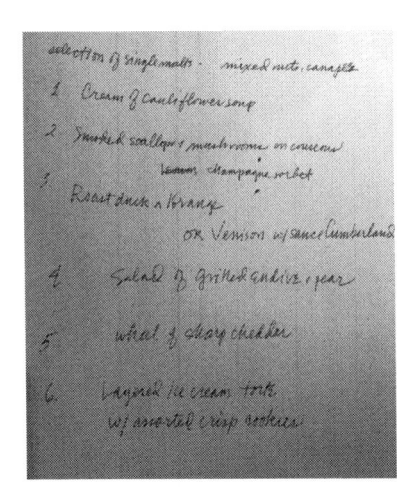

> selection of single malts · mixed nuts, canapés
> 1. Cream of cauliflower soup
> 2. Smoked scallops, mushrooms in couscous
>   lemon champagne sorbet
> 3. Roast duck à l'orange
>   OR Venison w/ sauce Cumberland
> 4. Salad of grilled endive & pear
> 5. wheel of sharp cheddar
> 6. Layered ice cream torte
>   w/ assorted crisp cookies

I'm filled with gratitude that you're so good at this, thank you.

Also, side note, Magnus's puzzling was decided upon with you in mind.

∼

And a very big thank you to Keira Stevens for narrating and bringing Kaitlyn and Magnus to life. All the way up to book 12 so far, you're amazing. I'm so proud that you're a part of the team.

∼

And thank you to Shane East for voicing Magnus. He sounds exactly how I want.

∼

Thank you to Gill Gayle and Emily Stouffer for believing in this story and working so tirelessly to bring Kaitlyn and Magnus to a broader audience. Your championing of Kaitlyn means so much to me.

∼

Thank you to my daughter Isobel and her husband Joshua Waier for consulting on the big fight scenes. I called Isobel one day, asking for help with the restaurant scene, explained what I needed, and a few moments later, Isobel had thought of Kaitlyn reliving that first disaster — the YouTube video that started it all, but winning this time.

Joshua helped with the scene happening at the same time back at the castle, the storm clouds up to the heavens in two places at once and the fire.

And then a whole 'nother phone call, Isobel helped with James's invasion of the Dunscaith castle. Thank you for planting the seed, that's one of my favorite things ever.

∼

Thank you to *Jackie Malecki* and *Angelique Mahfood* for signing on to help admin the big and growing FB group. Your energy and positivity and humor and spirit, your calm demeanor when we need it, all the things you do and say and bring to the conversation fill me with gratitude.

You've blown me away with a timeline of dates, new Facebook pages for the characters, Instagram pages, a rocking video, and your interest in a new book about the series, so many things. So many awesome things. Your enthusiasm is freaking amazing. Thank you.

∼

And thank you to *Anna Spain* for continuing to run the weekly book club, and for going live to answer questions about the stories. It means so much to me (and others in the group), I know it takes devotion, thank you for that.

~

I have a new venture, Patreon, and thank you to those of you that followed me there whether it's fan level or 'I love Liam and Blakely' tier, or both. Thank you for being a part of the magic, Tasha Sandhu, Jackie Malecki, Angelique, Paula Seeley Fairbairn, Diane Porter, and Sandy Hambrick for being the very first.

~

Which brings me to a huge thank you to every single member of the FB group, Kaitlyn and the Highlander. If I could thank you individually I would, I do try. Thank you for every day, in every way, sharing your thoughts, joys, and loves with me. It's so amazing, thank you. You inspire me to try harder.

And for going beyond the ordinary to the most of the posts, comments, contributions and discussions, thank you Anna Shallenberger, Diane M Porter, Linda Rose Lynch, Nadeen Lough, Alicia Jay, Kathleen Fullerton, Sarah McDuffie, Sarah Bussey, Christine Todd Champeaux, Christine Ann, Carol Wossidlo Leslie, Cindy Straniero, Cally Symms, Cynthia Tyler, Kaitlyn loves Magnus, Cheryl Rushing, Tina Rox, Anna Spain, Meg Stanley, Teresa Gibbs Stout, Retha Russell Martin, Kathi Ross, Stephanie Walden, Lori Balise, Christine Cornelison, Stacey Eddings, Holly Bowlby, Irene Walker, Nancy Josey Massengill, Crislee Anderson Moreno, Lisa Duggan, Paula Fairbairn, Kathy Ann Harper, Jessica Blasek, Melissa Crockett, Mitzy Roberts, Kelly Kennie, Jennifer Brown, Sherie Myles, Amy Brautigam, Marie Smith, Karen Scott, Diane McGowan, Amanda Thomas, Dawn Underferth, Heather Schmueckle, Samantha Aishman

Springs, Shannon Sellstrom, Kim Curtner-larson, David Bowlby, Lillian Llewellyn, Dee Mecklin, David Sutton, Marisa Mitchell, Sandy Hambrick, Jacqueline Modell, Jessica Pickle, Melissa Hallman, Toni Plonowski, Holly Kahn, Jeanne Mullock Bills, Fleur Garmonsway, Dorothy Hobbs, Noelle Blosser, Connie Pine, Erin Swearingen, Linda Jensen, Sharon Carr, Jenny Thomas, Barbara Snavely, Liza Gee, Tara Svenkerud, Cari Ritchey, Andrea Gavrin, Darcy Ortuso, Kari Cowley-Quigley, Tracy Drew, Pamela Barker, Sandy Burinda, Cathy Calcagno, Lorelei Scarbro, Molly Lyions, Maureen Woeller, Enza Ciaccia, Michelle Lisgaris, Mary Briarton, Susan Norman, Kate Collins, MarKaye Larson, Samantha Bowman, Michelle Lynn Cochran, Catherine Sebree, Kalynne Connell, Jessica Hufnagel, Tracy Eichler.

When I am writing and I get to a spot that needs research, or there is a detail I can't remember, I go to Facebook, ask, and my loyal readers step up to help. You find answers to my questions, fill in my memory lapses, and come up with so many new and clever ideas... I am forever grateful.

This time I forgot what I had asked before, thank you Chrystal Hicks for reminding me!

Thank you to Angelique for your record keeping, the family tree/timeline you've created. More than once I had to ask for help and you were quick to tell me when Katie was born!

I couldn't remember if Quentin was a Colonel or a General. Thank you to everyone who knew: Margo Machnik, Amy Kehler, MarKaye Larson, Angelique Mahfood, Diane M Porter, Cally Symms, Holly Bowlby, Cheryl Rushing, Carol Wossidlo Leslie, Rachael Temaat, Maria Sidoli, Meg Stanley, Melanie Gilbert, Dee Mecklin, Nancy Josey Massengill, Alicia Jay, Sylvia Guasch, Toni Escudier Plonowski, KaitlynlovesMagnus, Susan Colette Johnston, Sarah Bussey, Cristen Killay, and Stephanie Ferrero!

I was offered help on a Facebook Live video too, but I took it down because of tech difficulties. I'm very sorry if I missed your suggestion, but thank you all so much for your help.

∼

And when I ask 'research questions' you give such great answers…

I asked:
So the gang have some day to day living to do in Kilchurn in 1705.
What is a moment you think they should have? For instance, a harvest festival…or a kid birthday party…

I got so many great ideas, many I had already thought of and had written into the story, but I especially loved the idea of the American gang celebrating Fourth of July, playing kickball, and feasting for Thanksgiving.

Thanks to Meg Stanley, Leah Krakowski, Sheila Maxey, Jenniffer Vasiento, Shirley Carlyle, Gabrielle Joles, Jessica Reiter Cruz, Christine Ann, Stacey Eddings, Melissa Russell Hallman, Sara Bacher, Jessica Pickle, Mikaela Bogard, Deeanne McKenzie Pugh, Michelle Lynn Cochran, Anna Spain, Debby Casey, Julia Lane Dunne, and Azucena Uctum for those ideas!

I asked:
The gang are at Kilchurn Castle and lo and behold, a Young Widow comes to dinner as a guest.
What is her name?
And name a characteristic about her. (looks, speech, or manner)
There were so many imaginative wonderful answers.
First I picked Tori Smith for her answer: Lady Rebecca… she has auburn hair, freckles and bright green eyes.

Then I changed her name to Mariposa Flatts's answer: Sophie - perhaps a doctor or scientist.

I included both because Rebecca is also there...

I also asked about Agnie MacLeod (though I kept 'who' as a secret):

There is a new character, a female. She has access to the time vessels and has been intricately involved in some of the story.

I already have ideas, but I thought it might be fun to ask this one...

Where and when is her lair?

It can be anywhere in the world, any time 1552 and up... though, maybe the trailblazer has been used?

Wee don't know, so maybe she is even farther back. what i'm saying is: There are no wrong answers.

Have fun!

I got so many great answers, but unfortunately didn't pick a place yet, perhaps in the next book it will reveal itself...

At one point Lady Mairead asked her own question, in the form of a poll, here is your answers... The Upper East Side wins!

> **Lady Mairead Campbell Delapointe** created a poll.
> Admin · June 29 at 9:06 AM
>
> I am considering a purchase of real estate, in the year 1926.
> I am trying tae decide on where, perhaps ye hae an idea?
> This, I am told, is a poll, please answer promptly as I hae a party this eve with Pablo and I canna miss it.
>
> Added by Lady Mairead Campbell Delapointe
> Upper East Side, New York
>
> 86 votes

If I have somehow forgotten to add your name, or didn't remember your contribution, please forgive me. I am living in the world of Magnus and Kaitlyn and it is hard some days to come up for air.

I mean to always say truthfully, thank you. Thank you.

∼

Thank you to *Kevin Dowdee* for being there for me in the real world as I submerge into this world to write these stories of Magnus and Kaitlyn. I appreciate you so much.

Thank you to my kids, *Ean, Gwynnie, Fiona,* and *Isobel*, for listening to me go on and on about these characters, advising me whenever you can, and accepting them as real parts of our lives. I love you.

ALSO BY DIANA KNIGHTLEY

Can he see to the depths of her mystery before it's too late?

The oceans cover everything, the apocalypse is behind them. Before them is just water, leveling. And in the middle — they find each other.

On a desolate, military-run Outpost, Beckett is waiting.

Then Luna bumps her paddleboard up to the glass windows and disrupts his everything.

And soon Beckett has something and someone to live for. Finally. But their survival depends on discovering what she's hiding, what she won't tell him.

Because some things are too painful to speak out loud.

With the clock ticking, the water rising, and the storms growing, hang on while Beckett and Luna desperately try to rescue each other in Leveling, the epic, steamy, and suspenseful first book of the trilogy, Luna's Story:

Leveling: Book One of Luna's Story
Under: Book Two of Luna's Story
Deep: Book Three of Luna's Story

ABOUT ME, DIANA KNIGHTLEY

I live in Los Angeles where we have a lot of apocalyptic tendencies that we overcome by wishful thinking. Also great beaches. I maintain a lot of people in a small house, too many pets, and a to-do list that is longer than it should be, because my main rule is: Art, play, fun, before housework. My kids say I am a cool mom because I try to be kind. I'm married to a guy who is like a water god: he surfs, he paddle boards, he built a boat. I'm a huge fan.

I write about heroes and tragedies and magical whisperings and always forever happily ever afters. I love that scene where the two are desperate to be together but can't because of war or apocalyptic-stuff or (scientifically sound!) time-jumping and he is begging the universe with a plead in his heart and she is distraught (yet still strong) and somehow, through kisses and steamy more and hope and heaps and piles of true love, they manage to come out on the other side.

I like a man in a kilt, especially if he looks like a Hemsworth, doesn't matter, Liam or Chris.

My couples so far include Beckett and Luna (from the trilogy, Luna's Story) who battle their fear to find each other during an apocalypse of rising waters. And Magnus and Kaitlyn (from the series Kaitlyn and the Highlander). Who find themselves traveling through time to be together.

I write under two pen names, this one here, Diana Knightley, and another one, H. D. Knightley, where I write books for

Young Adults (They are still romantic and fun and sometimes steamy though, because love is grand at any age.)

DianaKnightley.com
Diana@dianaknightley.com

ALSO BY H. D. KNIGHTLEY (MY YA PEN NAME)

Bright (Book One of The Estelle Series)
Beyond (Book Two of The Estelle Series)
Belief (Book Three of The Estelle Series)
Fly; The Light Princess Retold
Violet's Mountain
Sid and Teddy

Printed in Great Britain
by Amazon